THE
RICH BOY

KYLIE SCOTT
NEW YORK TIMES BESTSELLING AUTHOR

Photographer: Michelle Lancaster @lanefotograf
Model: Chase Mattson
Cover Designer: ByHangLe
Editor: Angela James Edits and Alpha Beta Inc
Copyedit: L B Edits
Proofreader: Ela Schwartz
Formatter: Champagne Book Design

ISBN: 978-0-6484572-8-2

PLAYLIST

"Tempo" by Lizzo (feat. Missy Elliot)

"Going to California" by Led Zeppelin

"Lover" by Taylor Swift

"You're the One" by Greta Van Fleet

"All of Me" by Billie Holiday

"All the Good Girls Go to Hell" by Billie Eilish

"Fuck It I Love You" by Lana Del Rey

"Rocky Mountain High" by John Denver

"Circles" by George Alice

"All Loved Up" by Amy Shark

THE
RICH BOY

CHAPTER ONE

"IT IS A TRUTH UNIVERSALLY ACKNOWLEDGED, THAT A SINGLE MAN in possession of a good fortune, must be in want of a wife."

I slip my pen into my apron and rest my elbow on the bar. "And I take it you're the single man in this particular instance?"

"I am," says the new guy with all due seriousness.

"Any ideas who the lucky lady will be?"

"You."

"Huh." I frown, feeling mostly bemused. My Jane Austen T-shirt aside, this seems a little excessive. "Has this ever worked for you as a pickup line?"

"Never tried it before. How am I doing?"

"Well, there's one main problem."

"Just one?"

"Not to come across as a gold digger or anything, but since you raised the subject, you get that I'm going to need proof of this supposed fortune, right?" I ask. "What with you currently working as a busboy and all."

"Harsh, but I can see where you're coming from. What evidence do you need?"

At the other end of the bar, the manager pours a drink while not so subtly watching us out of the corner of his eye. Same goes for the other waitress on duty. Perhaps they dared him to talk to me. Bet him whatever amount of dollars to see if he can get me to agree to a date before standing me up and making me look the fool. Nothing surprises me here. There are reasons staff turnover is so high. For starters, Rob, the manager and owner of the dive bar, is an asshole who enjoys being unreasonable and inflicting his shitty sense of humor on others. While Kari, his new girlfriend and my fellow waitress, is somewhat of a raging bitch.

Not that the new dude isn't cute. Don't get me wrong; his attentions aren't entirely unwelcome. Truth be told, I've been oh-so-subtly checking him out ever since my shift started. He's in his mid to late twenties, at a guess. And I've been observing how good his rear looks encased in faded denim as he bends over tables to wipe them down. I've noticed the cool-looking tattoo only half-visible beneath the sleeve of his T-shirt. Then there's the way his thick longish dark hair has a tendency to artfully fall over his forehead as if he were some cinematic hero.

As for his face, let's just say he has a nice one.

So given that he's about a ten physically, and I'm a high six at most, you can understand my suspicions. But we haven't hit the evening rush yet and time feels like it's crawling, so the new busboy is pretty much the highlight of my shift. And a little harmless flirting can be fun. Especially when the dude knows Austen and the work environment is as dire as this one.

"Let me think." I give my long blond braid a tug. "Asking to see bank statements seems crass. Also, they could be falsified."

"True."

"But bringing me a suitcase full of cash seems...excessive."

"Probably be really heavy too."

"Hmm."

He sighs. "Tell you what, why don't I just go ahead and get you a ring?"

"You mean an engagement ring to celebrate our impending nuptials?"

"Right." He crosses his arms. And I did not get distracted by the movement of his muscles beneath his tanned golden skin.

Nope. Like the well-bred young lady I am, I keep my gaze glued to his pretty green eyes. "What if I prove my good fortune and excessive wealth by buying you the perfect ring?"

"All right, then. Just make sure you get something big and flashy without being ostentatious or over the top. No one likes that."

"Understood."

"Great. Materialistic, but acceptable. What was your name again, good sir?"

"Beck." He holds out his hand and we shake. His hand is big and his grip firm, but not overly so. "Can I just call you 'wife'? That's easy to remember."

"Ha. I'm—"

"Alice. I know."

"Nice to meet you, Beck." I retrieve my hand and pull my pad and pen out of my apron. "Now, as great as this has been, I have customers to serve."

"One last question. Would you like to go out sometime? With me?"

I pause.

"I hear they have great coffee and pie at the bakery."

"Yes, they do. But I don't think we should move too fast. We've only just settled the marriage question. Already moving on to coffee seems like a big step."

"That's a fair point and I certainly wouldn't want to rush things. It's just that there are a few things I'd like to discuss regarding our upcoming nuptials. The floral arrangements, in particular. You can never start planning that too early. What font to put on the invitation. That's a close second. You can't just roll with Comic Sans and think it's going to be okay. Then of course there's your trousseau to be organized. I could help with that." He's amusing, I'll give him that. But are his intentions pure? That's the question. "What do you say, wife?"

"I'll think about it."

And oh what a smile. The swoon is strong with this one. "Good."

The bar is located way back from the water. It also lacks the wine or craft beers list that other, cooler bars in the Santa Monica area have. Our clientele reflects this. We've had a busy night with the regular crowd shuffling in along with tourists in search of cheap beer, loud music, and big-screen TVs.

Regulars and those wanting service this century sit in my section. My tips are okay. I'm polite and affable, without being overly familiar. It's a fine line. Some dickheads, however, will never understand that being a waitress doesn't mean you're there for their sexual gratification. Tonight, that dickhead's name is Phil.

"There you go, sweet-thing," he says as he drops the twenty-dollar bill onto the ground. "Oops. How clumsy of me."

This is not a new game. I keep the smile plastered on my face as I pick up the money. I crouch down, one hand holding my shirt in place to avoid gifting the asshole a shot of my bountiful cleavage (a common habit among bargirls). But there's nothing I can do to stop my black jeans (dark colors match my soul and it's important to accessorize) tightening over my equally bountiful ass. Most likely, watching me do this is as close as this man ever gets to real live action. Phil is a sad sack of shit.

"Keep the change," he says, licking his lips.

As tempting as it is to smack him upside the head, I smile and walk away.

"Don't," says a deep voice behind me.

Next comes Phil's outraged spluttering. "Get your damn hands off me!"

"You don't touch her." Beck's grip on the dickhead's arm is

fierce. And Phil is no match for the new guy. "Not without her permission."

"I wasn't gonna—"

"You were."

"What's the problem?" Rob appears all red in the face from hauling his ass out from behind the bar in a rush. "Beck, Jesus, let him go. Phil, buddy, you okay?"

"This idiot just assaulted me." Phil puffs himself up, rubbing at the red marks on his arm. "Almost ripped my arm off."

"He was going to grab her ass," says Beck, voice tense.

"Are you serious?" Rob looks to heaven. "He was just playing around. The girl can take a joke, right?"

The girl, me, just sighs. Then I smile. A smile doesn't seem like much of a lie in the general scheme of things. But Beck's eyes widen in surprise. What the hell did he expect? I need this job.

"Very sorry about that, Phil," says Rob. "It won't happen again."

"It better not." The dickhead gathers his wounded pride and heads toward the door. The people around us return to drinking. It's over.

"Pull that sort of shit again and you're fired," snarls Rob. "That guy is a valued customer. He's in every other night spending money and tipping well, understood?"

Beck just nods.

And with gritted teeth, I go back to work.

"Does that sort of thing happen often?"

It's two in the morning and the last drunk has stumbled off. Kari and Rob left at around midnight when things started slowing down. That's when I get to tend bar for a while. Rob doesn't like me being back there when he's still working because, and I quote, "I take up too much space." So yeah, only Beck and I are left to clean up. Music plays softly on the stereo and the street outside is mostly quiet.

"Occasionally," I answer, wiping down the bar. "Comes with the job. Thank you for trying to save me from sexism, but I can look after myself."

Silence.

He starts putting chairs up on the tables, getting ready to sweep and mop the floor. At least I don't have to do it all on my own. Rob is such a cheap shit. It's been weeks since the last busboy just decided to not show up.

"I'm looking for another job," I say, not liking the silence. "Though it's not easy with the hours they have me on here. All in all, I kind of hate the place with the fire of a thousand suns. But please don't tell him that."

"Your secret's safe with me." He smiles. I smile. We all smile. The air is cleared. Good.

"So what's your story?" I ask.

Apparently I have a thing for the lean muscles in his arms, because when he pushes the broom around it's this close to being a sex thing. Takes me a moment to remember what I was doing, i.e. restocking the fridges and liquor shelves behind the bar. The new guy looks like good times and heartbreak. I should definitely know better.

"I suppose that as my future bride you have a right to know of my dark past," he says, expression grim.

"That bad, huh?"

Again he flashes a smile. "Nuh, not really. Decided I didn't like the path I was on so I got off it. Been traveling this great nation of ours and seeing the sights ever since."

"You're a wanderer, then."

"Guess you could say that. Hope it won't be an impediment to our future happiness? A life of love on the road has much to offer."

"I'll keep that in mind." I smile and straighten from packing some beers in the fridge. Think it over. Seems the likelihood of his interest in me being a bad joke encouraged by management is nonexistent after tonight's scene. But we're still talking around exactly what might be happening here. "After much consideration, I have decided that what you're actually after is meaningless sex, as opposed to the holy state of matrimony. I don't blame you for getting the two confused. It happens often."

His dark brows draw together, a hand going to his heart. "You doubt my intentions? I'm wounded, Alice. Wounded."

"Still after a wife to go with your good fortune, huh?"

"Absolutely." He recommences sweeping the floor. "But not just any wife. No. It must be you."

I smile and shake my head.

"You must allow me to tell you how ardently I admire and love you."

"Your knowledge of Austen is impressive, I'll give you that."

"Why, thank you. It's my stepmom's favorite book. She used to make me watch the movies with her all the time. Never thought that'd actually come in handy, but here we are." He smiles once more and my stupid knees go weak. I need to gird my loins or something against this man. "Though, to be clear, I wouldn't turn down meaningless sex with you until such time as you're ready to commit, of course."

"How very kind of you."

"Not a problem," he says. "We could try it as a baby step toward working our way up toward having coffee. Take it slow, like you said."

I bite back a smile. The guy is an outrageous flirt. "Do you normally jump straight to offering a girl your hand in marriage?"

"No. Like the lines from Austen, it's a new thing I'm trying."

"Any reason in particular?" I ask.

He ponders the question for a moment. "Life is short."

"True."

"Is the mop and bucket in the storeroom too?"

So that's all the explanation I'm getting. Okay. "Yes, it is."

We work in silence for a while. I'd like to say his presence doesn't affect me, but that would be a lie. Because almost every time I sneak a look, he's sneaking a look back. And he's smiling. If only he were less cute or something. Because the truth is, I might be a bit doomed here. Lust at first sight in the workplace is kind of a pain in the ass. Same goes for advanced flirting leading toward possible copulation. There's a myriad of ways getting involved, even just a smidgeon, could go wrong. Though apparently he doesn't intend to stay long and I'm doing my best to get the hell out of here. Ah. The elusive yet pervasive dream of working somewhere management isn't complete and utter trash. These days, it's all that keeps me going.

In the meantime, there's the prospect of a dalliance with Beck to be considered. And considering it, I am. If for no other reason than it'll give me an excuse to run my fingers through his beautiful hair and mess it all up. It might just be my new life goal. At least for this week. His hair and his lips and his arms. Those are my favorites, for now.

Before closing up, I touch up my eyeliner and lip gloss. It's been a long night, but I like to look nice for myself. That Beck will also be seeing me is just a bonus.

"Question," I say at around three a.m. as we finish locking up. "You hungry?"

"Answer. I could eat."

"Then follow me."

"Yes, ma'am."

The diner is within walking distance on Wilshire Boulevard and can best be described as low-key. However, it serves coffee and a half decent burger and fries at odd hours, when I most require these things. Therefore, it has my heart. Beck doesn't seem put off by the faint film of grease on everything and smiles at the 1950s kitsch aesthetic. Thereby passing another of my tests.

"You haven't told me your story," he says once we're seated in a booth and have ordered.

"I finished my degree and realized it was basically good for nothing and there were next to no jobs available anyway. Or at least nothing that appealed. Teachers and librarians are fighting for every scrap of funding they can get while newspapers are folding. The publishing industry is going through serious cutbacks. Majoring in English Lit may have been a mistake." I shrug. Truth is, I got stuck for various reasons. But this explanation is easier to swallow. "Figured if I was going to wind up serving then I'd like to do it somewhere I can walk along the beach now and then, without getting stuck in traffic for hours."

He nods. "Makes sense."

"I thought so. I'll figure out what I want to do with my life eventually."

"No rush. Good that you can take the time and space to figure things out for yourself without anyone pressuring you."

"Just the student loans hanging over my head," I say.

His answering smile is brief and small. "Grow up around here?"

"Close enough; San Bernardino," I say. "What about you?"

"No, I'm half a country away from home and intend to keep it that way. Though maybe half a country away is still too close. I hear Iceland's nice this time of year."

I raise my brows in question.

"Family." He shrugs. "What can you do?"

The waitress delivers our food, filling up the table with Beck's order of half of the breakfast menu. Without hesitation, he proceeds to devour it all. If I ate that much, my ass wouldn't fit in the seat.

"Want some?" He offers me a forkful of pancake, dripping with syrup. "It's good."

"I'm fine with my burger. Thanks." And I'm curious as heck about his family, but pressing him further wouldn't be polite. Dammit.

"So what are my future wife's favorite hobbies and/or interests?"

"Hmm." I stick a fry in my mouth and chew, thinking it over. "Reading, films, music…the usual. You?"

"Lots of things."

"Such as?"

"I don't know…hiking, rock climbing. Stuff like that."

"So basically I like to sit still and you're all about being busy and athletic. We have nothing in common."

"No. Wait. I can change," he jokes. "Give me another chance."

"You shouldn't have to change." I swirl another fry in some ketchup. "I'm sure you're perfectly fine just as you are."

All humor is gone from his face now, his expression blank. The look in his eyes, though, is dark and unhappy. It would seem I've hit a nerve. So of course, I do the worst thing possible and babble.

"I mean, what is even the point of being with someone if all you want to do is change them?" I ask. "If you and your significant other were both exactly the same, where's the interest or challenge in that? Do you just live in each other's pockets until the day you die? You'd have to run out of things to talk about pretty fast, right?"

Nothing from Beck, but a line is now embedded between his dark brows. A moment ago, he seemed all good humor and confidence. Now, however, he almost seems kind of lost. Something I'm more than familiar with these days.

"Beck, are you okay?"

He blinks, coming back to life. "Sorry. What were you saying?"

"Nothing; it's fine." My face warms and oh my God. Blushing is so fucking annoying. Be gone, foul anxiety. "I was just...."

"Imparting wisdom to me."

"Sure. Yeah. The combined wisdom and experience of my twenty-two years plus a degree I have yet to find a use for. Please take it with all due seriousness."

"I'll do that." The tension he's feeling seems to ease. His shoulders relax; his hands gesture around him. "I like this place."

"Me too."

"Probably not quite right for a wedding, though."

"Probably not," I agree. The weird mood has lifted. I want to ask him what it was about, but I don't know him well enough to pry. So instead, I settle for staring at him. Good Lord he's pretty. I've said it before and I'm sure I'll soon be saying it again. While I feel sort of bad for objectifying him, what can you do when he's right there breathing and existing and getting all up in my face? More importantly, I like him. Not a thing that happens often. And he can quote Austen. Still, rushing in doesn't feel right. "I bet you've got a girl in every town you've been to."

"If you're asking if I've spent all of my time wandering alone, then the answer is no," he says. "I've met lots of different people, worked lots of different jobs. Spent a lot of time staring out Greyhound bus windows, too."

"Hmm."

"What about you? Do you make new friends and acquaintances at the bar often?"

"No, not normally."

He stares at me and every damn time he does it my nerves start to tingle. But it's only chemistry, sexual attraction. Nothing to get my panties in a knot over. In all likelihood, it's the reptile part of my brain indicating his sperm is of interest and how he might make a good protector for me and our young. There's no actual bond between us. Not really.

"I've reached a decision," I say.

"Regarding?"

"You." I put down the fry and wipe my hands on a napkin. "I'm not taking you home with me tonight."

"You're not, huh?"

"No," I say, though my voice wavers with my lack of conviction.

The way he watches me, the look in his eye, it's as if nothing has ever been half as interesting as what just came out of my mouth and he can't wait to hear what I have to say next. A girl could get drunk on this kind of attention. But hot males and I do not have a good history. It's your usual pathetic backstory. Heartbreak, shattered dreams, and angsty songs played on repeat for weeks on end annoying the living shit out of everyone in the vicinity.

Much safer if my pants remain fastened. At least for the time being.

"Okay," he says.

"Assuming, of course, that all of this flirting is leading somewhere and you were interested in going home with me?"

"It is and I am."

A group of butterflies is called a flutter. And that's exactly what's going on in my stomach right now. "Perhaps another night, then..."

All of the smiles he flashed me before were nothing compared to the smaller, more thoughtful one he gives me now. Holy shit. My heart hammers inside my chest and my brain is both dazed and confused. I am utterly beguiled. That's the word for it. This man is the perfect mix of funny, gorgeous, and intriguing. "No rush. After all, we have the rest of our lives together. And, when you're ready, I'm happy to wait through however many bouts of meaningless sex before we go all the way to coffee. Whatever it takes for you to feel comfortable."

I shake my head. "You know, I honestly can't decide if you're crazy, comedic, or something else entirely."

Beck just grins.

Down at the beach, all is pretty much quiet and still. Most of the attractions on the pier shut down hours ago. I don't usually come here in the early hours of the morning, but Beck was interested so here we are. Guess neither of us want the night to end. Which is wonderful. The sand is cool under our feet, the moon low. In a few hours, it'll be dawn.

"I'd like to hold your hand, if that's not too forward."

"I think that would be okay." I place my palm in his and he immediately laces our fingers together. His skin is warm, his hand large. It suits his size. Yet we seem to fit together just fine. Without being told, he shortens his strides so I'm not left behind or dragged along.

"I think taking it slow is the right idea, at least for the next forty-eight hours or so." His expression is thoughtful, gaze looking out at the water. "We want to build a solid foundation for our marriage."

"Right," I drawl. "Dare I ask, have you been married before?"

"No, I haven't. What about you?"

"Nope," I say.

"Then our expertise is on the same level." He gives my fingers a squeeze. "I have a good feeling about this, Alice. A very good feeling indeed."

Waves lap at the shore, the sound soothing. After all the noise at the bar and then the bright lights at the diner, it's good to be outside in the clean ocean air. To stare off into the distance and think not particularly deep thoughts. My feet hurt and my head is tired, but the company is lovely. He has the hem of his jeans rolled up, toes digging into the sand. And his bare feet are every bit as attractive and interesting as the rest of him. Toes have never particularly titillated me before, yet here we are.

"Never really spent much time at the beach," he says. "More used to the mountains."

"There're no sharks in the mountains." A random but relevant comment. Shark week made an impression on me. "So it's probably safer."

"Yeah." He scratches at the dark stubble on his chin. "It does have that going for it. Though they do have Bigfoot up in the hills."

"But does he actually attack people or is he more of a hairy introvert who just wants to be left alone?"

"The latter, I think."

"Can't believe you rock climb. Isn't that hard?"

"Well, it's not always easy."

"You use safety harnesses and wear a helmet, right?"

He winces. "Ah, not so much."

"You free climb?" I tear myself free of his grip and turn on him. "Beck, that's dangerous. People die doing that."

"But it's cool, right?"

"Are you doing it because you think it's cool?"

He shakes his head. "No. It's for the challenge. Me against the mountain. See, there's not just the physical aspect, but there's the mental fortitude required as well. It's an amazing experience."

"I don't even know why you bother flirting with me," I say. "I think staying up past my bedtime to finish a book is a perilous and exciting adventure."

"Climbing is a calculated risk and I am as careful as can be. Promise not to make you a widow anytime soon, if that helps."

"Thanks. I think you're very brave."

He just smiles.

Meanwhile, my frown is intense. I can feel it. While this has been fun, it makes no sense whatsoever. Insecurity is a bitch, but it's not always without cause. "You know, at first I thought you were just talking to me because Rob dared you or something."

"You did? Why would you think that?" He frowns back at me.

I just shrug. No need to delve into my various complexes and issues right here and now. Or ever, for that matter.

"Let me state unequivocally for the record," he says. "I'm not here to hurt your feelings or lead you on, okay?"

"Okay."

He motions me closer with his hand. "Now you say it back to me."

"Ah, I'm not going to hurt your feelings or lead you on."

"Thank you," and he says it so sincerely. Guess I'm not the only one who's been screwed over in the past. "Now what do you think about our future prospects, wife?"

"I still think we're complete opposites."

"So according to your comments over dinner, we will therefore have much to discuss for the rest of our lives." He steps closer. Moonlight and shadows make him even more handsome. A little dangerous and a lot mysterious. The breeze tousles his hair and he stares back at me, calm as can be. He keeps his emotions well contained. I can't read him at all. Though the comedy seems like a type of protection, a sleight of hand to hide his real feelings. I can't talk; sarcasm and wit are my crutches of choice.

"I didn't think you were paying attention," I say.

"Of course I was." He takes another step closer. Our chests are almost touching now and his gaze never leaves my face. The heat of his body is intense, the pull of him extreme. Like he's this giant magnet I want to fall into and crash against. Stupid of me not to take him home tonight and get naked, preferably with no lights on. A real lost opportunity. How often does someone of Beck's caliber come along? Answer: next to never. "According to the rules of taking it slow, Alice, I'm not allowed to kiss you yet. Which is damn hard when you're looking at me that way."

"There are rules?"

"You don't know them? To be exact, I'm quoting article five subsection seven."

"That one, huh?"

"That's right. No kissing on the first date. And definitely no head."

A laugh stutters out of me. "Oh. What a shame."

"It is. But we can hug it out and discreetly feel each other up over our clothing," he says, his voice low and hypnotic. "If you like."

"Actually, that sounds quite nice."

"I was hoping you'd feel that way. All right, then." He holds his arms open. "I'm ready."

We're so close I barely need to move to be in his embrace. My arms go around his waist and my cheek rests against his pec. Arms wrap around me, holding me tight. He smells amazing, warm man flesh with the faint hint of sweat and the lingering scent of his aftershave. Combined with the salt air, it is all things good and right in this world. I could get high off of him, no problem. He holds me against him while his other hand is busy giving me a neck rub. The pads of his fingers stroking over my skin before kneading the muscle with just the right amount of pressure. The man knows what he's doing. I give this hug eleven out of ten.

Meanwhile, his face is buried in the top of my head, sniffing at my long blond hair. He's not even being discreet.

"I probably smell of stale beer," I say, trying to be helpful.

His chest moves slightly as he chuckles. "No. It's something floral."

"Hibiscus."

"Ah. Pretty."

It's actually from a dry shampoo because I'm two days past needing to wash my hair. Though he doesn't need to know this. The length of my leg hairs would also probably scare the man, but such is life. Sometimes a girl just needs to go natural. Also, I wasn't in the mood or anticipating getting this close with anyone. At least, not tonight. Being female can be ridiculously high maintenance.

But back to the hugging.

It's funny, his body is hard yet comfortable and the way he holds me is nothing less than swoon worthy. Like I'm treasured and protected. But also wanted. And with my breasts squished against his chest, he can no doubt feel my hard nipples reacting to his touch. Oh well. With his firm hand now working its way up and down my spine, going a little lower each time, teasing us both, there's no innocence about this embrace. Something is also happening in his pants.

"Isn't this nice?" he whispers. "And so chaste."

"You know, I was just thinking that."

His palm eases over the top of my ass cheek, fingers digging into the flesh just a little, grabbing hold of me. I slide my hands under the hem of his T-shirt, needing to feel his skin. Hot, smooth, and perfect. It's a visceral thing, the need to get closer. I rest my chin on his chest, staring up at him. Being this close gives me full body tingles. In this low light, his gaze is all dark and mysterious. And very sexy. The man makes me so giddy I can't think straight. Too many sensations, so much yum. It wouldn't take much to reach up and press his mouth to mine. How tempting. I can barely even remember why I thought waiting to go further was a good idea. Caution means nothing when your blood's running hot and your hormones have been so thoroughly agitated.

Then, I ruin it all by yawning. My jaw even cracks nice and loud. "Oh God. Sorry."

He laughs. "Think we better call it a night. Let you get some sleep."

"Yeah. I guess so."

"Want me to walk you home?"

I shake my head. "It's fine, thanks."

And he just stands there and looks at me for the longest moment. If only I could read his mind. I don't know why this gets to me so much, all of the attention he's showing. But it does. My body adores the way this man watches me as if nothing else matters. The complete focus in his gaze. Already I'm learning there's nothing half-assed about Beck. A change from the last few guys I dated. Not that we're dating. I don't actually know what this is.

"I'll see you tomorrow, right?" he asks, hand resting low on my back, thumb rubbing back and forth against the cotton of my shirt.

"Right." I smile. I can't wait.

CHAPTER TWO

WHEN HE WALKED INTO WORK THE NEXT DAY, I FELT LIKE I COULD breathe again. Like I'd been bracing myself, expecting him to disappear, expecting to be disappointed. I don't want to feel this way. I don't want to be this invested. It isn't wise. I kind of also dressed up for him, but also for myself. Sixty/forty maybe. I don't know. But one of my favorite outfits is a pair of skinny jeans that hug my ass and a short-sleeved black button down with a stand-up collar. Makes me feel fancy, especially with my hair braided and small silver hoop earrings.

I have it so bad for the boy. God help me.

And hey, odds are good that he will lose interest. Get distracted by one of the babes who frequent the bar or something. Lord knows he receives enough attention. Not that I was watching him all night. But I was sort of watching him all night. What can I say? He's very watchable. Or maybe he'll get sick of the place and its dumbass management and leave. Who could blame him? And yet, after closing time, when it's just he and I...

"Would you mind disposing of these for me please, wife?" he asks, depositing a collection of numbers and names scrawled on pieces of beer mats, dockets, and other strips of paper on the bar.

"You sure you don't want to keep any of them?"

"Nope."

"Okay." I sweep them all up in my hands and drop them into a trashcan. "Why does giving them to me feel like a statement on your part?"

"Because it is," he says. "Sometimes it's important to not only do the right thing, but to be seen doing it."

"Huh."

"That's some wisdom from my stepmom."

"Are you close to her?" I ask.

"Yeah. Reasonably so." He turns his face away. "Like I said, complicated family."

"You must miss some of them, though, right?"

"Sure." The dismissive way he says this is less than convincing. "Some of them."

"Don't you get lonely, moving from town to town?"

For a long moment, he just looks at me. The hint of sadness in his eyes giving way to something else. Happiness or hope maybe. It's hard to say. Beck is a mystery I long to unravel.

"Not when I'm with you," he says. "When I'm with you, wife, I'm exactly where I want to be."

"Smooth."

He grins and leans the broom against a table, resting his elbows on the bar. "Do you have any phone numbers you feel the need to dispose of? No pressure."

"Ha. No pressure." I smile. "But no. I don't accept numbers."

"I hope you'd accept mine. If I had a phone."

"You don't have a phone?"

"No." He shakes his head. "When you have a cell, then people you don't necessarily want to be able to contact you can do so and it's just a steep path straight into hell so far as I can tell."

"Ah."

"If it was just you sexting me that would be fine. But it inevitably wouldn't be." And at these words his mask slips once more. Just like last night in the diner when he went blank and distant. Only this time, his jaw is rigid. Seems like whatever he's trying to outrun isn't behind him just yet. But I guess that could be said of most of us and our emotional baggage.

I hate seeing him hurt or upset. "If you had a phone, I would definitely accept your number."

His answering grin is the slow sexy one. It turns my knees to water. "I'm very glad to hear that, Alice. How about a drink?"

"Not a problem. What would you like?"

"Whatever you're having."

"We're having a drink together? All right, let me see." I set up two shot glasses and pour the Don Julio silver tequila. If I hadn't already cleaned up the bulk of the bar I'd have made us margaritas. But maybe another time. It's a warm late summer night and tequila feels about right.

"You're not messing around," he says.

"Nothing says you're serious like tequila." We each pick our glasses, clinking them together before downing them in one. The liquor warms my throat all the way down. Shots are always a bit dangerous. But then everything about this man feels dangerous. To my head and my heart and my loins combined.

He does a little bow. "Now I would like to ask you to dance."

"Are you sure we're up to that? What do the rules say?"

"Since dancing is basically just hugging and rocking back and forth a little, strictly speaking, we would still be in accordance with the rules. As long as you can restrain yourself from attempting any ass grabbing, that is."

"Well, I'll do my best. But no promises."

"May I check out your playlist please, wife?"

I pass him my phone, wandering around to the other side of the bar. He takes his time selecting a song, smiling, frowning, and even snorting at some of my music choices. Judgey, much? Finally, "You're the One" by Greta Van Fleet starts playing over the stereo system. You really can't beat it for a slow rock ballad. He has taste. And I stand there like an idiot, unwilling to make the first move. Again he simply opens his arms in invitation.

"I'll try not to step on your toes," I joke, getting nearer to him.

"Stomp to your heart's content. I can take it."

Where to touch him…his broad shoulders seem like the safest choice, so I rest my hands lightly there. Meanwhile he slides his arms loosely around my waist. The moment I touch him, enter into his personal space, it's not awkward anymore. It's exciting and thrilling and a thousand other things. But not uncomfortable.

"Don't forget to leave room for Jesus," he says.

Only we don't. With each sway of our bodies we get closer until any kind of spiritual figure would have definite issues getting between us. But I figure Jesus has better things to do at this hour anyway. After a long night at work, my feet hurt and I probably smell suspect, but none of it matters. My heart beats hard and his arms surround me. I'm exactly where I want to be. Never would I have thought of my workplace as having any hint of a romantic vibe. Only it's him and me alone again. Anywhere would do.

"All of Me" by Billie Holiday comes on and we neither stop nor speak. We just keep moving to the music. My hands creep up to the back of his neck where his skin is bare and warm to the touch. His eyes are the most amazing shade of hazel. Like some lovesick fool I could stare into them for hours. I don't think I've slow danced with someone since high school. Don't get me wrong, there have been memorable times in my adult life. I've been given roses and taken to dimly lit restaurants. But being here with him is quickly becoming peak romance.

Next is "Lover" by Taylor Swift and we dance on. He doesn't try to kiss me so I don't make a move either. There's no need for more just yet. Doing this, being this close, is beautiful. I want about a hundred more moments like this with him. Possibly a great deal more.

When the music stops, we gradually still. And there's this moment when it's just me and him and the city around us seems perfectly silent. How good it is to simply be in his arms and to have the full focus of his attentions. To know that maybe, just maybe, I'm safe here with him. The chambers of my heart fill up with him, one by one, and it's both wonderful and terrifying.

"That was nice," he says in a low voice.

"Yes, it was."

He looks down, taking in the way our bodies are pressed together. "Baby Jesus would be appalled."

"I do so hate disappointing infant gods."

"You know, fifty years from now we're going to look back on tonight and you're going to regret not taking the opportunity to feel me up," he says. "Just going for it and grabbing my junk like you own it."

"Oh my God, Beck." I laugh. "That was such a perfect romantic moment and you just killed it."

"I did?"

"Dead and buried."

He scratches at his head. "Well, shit. I was only being honest."

"Of course you were."

With a smile, he takes a step back. I miss him immediately. The heat and the feel of him. Maybe I should have taken him home last night. Though this slower pace has a sweetness and heat I can't help but enjoy. Despite the crazy things that come out of his mouth and the insane cravings he inspires in me just by existing. Damn the man.

"So," he says.

I break out in gooseflesh from the way he looks at me. As if not only am I the only woman in the room (which I am), but quite possibly on the whole damn planet. As I've mentioned before, his attention is addictive.

"How about I get the mopping done and then take you on a second date to the diner?" he asks. "See if I can't bring the romance back to our burgeoning long-term relationship."

"A second date, huh?"

"It's a big step, I know. But I think we're ready. What do you think?"

I nod, my stomach turning upside down. "Let's do it."

The more time we spend together, the more I feel and the harder I fall. It's inevitable. The next night after work, we grab some pizza and walk through downtown. This has fast turned into a habit, us spending time together after work. Delaying the moment when we both go our separate ways. And yet I still haven't invited him home and he's made no further moves. Maybe if we don't rush things he'll grow to like the place and/or me and stay a while. That would be nice. Though there's also the faint fear that if we have sex then all of this amazing thrilling sexual tension will disappear. We'll be nothing more than two strangers who happen to have seen each other naked and in potentially awkward positions. Hookups are all well and good. But when it comes to him, I want more.

"I think I need that shirt," he says, nodding to a shop window.

"You don't find the mix of fluorescent leopard and zebra print somewhat aggressive?"

"But they have a dress in that print too. We could match."

"That would be something."

"And we'd never lose each other in a crowd."

"True." I oh-so-gracefully deal with a string of cheese attached to my chin. In the next shop window are a selection of formal gowns. All of them sleek and beautiful and so not my size. "For a while when I was little I wanted to be a fashion designer."

"What changed your mind?"

"I suck at sewing. No patience for it at all."

"Ah."

"But I would draw all of these pictures and Mom and I would

look through fashion magazines and sites together. It was one of our bonding things. That and books."

High up above, the moon peaks out from behind gray clouds. Being with Beck is, as always, enjoyable. The flow of conversation comes easy as if we're old friends. Then there's the way he watches me...it's safe to say my needs are growing. "Want" is too small and passive a word. I need to crawl all over him, to feel his heat and taste his skin. No matter my fears, it may be time to heed the call to action and make a move. I'll overthink it first for a while just to be sure.

"What did you want to be when you were growing up?" I ask, dragging my mind out of his pants.

His grin is wide. "Professional skateboarder."

"Cool. Were you good at it?"

"I know my way around a half pipe."

"So what changed your mind?" I ask.

The line between his brows returns. I hate that line. He stares out at the palm trees and sighs. "It's just a stupid kid's dream, right? Like wanting to be an astronaut or a fireman. You grow up and realize that's not how life works. Just because you like the idea of something doesn't mean you've got what it takes to make it to the top in that field."

"I don't know about that. Don't people now have three to five different careers over the course of their lives?" I ask. "You said you already changed the road you were on. What's another diversion if it leads to possible future happiness?"

"Pretty sure even busboys earn more than most skateboarders."

"You may have a point." I wave my fist at the sky. "Damn you, adulthood, with all of your inevitable debt and bills and endless cycles of existential crises."

He smiles. I made him smile. Victory.

A big fat drop of water hits my cheek. Sure enough, the

heavens open and down comes the rain. We run for cover beneath the shop awnings. "Perhaps I shouldn't have taunted the gods."

"Perhaps not," he says.

"If skateboarding isn't your destiny, then where do you see yourself in ten years?"

He makes a humming noise. Much thinking is obviously going on. "Sitting on a porch with you watching our children frolic in the front yard."

"Oh, we're having children now, are we?"

"Guess that's up to you."

I shake my head. "This time answer the question seriously."

"Okay." He sighs. "The grim reality is, I'll probably be back in Denver working for the family business."

"The one you're currently AWOL from?"

"Yep. This pleasant break from all of the bullshit will end eventually. I'll go back and do what's expected of me." And he doesn't look happy about it either. "What about you?"

"I don't know. I think I'd like to do some post-grad study. But the cost involved..." I let the thought dwindle away. One day I'll figure it out and find my motivation. Stop being the runt of the family. My brother is in IT and is doing great. But then, he was always top of his science classes. Meanwhile, I had my nose in a book and my head in the clouds. Real life can be hard for a dreamer who lives mostly inside their own head. Or maybe it's just bouncing back from disappointments that takes longer. Hard to move forward when your mind has a penchant for torturing you by reliving your worst moments and undermining your confidence. Sometimes I really am my own worst enemy. One day I'll grow up, get a better job, and be a great success. Make my parents proud. Anytime now would be good.

I finish the slice of pizza and commence wiping my greasy fingers with a paper napkin. Oh, awesome. An oil spot marks the front of my pale blue shirt.

"Come here." He catches my chin, carefully wiping beside my lips with his own napkin. "Wife, you're a hot mess. Emphasis on hot."

Maybe this is it. Maybe now he'll finally make his move. After all, you couldn't ask for a more romantic setting. Rain and misty streetlights. Just me and him and a whole sleeping city. Apart from the drunk down the way shouting out lyrics to a Led Zeppelin song. Someone yells at him to shut up from a nearby building. Such is LA.

"But that song's a California classic," I murmur.

"Like and/or lust in her eyes and tomato sauce on her lips."

"At least it's not in my hair." And we're standing so close, but all I want is to get closer. The man makes me greedy. "Beck?"

"Hmm?"

"What are you thinking about?"

"Stuff. Important stuff."

"Oh, really?" I smile. "Are you going to kiss me?"

His gaze fixes on my mouth, pupils large and dark. "Kiss you?"

"Yes."

He brushes the pad of his thumb slowly over my bottom lip. Such a small touch yet it echoes through me making every nerve ending sing. This man is magic. He licks his lips and I can almost taste him, I swear.

"I should," he says, his breath leaving him on a sigh. "But I'm not going to. Not yet."

"Why not?"

Instead, he takes me in his arms, fitting his long strong body to mine. Of course, this is all nice and good and even beginning to get a little familiar. The scent of him and the way he rests his cheek on top of my head. I tighten my arms around his waist, pressing myself up against him. In response, one of his hands slides down my back, grabbing hold of my ass. Nothing subtle about the move, but I don't mind. We're as wound around each other as we can manage on a city street. As close as we can be while fully dressed.

"I will kiss you," he whispers in my ear. "When the time is exactly, perfectly, without a doubt, right."

"That'd better be soon."

"It will be."

Here's the thing...dick is, generally speaking, readily available. What's rarer is liking the person with the appendage. It presents something of a quandary if you're attempting a simple straightforward sort of existence. Not that I know what I'm doing with my life. Let's not pretend I have a clue. But wanting to talk, spend quality time together, as opposed to just playing naked before moving on, is tricky. Sex becomes much less meaningless when you grow feelings for the guy. When you can't stop thinking about him and want to know his opinion about pretty much everything.

And that's a little scary because feelings are the worst.

Then there's the complication of us working together. Though, to be fair, it might not be an actual impediment so much as me searching for reasons to try and slow down my head and my heart. Any opportunity to guard against future hurt has, however, long since passed. Let's be honest.

"Food?" he asks as I lock the back door.

We've known each other for four days and we already have a coupledom routine. This is crazy.

"Wife," he says, placing a hand low on my back. "You're frowning. What can I do?"

"Just thinking."

"About what?"

Further revealing my various neuroses and assorted fears regarding his interest in me won't help anything. I shake my head, shove the keys into my handbag, and tell him a lie. "It was a busy night, is all."

"Yeah, it was."

Unresolved sexual tension fills the dark alley along with the scent of garbage. He smiles and, as usual, my stomach turns upside down and inside out. It's messy and gravity defying, the effect he has on me. If only he didn't make me feel things outside of the crotch region. Life would be so much simpler. I don't believe in love at first sight or even within the first few weeks of acquaintance, to be honest. It's too Hollywood. Too extreme. Yet while I'm not exactly sure what this is, it feels important. And given we both have the next two days off, now is the time to figure it out.

"Are you up to being wooed over ketchup and fries? Or we don't have to go to the diner," he says. "I mean, if you're not in the mood or whatever. We could do something else. Go for pizza again or take another walk on the beach, maybe?"

My brain has stalled. I have nothing. "Um..."

"Or I can just walk you to your car, if you want. Say good night." Now he's frowning too. It's contagious, apparently. "Say something, Alice. You're making me nervous and I'm not used to it."

"Which is weird given how it's basically my state of being."

"What's wrong?"

"Nothing, I'm just...I'm thinking. I need a minute."

"One minute." He holds his plastic wristwatch up to his face. "And...go."

"Very funny," I mumble.

Beck doesn't own a car. He says he doesn't need one. When he decides it's time to move on, he just catches a bus or train into the next town. In the meantime, he's living in a hostel nearby. Further proof that this is all temporary. A dalliance. An opportunity only open to me for a limited amount of time so I should make the most of it while I can. That would be the smart thing to do. Thinking about how much I'll probably miss him when he's gone would be less smart, however, yet unavoidable for various reasons.

What are my options? If I'd never met him that would have been sad. He makes me laugh. Hell, the last few days I've actually *looked forward* to work. And attempting to friend zone him would never have succeeded. The thirst is real. Though even in that impossible instance, it still would have sucked when he left. I think my anxiety has now mentally covered every possible scenario between us. Enough of the dithering.

I take a deep breath. "I've reached another decision."

"Hmm?"

"Yes," I say. "The time has come. I think we should just fornicate and be done with it... Beck?"

Only he's not listening.

Instead, he's staring over my head into the nearby parking lot that the alley leads to. A shiny luxury SUV sits beneath the one lone crappy light. Many is the night I've run to my car terrified of stalkers. From the back of the car emerges a man with a silver head of hair wearing a three-piece suit. Someone else waits in the driver's seat, barely visible behind the dark tinted glass.

Beck's jaw firms, a muscle popping out on the side. He is not a happy camper.

The stranger just stands there, watching us. Until finally, he speaks. "I didn't think you'd want me to come inside."

A grunt from Beck.

"If you'd have answered your cell, I wouldn't have had to come."

"Got rid of it months ago," says Beck. "What are you doing here? I thought I made it pretty clear I wanted to be left alone."

"You did, but I'm afraid I have some bad news." He sighs heavily before walking closer. An unimpressed gaze takes me in for all of a second before returning to the man at my side. Brows drawn in tight, he says, "Beck, your father..."

"What about him?"

"He's dead."

Oh no.

"What?" Beck stiffens. "How? When?"

"Eight days ago of a heart attack," the man reports, not unsympathetically. "It was quick; he didn't suffer."

Beck just shakes his head. I slip my hand into his and his fingers tighten on mine. Like he needs something or someone to hold on to.

"It took us a while to find you." The man inhales, wrinkling his nose at the smell. "You need to come home. They're delaying the funeral for you, but they can't wait much longer."

"People will talk," says Beck in a mocking tone.

"People always talk. But the point is you should be with your family right now. They need you."

Beck nods sharply. "Wait for me in the car."

The man doesn't hesitate, just about-faces and does as told. Suddenly I'm not so sure I know the person whose hand I'm holding.

Beck scowls at the luxury vehicle in silence.

"I'm so sorry," I say. Not really knowing what the hell else to say. And even though all I want is to be there for him, there's an awful, selfish part of me that's whispering that this is where it all ends. That this fancy black SUV is about to whisk him away forever, before we were ever actually together.

He looks at me like he's surprised to see me there. But his grip tightens. I don't want to let him go either. "Alice."

"Hey. Are you all right?"

"No, not really," he says. "I want you to come with me."

"What?"

Next he looks at the building, mouth skewed with distaste. "I have to go and you hate this place anyway. You said so. Come with me."

"Where to?"

"Denver, Colorado. It'll be an adventure."

"Beck, you're going home to bury your father. Do you really think now is the right time for—"

"We're in the middle of something here," he says, clutching my hand to his chest. There's a manic energy to him now. An edge I haven't seen before. If the cool and amusing persona is his mask, then this is a big part of what lies beneath. An iron will. I know because he's currently trying to bend me to it. His grip on my hand and the look in his eye couldn't be more intense. "Aren't we?"

"Yes, but…"

"I'm not sure when I'll be able to come back, is the thing. My family is complicated." He swallows. "Come with me. Please."

"What, and just leave everything behind?"

"Yeah. For a little while, at least," he says, leaning in close. "Don't you want to see where this goes?"

"Beck…"

"I don't want to go back on my own."

My mind is in chaos. Too many thoughts and feelings and questions. And all I can keep thinking is that I've got two loads of laundry to do tomorrow. That I'm due at my parents' tomorrow night for dinner. That there's a crushing student debt hanging over my head. So much everyday nonsense. But that nonsense is my life. The mystery that is Beck and the thrill of being with him…it shouldn't replace the small amount of stability I have here. I know better than to throw caution to the wind and put my life on hold for a guy I just met. Even if I have feelings for him. "I can't just up and leave for someone I've only known for four days, Beck. I'm so sorry for what you're going through. For losing your father. But I can't."

His face takes on that aloof expression I hate, and he gives my hand a final squeeze. The smile he gives me is all things false in this world. "Sure. I understand."

I've let him down. Fuck it, I've let both of us down. Being an adult sucks. "You better go. They're waiting."

"Let me, um...I'll walk you to your car first."

"Okay. Thanks."

Something inside my chest hurts. And it only gets worse when he waits for me to lock myself in my vehicle before giving me another grim smile and tapping his knuckles once on the roof of my old sedan. For a long moment, we just stare at each other. We're saying goodbye. That's the truth and it's fucking awful. I start the car engine and he stands there in the dirty little lot, watching me leave, while I watch him in my rearview mirror. Doing my best to block out the pain and remember every last detail. Everything about him and how being with him made me feel. Going, going, gone.

There's something messed up about me watching the sun rise. Given how deeply I appreciate my sleep and that I have no particular spiritual leanings, it just shouldn't happen. Especially once you factor in my crazy work hours. There is no excuse. Yet here we are.

I sit on my crappy little patio as the sky turns grey, violet, white, yellow, and orange over Los Angeles. The smog and urban buildup is a nice touch. I have my earbuds in, listening to the small playlist Beck made me. Greta Van Fleet, Billie Holiday, and Taylor Swift on repeat. An awful bottle of white wine sits almost empty at my feet. All in all, the scene is quite pathetic.

But I made the right choice. Or did I?

What I should do, is call a friend and talk it out. That's what a normal person would do. Only, Natasha who used to work at the bar moved to New York, and with the time difference she'll already be at work. And Hanae, my roommate from college who is now living in San Diego, has bad insomnia. So if she's actually asleep there's no way I'm going to risk waking her. Mrs. Flores next door is seventy-eight and also needs her sleep. Same goes for my sister-in-law with a small child. I am all alone with my wallowing in self-pity.

It's too bad that I only have a handful of options. But, the thing is, I'm a bit of a shitty friend. I never set out to be, yet somehow I just let it happen. Over the last year or so I've become awful at keeping in touch with people and showing up to things. Friends from high school and college have all sort of drifted away. Reaching out now in my time of melodrama feels off. Maybe it's what Beck and I had in common: we're both a bit lost and alone when it comes to living our lives right now. I could call Mom. She wouldn't mind. But what if she decides to be sensible and say that pining for someone you've only known for four days is stupid? No, thank you. I'm in need of empathy, not admonition.

I hope he's okay. Both of my parents are still alive. The idea of one of them passing is horrible. Of someone who's been such a huge part of your life being gone. Then there's the whole part where he'd said he wanted to steer clear of his family for the foreseeable future. Now he's going to have to deal with the loss of his father and all of them en masse. Poor Beck.

I swill down the last of the wine, wincing because it's not only warm but acidic and generally disgusting. Damn me and my cheap alcohol. However, it was the only thing I had in the apartment. Stupid to be lonely when you live in a city surrounded by millions. Makes no sense at all. But I miss him. Dumbass feelings.

Guess I might as well put my half-drunk ass to bed. Get up later and do laundry and get some groceries and go through the motions of my normal life. Because that's what I'm back to...normal. The word never felt so small and sad.

Back at work, Rob is infuriated by his latest busboy's desertion. I try to explain about the deceased father and everything, but it doesn't help. Rob keeps right on yelling. The man is a bag of dicks. Anyway. Pretty sure Beck isn't coming back anytime soon and doesn't need the job or the money. Not after seeing the luxury vehicle and the dude in the slick suit taking his orders.

What was with that and who the hell is he? These are both questions I'd dearly love to have answered. Though the likelihood of this happening is low. Google could possibly answer these questions if only I knew his last name. Since he was working for cash under the table, not even Rob can tell me, if he were so inclined.

Beck and I never really discussed family or finances. Not in depth. Though you don't normally get into personal shit like that within the first few days of knowing someone. It takes time to build trust. And we had plenty of other things to talk about. But maybe he really is a single man with a fortune. How bizarre. My parents are both schoolteachers. That's how they met and fell in love. We were okay, but not rich or anything. Any knowledge of how the other half lives is restricted to TV and the internet. I can't imagine the Beck I knew collecting dirty glasses and mopping the floor being waited on hand and foot. It just does not compute.

Two and a half days since he left and my heart is still hung over. I want to see him again. Best not to hold out hope, though. It just leads to further harm.

Meanwhile, work sucks. It's twice as busy now that we have to clear tables as well as take orders. Kari is also being even more useless than normal and half her customers move to my side. But more importantly, Beck's absence feels huge. My whole world is smaller and less special somehow. No sharing smiles with him. No listening for his voice among all of the noise. No end of the night/ early morning walks on the beach, dancing, or eating at the diner. Without him here, I feel like I'm back to just going through the motions. Not even wearing my favorite navy boho-style shirt is helping.

I need to get a life. That is the big ugly truth. The hole inside of me can't be filled with love interests or other distractions. My happiness is my own job. I just need to figure out where to start.

Halfway through the night, a big dude in a black suit sits at one of the tables. He puts down some money and gives me a bland impersonal smile. "Diet Coke. Keep the change."

"You only want the soda?"

His hands rest on the table in front of him, fingers laced. "That's right."

"This is a fifty-dollar bill."

"Yes, it is."

"Okay, then."

I fetch him his drink while he plays with his cell. And that's it. He sits there sipping his diet soda. After an hour is up, he orders another, leaving a second fifty-dollar bill on the table. The process is repeated. Aside from his excessive tipping, there's a strange formality to the man. I don't know how else to describe him. But the night is busy and I don't have time to think about it. Though he keeps watching me. Which is more than a little creepy.

"Are you sure there's nothing else I can get you?" I ask, upon delivering his third diet soda of the night.

"There is something I'd like to discuss when you take your break." A statement like this deserves red lights and warning bells.

"I'm in a relationship," I lie.

"Nothing like that," he says in a rush. "Beck asked me to pass on a message to you."

My heart stutters. "Beck?"

"Yes." The man's brows rise. "You are Alice, aren't you?"

"Yes. Yes, I am. And I already had my break earlier." As per usual, I spent said break hiding out in the lady's bathroom sitting in a locked stall (with the toilet seat down). It's the one place I can usually rest my feet uninterrupted for five solid minutes. "What's the message?"

"That I'm here in case you change your mind."

Huh. "That's what he said? That's everything?"

"Yes, miss," says the big buff man. "My name is Smith and

I'll be in the bar every night between eight and two for the next week. Then I'll wait out in the parking lot to ensure you get to your vehicle safely. Those were my instructions."

I don't know what to say.

"And should you decide to change your mind, I'm to get you to Denver."

Someone calls for me, but I ignore them. "Is he all right?"

"I can't say, miss."

"Well, who is he?" I ask. "I mean…this is a lot. It's not exactly normal behavior, if you know what I mean?"

"I know what you mean," he says. "But I can't answer that question either, sorry."

"Are you also supposed to be tipping me this much?"

His smile is more genuine this time. "Your time is valuable and I'm instructed to cover those costs."

"Okay." This is all well beyond my range of experience. Someone is yelling "waitress" on repeat, but I need a minute. Possibly two. "Are you a friend or an employee or what, exactly?"

"A driver, miss."

"So this isn't all some weird involved human trafficking setup, then?" Maybe I shouldn't have said that, but I don't know. It made sense for a second inside my head. And you can't be too careful.

Smith's eyes widen. "No, it's not. You're welcome to photograph both me and my vehicle and send them to a friend or family member, if you like. We could even go by a store and purchase a Taser and pepper spray if it would make you feel safer."

"That's very considerate of you."

A nod.

Now Rob is yelling at me too. Something about getting my fat ass back to work. I hold up a hand, needing another moment to sort out my life. As I see it, the main points regarding arguments for and against going with Smith include: My job is shit. My apartment isn't much better. In fact, nothing is keeping me in

LA right now, when you get down to it. It's not like my family rely on me for anything.

"Have they had the funeral yet? Was it hard on Beck? Was he close with his father?" I clamp my mouth shut, then finally manage to ask the only question that matters. "Do you think it would help, if I was there?"

"I'm here, aren't I?"

Before I do anything, further proof is required. "Can you get him on the phone, please?"

The big man presses some buttons and, sure enough, Beck appears on screen. Instantly I move closer. Still, his voice is hard to hear over the music. "What's up, Smith? Is she okay?"

"She'd like to talk to you, sir." He angles the cell my way, not letting me hold it. Guess he's tetchy with his belongings. Or maybe he's keeping an ear out for further instructions.

Beck smiles. But it's a tired, weary one. "Wife. Get on the plane."

"You're not the boss of me."

"No. But I'd like to be. That'd be fun. Or you could be the boss of me. Whatever." His gaze shifts to something off screen for a moment and his smile dims further. Dark circles linger under his eyes. "Wish you were here."

"Me too."

"Here's your chance then," he says. "You want to be with me and I want to be with you. Enough excuses. Take the leap, Alice. Promise I won't let you fall."

I sigh. It's so damn tempting.

"I'm sorry, I have to go. Things are happening here."

"Okay."

"You're safe with Smith. I promise." And he's gone.

The screen blanks before returning to a close-up picture of a Persian cat. Smith turns the cell over, expression set in stone. I would not have picked him as a cat lover.

But the important thing here is that Beck is going through a tough time and wants me with him. That's the clincher. He also asked me if I wanted an adventure and the truth is I do. I really do. I'd even go so far as to say I'm due one.

Not sure there's actually any argument for the con side.

"One moment, please," I tell Smith before heading toward the bar. I slap my apron, pen, and order pad on the counter. "I quit, Rob. You're such an utter cock-splash. I don't want to work for you anymore. Haven't for a while now."

A red flush emerges beneath his white skin and Rob stammers something unintelligible before working his way up to shouting abusive words at me. He's not even original. You could read any of these insults on a bathroom door. Meanwhile, Phil the dickhead sits at a table with an odious smile on his face when he sees me coming his way. The man looks directly at my tits and licks his lips. He's so gross. Seriously.

"Excuse me. I just need to borrow this for a minute," I tell a dude at a table nearby as I pick up his glass of beer. With a polite smile, I pour the cold liquid into Phil's lap. It feels good. Really good. Then he's yelling too. Other people, however, are laughing and clapping. Maybe they think it's a show or something. Whatever. I'm done.

"Thanks, buddy," I say to the guy whose beer I liberated and slap down one of Smith's fifties on his table. "Next round's on me."

"Ready, miss?" Smith asks.

"Let's go."

CHAPTER THREE

"Nice Taser," says Beck, standing outside the hangar, hands in the pockets of his black suit trousers. His dark shoes are shiny, his button-down is white, and his black tie has been pulled askew. His hair is still a bit long, but artfully styled. In fancy clothes with the tattoo covered, the overall effect of him is quite different. A little intimidating, even. "Used it on anyone yet?"

"Not yet."

"No?" he asks. "Well, the day is still young and you haven't met my family."

Carefully, I finish descending the stairs of the very shiny private jet with Taser in hand. Smith insisted I have one so I'd feel secure. I may have briefly had second thoughts after he still refused to give me Beck's last name since he didn't have permission to disclose same. And why the hell is his identity such a mystery? Anyway, in my black jeans with a matching T-shirt and cardigan, I feel decidedly underdressed. But then being in Beck's general vicinity I feel like I'm a nonentity. His face is made for billboards and the silver screen. I should be asking for his autograph, not contemplating whether or not flying halfway across the country officially makes me his girlfriend. And yet here we are.

"How are you?" I ask.

"I'm okay."

"Are you really? Because it's okay not to be."

He does a one-shoulder shrug and stares at me. With his pale face and subdued gaze, he looks as if something or someone has been sucking the life out of him. About what you'd expect from a person dealing with a death in the family. I want to take up sword and shield to protect him. Ride in on a white stallion like a kick-ass princess, et cetera. But I can't guard him from this pain.

"I'm better now you're here," he says softly.

And I'm beyond happy to see him. I am. Though a lot has happened since my resignation yesterday and today's arrival in Colorado.

Smith had been keen to leave last night, or early this morning, but there'd been a couple of things I needed to do. Given I had no idea how long this adventure would last, or quite where it would take me, I needed stuff. Clothes, cosmetics, the usual. Along with the chance to wrap my head around what was happening. My potted plant, Gretchen, needed to be placed under the care of Mrs. Flores and then I had to call my parents and do some explaining. Their reactions to me leaving my job (permanently) and California (temporarily) were not encouraging. But I'm a grown-ass woman and my decisions are my own. There's also been some dwelling on my part over what Beck's lies of omission about his life actually mean. If they matter. If he owed me the truth about his background sooner. Even though, at the end of the day, we haven't known each other very long, I choose to take a leap of faith and get on the plane.

"So...that jet has big comfy leather seats and the fanciest bathroom I've ever seen," I say. "The bedroom wasn't bad either. So I guess the question is, how good is your fortune exactly?"

He grabs the back of his neck and looks away. "You can't say I didn't warn you."

"Hmm."

"If you chose not to believe me, that's not really my fault."

"Is that so?"

"I'd come closer, but I'm kind of afraid you're going to use that on me." He nods at the Taser. "What do you think are the odds of that happening?"

"Probably pretty low. I'm quite fond of you, actually. Deep down."

He cocks his head. "How deep, exactly? Just out of curiosity."

"I have questions."

"I know you do. But first, would you mind if…" Oh so carefully, he takes the Taser from my hand and passes it to Smith who happens to be walking past. The driver places it and my battered overnight bag into the back of a waiting large shiny Range Rover. Like everything related to this version of Beck, it looks new and expensive. Way out of my price range.

"Can I touch you?" he asks.

"I wish you would."

His hands cup the sides of my neck, thumbs softly sliding over my jaw. The way he looks at me is…I don't even know. It's like there's this roiling mass of emotion inside of me trying to get out. The man gives me goose pimples all over. And when his lips touch mine, everything is better and worse. On one hand, it's not enough. I want to crawl under his skin. Get inside his head and find all the answers I seek. On the other hand, it's fucking perfect. His tongue in my mouth and my hands fisted in his nice neat shirt. He explores my mouth like he's already claimed ownership and fair enough. Because we're not doing this in half measures. Our mouths stay melded together in a wet and hungry kiss that goes on and on. Six whole days of crazy coalescing into this one moment. Nothing outside of this matters. We're both breathing heavily when he stops and rests his forehead against mine. I can taste him on my lips and he is delicious. Neither of us lets go.

"Been wanting to do that for a while," he says, voice low and rough. "I'm really glad you're here."

"Me too. I missed you."

He takes my hand in his and leads me toward the car. His smile is back. Maybe not as wide as normal, but it's there. Despite being a mile higher location wise, I breathe easier being with him. He swings our joined hands between us and there's an enthusiasm or boyishness to him that is nothing less than charming. "Hope we didn't make Smith blush."

"How long has he worked for you?"

"He's been with the family since I was a kid."

"Then I'm sure he's seen worse."

"Alice," he says, nose wrinkled, "are you insinuating you weren't my first kiss?"

"I wouldn't dare. How old are you, by the way?"

"Twenty-six."

"Long time to wait for a kiss."

"To quote our dear friend Miss Austen: 'The distance is nothing when one has motive.'"

"Nice."

"Thank you." From a back pocket, he takes a pair of Ray-Ban sunglasses and slides them on. "Though it was a pretty great first kiss. I can see how you might get confused."

I just shake my head. "God, I missed you."

"Good. That's good."

"I'm like wildly underdressed."

"You're fine," says Beck, opening the car door and climbing out. "You're wearing the right color and everything."

I glance again at the couple of gentlemen entering the house. They're wearing neither jeans nor T-shirts. Nope. They're dressed like Beck.

"What, black? Oh my God. That's why all these cars are here?" Shit. Hurriedly, I follow him out of the vehicle. "I can't just turn up at your dad's funeral."

"Eh. You kind of already did."

"Maybe Smith could drop me somewhere so I can buy a decent outfit. Or I can just grab an Uber." It'll bite into my savings, but oh well. "You go inside. It won't take long."

"Stop worrying."

Easy for him to say. My shoulders are creeping higher and the sweating situation isn't good.

We're standing on the front steps of a sprawling gray stone chateau. And on a street crowded with impressive real estate, this one outshines them all. If the iron gates and hedge lined driveway leading to immaculate lawns and gardens didn't spell it out already, it's obvious we're deep in rich people land. On the drive over, Beck distracted me, pointing out various Denver landmarks and so on. With Smith in the car, I couldn't ask all the things I wanted to. I did tell him the story of my grand exit from the bar, but we need privacy to really talk things over. Judging by all the people around, I highly doubt we'll be getting it anytime soon.

"What are you, Denver royalty or something?" I ask.

He smiles. "You're funny."

While Beck is as calm as can be in the face of all this, I am distinctly less so. "This is a bad idea."

"Come on, it'll be fine," he says, leading me inside. "You're here with me. That's all that matters."

He's right. I take a deep breath and try to squash down my feelings of inadequacy. They might all be perfectly valid, but it doesn't make them relevant. As hard as it might be to get it through my head, Beck's father's funeral isn't all about me.

Beyond the double wood doors, people spill out of rooms on either side of a large two-story foyer. Everyone is dressed in immaculate black suits and elegant dresses. Servants in neat uniforms circulate with trays of drinks and appetizers. High overhead hangs a beyond spectacular chandelier. And already, people are looking at us. Not surprising. My sneakers squeak on the marble floor. Dammit.

"There you are," says a tall dude about a decade older than Beck. They actually look a little alike. Only this guy's dark hair is cut short and there's none of the boyishness left in his face. His dark suit is tailored to perfection. It's like he's the poster child for suave and serious. He gives me a brief glance before raising a brow at our joined hands. "Meeting in the library. Now."

"Alice, this is my half brother Ethan," says Beck, though the dude is already walking away. "Ethan, this is my Alice."

I go to smile in greeting, but then I don't. Because this is a funeral and not a smiling occasion. Not that his brother is even looking. Ethan just raises a hand in a brief wave-like gesture as he cuts through the crowd.

"Guess we better go." Beck moves to lead me on.

"I don't think he meant me."

"But we're sticking together, right?" he asks, bringing his face in close to mine. "I mean, I think we should. You're not safe among this crowd without your Taser, Alice. Someone could try to trade you in for some new Louis Vuitton or the latest Gucci or something. Fuck knows what could happen without me here to protect you."

"Beck..."

The man is a force of nature. Or I just suck at telling him no. A bit of both, maybe?

Then a woman steps out in front of him, drawing him to an abrupt halt. I half stumble into his back. All around us, everyone seems to be paying attention to this encounter, the chatter falling quiet. I have a bad feeling about this.

"You've been avoiding me," says the woman, placing a hand on his chest. The touch does not seem familial. She's pretty and petite with dark hair and tanned skin. And in her black sheath dress, stiletto heels, and diamonds dangling from her ears, she fits in perfectly. I, on the other hand, do not. Beck's fingers tighten around mine as if he's worried I might try to bolt.

"Yeah." Beck nods, taking a step back to remove himself from her reach. His tone of voice is distinctly unhappy. Angry, even. "And I one hundred and ten percent plan to keep on doing so."

We're off again, angling around the now furious woman and moving through the crowd even faster than before. I'm basically being dragged in Beck's wake, his grip on my hand resolute.

"Who was that?" I ask, trying to keep up.

"Someone who lost my good opinion."

"I see." I do not see. In fact, I have no damn clue about this or anything else going on around us.

We turn right at a grand piano and head down a hallway lined with formal family portraits, paintings of landscapes, and the occasional antique-looking side table, each topped with a vase overflowing with white roses. A dozen or so people are already gathered in the library. A large room full of books and dark polished wood. Every eye in the room looks our way. Some curious, some speculative. None of them particularly welcoming.

"Close the doors," says an elegant elderly woman with short white hair, sitting in a chair that's only marginally smaller and less grand than a throne. Her gaze fixes on me and she frowns. Pale fingers tighten around the ornate silver head of the walking stick she's holding. "Hurry up. Sit down so we can get started."

Beck closes the double doors as ordered before guiding me toward the only empty chair in the room, a leather wingback. I take the seat while he perches on the arm. Several people give me side-eye. I sit back as far into the seat as possible, hiding from the light of day. Or at least their piercing gazes. Mom once wrangled me an invitation to a neighbor's party when I was eight. Neither the birthday boy nor his friends wanted me there and they were not shy about letting it be known. That's sort of what this feels like. I worked two jobs during college. But I bet no one here has ever experienced money problems. I am so out of my depth. Also, I should have worn more deodorant because nerves.

A man in a three-piece suit sits behind the desk. He shuffles some papers and clears his throat. "Shall I begin?"

The elderly lady nods in a regal manner.

"This is the last will and testament of Jack William Elliot Junior. This document revokes all wills and other testamentary dispositions that I have previously made. Mr. Rahul Nair Esquire is hereby appointed as executor—"

"Just give us the basics, Rahul," she interrupts. "I don't want to be here all day."

Rahul's lips tighten at the order. "All of my shares in Elliot Industries are to be divided equally between my four children, Ethan, Emma, Beck, and Henry. My youngest son's interests will be controlled by my eldest son, Ethan, until Henry is twenty-one years of age."

A woman gasps. She's around forty and wearing a formfitting black suit. I've never met a supermodel, but she could probably be one. "But what about me? I'm Henry's mother, for heaven's sake!"

The lawyer shuffles through the paperwork for a moment before finding the relevant information. "To my wife, Giada, I leave the Bertram Street residence and twenty-million dollars. A fund to continue paying staff wages and to maintain the residence and grounds has been established. The fund will remain in force for as long as the residence remains in the family."

"Is that all?" Beige manicured nails dig into the shoulder of a teenage boy beside her. He winces, wriggling out from beneath her grip. "It can't be. I can't possibly be expected to live on just that."

At this, someone snorts. I don't see who.

"Forced to stay in that horrible museum for the rest of my life. I won't do it!"

"Continue please, Rahul," says the old lady, ignoring the drama.

"Yes, Mrs. Elliot," he answers. "The cottage on Cape Cod goes to my ex-wife, Rachel, along with my apologies. You were right, I was an ass."

A stylish middle-aged blonde laughs at this, before quietly sighing. "Yes, you were."

"Apart from the established trust funds for the grandchildren and some smaller bequests to longtime staff members and other various donations, that's basically it," says the lawyer. "The rest of his belongings and properties are to go to the four children. Any unwanted items are to be sold at auction with the proceeds to be divided equally among them."

Through all of this, Beck sits perfectly still. He might as well be a statue. His posture is perfect, the expression on his face set. Whatever he's thinking or feeling is buried deep.

A different woman, who was seated beside Ethan, rises to her feet with a smile. She's early to midthirties at a guess. "All of the years of bullshit and manipulations and he does this. Just breaks the pie into four easy pieces. Fuck me."

The elderly lady, Mrs. Elliot, knocks her walking stick against the floor twice. "Language, Emma."

"Sorry, Grandmother. But seriously...you have to see the joke in all of this."

"It's no joke," cries Giada. Tears are making tracks through her heavy makeup. Can't help but feel that it has more to do with her bank balance than burying her husband.

"If you honestly can't survive on twenty-million cash and real estate worth at least twice that then I guess it's time to go back to working for a living." Emma shakes her head. "Or you could play to your strengths and marry another rich old man, I guess."

"Emma," Mrs. Elliot growls. "Enough."

But Giada is already on her feet and storming from the room. How she can run in heels that high I have no idea. I'd break an ankle or fall on my ass.

"Darling," says the sophisticated blonde with the cottage on Cape Cod. "That was unkind. It's also neither the time nor the place."

"Yes, Mom." Emma takes the empty spot next to the teenage

boy, sliding an arm around his shoulders. But he just shrugs her off. She smiles, undaunted. "Welcome to the Billionaires Club, kid."

"Can't touch it for five years so what does it matter?" Henry, the teenager, takes a cell phone out of his pocket and gets busy doing something.

"Like your trust fund doesn't keep you in designer sneakers and sports cars and whatever other nonsense you feel you need," says Mrs. Elliot. "That will be all, thank you, Rahul."

In silence, the man gathers his papers and rises to his feet. "Each of you will receive a full copy of the document today. Don't hesitate to contact me if you have any questions. I will begin executing the relevant provisions in the very near future."

"The sooner the better." Mrs. Elliot's gaze fixes on the door through whence the angry widow just retreated.

Rahul nods. "Of course."

"Thank you, Rahul," says the Cape Cod lady.

Ethan, the big brother, stands up and shakes his hand. There's some murmuring, but I can't hear what they say. Not that it's any of my business anyway.

And then the lawyer is gone. It's just the family, and me. Some of the stiff formality of the occasion seems to ease with his departure.

Beside me, Beck is now scowling at the floor. If he had laser eyes, he'd have long since burnt a hole in the parquetry. Guess he just joined the Billionaires Club too, if he wasn't a member already. Seems like everyone around here must have had some sort of trust fund. Because, holy shit. The kind of money they're talking about…it's a lot. More than my brain can handle. Money like that requires a high-class girlfriend. Someone from the right social set. Not me. Yet here I am—the girl whose hand he's holding on to like it's a lifeline. I wish there were something more I could do for him.

"He said I was out." Beck's forehead is furrowed. "That he was changing his will."

Ethan's stern gaze gentles. "Dad said a lot of things."

"It feels weird not having him here, glaring at everyone and being disappointed in our life choices," says Emma, ruffling Henry's hair. He half-heartedly tries to duck away from her. "Speaking of which, who the hell are you?"

I sit pinned beneath her gaze.

"She's my Alice," answers Beck.

"Is she?" Emma's brows rise. "What does Selah have to say about that?"

"I didn't ask."

"I assume she's staying?" asked Mrs. Elliot. "I'll have a room made up."

"Thank you," said Beck. "But that's not necessary, we can—"

"It's necessary."

Henry smirks. "Cock blocked by Grandma."

Mrs. Elliot strikes her walking stick once hard against the ground, a pink tinge emerging beneath her white skin. "Language. All of you, go and circulate, we have guests. You will keep all mention of my son's will from your lips. I will not have Jack's funeral marked by petty squabbling. This family will show a united front. And Beck, make sure your mother doesn't meditate on the front lawn half-naked again. I have no interest in explaining her odd habits to the neighbors."

"I'll talk to her," says Beck.

"Good. Rachel, see to the girl, would you?"

"Of course," says the Cape Cod lady, giving me a small smile. Wait. Am I *the girl*? And if so, what does seeing to me entail? Then Rachel, Cape Cod lady, follows the old dame out. Guess whatever it is can wait until later.

The moment they're gone, Emma puts her feet up on the stone coffee table. The red heel is a stark contrast to the black patent leather. Those shoes probably cost more than I make in a month. Like her mom, she has a light tan appearance with perfect lips and pale blond hair. Only hers is straight and shoulder length.

"So," she says, gaze on Ethan, "you'll be the next king of the castle, but we've all got equal stakes. This should be interesting."

Ethan just grunts.

"Or at least it will be in five years' time when you lose control of Henry's vote," she amends. "It's funny. I always thought Dad would shut me out on account of having a uterus and all."

"No. You earned your place," says Ethan.

"And I didn't, I suppose?" asks Beck, easing his hand from my hold.

His brother stares back at him, face blank. "Nobody wins points for leaving when the going gets tough. You know that."

"He made it impossible for me to stay."

"Oh, grow the fuck up." Ethan's gaze is cold and hard. "He tested us all in different ways. You're the only one who decided to disappear because your delicate little feelings got hurt."

"Would both of you fucking stop it?" says Henry, jumping to his feet and heading for the door.

Emma sighs. "Kid, it's okay..."

But he's already gone.

"Well done, morons. I need a drink." Emma's head rests against the back of the sofa. She pulls out her cell and sends a message. At least, I assume that's what she did since there's a knock on the door a minute later.

"About time," she mumbles. "I'm dying here."

Beck and Ethan just keep on glaring at each other. This is not a happy family. Lots of underlying tensions. Oprah and Dr. Phil would have a field day. A death in the family is meant to be difficult, times of change always are. With the complicated family dynamics and the amount of money involved, however, it seems to be the usual amount of stress times about a hundred. As they say, money can't buy you love.

A handsome man in yet another well-tailored suit wanders into the room. Dark hair, dark eyes, olive skin, and cheekbones you could cut yourself on. He closes the door behind him, looking around at each of us with interest. Though his gaze rests the longest on Emma who dramatically says, "I need a drink."

"You need a hell of a lot more than that," he says. "But at this stage, a strong drink can't hurt."

"The therapy and medication can and will come later, rest assured." She waves a hand grandly in the air. "Alice, this is Matías. Matías, meet Alice. Consider yourself introduced."

He smiles and moves over to a well-stocked drinks trolley. "I'm the trophy husband."

"Wait," says Emma, massaging her temples. "We're back together?"

"Nope. Still getting divorced. Thank God."

"Oh, good. It's been a busy week, but I didn't think I'd have forgotten something like that."

"It's just that trophy divorcé doesn't have quite the same ring." Matías looks up from the drinks trolley. "What's wrong, your Botox bothering you again?"

Emma raises her middle finger. "If I have a headache, it's because my father just died, and two of my brothers are behaving like children, while the one who actually is a child is being raised by a cannibal in Jimmy Choos."

"Isn't Giada a vegan now?" asks Matías, pouring whiskey into five tumblers. "Thought Lise talked her into it a few months back."

Beck just shrugs. "Don't look at me. I have no idea what my mother's been up to."

"Speaking of which, Lise was so proud you'd cast off the capitalist yoke in favor of undertaking a journey of spiritual discovery across this wide land," says Emma. "Finally following in her footsteps."

"Yeah." He winces. "That was not what I was doing."

"What's wrong? Didn't you find your Patronus?"

"How much is her woo-woo company worth now, anyway?" asks Ethan.

"I don't know, forty million or so?" answers Emma. "The organic herbal-flavored waters seem to be doing particularly well for her."

Ethan shakes his head.

Matías starts passing out the drinks. First to Beck and me, followed by Ethan and Emma. The tumblers are a beautifully cut crystal, heavy in the hand, and the liquor smells delicious. Like honey and cinnamon. Far better than anything we had on the top shelf at the bar.

"The Macallan?" asks Ethan with a brow raised in amusement.

"Why not? He ain't here to stop us." Matías smiles. "To Jack."

"To Dad," says Emma in a quiet voice.

We all drink. The whiskey is indeed superior and smooth. Though it's largely wasted on me, a vodka or tequila drinker from way back. For a moment, no one talks, everyone reflecting on the deceased or enjoying the high-priced liquor. Everything is silent since any noise from the rest of the house is smothered by the thick old walls. The couple of hundred people might as well not be out there. But the illusion is broken as soon as Rachel opens the door.

"Ethan," she says, tone ever so slightly reprimanding in the way only a mother's can. "The mayor would like to talk to you."

He nods. "I'll be along in a moment."

"And I believe your grandmother expected you to socialize," she says to Emma before slipping back out into the hallway.

"'O Captain! My Captain!'" Emma rises to her feet, taking

her glass with her. "On my way. C'mon, ex. If we let the wives ogle your ass, I might not have to trade pleasantries for quite so long."

"That sounds like a whole lot of no fun," says Matías. "Beck, we need to talk. Sometime soon would be good. I know you said silent partner, but disappearing on me for six months was a little quieter than I expected."

Beck nods. "I'll be in touch."

"Good."

Only Ethan remains, draining the last of his whiskey. He gets to his feet and rolls his shoulders. "Well?"

"I want the Heritage." Beck stares back at him, gaze serious. "Outright."

"Can't say it's a surprise." Ethan's lips are pressed into a fine unimpressed line. "All right, it's yours. But that's all. You're going to have to earn back the trust of the board and shareholders on your own. Don't think Emma will help you either, after the mess you left. And remember, I'll be watching."

Beck just nods.

Ethan pauses at the door. "Nine o'clock at my office tomorrow morning for the paperwork. Just remember, you owe me. Because I won't forget."

CHAPTER FOUR

"THIS REALLY IS AN EXTRAORDINARILY YELLOW ROOM."

"You haven't been in here before?" I ask, opening drawers and cupboard doors, trying to track down my meager belongings. Turns out that being allocated a room also means someone will have already unpacked for you. I'm not sure how I feel about this. My favorite cool battered brown boots look distinctly low class sitting in the bottom of the antique armoire. At least I have my own bathroom attached. If I had to go looking for one in the middle of the night, they'd probably need to send out search parties.

Beck lies back on the grand canopied bed, hands behind his head and legs crossed at the ankle. "Don't think so. Pretty sure I'd remember this amount of chintz."

"How many bedrooms does this place have?"

"Only eight or so."

"Only."

He laughs.

"So, your fortune is very good indeed."

"It is after today," he says, voice subdued once more. "Guess you're owed a story just about now."

"That would be nice. I won't lie; I'm curious as all hell. But if you're not in the mood, I understand."

"Sit, then, and let me regale you with a tale."

"You sound like a bard." I sit on the end of the bed, getting comfortable, and stare at him. "Beck, if your grandma catches you with your shoes on the bed you'll be in big trouble."

"Nuh," he says. "She'll just give me the look of disappointment. It's her majordomo you got to look out for. That man is plain mean."

Downstairs, the wake is finally winding down. We'd speed walked through the crowd looking for his mother, as per his grandmother's instructions, but that was as close to socializing as we got. Any snippets of conversation I heard were about art gallery openings and how the dollar was trading. I've never felt more like the hoi polloi than I have today. At any rate, his mom, Lise, was nowhere to be found. Beck didn't seem especially concerned. If anything, he seemed relieved. He mumbled something about her probably deciding to leave early and then let it go. Seems she might be less than dependable when it comes to supporting her son. The woman who'd stepped into our path earlier had disappeared as well, thankfully. There's been enough drama for one day. Sheesh.

In lieu of dealing any further with his family, he took me on the scenic route to my room, via the kitchen. Here he liberated a tray full of appetizers (figs with bacon and chili were my favorite), two bottles of red wine (Beck is already halfway through the second), and here we are. Alone at last in the room where all things yellow, floral, and expensive come to die, apparently.

Not that I mind. Alone with Beck, having just him and me time, is soul-stirringly good. Watching him, listening to him, I can't keep the smile off my face. Odd, given that there was a funeral earlier, but maybe we should celebrate life on days like this. If I wasn't here...in all likelihood, he'd have been hiding out, getting drunk alone in his room right now, dealing with all of this on his own. The mere thought makes my heart hurt. An array of emotions have crossed his face today. Happy, sad, and all of the variants in between. Angry and hurt, lost and weary too. And I don't always know the right thing to say, the correct way to comfort him. But any lingering doubts I had over throwing in my job and getting on the plane are gone. Because he shouldn't ever have had to face today alone.

I know in my bones I made the right choice.

"What are you looking at?" he asks.

"You." Fuck, I love his smile. And his long body and his mind and all the rest. So doomed.

"How long can you stay?" he asks, his happy turning more serious.

"Beck, I only just arrived. I haven't really made any decisions..."

He runs his tongue over his teeth. "Okay. Challenge accepted."

"What?"

"I'm going to convince you to make your move here permanent." And he's so matter-of-fact about this. If only I had an ounce of his confidence. Because while this statement is beyond flattering, it's still a bit bewildering. He's a rich good-looking guy, he could have anyone he wants. So why me?

No way am I letting my insecurities out to play, however. "Maybe we should take things one step at a time. Why don't you just stick to you telling me your story for now?"

"For now...okay. Here we go." He takes another swig of wine straight from the bottle before clearing his throat. "Once upon a time, a canny bastard by the name of Jack Elliot decided working in his uncle's grocery store his whole life was a bad deal. The pay was crap, the hours were long, and his cousin took every possible opportunity to lord it over him."

"What a jerk."

"Indeed he was," agreed Beck. "Now, being your typical Scotsman, Jack was good at three things. Fighting, talking shit, and saving his pennies. Through this mad combination of skills, he bought up real estate. Started small and worked his way up. That turned out well for him. Especially once he started moving into building and developing as well. Next, he decided to invest in friends' businesses. Helping them grow while charging them a bundle in interest on these loans. Sometimes, when they couldn't pay him back, he'd also help them by buying them out at below cost."

"How literal are you being about the word 'friends'?"

His smile is tight. "There are some really good reasons why people don't like my family."

"Got it."

"Didn't matter about the money, though. Jacky boy still wasn't accepted by the elite and didn't that piss him off?" He smiles to himself, reading the label on the bottle of red. "So, he did what any sensible rich upstart would do and got himself an old-money society darling for a wife. The one and only Catherine Greenway of the Colorado Greenways Shipping Company."

"Your grandmother?"

"That's right. They could even trace their lineage back to some minor European royalty. Definite bonus points for that." His gaze moves from the ceiling to me, a line forming between his brows. "What are you doing all the way down there?"

"Listening to you."

"Be easier for you to hear if you were closer," he says. "And I wouldn't have to project my voice so much. It's really quite delicate. I may have forgotten to mention that."

"Your voice is delicate?"

"It's more my throat." He fake coughs. It's a pitiful thing. "See?"

"That is sad."

"Right?" As if his long lean body weren't temptation enough, the man has these beautiful hazel eyes that he knows how to use to effect. Not to mention the dark lashes he's currently fluttering in my direction. "C'mon, Alice. There's only three hundred and eighty-five cushions on this monolith of a bed. I'm sure you'll be comfortable up here beside me."

"Beck…"

"I've had a very hard day. Don't you want to comfort me?"

"You know I do."

"And yet you're still at the wrong end of the bed."

Whether or not I want to be all over him is not the question. I drop my head back and stare at the high ceiling with its fancy decorative molding for a moment before giving him my serious look. "After that kiss at the airport, I very much want to be closer to you. But allow me to take this opportunity to mention that there is no lock on that door."

"Really?" He screws up his face. "Bet that's why she chose this room. What a sneaky, possibly bordering on evil, grand-mother she is."

"If it makes you feel any better, I was probably never hav-ing sex with you in your grandmother's house anyway. There's just something innately wrong about that. Especially now that I've met her," I say. "I'd be imagining her looking at me disap-provingly for messing up the linens the whole time. A real mood killer."

First he laughs, then he frowns. "Hold up, sex? Who said any-thing about that?"

"It isn't what you had in mind?"

"Absolutely not."

"Oh. I thought 'comfort you' was a euphemism."

"What a dirty mind you have. Not to mention checking for locks on the door. Who even does that?"

"Sorry."

"Look, Alice," he says, face set in the most serious of expres-sions. "Don't get me wrong. I really like you as a person. I just don't feel as if we're quite there yet."

"You don't, huh?"

"No."

"And yet I'm meant to be moving permanently to Denver

now at your say-so. Okay, then. My bad." My brows rise. "Wow. How awkward."

"Us being in the same city and having sex are two very different things. And don't be embarrassed." He sighs. "It's just, if we rush in…"

"Yes?"

"Taking it slow is best, letting the emotions and connection between us build." This is all said with various complex hand gestures. A kind of rolling and turning motion. Not really sure what any of it means. Where does the playful banter end and the truth begin? Or maybe I'm just not used to anyone wanting to attempt serious and slow with me. In today's dating world, it is kind of an outdated notion. Especially around about the time he flies me a couple of states in a private jet. "So, Alice, would you care to cuddle? It's just like hugging only done horizontally."

"Sure. That sounds nice."

I settle in beside him on the bed. The empty bottle of red wine sits abandoned on the bedside table. Beck slides one arm beneath my neck, the other over my hip. Both urge me closer. He smells good. But then he always smells good. The heat of his body and the small smile he gives me are all so deeply personal. Just for me. It's like we're back in our own little bubble and nothing else matters. Despite the luxury accommodations.

"Hey," he says, voice deep and low.

"Hi."

I slide my palm over his chest, fingers toying with his black silk tie. One of his hands slides down, over my hip and onto my thigh. Low enough to draw my knee over to rest on his leg. We're basically plastered all over each other from top to toe. With the tip of a finger, he draws circles on my back. It's relaxing. The cadence of my breath soon matches his. In and out, nice and easy. We're a world away from the tension that was running through him downstairs.

"Comfortable?" he asks.

"Very." I smile, inching a little closer. "You were telling me about Jack and his amazing marriage."

He stares up at the ceiling. "Not really much more to say. She came from old money, but a dwindling fortune. He had no pedigree, but serious cash. It was a match made in capitalist heaven. They tolerated each other enough to produce Jack Junior and he in turn fathered the rest of us. More money was made. More friends were lost. So on and so forth. On and on it goes."

"And this is where you grew up? Among all of this grandeur?"

"Some of the time," he says. "Mom was a model. She was from Denmark originally."

"Hold up. Your mom is Lise *Olson*?"

"Heard of her, huh?"

Shit. "Just a little. She was in all the fashion magazines my mom used to buy when I was growing up." Mom would never have been able to buy any of the brands we used to lust after—not with what she had to squirrel away for my college fund. But at least she could afford the magazines, and we spent more than a few evenings sighing and dreaming over them.

"That's her," he confirms. "The amount of fellow students at boarding school who kept pictures of her under their beds was... disturbing to say the least."

"Ew."

"You said it." He sighs. There's been a lot of sighing today. "Anyway, she and Dad got involved. When Rachel, Ethan and Emma's mom, found out about it, she divorced him. By then, Mom was pregnant with me. Accident or not, who knows? But I had the distinction of being the first and only family bastard of the last few generations."

"People still care about that sort of thing?"

"Some do," he says. "They didn't last long together. With the proviso that I took on the family name, Dad set her up in a flashy New York City apartment as far away from him as he could manage while still keeping me in the country. A couple of times a year I'd come west to spend quality time with him and learn how to be a man. Or at least, that's how Dad put it. Mostly I rattled around some penthouse or mansion, made awkward conversation with his latest lady friend, and hung out with the rest of the family while he worked all hours of the day and night. *Money doesn't make itself, son.* That's one of the Elliot family mottos. Up there with, *always have a prenup, super yachts are a shit investment,* and *when in doubt, diamonds should shut her up.*"

I rest my cheek on his shoulder. "Yikes. Sounds lonely."

"Everyone's lonely sometimes."

"You've said that before."

"Well, it's the truth," he mumbles. "So that's my origin story."

"You must have some good memories with your dad, I hope."

"Sure, some. Don't take my moaning too seriously; my childhood wasn't so bad. I had every toy you could ask for. Trips to Europe. Stuff like that. And when Rachel found out he was just dumping me to go work, she took an interest. Started taking me to ball games and movies. Made me sit through *Pride and Prejudice* with her more times than I can count. Encouraged Emma and Ethan to do things with me too." His hand slides through my hair, twirling it around his finger. "Alice, you mind if that's enough for now? I know you've still got questions, but—"

"It's fine." I did have more questions. Mainly about how he came from a history dripping with wealth to being a busboy in a crappy LA bar. And maybe also some questions about how he wound up slow-dancing with the waitress after closing. But now clearly wasn't the moment. "I really am sorry about your dad."

"Yeah, me too. That was a shitty day," he says quietly, his eyelids squeezing shut. "It's weird, the idea of someone just being gone."

"My nan died of a stroke a few years ago. But she lived on the other side of the country and I didn't really know her well."

For a moment, he says nothing. I always wanted the ability to portal for a superpower. Right now, however, being able to read minds would be useful. His hold on me tightens, fingers pressing in a little. "If I haven't already said it ten times before, I'm glad you're here."

"I'm glad I'm here too."

"Master Beck," a loud and stern voice announces.

Beside me on the bed, Beck stirs with a groan. Guess we fell asleep. I check my watch, and sure enough, it's almost nine p.m. Hours since we had our impromptu appetizers picnic and he told me a little about his life. We both sit up, stunned by the intrusion. Maybe I should have wedged a chair beneath the door handle or something. Though I've only ever seen it done in movies so no idea if it actually works.

"Your grandmother thought you might have gotten lost on the way to your room," continues the man. With the hall lit bright behind him, he's just a big shadow standing in the open doorway. "Allow me to escort you back."

"Not necessary, Winston," says Beck. "But thanks for the thought. Tell Grandma that I can find my way just fine and will do so in a moment or two."

"I'll wait for you in the hallway then, shall I?"

"Oh, and Winnie?" Beck's voice hardens. "Don't walk in on Miss Lawrence again."

"I knocked," says the man. "You must not have heard me."

"Knock louder next time and wait for her to answer. You know how Gran abhors bad manners."

"Almost as much as she dislikes unplanned additions to the family."

The two just stare at each other. Then the door shuts without further comment.

"That's the majordomo I warned you about." Beck shakes his head. "Used to scare the crap out of me as a kid. You have to admire his total dedication to being a dick."

"Was he taking aim at you being born out of wedlock or me being a money-grubbing ho who can't be trusted with your sperm?"

"Both, probably," he says. "The man can multitask like you wouldn't believe."

"I feel like I'm a teenager all over again."

"Gran can be somewhat old-fashioned, overbearing, and generally an all-around control freak." His gaze is unhappy. "Sorry about that."

"Lucky we weren't doing anything interesting."

"Hmm." He shoves a hand through his messy hair, looking all tense again. "You are safe here, Alice, I promise."

"Well, from the living, sure. That asshole out in the hallway doesn't scare me. But what about ghosts?" To be honest, I'm a bit miffed about being separated from him at this hour. If we weren't ready to sleep together in the figurative sense, I at least liked the idea of doing it in the literal sense. And now this rude douche-canoe majordomo dude is cheating me out of even that. I scowl. It's even possible I pout. I wouldn't put it past me.

He smiles. "Ghosts?"

"It's an old house, isn't it?"

"Yes, it is. Though to my knowledge, no one has actually ever been murdered here," he says. "Which isn't to say Catherine the Great doesn't have a temper. Gran's made Denver shake with fear a time or two. But still…no gruesome killings in this house as far as I'm aware."

"Yeah, but what if there were some genteel type who just became overwhelmed with the amount of chintz in this room and up and expired? It would have looked like natural causes when really it would be like the house itself had turned against them, just like in a movie."

His brows draw in tight. "You know, I never thought of that."

"It could happen."

"Oh, it totally could. Death by florals. What a fucking awful way to go." He seizes my hand, kissing my knuckles and making me laugh. "Beloved Alice. Please don't die on me through the night. It would really bum me out."

"I'll do my best."

"That's all I can ask." And he's smiling again so my work here is done. He drops my hand and climbs off the bed. "Be brave. I believe in you. Good night."

"Night."

Not sure what I was expecting exactly, but no one came in to open the curtains, stoke the fire, and serve me tea and toast in bed the next morning. Of course, it isn't the nineteenth century, so there you go. I shower and dress, blow dry my hair, and all the rest. There's nothing like winged eyeliner for boosting confidence. Another pair of jeans, a clean T-shirt, and my favorite boots complete the ensemble. It's about the best I can do. The rich will have to take me as I am. I'm not one of them and I never will be.

The house is silent. I tiptoe down the fancy staircase, unsure where exactly I'm supposed to go and what I'm supposed to do. No response from the text I sent Beck. (He gave me the number on the ride from the airport.) Maybe if I head down to the front gates I can call an Uber to come take me to the nearest coffee and mall. It sounds like the best plan.

"Miss Lawrence."

I jump. "Shit. You scared me."

Winston, the majordomo, has a face set in stone. Nothing

seems to occur on it. Nothing changes. "Miss MacKenna is waiting for you in the drawing room."

"Right. Where is that again?"

He nods to the room to my left.

"Thank you."

Winston turns and heads up the stairs. Bet he's off to check my bag to see if I've stolen anything.

Inside a cream room with gold accents, Rachel sits sipping a cup of coffee and perusing an iPad. Perhaps I'm finally going to find out what Grandma's "see to the girl" comment meant. I'm half afraid, half curious. Also, I note that no one offered me a caffeinated beverage. Assholes. I also don't tackle the woman and steal her coffee. It's called self-restraint.

"Good morning," I say.

"Alice." Rachel sets the delicate coffee cup aside and gets to her feet with a smile. She's wearing a pale green pencil skirt and blouse. Her blond hair is pulled back into a chignon. The woman is polished to perfection. I doubt a speck of dust would even dare sully such flawlessness. "Let's get moving. I have a meeting in an hour so I don't have much time, unfortunately."

"Get moving where?"

"No one told you? We're going shopping." She strides toward the doors, accepting her tan woolen coat and handbag from a waiting maid who seems to appear out of nowhere. The help sure move quick around here.

"Oh good," I say. "I was hoping to pick up a few things."

"Great. Let's talk in the car."

At least going shopping will get me out of this mausoleum and away from Winston. I check my cell, still no answer from Beck. But then it's half past nine and he was going to be in the meeting with his brother. I slept late, what with the time difference and drama of yesterday. Guess I'll catch up with him later.

Walking with all due grace on her tan pumps, Rachel slides

into the backseat of a Rolls Royce. A different driver than Smith holds open the door for her. I head around to the other side and open my own door despite the driver's weird glance. Inside are ridiculously comfortable and soft tan leather seats. Rachel has a classic kind of beauty. Wide blue eyes, a straight nose, and nicely shaped lips. Yet another woman in the family who could have easily been a model. Beck's dad sure had a type. Which yet again makes me wonder what I'm doing here. Though Beck isn't his father and my insecurities need to remember this fact.

"I guess this is all a lot to take in," she says as the engine purrs to life and we start moving forward.

"You could say that."

"Beck is a good boy. Or a good man, rather."

"Yes, he is."

She nods. "It won't necessarily be easy if you decide to stay. If you continue seeing each other. The family is…complicated. But I'd imagine Beck will make it worth your while."

No idea if she's after information or not, but I keep my mouth shut.

We drive in silence, the elaborate gardens and grand houses giving way to mini-mansions that are no less impressive. I grew up in a three-bedroom bungalow in a nice enough area. Nothing like this.

"Are we going to a mall?" I ask.

"Yes, Cherry Tree."

"Do they have Old Navy or Nordstrom Rack?"

Rachel just blinks. "I'm not sure."

"It's just…I'm on a budget."

"Alice," she says, her hands stilling on the iPad. "You don't need to worry about that. Arrangements have been made."

"What do you mean?"

"I realize this might seem a little odd, but I'd ask that you trust me."

"Trust you with what exactly?"

"Here we are," she says.

We're already pulling up to the curb outside a sprawling and rather magnificent mall. It's all glossy brown and black stone and quite possibly the grandest shopping complex I've ever seen. Chances are, I couldn't afford a coffee in this place. A man in a gray-checked two-piece suit stands waiting on the sidewalk. He's about a decade older than me and a hundred times more stylish. The aqua-colored tie confirms it. Behind him stands an older lady in a silk floral jumpsuit. I'm not just out of my depth here, I'm drowning.

"They're personal shoppers." Rachel searches in her handbag, pulling out a black credit card. "They'll help you today. Just give them this."

"Is that Beck's?"

"The card? Yes."

"No." I shake my head. "I'm not...that's not something I'm okay with."

For a moment, she just looks at me. "Alice, you have ethics and I applaud that. It's refreshing, really. But the fact is, you're dating an Elliot and in this town that means something. I don't mean to be harsh, but the way you look now does not fit into this world."

"I know I'm not as—"

"Now, I do not doubt that you have a wonderful personality. But I repeat, you do not fit," she says in a not unkind voice. "And while you're part of this world, you need to. Otherwise, you're going to cause unnecessary friction for both Beck and yourself. With his family, his friends, people he does business with...pretty much everyone."

My secondhand Levi's feel so judged right now. Which is bullshit because I love them. And yet.

"It is not going to be smooth, Beck sliding back into his old life here. Especially not with Jack's death. Beck ruffled a lot of feathers when he left the way he did and now again with bringing you here. If you let the personal shoppers help you, then you'll be one less thing he needs to worry about."

"Since you have his card, I take it Beck knows about all this?" I ask.

"When I saw him this morning, I told him I was taking you to lunch and that there might be extra expenses."

"So you didn't tell him."

She stares off into the distance with a faint line between her brows. "I find matters like these are often best sorted out between us girls."

These fucking people.

"It's your choice of course, Alice," she says. "All I can do is encourage you to see the big picture and move forward in a way that will bring you the best chance of success."

For a moment I just sit there, staring at the hands in my lap, at the chips in my black nail polish. Also, my cuticles are a mess due to me picking at them. One of many annoying nervous habits. It feels like control is being stripped from me and I don't like it. At least Beck isn't behind any of this bullshit. And as much as I'd like to tell Rachel what she can do with her opinion, she was one of the few people who was kind to Beck when he was left alone by his dad as a kid. There's a lot to consider.

But do I want to fit in with his family? That's the question.

I definitely don't want him to think I'm here for his money. However, I don't want to reflect badly on Beck, either. This is the truth of the matter. And tensions are indeed running high. God knows what he's going through dealing with everything right now. God knows why exactly I'm even here. However, while I am, I want to be a good thing in his life. Something he doesn't need to worry about.

She holds out the card with a sympathetic smile. "Every relationship requires compromise, I'm afraid."

True enough. I'm just not sure about this particular one. The card is thicker, heavier than anticipated. I slip it into the inside pocket of my handbag for safekeeping. If money means power in this world, then I'm holding on to what little control I have. A cold wind slaps me in the face. The Rolls engine purrs to life and Rachel is gone. I hang my head back and look at the clear blue sky. Given how my day is going, it's amazing a passing bird doesn't just shit on me. Honestly.

"Hi," I say to the waiting dynamic shopping duo. They're so sophisticated. Bet they sit front row at fashion shows. "I'm Alice. Um, I don't know what you've been told, but just a couple of outfits will be more than enough. No need to overdo it, right?"

They share a silent look.

I'm sequestered in a changing room larger than my apartment. It has plush white carpet with a couple of matching sofas, and ginormous gilt-edged framed mirrors. People rush back and forth fetching lingerie, shoes, evening gowns, active wear, and everything in between. Not all of the outfits fit. I won't even try all of the suggested outfits on (beige people shouldn't wear beige). However, we've managed to find a few different things that work. There's a garment rack full of rejected outfits, another of possibly maybes, and half a rack of yes please.

And in walks the woman Beck admitted to avoiding at the wake. Yikes.

"Not bad," she says, looking me over before directing a young man to deposit a collection of shopping bags from various stores to one side of the room.

Considering the amount of Spanx I'm currently wearing and the fact that I can barely breathe, you'd think I'd at least earned a solid good. The black Oscar de la Renta–pleated stretch-wool midi dress I have on is nothing short of beautiful and I wish to be

THE RICH BOY | 71

buried in it. Same goes for the leather booties. So maybe despite all of my protestations and fears about selling out, I like expensive-people fashion sometimes after all. Label me a hypocrite.

I am, however, done for the day. Normally I like shopping. I even love it. But three hours of people trying to convince me I'd look great in neo-mint (whatever that is), yolk yellow, and electric blue, before attempting to sell me on feathers, puffy power shoulders (while I respect Anne of Green Gables it's a hard no from me), and a silk boiler suit, is a lot. More than I can handle, apparently. I won't be coerced or bullied into getting anything that doesn't feel like me. And while the personal shoppers aren't happy, that's not my problem.

"Hi," I say. "I'm Alice."

Her gaze jumps to mine. "Sorry. Selah. Nice to meet you. We crossed paths briefly at the wake. You might not remember."

"I remember."

A nod and she looks away. "I'm Rachel's assistant. She sent me over to check on how everything was going."

"Fine. I think we're about finished."

Nothing from her.

"What line of business is Rachel in, by the way?" I ask, curious.

"It's her department store you're standing in," answers Selah. "Or rather, her family's."

Holy shit.

Everyone's heard of the Mac Department Stores, though there's only a few of them in the country. Mac is where the seriously rich shop. Before today, I'd never even bothered stepping foot inside one. A solid choice, considering the dress I'm wearing costs over five thousand dollars. The personal shoppers tried to get me to stop looking at price tags, but curiosity wins every time. And the running tally kind of makes me want to hurl, only I'd ruin my pretty shoes.

"Rachel wanted to make sure we're covering all bases." Selah walks around me inspecting the dress. I'm honestly not used to people caring about how I look to this degree. The level of attention is a combination of weird, kind of nice, and awkward. Though having it come from this particular perfect petite brunette doll is daunting. Don't get me wrong; I have self-esteem despite my various neuroses. But I also have suspicions about where she fits into Beck's life.

Which is when my cell vibrates from where it's sitting over on one of the sofas.

Beck: Forgot to mention Rachel wants to take you to lunch.
Me: Yeah…
Beck: Sorry about that. Meeting ran overtime. Everything okay?
Me: It's fine. Hope your meeting went well.
Beck: Tell you about it later. Lawyers up next. Wish me luck.
Me: Good luck. x

I'll tell him about my day (and possible list of grievances against his family, society, and the patriarchy) later. He's got enough to deal with right now.

"Hello! What do we have here?" Emma, Beck's half sister, sweeps into the room. Privacy is just not a priority with these people. "Oh, I like that dress on you."

"You do?" I check myself once more in the mirror. "It feels great."

"Excellent."

"The new Fendi Baguette came in, I see." Selah gives the green velvet handbag on Emma's arm a covetous look. "Very nice."

"Isn't it just? I've only been waiting forever." Emma casts an eye over the collection of clothing hanging on the racks and packages spilling off the second couch and onto the floor. "Who's been shopping?"

"I picked up a few things for her," says Selah.

Emma snorts. "Beck is gonna regret that. Trusting the ex with your money...most unwise."

"Speaking from experience?" Selah cocks her head.

Emma sits on one of the sofas, crossing her legs and swinging her foot back and forth. "I'll have you know, Matías disapproves of my wealth. He said, 'Only he who has spirit ought to have possessions.'"

"What?"

"Right? I hate it when he quotes Nietzsche at me."

Selah wrinkles her nose. "Like nihilism ever made anybody smile."

"This is my point," says Emma. "But no, we're all soulless capitalist scum addicted to material goods and out of touch with the common people, apparently."

"Nietzsche wasn't a nihilist," I say, almost without thinking. My favorite English Lit professor had a thing for Nietzsche's early period, and could quote the *Birth of Tragedy* almost verbatim. "And he didn't care less about the common people. He just worried that people's possessions would become their focus, instead of culture and spirit and the things that really matter. Art. Literature."

There's a pause as they both turn to me. Selah's eyes narrow and there's something new in her gaze. Like she's looking at me for the first time. Really looking. Not that she approves of what she sees.

Emma smiles and shrugs. "Well, I don't know about Nietzsche, but Matías was wearing a Brioni suit when he said it. So you'll forgive me if I misread the context. There were some mixed messages coming through."

I smile graciously and let them return to their conversation.

Meanwhile, my head is busy. So Selah and Beck did used to date. Given the weird vibe and animosity between them (at least on his part) it certainly makes sense. And she's obviously a part of, or still lurking on the fringes of, his family life and fortunes.

Interesting.

A man walks in with a tray of glasses and a bottle of something in an ice bucket and places it on a small table. At times like this, it feels a little weird not to be the one doing the serving. Another reminder that I'm not one of the rich people and do not belong here. No matter how great the dress. And the dress is really fucking great. When Beck is ready to replace me with someone his family finds more suitable, I'm taking the dress home to ease my heartache. The booties can come too.

Selah starts pouring the champagne. "Some Dom. Thought we might be in need of refreshment by now."

"I think we're done here," I say.

Pausing her pouring, Selah inspects the racks of clothes. "Which ones are you keeping?"

I nod to the smallest collection.

"We might need to go further afield if that's all you could find. I'll reach out to some contacts at other stores and a couple of designers who are good at plus size."

"No need. That'll be plenty."

Selah opens her mouth, then closes it. "All right. Tell you what, why don't I finish up here while Emma accompanies you to the salon and spa?"

"You're not cutting my hair." This is not a suggestion. This is a statement.

"It won't be me taking her, I've got a meeting. Someone else will have to wrangle the new girlfriend." Emma sips at her champagne. "You do need a trim, though. I can see the split ends from here. And a keratin treatment and some highlights wouldn't hurt you either."

"Her skin is going to take some work," adds Selah. "And those brows..."

Emma nods. "The ragged claws you're calling nails definitely need fixing."

"I'm not even going to comment on the length of her leg hairs."

"You just did." I frown. What a pair of assholes.

"C'mon, Alice," says Emma. "I'm sure Mommy Dearest already gave you the lecture. You know, *can't embarrass the fam* followed by *you'll still look like you—just the best most expensive version of yourself.* That sort of thing."

"Yep."

Emma just shrugs. "What can I say? She's mostly right. This is mostly for your own good. Not to be unkind, but people were asking who the hobo with Beck was yesterday."

"What?" I ask. "Wow."

"Yeah. It's harsh."

"Very."

"And I kind of have to agree with them," says Emma.

"I don't think I like you after all."

Selah laughs. "No one likes her."

"Oh, my sweet summer child." Emma's smile is benevolent. "We're not here to be liked. We're here to get shit done. You think you're getting new threads because Grandma actually likes you or wants you here? It's because she wants Beck back under control. At least, I'm guessing that was her message to Mama yesterday. Best make the most of all of this while you can because you never know what tomorrow will bring. Now quit your whining before you give me a headache."

I say nothing. Sometimes keeping your mouth shut works best. And she's not telling me anything I didn't know or at least suspect. But still...to be honest, when it comes to today's she-nanigans, I'm more averse to the idea of people trying to inflict change on me than I am to getting pampered. It's worth remembering that Beck likes me how I am. At least, I think he does. He never mentioned me being fundamentally lacking in all the ways and needing the overhaul they clearly intend to perform. Maybe it slipped his mind?

No. Nope. This I will not believe.

This is all such a trap. The clothes and accessories and so on. When do you stop and feel like you're enough? Pretty enough, smart enough, good enough? There's an edge of desperation to it all that makes me uneasy (even more so than general). And yet I want to fit in and make Beck proud. But look at me, I'm like the anti-Selah. Big where she's little, clumsy where she's graceful. No way will I ever compare. Guess I'm just going to have to settle for being me. Albeit a slightly slicker version of same.

"I'll take her to the salon and spa," says Selah in a not so happy tone.

"Aw," says Emma, "what a lovely bonding experience that'll be for the two of you."

I down the Dom. It's not bad. "Fine, I'll go. But I can find my own way. I'm sure Selah has better things to do. Where did the clothes I arrived in go?"

Selah doesn't even hesitate. She also doesn't meet my eyes. As liars go, she kind of sucks. "Probably sent to the dry cleaners. Wear one of the new outfits."

"Are you lying to me?"

Emma cackles like an evil witch on her way out the door. "Have fun, ladies!"

"Selah, did someone throw my stuff out?" I ask with more than a tad of aggression. "Because that is not okay. At all."

Her eyes and mouth widen. Not sure if it's fear or surprise or what. "Now, Alice…"

"You are fucking kidding me."

And Selah gives me a most put-upon expression, accompanied

by a heavy sigh and tired eyes. "Look, I'm not sure, but it wouldn't surprise me. Rachel's instructions for you were detailed, to say the least."

Curbing my need to swear is a major victory. These people are the worst. If anything has happened to my Austen shirt I will burn something down.

"But I'll see what I can do about finding them."

"Thank you." I do not sound appreciative, but oh well. It's been a long day.

"As for the other matter...look, we don't have to like each other. Given the situation it would be bizarre if we did. But just because I'd make a convenient villain doesn't mean I am one."

I think it over. "Out of curiosity, are you going to be making a play for Beck?"

"He and I have some things to discuss."

"Not sure he'd agree with you."

Her lips flatline. "That's between me and him."

"You're right, we're probably not going to be friends," I say. "But I don't have the energy for making enemies. At least, not today."

"Let's just be superficially nice to each other and get this done, okay?"

"Get what done, exactly?"

She finishes her champagne. "It's just a tidy up. I don't know why you're making such a big deal out of it."

"Because I basically like me how I am and don't see the need for radical change just to please you asshats?"

"Wow," she says, brows raised. "Did you pick the wrong boyfriend or what?"

It would be great to hit something. Even being pretend-nice to these people is hard. "All of this isn't for Beck; it's for his family."

She just smiles. "Same thing, Alice. They're the same damn thing."

CHAPTER FIVE

"**M**ISS, CAN I HELP YOU?" ASKS THE BELLBOY.

I'm standing outside a spectacular big old hotel, generally getting in the way, and cluttering up the sidewalk. I don't know what I'm doing here. Maybe this is a mistake. I've stayed in many motels over the years, but never an actual hotel. Mom and Dad were into camping trips for family holidays and it's not like I've had the money to splash out. Yet here I am.

After the salon and spa, Selah shoved me into the back of another vehicle. The driver could have dropped me at the wrong place. Though given the recent turns my life has taken, probably not.

"Miss?" the boy repeats.

At least I now look the part with my glossy ponytail, perfectly painted black nails, and makeup. I feel like chonky Cinderella. Never has my cat-eye eyeliner been so perfect. My designer jeans are high-waisted with pleats, worn over a white T-shirt bodysuit, with a black Burberry trench, and a sweet simple pair of Manolo Blahnik suede flat mules in black. This is my casual outfit. Because even if the weather allowed for it, flip-flops and denim cutoffs aren't done in Beck's world, apparently. I picked out a couple of other outfits for more dressy occasions. At least the family can no longer accuse me of being a total embarrassment.

"I—I, um..." I stutter. So just a seventy percent embarrassment then.

"It's fine. I've got this, Sam." Beck strides out of the beautiful boutique hotel in a navy suit. When he looks me over, he's doing the careful blank face thing again. "Don't I know you from somewhere?"

"They attacked me with your credit card."

He sticks his hands in his pants pockets. "Rachel only said she was taking you out. Said she wanted my AMEX in case something caught your eye. I assumed several somethings did because the concierge mentioned they dropped off your things earlier."

"I don't mean to be overdramatic, but...they did things to me," I say. "What do you think?"

"What do *you* think?"

"What do I think you think or the other way around?"

"The other way. I think." He frowns in thought. "It's been a long day."

I look down at myself. "I'm not sure. I guess I like it. Some parts of it, at least."

"Well, I like the parts that you like."

I smile.

"But mostly I just like you."

"Thank you. I like you too." I take a small step forward, pressing my lips gently against his. An innocent enough kiss, given we're in public, if a slightly long one. The minute I'm close to him, everything feels better. Like I belong right here regardless of hair, waxing, or designer goodies. "Couldn't help but notice the name on the building. I guess hoping the Heritage was just like a coffee cart or something was kind of stupid of me."

"We do have a coffee shop here, if that counts?"

"Not a bit. What else do you have?"

"Allow me to show you, fair Alice." He holds out his elbow for me to take. "Welcome to the Heritage."

There's lots of glass, painted black walls, and various art deco features. Makes sense since it's got to be about a hundred years old. Farther in, dark paneled wooden walls lead up to antique light fixtures hanging on the high ceilings. Velvet sofas, long low coffee tables, and leather wingback chairs. Modern art mixed with more old-world type antique pieces and large fresh flower arrangements. This hotel is so cool it hurts.

And everyone seems to be watching us. Staff and guests included. One person even pulls out a cell and takes a picture, for fuck's sake. How rude. Beck either doesn't notice or doesn't care. Guess he's used to this level of attention. But it kind of makes me grateful for the clothes. They act as armor against all the inquiring eyes. Either that or these people are undermining my sangfroid. I don't know. The shoes are pretty and the trench is kind of cool. I take comfort in this.

"We have a gift shop, barber shop, cocktail lounge, and a restaurant." He nods to the people behind the lobby counter and guides me toward a bank of elevators. "I know they look old, but they work."

"They're beautiful. This whole place is. And it's yours now?"

"I'm in charge," he says as we step into the elevator. He pushes the button for the level before the top floor. Floor fourteen. Guess we're taking a tour of the place starting at almost the top. Whatever. I'll follow him anywhere. "But it's still owned by the company at present. So I have family and other stockholders to answer to until the sale goes through."

I nod. The elevator kicks off with the subtle clanking that modern money just can't buy.

"What are you thinking about?" he asks.

"Lots of things."

"Such as?"

"Well…this place is seriously impressive for starters."

"You ain't seen nothing yet."

I stare at the floor for a moment. Elevators are so awkward. "Did you notice people staring at us downstairs?"

"It happens." He shrugs. "Just ignore it."

"Are you at the top of the most eligible bachelor list in this town or what?"

"The state list and I'm number two. Ethan holds the top place."

Fuck me.

"It's not who I am, Alice," he says, tone particularly persuasive. "It's just a side effect of the money. Ignore it, okay?"

Easy for him to say.

We arrive at the fourteenth floor and he draws a keycard out of his pocket. Whatever he wants to show me is down the end of a hallway lit by more cool old light fixtures. There's an energy to Beck now that's been absent since he was in California. Not that I expected him to be ecstatic when his father had just passed. But it's nice to see him excited about life again.

After opening the door, he looks at me with a smile. "Go ahead. Have a look."

"Okay."

I head inside, taking my time checking everything out. If this is a big deal for Beck, then I want to give him his due. And it obviously is, because the man watches me like a hawk the whole time. The walls are painted graphite and the furniture is lush, just like downstairs, and upholstered in different shades of blue. A large open area has a living room, a long wooden dining table, and a galley kitchen with shiny white stone benchtops. There's also a fireplace, ginormous TV, a bar and wine fridge...basically every luxury you could want. Floor to ceiling windows look out onto LoDo and there's an outside sitting area with its own fireplace and Jacuzzi. It's a lot to take in for a basic bitch like me.

"Are these the penthouse apartments?" I ask, heading to one end of the room. A study with a cluttered bookcase is the next thing I find, followed by a bathroom with pristine white tiles.

"No, those are upstairs. They're double the floor space."

"Wow."

"They are nice," he admits. "But I thought it best to keep those available for guests. This one is just for personal use. Figured we didn't really need a grand piano or two extra bedrooms at this stage anyway."

"This one is for the family?"

"If by family you mean you and me."

I don't know what to say. I'm starting to get the feeling I'm overusing the word "wow." There's every chance I'll never become acclimatized to his wealth. Or at least, I hope not. Imagine taking this kind of beauty for granted. But on the other hand, Beck and I are finally getting some privacy. This is splendid.

"Actually thought Dad would have evicted me when I left," he says, voice contemplative. "But he didn't. Guess the old man was more bark than bite sometimes. At least when it came to his children. The things you learn when it's too late."

"This is where you lived before you went wandering?"

A nod as he leans against the closed door. "Lived and worked here. I oversaw the renovations last year. It was my project to prove myself to dear old Dad and the board."

"You must be proud," I say, heading toward the other end of the room. "This apartment is amazing. It's a beautiful hotel, Beck."

"Thank you. A lot of people worked hard on it."

"I'm sure they did. But this place is your baby, isn't it?"

He smiles.

And I just wait.

"This place...a lot of people thought it was worthless. Thought we should basically gut it and start over. More cost effective that way. Modern and flashy brings the people in, gets them spending. The board wasn't interested in the history of the place or its story."

"But you were."

He shrugs. And it's such a careless gesture, but his smile still lingers.

"You proved them wrong."

"We're making money; that's what matters."

"Don't dismiss what you did here. I think there's more than a little of the creative in your soul."

He snorts. "Elliots don't bother themselves with souls. Or consciences. Too inconvenient. We're built and raised to be money-making machines."

"You're more than that." I raise my chin. "And you know it."

"Do I?"

"Yes. You wanted more. You went looking for more, remember?"

"And yet here I am, right back where I started." He licks his lips, turning away. "Eventually, my plan is to build myself an empire by turning this into a chain of boutique hotels. Along with some other investments I've been nurturing."

"That's incredible."

"The things you can do with money, huh? And yet you still won't let me buy your love," he jokes.

"Would you even want it if it was for sale?"

For a moment, he just stares at me. "Good point, dearest."

He follows me into the bedroom where a massive bed takes pride of place, made up with white linens. There's also some very cool charcoal-colored vintage style wallpaper and a pale blue chaise longue just perfect for reading. But back to the bed. It's orgy size. And there's only one.

"Wherever will I sleep?" I ask, testing the mattress with a hand for softness. Just the right amount of firm and bounce, thank you very much.

"Wherever you want."

"And where will you sleep?"

"Wherever you want me to. With my jammies on, of course. We wouldn't want to rush things."

"Wouldn't we? Remind me why not again."

"My naughty Alice. What a delight you are."

"The problem here is, you think I'm joking."

"Oh, trust me. I take you very seriously indeed." It might just be me, but Beck's voice seems to have dropped about an octave. And it is sexy times music to my ears. He leans his back against a door jamb. Yes, there is definite heat in the man's eyes. "Bathroom and closet are through here."

"No need to move. I'm sure I can squeeze past you."

"If you insist."

And I take my time easing past him too, using tiny sidesteps into the short hallway. I also may or may not be pretending the doorway is half the size it actually is. Who cares about a pretty apartment when I have this pretty man so close? I notice Beck doesn't move an inch, letting my breasts brush against his hard chest. Though there's like at least four layers of cloth between us, my pussy tingles and nipples harden. And we maintain eye contact the entire time. I couldn't look away if I tried. Getting up this close and this personal with him more than makes my day. Given a little time and a lot of privacy, the things we could do in that big bed. I've never had the opportunity to mess around with a man in a suit before. It's a positive life experience.

"Feel free to go back and forth a few times," he says in the sexy low voice. "You could even turn around if you like."

"Oh?"

"I've always had the utmost respect for your gorgeous ass."

"You say the sweetest things."

"'I do sometimes amuse myself with arranging such little compliments.'"

"You were so hot right up until you quoted Mr. Collins," I say, referencing *Pride and Prejudice*. "I was totally going to rub my butt against you."

"It'll never happen again, I promise." He leans forward, pressing a soft kiss to my lips. The firm warm pressure of his mouth is divine. "You are so fucking beautiful."

"I think Mr. Collins should have just led with that. Who knows where it might have gotten him."

His hands clench at his sides. Like he wants to reach for me but is holding back for some reason. So I reach for him instead, smoothing my hands over his suit jacket, straightening his tie.

"I do like the business look," I murmur.

"Is that so?"

"Mostly I just like you."

His gaze runs over my face. Still hesitating for some damn reason. For all that he talks a good talk, there's doubt in him since he's been back in Denver. And while I'm used to it from me, I'm definitely not from him.

"Beck, kiss me, grab me...do what you want."

And there's a flash of a lusty grin before he's on me. His hands cupping my face, fingers sliding into my hair. And his mouth... Good God, does the man know how to use his mouth. Warm lips and skilled tongue and he takes as much as he gives. The soft gentle kiss before was a lie. This is the real Beck. Full of heat and emotion. Whoever or whatever taught him to hold back, to rein himself in, needs a good kick in the pants. Because when he kisses me like this, he makes my head spin and my body ache. His teeth nip at my bottom lip before sucking away the sweet pain. Then he's feeding me deep wet kisses that I just might die if I have to go without. Melodramatic, but true.

When he pulls back, we're both breathing heavily. His thumb carefully swipes the side of my mouth. "I'm afraid I messed up your makeup and fancy hairdo."

"You're wearing a little lip gloss yourself."

"If I haven't said it yet today, I'm glad you're here."

"Me too."

"Isn't this better than staying at Grandma's house and getting busted by Winston like a pair of horny teenagers?"

"It sure is. Though there's still a serious moral quandary to be discussed. What do the dating rules say to do when there's only one bed?" I ask with my best attempt at a coy smile. It's probably not very good. I'm more of a lusty beast when it comes to this man. What can I say? He makes me ache. I rest a hand on his chest, feeling for his heartbeat. Hard and steady. A lot has changed since LA, but the chemistry between me and him is alive and well. The growing bond between us.

"And there's not a single other room available in the hotel or indeed the whole city," he reports. "I already checked."

"Gosh darn it."

He clicks his tongue. "Such language coming from a young lady. Why I never. What do you think of the rest of the place?"

I grin before letting my arm drop and turning to check out the walk-in closet. "Motherfucker!"

"What's wrong?" he asked, sounding startled.

"Um, Beck?"

"Yeah?"

"It was just you living here, right? By yourself?"

"Yes." He rests his hands on my hips, leaning his chin on my shoulder to look into the not-small room. "How about that."

"You don't by any chance happen to own a sizable collection of designer handbags, do you?"

"Can't say that I do."

"How about women's shoes?"

"Nope. None of them either."

I sigh. "I was worried you'd say that. How much of the room exactly does your stuff take up?"

"My things are in the first set of drawers on this wall here and about half of the hanging area on the left-hand side. But as you can see, they've actually pushed my custom suits back to make room for more of your dresses and coats." He helpfully points this out, fingers flexing against my hip. "I never bothered with the display cases on the back wall, which is good since they're now full of your purses and so on. And it looks like my shoes have all been moved to the bottom rack. The rest is yours."

"Fuck me."

"Absolutely. Eventually. In the meantime, let's take a closer look, shall we?" He moves me a little to the left with the pressure of his hands on my hips.

"I can't believe they did this."

The room is done in a soft gray and it's basically walls full of drawers, hanging space, and a couple of big mirrors. In the center of the room is an island featuring yet more drawers with a plush sofa at one end with a makeup table and chair at the other. And from what I can see, all of it is full.

Beck starts pulling open drawers. "What have we here? Scarves, gloves...that's a bit boring. Where's the good stuff? Ah. Here we go. Panties, bras...yeah, nice extensive collection of lingerie. Now this I approve of."

"You've got to believe me—I did not okay this." My heart is pounding, my lungs working double time. "I would never just spend your money this way."

"Hey—"

"A few outfits, that's all I agreed to. I figured you probably wouldn't mind. To help me fit in with your family and everything. Rachel said it was important." When in doubt, never be afraid to throw the nice rich white lady under the bus. "We can probably take it all back, right?"

He holds up a pair of vintage-styled, see-through, black boy-leg briefs. "Why would we do that?"

"Because it's way too much."

"Dearest." He stops, sets down the underwear, and sighs. Next, he slides his arms over my shoulders, giving me a smile. This is the one that says I'm amusing him. Thank God he isn't angry. "You need to breathe. Want me to give you mouth-to-mouth?"

"I'm so sorry."

"It's not your fault. Never apologize for shit you didn't do. Another one of Mom's quotes. Though that's not how she worded it exactly."

"What was your dad's take on such things?"

"Dad never apologized regardless of who was to blame. Never admit culpability. Get a lawyer on the phone. 'Plausible deniability' was his middle name." He leans his forehead against mine. "Alice, so long as you like the things, it's fine."

"It's not really."

"What would your mom say?" he asks, tone curious.

"That no one woman could possibly need this much stuff. Though she would also check out which designers were present and do some drooling." I sigh. "She'd also say women apologize far too much for things that either aren't a problem or aren't their fault. So I guess our mothers have that in common."

"I agree with them. Anything you don't want, send back. It's your choice."

I frown some more.

"You have bewitched me, body and soul. And I don't need you to change a single hair on your pretty head for me. You know that, right?"

"Quite a few of those hairs have already been chopped, dyed, and changed." I smile. "But thank you. It's nice to hear you say it. I feel like a gold digger."

"Don't be silly. I have the money and enjoy spending it on you. End of story." He kisses the tip of my nose. "But if you don't want it, send it back. If, however, there's stuff in here you do like, then keep it. Let me spoil you a little."

"This is a lot more than a little."

"Here's the thing." He wraps his arms around me, pulling me in against his body. "If you're worried this early in our relationship about us not being financially equal, the only way I can fix that is by giving you half of my net worth."

I gasp. "That is not funny."

"I almost want to do it just to see the look on your face. And Ethan's. It is not an understatement to say my brother would lose his shit completely. Could be fun."

"Please be serious."

"I am being serious. You can't let all of this freak you out," he says, calm as can be. "I get that you didn't have any warning about me coming from money when we met, but it is part of my world. And you want to be part of my world, right?"

I just look at him.

"And, no, I'm still not suggesting I needed you to change for me."

"Then what are you suggesting?"

"That I have the money, first due to my trust fund and now the inheritance. It's not going anywhere. We might as well enjoy it."

Easy for him to say. "Beck, do you see how I'm kind of caught between being a money-worrying pain in the ass and feeling like I'm using you here?"

"You're not using me," he says, voice bordering on angry. "Believe me, I know exactly how that feels. Look at me."

I do as told and his knuckles gently caress my cheek. "I don't want to wreck this," I explain. "I'm just so far out of my element."

"Let it go and enjoy the things. Things can be fun." He gives me a lopsided smile. Quite possibly the most endearing one in his arsenal. My knees instantly go weak. The power the man has over me is breathtaking. But still, there's an opportunity to ask a question here. And the only thing I love as much as having Beck's attention, having him touch me, is getting to learn more about him.

"Though if you were having fun, why did you leave all of this to clean tables?" I ask.

"Because I had to find you."

I pause. "That's a pretty great line."

"And Austen didn't even write it." He pulls back, slipping his hands into his pockets. "I had to get my head sorted out and I had to find you. Think I did a pretty good job on both counts. Though especially the last one."

"Oh God. You're giving me feelings again."

"Sorry about that."

"No, you're not."

"No," he says with a soft smile. "I'm really not."

"So I met Selah today."

Beck freezes with the smoked prime rib sandwich ordered off room service halfway to his mouth. "Did you now?"

"Mm-hmm."

"That explains it. Between her and Rachel, I'm not surprised you now have a closet to rival a Kardashian."

I point a fry in his general direction. They're damn good fries and the burger wasn't bad either. A blob of ketchup is hanging off a finger so I suck that off quick smart. Yum.

Meanwhile, he sits there, frozen, staring at my mouth.

"You okay?" I ask.

He blinks. "Huh?"

"Let's discuss you and Selah…because I'm getting the feeling there's a story there."

"Why am I always telling you my stories, and you're never telling me yours?"

"You haven't told me that many and I'm happy to trade you tale for tale."

"Deal," he says. "You go first. I'm still eating."

"What do you want to hear about?"

He ponders this for a moment. "How about your first love? What competition am I up against here?"

We're on the apartment's terrace, sitting opposite each other on couches with the fire going to warm the chill of the autumn air. Our first night alone together in Denver. Stars twinkle overhead and the sounds of the city are far below. It's lovely.

"My first serious boyfriend was during my last year of college." I abandon the remaining fries and stack up any empty plates before settling back into the comfy seat. "His name was Paul."

"I hate him already."

"You don't like the name Paul?"

"I have no opinion regarding the name Paul. I just hate this one in particular for reasons that shall remain secret."

I bite back a smile. "Okay then. So Paul was on the football team. I thought I was so lucky to have gotten his attention. To have such a big man on campus for a boyfriend. He and I spent lots of time together going on drives and watching the stars and hanging out in my room. We both had hormones so sex was soon involved. What didn't occur to me for a long time, or at least didn't initially bother me, was that we never really hung out with his friends. Now and then we'd do something with mine, but never his. He made all of the usual excuses. How he wanted to keep me to himself, that we had so much fun alone with no pants on, that his friends were boring immature jerks only interested in keg parties...you know."

Beck just watches me, his sandwich forgotten.

"But the fact was, he was embarrassed to be seen with me. I wasn't one of the skinny cool girls."

His gaze darkens. "Knew I hated Paul for a reason."

"So that's the story of my first love."

"You loved him?"

"No." I smile. "I just thought I did. Idiot didn't even give me my first vaginal orgasm."

"Now that's a story I need to hear and don't spare any details."

I shake my head. "We're trading tales here. It's your turn now."

"Fine. But I would point out that I asked for the story of your first love."

"Honestly." I frown in thought. "I don't think I've ever been in love."

"Okay. Interesting." He wipes his hands off on a napkin before taking a swig of beer. There's a masculine grace to even his simplest movements. And the way his throat works when he swallows. I'm more than a little gaga over this man. "Selah, huh? The story of Selah is, my father decided she'd make a great starter wife. Looked good, had a trust fund, came from the right family, wouldn't give them too much trouble over the prenup. So he talked Rachel into giving her an internship and then set about putting Selah in my path. Like an idiot I fell for it, even bought her a ring."

"Did Selah know about your father's plan?"

"That she did. His people had given her all of the inside information. My likes and dislikes. Places I went, things I did, people I'd dated, that sort of thing."

"Shit."

"Indeed." He turns his head, staring out at the city lights and the mountains in the distance. It's a breathtaking view though it has nothing on him. His expression, however, is a long way from happy. "Selah was all-in for the status and wealth of marrying an Elliot. It was Rachel who put two and two together and started asking the right questions. She and Dad had this huge fight. Then Selah finally admitted everything to me and...yeah."

"Did she love you?"

"Does it matter?"

"But you obviously loved her, right?" I ask. "I mean, you bought her a ring."

Beck's forehead furrows. "I don't know. I think she made sense to me, more than anything. She fit into the life my father and I supposedly had planned out. My great big successful future as part of the Elliot dynasty. Not exactly romantic, but there you have it."

"I'm sorry."

"I'm not. If I hadn't gone through that then I might not have seen how small my world was and what a cold emotionless void my future was shaping up to be. I was turning out just like dear old Dad. The things we do to please people, huh?"

"But you and her never lived together?"

His tongue plays behind his cheek. "No. She suggested it several times, but I kept putting it off for some reason."

"You were ready to give the woman a ring, but not a drawer."

"Telling, isn't it?" he asks, his voice wry.

I take a sip of my drink. "Question. If Selah already has money and position, why is she working as your stepmother's PA?"

"Answer. Because she has her own daddy issues. Her old man believes her life goal is to marry well and produce heirs. He won't let her get a foot in with the family company."

"Jesus."

"And since he has a lot of friends, the chances of her finding a job in this town are...not good. Rachel is about the only person who'd stand up to him. But she's making Selah work her way up. Kind of amazed she kept her on after the shit with me went down."

"Do you resent that?"

"Are you my therapist now?" he asks with a smile.

"No. Just curious."

"We all make mistakes. And just because Rachel's giving her a second chance doesn't mean I will be."

"Okay. So that's why you went wandering?"

"It's part of it." He sits back with his beer, the flames from the fire casting shadows across his face. Making the sharp angles of his cheekbones and the cut of his jaw even more prominent. "Thing is, if everything hadn't gone to hell, I wouldn't have found you. A woman who almost has a panic attack when I spend money on her. A woman who now owns almost every drawer in the apartment."

"Ugh. Don't remind me."

"I wouldn't have walked away from all of this and gotten some perspective."

"Is that what cleaning tables did for you?" I ask.

"What I discovered is, that it's not until you get completely away from your family and all of your support systems and have to stand on your own two feet that you find out who you really are. Living without the money and Elliot name, I'd never had that before," he says, voice thoughtful. "Of course, I could have made a phone call and gotten it all back. Dad would have sent the private jet to fetch me. With a bit of groveling, I'm sure all would have been forgiven."

I nod, nursing my drink. "But you didn't."

"I survived the trials and tribulations of minimum wage." His tone is heavy on the self-mockery. "Like millions of my fellow citizens."

"And now you're back."

"Yes, I am."

"With a girl who's the exact opposite of your ex."

He raises a brow in question.

"Physical, financial, social status…they're all very different."

"Okay," he says, straightening up and leaning forward. "Time for me to play therapist here for a minute. Let me make this very clear. You are not some juvenile rebellion on my part. I am not trying to lash out at my dead daddy or any other assorted members of my family by being with someone from beyond their circle. I set out to learn about the world outside of the Elliot bubble and wound up finding someone who likes me for me and not my money. Someone who is funny and hot, and who I very much like spending time with. You. Are you hearing me?"

"Yes."

"Good." He sighs. "Furthermore, I am not Paul. I'm neither using you nor embarrassed by you. Nor am I sexually incompetent."

"But I only have your word for that now, don't I?"

He tips his chin. "Be precise. Which part of my diatribe are you casting doubt on exactly?"

"The claims of expertise when it comes to fucking."

"Alice, Alice, Alice." He clicks his tongue. "If you think I'm putting out now just to prove a point or to meet your dare, you are very much mistaken."

"We need to discuss this whole waiting thing," I mumble. "Please give me a full and thorough explanation for why this is necessary again. Especially since we're now officially sharing a bed and living space."

"I just think it's best we wait." And he says it so casually. Like it's already decided and that's that.

"Why?"

"Lots of reasons."

"Such as?"

"Actually, there's just the one. The solidity of our relationship," he announces. "Now, this is all very cutting-edge science, I assure you. Try your best to keep up. You see, I'm basing my hypothesis on my own past experiments in this particular field."

"I'm listening."

"This may shock you, but in every relationship I've had up until now sex tends to enter the equation quite early on. And each and every one of those relationships failed." He holds out a hand like he's presenting something. Like he's a magician as opposed to a sexy moron. "In summation, it is my belief that fucking too soon quite possibly fucks things up long-term."

I wrinkle my nose. "No."

"Yes."

Give me strength. "Or maybe you just weren't compatible with these other people."

"Maybe."

"Or either you or they weren't ready or looking for a relationship at that particular point in time."

"Perhaps."

"Or there could have been trust issues or a hundred other reasons why relationships fail that have nothing to do with sex."

"Yes. Quite possibly," he agrees. "Or, I'm right, and we should take it slow."

I need alcohol. Lots of it. "So none of my very valid points matter because you've already made up your mind."

He says nothing.

"You know, this is probably me overthinking shit. But I'm actually feeling slightly slut shamed for wanting to have sex with you sooner rather than later."

"What?" He scowls. "No."

"I thought taking it slow was this fun game we were both playing. But now it feels very much like you're wearing the pants of judgment."

His forehead furrows. "Alice, no. Absolutely not. We are going to have sex and lots of it, I promise you. We're just taking it slow."

"I officially hate that word."

"And this is not about me not wanting you. Do not doubt yourself," he says. "When I masturbate in the shower, you are the undisputed star of the show. Both morning and night."

I blink. "That was actually kind of hot. Say it again."

"That this is not about me not wanting you?"

"No. The other bit."

"Do not doubt yourself or us."

"Don't take this the wrong way, but sometimes I want to throw things at you," I confess. "Not necessarily sharp or even particularly heavy hard-hitting objects. But...you know...things."

There's laughter in his eyes now. "You want me to repeat the bit about masturbating while thinking about you, huh? Would you like to know specific fantasies or do you just enjoy me talking dirty to you in general?"

I'm not panting. That's someone else. "You can't tell me you've masturbated thinking about me and then ask me to wait to have sex. It's unreasonable."

"And yet I'm doing it." He collects the used plates and utensils to take back inside, returning with another couple of beers in hand. "Now, the next question is, why are you trying to rush things between us?"

"Perhaps I'm just interested in what's in your pants."

"Why didn't you say so earlier? I'd be delighted to send you a dick pic." He passes me a beer with a grin. "Dad always said to ensure our digital footprint was as light and legal as possible. But what with me having missed your last twenty-two birthdays, a nicely lit shot of my junk is the least I can do. I'll even pick out an arty filter for you."

I snort/laugh. So ladylike. "I'll be sure to use it as the wallpaper on my cell."

"I would hope so." He settles back in his seat opposite me. For all of the beauty of the stars and the city lights, nothing beats just staring at him. "What are you thinking about?"

"You know you use humor as a kind of defense system, right? As a way to keep people at a distance."

His brows rise. "I hadn't thought of it that way."

"Hmm."

"I wonder if we have a bit of that in common, hiding behind wit and sarcasm."

My mouth opens, but nothing comes out. I can't entirely

discount his words. Not when deep down I know there's an element of truth to them. So instead, I say, "Maybe."

"My first instinct is to say something clever here, so I guess that proves your point. But I'm going to resist the urge and just give you the truth." For a long moment, he stares at me. "I want this to work, Alice. I need it to work."

"But you'd be okay without me."

"I'd be alone without you. And you'd be alone without me. Is that what you really want?"

"Sometimes alone is safer."

"Sure," he says, tipping his chin. "I can say I'm not going to hurt you and mean every word. But things happen. Life happens. Us being together, trying to make this work, is a risk. I happen to think it's a worthwhile one and I'm hoping you do too."

And then it hits me. "You're afraid of being alone."

"No, I'm used to being alone. I've spent most of my life alone. And I'll take alone over being used or lied to any day of the week." He swallows. "But I'm betting that you're not out to do either of those things. I'm betting that you're the sweet funny woman I met in a shitty bar in LA whose smile made me a little crazy. Who laughed at my stupid jokes, invited me to her favorite diner, and held my hand when we walked on the beach."

"Beck..."

"I lay awake for hours thinking about you. Couldn't get you out of my head." His smile is pure. There's no other word for it. "I hadn't planned on hanging around in LA. But I had to go back for more."

"I was so scared you'd leave. I'd only just met you, but..." And I don't mean to say it, however, my idiot mouth just blurts it out. "This is all moving so fast. Apart from the sex, I mean."

Nothing from him. The expression in his eyes, however, is one of worry. It makes my heart hurt to see him this way. I rise and head over to his couch, curling up next to him. He slides an arm around my shoulders, drawing me close. Together is definitely better, he's right about that.

"You're not alone." I cover his hand with mine. "I'm here, Beck, and I'm not going anywhere."

"Okay," he says, voice low. "Thank you."

"Selah is an idiot. You're already the dream guy without the money or the name. You're officially too good to be true."

"Officially, huh?"

"Yep." I rest my head against his shoulder and watch the flames. We've both had enough real, angst, and honest for the time being. "Doesn't mean I'm agreeing with your whole philosophy of abstinence making the heart grow fonder or the relationship grow stronger, however."

"Just because you disagree doesn't mean I'm giving you the d." He taps his bottle against mine before downing some beer. "I think spirited discourse and an occasional disagreement is healthy in a relationship. Yay, us."

"Yay," I say drolly.

Beck kisses the top of my head before resting his cheek there. Everything is going to be okay. I'm like fifty-seven percent sure of it.

CHAPTER SIX

ECK AVOIDS MY GOING TO BED AND WAKING UP ATTEMPTS AT ENTICING
him into sex by simply being absent. He stays up late working
in the office then is gone by the time I wake. When I text him,
he says he's at the gym then heading straight to work. But I will
not be deterred. Just because other relationships he's been in hit
the wall doesn't mean we necessarily will. And he can't avoid me
on the mattress forever. It might be big, but it's not that big.

Emotions-wise, we feel more stable after the discussion the
night before. Which doesn't mean it's still not all a terrifying risk,
but here we are. Everything is scary if you look at it the wrong
way. But I want to keep looking at him and listening to him and
lying next to him for a good long time.

It turned out, Selah had found my clothes and they're in the
walk-in closet along with all of the new stuff. Thank fuck for that.
I'll have to remember to thank her. Though it kind of irks me to
acknowledge any of her good deeds, after Beck's story last night
and her part in the father's machinations. She hurt my boyfriend.
Not something I'll forget anytime soon.

While I don't mind being tidied up a little, I am not down
with having the original version of me erased. They actually did
a great job on the clothes and stuff. Most of it seems to be in the
colors I like and not so far afield of my own style that I don't recognize myself anymore. Of course, there's a few things I'd rather
remove a limb than wear. But all in all the personal shoppers know
how to do their jobs. As you'd expect from anyone who worked
for Rachel—she clearly knows how to take control of a situation.

Beck left me a note that he'd be busy until late afternoon, so it's time to play tourist. After I call my mom to let her know I'm both still alive and still with Beck. I also give her the full explanation about his money and his family. She's a little astounded, to say the least. And fair enough. I'm not even sure I've gotten my head around it all yet.

I walk over to Larimer Square to look around. Lots of cool boutiques and an Italian restaurant with awesome pizza and a Cucumber Lavender Rickey to die for. Got to love old-fashioned cocktails gone hipster. This is when my cell chimes, alerting me to a text.

Natasha: Hey.

Me: Hi! How you doing?

Natasha: Work, life, blah blah blah. What about you?

Me: Met someone, quit my job, and maybe moved to Denver.

Natasha: Maybe or did move to Denver? This is not an in-between kind of statement. Unless you're stuck halfway in Utah.

Me: Did. I guess. Guy I met comes from here.

And that's when my cell rings.

"I can't wait for you to text me," says Natasha, by way of greeting. "I need answers now. So you finally told Rob to shove it, huh?"

We used to work together at the bar before she ran off to New York. She knows the pain that is Rob firsthand. "I did," I say. "It was glorious. Called him rude words and everything."

"And now you're in Denver?"

"Yes. A guy came to work at the bar—let's call him hot busboy for the sake of this story—and we started flirting and stuff happened."

"Okay."

"Then it turned out he was rich and came from Denver and had to go back to Denver so eventually I went there too and that brings us up to now."

"Wait," she says. "He's rich? How rich?"

"Very. Think big wealthy dysfunctional family with lots of mansions and businesses and I do not fit in."

"But he wants you there."

I smile. "He does. Anyway, how are things with you?"

"I work, I date, I drink coffee. The usual." She sighs. "Tell me more about rich busboy. That's far more interesting. Nice catch, by the way."

"Please don't say that." I sigh. "I didn't set out to catch a rich dude or something. It just kind of happened."

"You're right. Sorry."

"He's the greatest. I really like him."

"You're using middle school speak. Give me specifics. How does he treat you? What's he like in bed?" she rapid fires questions. "What's his name?"

"Great. None of your business. And Beck Olson."

"Putting you on speaker so I can look him up."

"Okay." I wait. "What have you found?"

"You haven't looked him up yourself?" she asks. "What's wrong with you?"

"I wouldn't even know where to start answering that question." I stir my drink with a paper straw. "His stepmother gave me a makeover yesterday. Clothes, hair, makeup...the whole shebang."

"Why don't you sound happy? Normal people love makeovers. Especially when someone else is paying." She makes a humming noise. "Ex-fiancée is pretty. I hate her already."

"She's actually not that bad. At least she's been sort of nice to me."

"Fuck me, his mother is a supermodel."

"Crazy, right?"

"This is wild," says Natasha. "Oh, he is a very good-looking specimen. That jawline, that dark floppy hair. I think I'm in love."

"Don't make me hang up on you."

"Hey, there's a photo of you two together."

"There is? Where?"

"Denver Days. Looks like a lifestyle slash gossip site," she says. "If it makes you feel any better, the makeover you got worked a treat. You look very shiny. Lots of speculation about new mystery girlfriend and his return in the wake of his father's death. Not much else."

I put her on speaker, look up the site, and cringe. Photos of me in general are the worst. Though the outfit and hair are pretty great. It's from when we were standing outside the Heritage yesterday. I hadn't even realized there was a photographer around at that stage. "Hmm."

"I've never had a famous friend."

"You still don't. He's got the name and money, not me," I say. "I've never had random people digging into my private life before. This is so strange. Let alone living this lifestyle, having these things, which I've done nothing to deserve."

"Try to put the guilt aside and see it as weird fun as opposed to weird horrible."

"Yeah."

"You're telling yourself shitty things inside your head, aren't you?" she says, voice stern. "You need to cut that out. It's bullying. You're cute and cool and he's lucky to have you."

"Nat…"

"What would you say to me if I was being all self-doubty and whiny?" she asks.

"Pull your head of your ass, you beautiful goddess?"

"Exactly. Now go find a mirror and say it to yourself."

"Will do." I take a deep breath. "I love you."

"I love you too."

"Stand tall, shoulders back, and tits out," I say.

"That's the way." She laughs. "You've got this."

By the time I get back to the Heritage in the early afternoon, it's coffee time. Except the coffee shop is still handling a roaring lunchtime crowd and there's nary a seat to be found. So I head inside for the cocktail bar where it's not quite so crowded. Still, the bartender/mixologist is working her ass off and the waiter on duty is all but running back and forth from the kitchen to serve meals to many groups of people seated around the low tables. Seems like the Heritage is very popular.

I take a seat at the end of the bar and wait.

"Miss Lawrence." The waiter appears like magic. "What can I get for you?"

"Coffee, please. But there's no rush. I can see you're busy."

He puts the order into the computer. "I'll get that for you right away."

Sure enough, a couple of minutes later a coffee sits in front of me. I don't even bother asking how he knew who I was. The man is either damn good at his job, or Beck has been thorough in ensuring I feel at home here, or gossip has been going around. A mix of all three perhaps? Whatever.

"They called around. We can't get anyone else in on such short notice," says a voice nearby. A woman dressed in a black pantsuit. "It's going to be a couple of hours at least."

The waiter's face tightens.

"I'm sorry, I have to get back." She heads into the hotel restaurant next door. It's busy in there as well.

"Problem?" I ask.

The waiter, his name tag says Isaac, gives me a wary look. "No, Miss Lawrence. Just some members of staff are off sick. It happens. Everything is fine. Is your coffee okay?"

I climb off the stool. "You need help for a couple of hours? I'm a waitress. Tell me what to do."

His mouth just kind of hangs open.

"Isaac, I can help," I repeat.

"Oh, no. Mr. Elliot—"

"Won't mind in the least. I promise." I survey the room. "Tell you what, I'm going to start by clearing those tables and giving them a wipe down. You let me know what you'd like done after that."

And off I go. If I want to be part of this world then I need to be on the lookout for ways to contribute. This is a pretty straightforward way to help Beck.

Of course, the only downside to getting a whole bunch of new shoes is having to break them in. My feet are going to be sore by the end of the day. Lucky I wore low wedge booties with my Oscar de la Renta black sleeveless midi dress. Both are black so I mostly blend in with the staff. They don't seem to have a uniform in this area so much as just wear clothes that are black or white. Makes sense. Those colors tend to be easier to clean.

I raise a few eyebrows back in the kitchen, but it's easy enough to figure out where the dirty dishes go and where to find a cloth to clean off the tables. Isaac handles the computer for ordering and taking payment, while I deliver and do cleanup. We work well together and the time goes by quickly. It's actually kind of nice to be doing something in my comfort zone. Not that waitressing is how I want to spend all of my days.

By the time the extra person appears, we're edging into happy hour, so I hang around a bit longer to help out with the larger crowd. In fact, everything is going great right up until a group of four men walk out of the restaurant. And at the front of the group is Ethan. Beck's brother freezes in place at the sight of me carrying dirty dishes. The man has an impressive frown. I have never been quite so thoroughly disapproved of. Such condemnation. Like shame on me for existing in his general vicinity. These damn people.

"Alice," says Beck, stepping around his brother.

"Hey. Some of your staff are out sick. I'm just helping."

"Thank you. Let me grab those for you." He picks up the used glassware and follows me back into the kitchen. We both wash our hands before heading back out.

"You've got to be fucking kidding me," says Ethan as we return.

At least I look okay. The hairdresser and makeup artist gave me lessons yesterday. While he may not like what I'm doing, he can't disapprove of my appearance. "Ethan. Nice to see you again."

"She can't be doing this," he says to his little brother. "What'll people think?"

"Do people think? That's the real question." Beck's frown is not quite as fierce as his brother's, but it's not bad. "And as far as I'm concerned, she can do whatever she wants. Currently, she's choosing to help run this business. A family business until the sale goes through. How can you possibly fault her for that?"

"You want the board to take you seriously or not?"

"Of course I do."

"Having your new girlfriend join the kitchen staff is not the way to go about it," growls Ethan. "I realize her employment options are limited, given her experience. But if you need to keep her busy then Emma can get her involved in some charities or something more suitable."

My fingers curl into fists. Confrontation sucks, but I'm not about to stand here and take this. "Could we not talk about me like I'm not here, please?"

"You had Alice investigated?" asks Beck, his face still and voice cold.

"Of course we did." His brother doesn't even hesitate. Like it's the most normal thing in the world. Damn creep. "Most positive thing I can say about her is that I almost fell asleep reading the report. I know Dad setting you up with Selah pissed you off, but did you have to hit back by finding a woman who encapsulates average to quite this degree?"

Beck's jaw is rigid.

"But then you've always had a weakness for unloved and neglected things. It's how you first got your hands on this hotel."

Ouch.

But he isn't finished yet. "I suppose I should be relieved it's not some coked-up pop princess on your arm like last time."

"That's enough," I say, teeth gritted. My parents raised me to be nice, to be polite. But I'm not into being a doormat. Some people are just never going to like you for whatever reason and that's life. "You've said your piece, Ethan, and rest assured we're all in awe at your level of dickery. It's time, however, for you to think about leaving."

Ethan's nostrils flare in anger.

And the suit beside him makes a strangled sort of noise.

I care not. "Look around you; you're causing a scene. People are watching and listening and soon this'll be talked about all over town. Of course, no one expects any better from the likes of me. But you...that's not very Elliot behavior now, is it?"

Beck bites back a smile.

"I need you at that meeting tomorrow, Beck." Ethan's face is tense. "Don't be late."

"I'll be there," says Beck.

With a final glare thrown in my direction, his brother strides away with dude number three hot on his heels. The fourth member of the group, however, gives me a warm smile. "Nice to see you again, Alice."

"Matías. Hi."

A new waitress emerges from out back and Isaac gives me a smile. Guess I'm done waitressing for the day.

Without saying a word, Beck takes my hand and leads me toward the elevators. I didn't tell any lies. People are indeed watching. Matías follows a couple of steps behind us. But it isn't until we're in an elevator heading up to the apartment that the scene is discussed.

"Is dickery even a word?" asks Beck.

Matías cocks his head. "If it isn't, it should be. And your older brother's behavior certainly encapsulates the very essence of it."

"I hope you're not angry at me," I say. "But I'd kind of had enough. There's constructive feedback and then there's character assassination and his little speech was closer to the latter. For both of us."

"You were absolutely perfect." Beck raises my hand to his lips, kissing my knuckles. "I don't think I've ever had a girlfriend who'd been willing to protect me from Ethan before. I like it."

Phew. "What do you think is in the file on me?"

"Try not to let it worry you," says Matías. "They have files on everyone."

Beck smiles and says a whole lot of nothing.

"Coked-up pop princess?" I ask.

The smile falls from his face. "That was a long time ago."

"Months," agrees Matías.

"Years."

"Years is plural."

"Fine. More than a year ago, then." Beck frowns. "Don't make me look bad in front of my girl, you asshole."

Matías just laughs.

"Speaking of dubious things best not mentioned, what are you and Emma fighting over this week?"

"A soup tureen."

The elevator doors slide open and we head for home. Or at least, home for now. Who knows, once Ethan reports back about my latest disgrace I might be run out of town by Olson company employees carrying pitchforks. And Grandma & Co. will certainly not be impressed. God, this situation is complicated. Usually if someone's family doesn't like you there's little risk of it leading to all out corporate war.

How and when did my life get this interesting?

Beck opens the apartment's front door, holding it for us to go ahead. The view with the sun setting over LoDo is spectacular. Maybe tonight we'll get to use the hot tub. I head straight for the couch and take off my shoes and the little sock things. I arch my feet and stretch my toes. Oh, heaven is having bare feet after a long day. If such behavior is uncouth and Elliots aren't supposed to be seen barefoot in their own damn apartments then I definitely don't want to be one. Beck and I can just live in sin forever and ever amen.

"Matías, and I ask this respectfully as a friend, why in the ever-loving fuck would you want a soup tureen?" asks Beck, grabbing craft beers out of the fridge and passing them around.

"It's antique, silver, worth quite a bit."

"And yet it is still a soup tureen."

Matías makes himself at home, man-spreading on the opposite couch. "Told Emma I might use it for ice and beer at barbecues or just put it in the laundry for all those single socks you can never find a match for. She almost went into apoplexy. It was hilarious."

"How large are your legal bills, just out of curiosity?"

"We don't use the divorce lawyers for this sort of small stuff anymore," says Matías. "Having to send messages through them about every little thing sucked all of the fun out of it. We both prefer the direct approach."

"Correct me if I'm wrong, but are divorces meant to be fun?" I ask.

"He and Emma are having the time of their lives, apparently." Beck sits beside me, sliding an arm around my shoulders. His fingers play with my ponytail. "Don't feel bad. No one understands."

"You only get to divorce someone once," says Matías with all due seriousness. "We want to make sure we do it right."

I nod as if I understand. "Okay."

"Someday, if you two decide to get married, you'll understand."

"Of course, you could always go back to couples counseling," suggests Beck.

Matías screws up his face in disbelief. "Our divorce negotiations just hit their second year. You can hardly expect us to start acting like adults now."

Beck takes a swig of beer. "It's good, by the way."

"Told you," says Matías. "They're a great little microbrewery, but they need money to expand. Add some new lines, move into ciders as well, maybe."

"And they're solid?"

"The numbers add up. It's a bit bigger than we normally go, but I like them."

"You mentioned being business partners the other day?" I ask because, curiosity. The beer is more hoppy than I like, but it's not bad.

"When I got access to my trust fund at twenty-five, Matías and I started The Crooked Company," says Beck. "We do seed funding, specialize in helping small businesses. It's our way of counteracting the damage large companies like Elliot Corp. do."

"That sounds great."

"It is." The pride in Matías's gaze is unmistakable. "We work with small-batch distilleries and ice-cream makers, a rare book shop, vintage record store, electric bikes, a lipstick company, organic butchers, slow fashion, artisan donuts, food trucks, a service to help you set up your own edible garden, several different apps, and all sorts of things."

"With the added benefit that it annoyed the absolute crap out of Dad," says Beck.

I smile. "I can't imagine why with a name like The Crooked Company."

Beck winks at me.

Matías sets his ankle on the opposite knee, crossing his legs in the way dudes do. There's certainly no shortage of pretty men in bespoke suits in this part of town. If Emma did marry him for his looks, I can't fault her taste. His dark eyes are nothing less than entrancing. "For a waste of time and money it sure is earning nice dividends."

And they're all such high achievers. Then there's me, still not knowing what I'm doing with my life. Ethan might have had a point about my averageness. These people all have such purpose and drive. You can only float through life without a clue for so long. Right now, I'm not even earning an income and the idea of living off Beck does not appeal.

He clears his throat. "Beloved, did you happen by any chance to buy that chunk of rock sitting on the coffee table?"

"No."

"Ah."

"It's clear crystal, quartz or something, isn't it?" I ask.

Matías frowns at the thing. "Whatever it is, it's bigger than my head."

"Mother must have stopped by," says Beck. "It's probably to help protect us from bad vibes or something."

I set my bottle down on the coffee table. "This is good, but if you don't mind, I'm going to make myself a vodka and soda. Not really in the mood for beer."

"This is your home now too." Beck downs another mouthful. "You don't need to ask me permission."

"More than just a holiday, then?" asks the other man.

"Permanent, as far as I'm concerned," says Beck. "But perhaps she needs persuading."

"I've only been here for like forty-eight hours," I intercede.

Beck's silence speaks volumes. Underneath the hot and humorous exterior, he's a man used to getting what he wants. Guess it comes with the money. And perhaps his disguised alpha dog tendencies. However, I have yet to meet an Elliot who doesn't like control.

"Have a chance to look around yet, Alice?" asks Matías.

"I walked over to Larimer Square today. It was nice."

Beck cocks his head. "You went out?"

"For a little while," I answer.

"And Smith didn't take you?"

"It's only a couple of blocks."

"Yeah, but…"

Matías stares out at the view in silence.

"But what?" I asked.

"You didn't tell me."

"I'm telling you now."

This smile of Beck's is one of the lesser seen ones. And it's not the least bit genuine so it's just as well. "Well, I like to know what you're up to and I left instructions with the concierge. They were supposed to call Smith if you needed to go anywhere."

"They asked if I wanted a car and I said no."

Nothing from him.

"Is that a problem?"

It takes him a moment to answer. "I just want you to be safe and happy."

"And I was both, thank you. You're busy. You don't need me checking in hourly."

"No, but a message now and then to let me know how you're going and what you're doing would be nice."

Guess that's fair enough. Within reason. "All right. I'll consider that in the future."

"Thank you."

"But I'm not comfortable taking up Smith's time. Nor do I need a bodyguard. That kind of thing might be normal for your family, but it's not for me."

"Yes, but you're new in town and you're my girlfriend. So I'd feel better if—"

The doorbell chimes, cutting him off. Since I'm already on my feet I answer it.

"We're not finished talking about this," says Beck.

"Sure we are. You're just in denial."

In the hallway is a stranger carrying various bags, and Selah. A sure sign that the crystal isn't protecting us from shit. She flinches at the sight of me opening the door to Beck's apartment. Then she just stands there, looking at me expectantly. Why exactly, I have no idea. And again, I can't help but note all of the differences between us. She's just so damn perfect in so many ways. Except for the ones that matter, apparently. I square my shoulders. The girl will just have to get used to me standing in what was once her space, because I have no plans on going anywhere anytime soon.

"Damn." Beck appears behind me, placing his hand against the small of my back. "I forgot."

"Of course you did," says Selah, barging into the room.

"There's a charity gala tonight. They'll be including a memoriam for my father." Beck winces. "We're required to attend. Or I am."

I take a deep breath. "Right."

"You don't have to do this," he says.

"Of course she does," scoffs Selah. "It's part of the job. Alice, this is Tex, your hair and makeup artist. He'll set up in the bedroom. We're on a tight schedule so let's get moving."

And Beck is pissed. Guess I wouldn't want my ex in my home either. But the chill in his gaze is verging on arctic. "I'm certain Alice can handle this. Your presence is not required."

"Your grandmother called Rachel, who sent me," says Selah, dark hair immaculately drawn back in a bun. "Do you really want to take on those two?"

In response, he pulls out his cell, ready to make the call.

"It's fine." I place my hand on his forearm, giving it a squeeze. "Really."

"Are you sure?"

"Let's just get this done." Then I remember Natasha's words. "Who knows? I might even enjoy it."

Through all of this, Matías says nothing. Now he salutes me with his beer, one Elliot outsider to another. Makes me wonder how much of this sort of thing he's had to deal with over the years. If the pressure and interference helped push Emma and him toward their separation. Not a happy thought.

"Thank you," says Beck.

"Not a problem."

I stroke the stubble on Beck's cheek and he instantly moves closer, pressing his mouth to mine. This is not a chaste kiss, but neither of us cares. Audience and his weird-ass relationship philosophies be damned. I can feel the eyes on us and it just doesn't matter. His tongue strokes my own, his hand grabbing the back of my neck, holding me in place. As if I'm going anywhere. For all of his wanting to wait and playing it cool, there's an element of control to him in this moment. And it's hot as fuck. We're both breathing heavily, caught up in the moment. My head goes light and my sex squeezes tight. I grip his upper arms, half just needing something to hold myself up. The other half of me is admiring how hard his body is beneath my touch. I want to rub up against him, explore him all over. Every time we get this close, stopping gets harder and harder. The tension in his body and fervor in his touch tell me he's struggling too. In all honesty, the boy better be done with this waiting shit soon or else.

When he draws back, his thumb wipes over my damp bottom lip. "Whatever you want, Alice."

Good God this man makes me smile. Meanwhile, Selah looks like she sucked on a lemon. Everything is as it should be.

CHAPTER SEVEN

"**D**ON'T BE NERVOUS," SAYS BECK. "YOU LOOK BEAUTIFUL."

"I'll be nervous if I want to. I just won't let it stop me from doing anything."

"That's my girl."

He stands beside me dressed in a tuxedo and a smile. And holy fucking hell does he wear them well. Not to mention the dark hair styled into a pompadour and hazel eyes I could stare into for days. Then there's the warmth in those eyes when he looks at me...I might just swoon. I'm not sure if I've ever been truly seen before. Not like he sees me.

"We could have stayed home and had sex," I say.

He grins. "You called our apartment home."

"You're missing the point."

We arrived in a limousine, the first time I've been in one since prom. The gala is being held in the ballroom of a big hotel. Lots of ornate potted orchids and sparkling chandeliers. Selah and I had a robust discussion about what I'd wear. She wanted me in a sequined monstrosity and no way was that happening. In fact, I gave her the thing along with about half of the wardrobe contents to take back to Mac. For some reason, seeing all of the free space in the walk-in-closet soothed me big-time. Like maybe my life hasn't been turned upside down (albeit in wonderful ways) and I still have a little control.

That's the great thing about anxiety. There's always something to worry about. When things are going bad, they can always get worse. But when things are great, it can all be stolen from you at any moment plunging you into the darkness of the abyss. Sometimes I get really sick of the inside of my head.

Everything is fine. I've got this. And I'm going to keep saying it until it's the truth.

I don't normally wear dresses due to chub rub. Of course, you can get undershorts and other things to combat it, but I generally prefer pants. This, however, is a special occasion. The gown I chose is by Juan Carlos Obando, navy crepe (dark colors hide food stains), one shoulder and ankle length. It's simple and elegant and I love it. Some sparkle is added by Gucci block heel silver sandals and a bangle of white gold and baguette-cut diamonds. There're also beautiful diamond studs in my ears. I'm pretending they're all fake, like rhinestones or crystals. Because otherwise there's every chance I'd lose my shit over what they're worth. Being a billionaire's girlfriend is weird after so recently living on ramen noodles during the lean weeks.

The other thing about this jewelry is that I could have sworn these pieces weren't here yesterday. A string of pearls and matching stud earrings (my lifelong dream of being able to clutch my pearls can finally come true), a diamond pendant necklace, and a few other small things that probably cost a fortune have been placed in the closet. But not these. Maybe Selah just brought them over. I don't know.

At any rate, the lesson here is, you don't need to be a size zero to look good. But money certainly doesn't hurt. Especially with photographers roaming the place. For the society pages, I guess. We're stopped several times on the way in. My cheeks hurt from smiling.

A waiter escorts us to our table where Beck's grandmother is already seated and holding court with Ethan sitting beside her. Sad to say he looks almost as good in his tux as his brother does. I'm not shallow, however, so I plan to keep right on disliking him. Our entrance earns more than its fair share of attention from the other guests. And I'm drawing quite a few admiring glances along with the curious ones, which is nice. It must be odd being an Elliot and having people watching you all of the time, being so invested in knowing what or who you're doing. Some people need to get a life.

Selah is seated at the next table beside a handsome young man. The look she gives me is resigned. Not a smile, but not a frown. The look she gives Beck, however, is wistful. Sad eyes and rounded shoulders. If I'd fucked up so badly with him I'd proba-bly feel the same.

"Your ex is here," I say in a low voice to avoid being overheard.

"To be expected. Her family are big donors for the hospital."

"Did she manage to corner you earlier at the apartment?"

"Told her I wasn't interested in anything she had to say." His raises a brow. "You're not jealous, are you?"

"I don't know."

He pulls out my seat for me ahead of the waiter, his gaze thoughtful. "You shouldn't be."

"Reason doesn't often count when it comes to emotions." I sit, making sure my posture is perfect. The less cause I give Grandma & Co. to complain the better.

Catherine breaks off her conversation with the silver fox sitting next to her. She looks glamorous in a black velvet gown. "Beck. Alice. You missed the appetizers. I was beginning to think you weren't coming. Emma's absence tonight is disappointing enough."

"She's in Chicago on business," says Ethan. "It couldn't be avoided. You know that."

Catherine sniffs, unappeased.

Beck delivers a swift kiss to his grandmother's cheek, mur-muring something to her (apologies, most likely), before taking his seat beside me. He takes my hand under the table as the woman on his other side immediately engages him in conversation. So this is how rich people do charity and party at the same time. Everything is sparkly and shiny and top of the line. There must be at least a few hundred people here.

Five minutes later, Beck is still busy talking to the other woman so I guess I'll just occupy myself. No problem.

"You'll have to excuse him," says the woman sitting next to me. Ethan's date. Her skin has a bronze hue, a perfect contrast to her red silk dress. "Beck's used to everyone already knowing each other at these things. Whether it's from the country club or the arts gala or Aspen."

I give her a polite smile.

"Penny Hollis. I'm a lawyer at Elliot Corp."

"Alice Lawrence."

"You're the new girl in town causing all of the fuss."

What am I even supposed to say to that?

"Excuse me, miss." The waiter reappears with a vodka, soda, and lime, saving me from coming up with a reply to Penny's comment. Guess Beck ordered for me. I knew there were reasons I kept him around.

This time my smile is far more believable. "Thank you."

"So the woman monopolizing your boyfriend's attention is in investment at Elliot Corp. Next to her is a heart surgeon and her partner. Then there's the property specialist who's hoping to offload a penthouse onto Ethan," she reports. "The bored-looking blonde is the trophy wife of the older gentleman trying to sell Catherine on something. He's a big deal in media, out visiting from New York. And the rest you know."

"You attend these things often?" I ask.

"Often enough."

The beautiful blonde with the sandy complexion sure does look bored, throwing back champagne at a steady rate.

"If you marry for money you wind up earning it," murmurs Penny. "She used to be a pro-golfer, but he made her give it up so she could fit in with his schedule and lifestyle. I wonder how she feels about that decision these days."

Meals are brought out. A cut of beef sits atop roast potatoes with some sort of Italian tomato sauce and asparagus. Beck and I have to stop holding hands in order to eat, but I don't think the woman beside him stops talking long enough to actually get any food in her mouth. Her loss—the meal is spectacular. Beck shoots me a few quick smiles throughout all of this and that's all I get. I try not to let it bother me. It's another sink or swim situation and I have every intention of surviving and standing on my own.

"How long have you been working for them?" I ask.

Penny swallows her food, washing it down with a sip of red wine. "Going on a decade now."

"And you're from Denver?"

She nods. "Born and bred. It might be a big city, but it's still a small town at heart. I can't imagine living anywhere else. Have you had a chance to see much?"

"Only Larimer Square so far."

"Get Beck to take you up into the mountains. That's where the real beauty is."

"I'll do that."

Catherine gives me the occasional cool look, but I can deal with that. Given I am neither spilling my food nor dancing on the table, she really has nothing to complain about. Ethan ignores my existence entirely. Making it even odder that his date does not. Due to politics or politeness, I don't know.

"I'm just going to ask because that's how we find things out," says Penny. "Did Beck actually pick you up in a dive bar where he was working as a busboy?"

"Ah…"

"Because that's what Ethan told me and honestly I'm still having a problem picturing it."

"You and Ethan are close?" I ask because having no idea what

Beck does and doesn't want known means a diversion is required. I'm not ashamed and neither do I want to lie. But he does business with these people. I'm not particularly gifted at manipulation or subterfuge. Games of strategy are lost on me. Avoidance, however, I can do. After all, I've been avoiding both the questions and hands of idiots with varying blood alcohol levels in bars for years.

"We work together and we're friends. We're not an item though. I'm not foolish enough to attempt dating an Elliot." Then she realizes what she's said, and raises a manicured hand, the fingernails a perfect match for her dress. "Not that that's any reflection on you, of course. If the busboy story is true, then you didn't know the hornet's nest you were stumbling into. One might even say he won you over under false pretenses."

I take my time, thinking things through. That the story of Beck and my courtship is being discussed around town leaves a sour taste in my mouth. However, there's not a damn thing I can do about it. And what could I say here, really? I almost failed math, but my new boyfriend's a billionaire? I'm a waitress and underachiever by choice and trade? Beck is dating down in the eyes of many. I understand. That I'd kick his ass and be out of here on the next plane if he didn't treat me right regardless of any perceived inadequacies is between me and him. All of this is just further proof that making conversation sucks and people are the worst. Time to drink.

Penny swirls the wine in her glass. "You have the discretion part down. They should give you points for that at least."

And I keep right on saying nothing because apparently it's working well for me.

"I'm going to take your silence for assent," she finally declares. "Beck was always the black sheep of the family, but that's something else. Good for him getting out and doing his own thing. Even if it was only for a short while."

As tempted as I am to kick him beneath the table and have

him intercede, I don't. When it comes to him, curiosity wins out as always. What's the harm in letting the lady talk?

"Of course, Jack pushed him too far. He never thought Beck would actually up and leave. None of them did. When the apron strings are lines of credit the pressure to obey the family and company can be extreme." Gaze thoughtful, she stops talking to eat for a minute. "But now Catherine and Ethan are busily gathering their forces to show the board and the world a strong united front. And your boyfriend is part of that."

"Yes, he is," I say, because duh.

She looks over her shoulder to the table behind us where Selah is seated. The look Rachel's assistant gives us is somewhere between dislike and distrust. Fair enough. Next her gaze goes to the talkative investment specialist on the other side of Beck. The one taking up all of his attention. She's apparently no happier at this woman than she is with us. Interesting.

"Lots of competition for your position, Alice," says Penny. "I wish you the best of luck."

Instead of answering, I take a sip of my drink. Honest to God, I should win some sort of shutting-up award tonight. However, it's better to say nothing than to stick my foot in it.

"Everything okay?" asks Beck, sliding his hand up to the nape of my neck.

"Everything is fine."

"Can I get you another drink?"

"No." I need my wits about me with this crowd. Loose lips sink ships and all that. "Thank you."

Waiters collect the dinner plates, replacing them with dessert. A dark chocolate ganache with raspberry pulp on the side. If anything, it's a little too rich. Much like everyone present. Or maybe I'm just poor and judgey despite my new bling.

Up on the stage, a woman welcomes everyone and thanks them for their donations before introducing Beck's brother. Ethan rises from his seat and makes his way to the microphone to great applause. A picture of their recently deceased father appears on the big screen behind him. There's no mistaking the family resemblance. Jack is just an older, more lean and lined version of his sons. Like Catherine and Ethan his eyes are ice blue, his gaze dignified and hard.

"If I said my father was a saint I'd be lying," begins Ethan.

Startled laughter echoes through the room.

Catherine does not look amused. Then again, she rarely does.

"In fact, he'd probably haunt me for ruining his reputation," Ethan continues. "Jack Elliot was a hardworking man who dedicated his life to expanding the empire his father had begun. His commitment and focus to this task were absolute, as any of you who knew him can attest. Family loyalty was everything to my father. That his children would grow to understand and appreciate the devotion and sacrifices it takes to be an Elliot, and to be a part of this community, and to go on to contribute in their own way. That was his ultimate goal and vision, and it's what has brought us all here tonight. It's my honor to announce that a new wing will be built in remembrance of my father and his commitment to this great city and its people."

Applause fills the ballroom.

Ethan shakes the presenter's hand along with several others. People from the hospital or city officials, perhaps. I don't even want to imagine how much money a hospital wing would cost. But it's nice to see them doing something with the money besides buying another mansion. Amazing to think they can just make the decision to save lives and impact so many. It's hard to process what it would be like to have that much power.

Music starts up and the presentation is over. Catherine nods graciously to words of praise from those nearby. It takes Ethan a while to return to the table due to all of the back slapping and handshaking going on.

"Penny, good to see you," says Beck, resting his arm on the back of my chair. Looking as devastating as ever in his tux. "I was hoping to get your opinion on the Amari contract. My brother's keen, but I have some concerns."

They start to talk and I tune out, listening to the chamber orchestra. When Beck, Penny, and Ethan start discussing something about derivatives versus equities I decide it's time for a break.

Even the bathrooms are fancy with gray marble floors, walls, and bench tops. While I'm washing my hands, a woman around my own age introduces herself and asks me what school I went to. She seems somewhat perplexed when I tell her my local. Still, it's nice to get away for a while and stretch my legs. Less so to be met by the lady investment specialist from the table on my way back out. Her smile is all sharp teeth. Guess we're not going to be friends.

"You're Alice," she says like this is news.

I nod and try to edge around her, but she moves to block my escape. "You should know there's at least six women here tonight that your boyfriend's fucked. And those are just the ones I know about. He has a limited attention span. Once he gets his dick wet, it's all over. Apparently, he's a real animal in bed. But not so great when it comes to commitment. Look at poor Selah. She comes from one of the best families in town and he walked away without a second glance. So someone like you...let's just say that your time should be up any minute now. Better enjoy it while it lasts."

"Really?" I ask in a skeptical tone.

Her gaze snags on my diamond bracelet, lips twisting into a sneer. "That should come in handy. Nice and easy to hock back home in Cali, huh?"

"Is that it?" I cross my arms. Confrontation in general kind of makes me want to puke. But here we go anyway. "Are you finished with your mean-girl takedown?"

"Good question," says a familiar deep male voice.

"Ethan." The woman's eyes go as round as dinner plates. "I didn't see you there."

"You're done for the night, Jenna."

"What? But I was just—"

"Leave," he orders. "Now."

And the girl all but runs.

Ethan watches her go in silence before turning back to me. Still not wearing his happy face. But at this stage, I'm not sure he even does that emotion. "Tell me, Alice, do you dance?"

"I sway back and forth in time to the music if that counts?"

"That'll do." Ethan offers me his arm. "Let's go."

Only a few couples are on the dance floor. This time, there is definitely room left for Jesus. Ethan holds himself and me with a stiff formality. I bet he knows how to waltz and foxtrot and all sorts of things. I think I can remember how to do the Macarena. Something tells me he wouldn't be open to that suggestion. At any rate, the music is all wrong for anything half that interesting. We assume the standard waltz pose and rock back and forth.

"Thank you for running interference, but I could have handled it," I say when the silence between us starts to unnerve me.

A grunt.

"Is this the part where you warn me away from your brother?"

"Would it be any more effective than Jenna's mean girl routine?"

I wrinkle my lips. "No."

"I'll save my breath then."

"Not going to offer to cut me a big check to leave town either?" I say, because apparently all of those words I held in over dinner are now intent on spilling out. "Not that I'd take it. But you're much less high society gangster than I thought you'd be."

"High society gangster?" he asks, brows raised. "Really?"

I shrug.

"I can see why you two get along. You both have a peculiar

sense of humor." And the look on his face makes it clear exactly what he thinks of our shared brand of humor. Still, he's out here, dancing with me in public. Especially surprising given he's made what he thinks of me more than obvious.

"Cutting in," announces Beck, appearing beside us.

"Wondered when you'd notice she was gone," says Ethan.

"Something on your mind, big brother?"

"Maybe don't ignore your date next time. That is if you plan to keep her. I have to get back to the office. Have a nice night." Ethan takes a step back, giving me a nod and tugging on the cuff of his shirt, before departing the dance floor. Numerous people watch his exit.

Beck's gaze narrows. Unlike his brother, there's no politeness or messing around. He slides his arms around my waist, melding us together from chest to knee. "Was I ignoring you?"

I open my mouth to reply, then reconsider and shut it. Honesty isn't always helpful.

"Fuck," he mutters. "I'm sorry. That conversation probably saved Elliot Corp. somewhere between two and four million. Time I could have been spending with you. I won't get my priorities that wrong again."

It's hard not to giggle. "Are you serious?"

"Absolutely."

"Well, I had a nice chat with Penny. It was fine."

With my hands on his shoulders, we move slowly in time to the music. It's just like when we were in the bar, only completely different. Absolutely everything has changed apart from the way he makes my knees weak. And the way he looks at me like I've just replaced the sun as the center of the galaxy. That sort of thing can really go to a girl's head.

"This was a work function for you," I say. "Perhaps I didn't quite understand what that entails, but I do now."

"It's no excuse."

I shrug.

"Especially if it was bad enough that Ethan's commenting on it."

"Do your brother's opinions really matter?" I ask.

"Of us? No. Not in the least." He shakes his head. "Of me not treating you right? Yes. Very much so."

"Why does he even care?"

"We both grew up seeing our father treat the women in his life like shit," he says. "Neither of us want to continue the tradition. For Ethan, it means never getting serious with anyone. For me, it means getting things right with you."

"I think we're doing fine," I say. "Considering all of the recent upheavals and the fact that we've been dating for approximately two minutes now."

"Best two minutes of my life," he murmurs.

He looks into my eyes and, honest to God, I kind of lose touch with reality for a moment. Forget the world and our problems and everything else that matters. It's not fair. I never stood a chance of not falling far and fast for this man. Then some evil part of my brain reminds me that apparently six women in the room have gotten to crawl all over him naked while I haven't. And those were just the ones she knew about. Damn.

"Why did you just frown?" he asks.

"I didn't."

"You're not a very good liar, are you? Have you ever considered practicing in front of the mirror?"

"Beck, it's nothing."

"I disagree. Something just upset you and I want to know what it is."

I sigh. "Can't we just relax and enjoy ourselves?"

"I find honesty very relaxing and enjoyable. Don't you?" His hands sneak down to cover the uppermost curves of my ass. Our hips couldn't be any more publicly together without someone getting arrested.

"Fine," I groan. "Your friend Jenna cornered me in the hallway earlier and said some not so nice things. That's why I was dancing with Ethan. He walked in on the scene and sent her to her room. Not that I couldn't have handled it just fine on my own."

"Of course you could have. I was there when you handed my brother his ass, remember?"

I am validated. Hear me roar.

"What sort of not so nice things did she say?" he asks.

"Can't we just let it go? Please?"

"No."

"Ever heard the saying, other's people's opinion of you is none of your business," I say somewhat haughtily. "I actually got that off Instagram. Not sure who said it."

He just stares at me, waiting.

"Beck…"

"Whatever she said upset you and I'm thinking it might have been about you and me. Now I can't tell you it's bullshit and set your mind at ease if I don't know what it is."

Dammit. "She said that's you've slept with a goodly number of the women here and are only using me for sex before kicking me to the curb with the morning trash. That's a rough summation. I may have embellished slightly with the whole morning trash thing. But basically…yeah."

His jaw tightens.

"Little does she know we're not even having sex, huh? Joke's on her."

He looks away, his mouth a tight line.

"Aren't you supposed to be setting my mind at ease or something? With relaxing and enjoyable honesty?"

His gaze returns to mine, searching for something. I just smile and hope that's what he needs. "Alice, I'm sorry you had to deal with that."

"I'm a big girl. It's fine."

"Jenna wasn't lying about the other women."

"I know this is going to be hard for you to hear," I say. "But I never actually believed you when you insinuated that you were a virgin."

His smile is kind of pained. "I was always upfront with them. I never let them think that I wanted more. Not like I have with you."

"Good, I'm glad. On both counts." I link my hands behind his neck. "There are going to be people who don't like me. And there are certainly going to be people who don't like us together. But the thing is, they don't matter. It's up to you and me to decide what's best for us."

He nods all thoughtful-like. "You're never going to convince me that there's a situation where you should have to deal with this sort of shit. But you are also very wise."

"Thank you."

He leans down and I lift up and we kiss. No tongue so as not to upset his grandmother or other onlookers. But it's sweet just the same. Kissing him could never not be.

Then I remember. "Oh, in the interest of full disclosure, she also said that she'd heard you're an animal in the sack."

"Yeah," he says. "I started that rumor myself."

I laugh and on we dance. It's not such a bad night after all. But it's not done yet.

"Busy?"

Beck is slouched on the sofa at home, frowning at a tablet. "I missed a lot while I was away. It's going to take some time to catch up. If everyone could just stop sending me emails for an hour or two, that'd be nice."

"Hmm."

He's ditched the jacket, along with the bowtie. But on the

plus side, he's undone the top two buttons of his shirt, displaying the strong column of his neck and that dip at the base. The view is delectable. "There's a hotel for sale in Boulder that I want to take a look at. It'll need a lot of work, but it seems promising."

"Not the Stephen King *The Shining* one, is it?"

He smiles. "Ha. No."

"Still, that's exciting."

"Signed the papers with Ethan today to buy the Heritage," he says, still staring at the screen.

"Yeah?"

"Dad liked snatching up real estate in general. It's more stable than stock in most cases. Diversify or die. Got to make that money work for you."

"Well, you can tell Catherine if she doesn't agree to sell the Heritage I'll wear white after Labor Day and use the wrong fork at the next soiree."

"How shocking." He looks up with a grin. And freezes. "Dearest."

I walk over to the couch, perching beside him. The poor boy doesn't seem to know where to look first. My chemise is pale blue satin with lace edging. Shoestring straps, skirt brushing the tops of my thighs, and my breasts barely contained, let alone covered. There's even a matching thong. Not that he knows yet.

"Now, I can smell you on the pillow, so I know you are in fact sleeping in the same bed as me," I say. "You're just not around when I'm awake."

"It seemed safest. Though you're accommodatingly cuddly even fast asleep."

"Is that so?"

He nods slowly. "We've spooned. Just because you weren't conscious doesn't mean it didn't happen."

"That's a big step forward in our relationship."

"I thought so."

"It's a shame I missed it." And he really doesn't need his tablet so I take it and place it on the coffee table. Makes it much easier to climb onto his lap. Facing him, of course. I'm not messing around here.

"Alice."

I take his hands and place them on my thighs. "Yes?"

"Is this a declaration of war?"

"Hmm. I prefer to make love, not war."

"This is not going slow."

"To be fair, I never agreed to any of that. Waiting was all your idea and we've already established that it was a decision based on incomplete data."

"That may be so. But it's important to me," he says. "Let's take a moment here and discuss it further."

"There's no need. I already know and disagree with your reasons. But for the sake of getting along and mutual trust and respect, let's set a limit to tonight's activities."

"All right." Whatever his words, he's growing hard beneath me. Makes it impossible for me not to rock against him. He's thick and rigid and feels divine. Tingles radiate from my sex straight up my spine. He swears, low and heated. His hands grabbing at my hips. "Stop moving for a minute. I can't think when you do that."

"It feels so good, Beck." But I pause, reluctantly.

"You wanted to talk about limits," he says, face set. "I'm listening."

"You're a control freak, you know that?"

"Yes," he says. "But's it supposed to be a secret so don't tell anyone."

I wind my arms around his neck and rest my face on his shoulder. If he gets makeup on his shirt then bad fucking luck. I need a second to think. "You're driving me crazy. I'm not usually a sex monster."

"You're beautiful when you pout," he says, fingers trailing

up and down my arms. "The prettiest pouting, barely dressed sex monster in the room."

I take a breath and sit up. "All right, here's the deal. There's going to be making out, i.e. kissing along with over-the-clothes fondling. We've already done some of that so you should be comfortable with it."

"I accept your terms."

"And you already let me climb onto your lap so I assume that's okay too?"

A nod from him. "You are more than welcome to stay where you are."

"Good."

"One question." His gaze drops to my breasts once more. "Are you going to insist on wearing that while we're kissing?"

"Yes. It feels nice and it's pretty. I might sleep in it too."

"Flannel jammies feel nice," he says. "Or you could even wear long johns. Now there's an idea. Not only are they extremely comfortable and quite practical, but some might say rather beautiful in their own way."

"Do you have a lumber jack kink you need to tell me about?"

"No."

"Then no."

His tongue plays behind his cheek. "That's...actually that's fair enough."

"Glad we've reached an agreement."

"Torture me with your lingerie. I'm not afraid of you. Much."

Hand cupping the back of my head, he urges me close for a kiss. Our lips meet and his tongue slips into my mouth, stroking against mine. He's amazing at this. The man makes my head spin. And I give as good as I get, pressing my mouth against his, fisting my hands in his shirt. Neither of us holds back. Noses bump and teeth collide and maybe this is war after all. Though I'm pretty sure if that's the case, we're on the same side. Most of the time, at least. I'm doing my best not to move my lower body in case it's breaks the current making-out rules, but it's not easy. Every inch of him is hot and solid. And I'm melting all over him. He wraps my ponytail tight around his hand, palming my breast with the other. Everything in me is trembling when he brushes his thumb back and forth over my hard nipple.

That's what I want. More and more and more.

My lungs are laboring, heart pounding, and he growls. Actually growls into my mouth. Fucking hell. Maybe he did start the rumor, but he's an animal just the same.

"This is not slow," he snarls.

One hand on my ass and the other on my back, he flips our positions. Now I'm under him on the couch, holding on for dear life as he rubs his cock against me, working me to orgasm. Gaze glued to my face, his expression determined, he changes his angle and holy hell. My clitoris has never been so happy. It must be its birthday because this is the most spectacular present in recent history. Which makes it even harder to put an end to things.

"Wait," I pant. "Stop."

Immediately, he pauses. We're both breathing hard. There's even a sheen of sweat on his forehead. "What's wrong?"

"Holy hell that got out of hand fast. This…this isn't what we agreed to."

"Blame it on your lingerie. I like it a little too much."

"Hmm."

"Enough talking. I need to get you off. Right now."

And considering my nipples could cut diamonds, he was well on his way to doing it too. My sex flutters, empty and sad. Poor innocent thing. "Tell me this first, how does our dry humping session end? With you coming in your pants or…"

He just blinks.

"Let me guess, you were going to go fuck your fist again in the shower?"

"You say that like it's a bad thing." Twin spots of red stain his cheekbones and his pupils are dilated. "Is it a bad thing?"

"I propose a new rule," I say, slowing catching my breath. "Neither of us comes until we're coming together. And I'm talking penis in vagina. Us having actual intercourse."

Now he frowns.

"I'm sick of being left out of your sex life. You and your rendezvous with the liquid soap leave me out in the cold. And that is the exact opposite of a relationship."

"Alice—"

"I'm serious."

"Yeah. I'm getting that." He raises himself off me and sits further down on the couch. "Do you think this is going to pressure me into hurrying things along between us?"

"No, Beck. I am not trying to manipulate you." I sit at the opposite end of the couch, trying to breathe deep and think calming thoughts. Cock-blocking yourself is hell. "But I don't want to come without you. And I don't want you coming without me anymore either. If we're doing this, then let's do it properly."

He just looks at me.

"Well?"

"All right. Agreed." He rests his head back against the back of the seat, staring at the ceiling. "For a control freak, I have surprisingly little control around you. It's disconcerting."

"I'm not finished yet," I say. "I want to go to sleep with you and to wake up with you. Like a real couple."

"We are a real couple."

"Look…" How to explain this. "I've never lived with a boyfriend or a partner or whatever your official label is. Never even been on vacation with one. So I want this level of intimacy with you while we wait. I need it."

He thinks it over. "All right. But no more negligees or it'll be impossible for me to get any sleep. Your tits and sheer materials are apparently my kryptonite."

"Okay."

"Come over here," he says, holding out a hand.

I crawl to the other end of the couch, sitting with his arm around my shoulders. There's a good whole solid inch of space between our torsos. A necessity given the way his cock is straining the front of his pants. It's an impressively sized hard-on. I can't wait to see him in the flesh. But such thoughts are not helpful, so I stare out at the view. Beck, meanwhile, grabs a throw rug off the back of the couch and covers me from neck to toe. I won't be catching a chill anytime soon. Not that I was in any danger.

"Much better." He wraps a tendril of my hair around his finger. Apart from the air conditioner clicking on, everything is silent.

"Question. If I'd asked you to come home with me that first night we met, would you have?"

He makes a humming noise. "Answer. Maybe. Probably. Who are we kidding, I wanted into your pants. But the more I got to know you, the more I wanted you to take me seriously."

"I do take you seriously."

"Thank you," he says in a quiet voice. "In case I haven't said it yet today, I'm glad you're here."

"I'm glad I'm here too. But you don't have to tell me every day."

"Sure I do," he says with a smile. "I've got a couple of things going on tomorrow morning that I can't miss, but how about we go do something after? Just the two of us?"

"Like a date?"

"Absolutely like a date."

I grin. "I would love to."

CHAPTER EIGHT

T RUE TO HIS WORD, WE GO TO SLEEP TOGETHER (AFTER I'VE PUT ON one of his T-shirts and some sensible cotton boy shorts underwear) and he wakes me before leaving for work. There's nothing like waking up to a man in a suit handing you coffee and telling you he's ordered pancakes.

Quality level of life: nirvana.

We need to make more of an effort to eat the food filling the fridge, though. I'm a little horrified at the waste. However, Beck is so used to picking up a phone and having everything done for him. Not worrying about cost, just convenience. It must have been beyond strange when he walked away from this life. Though he seems to have slotted back in just fine.

But back to sleeping together. What with liking my own space, I wouldn't have thought I'd be a cuddle bunny. Having woken a time or two during the night to find us all over each other proves differently, however. The first time, he had an arm thrown around me, and the second time, I had a leg thrown over him. Asleep me adores being with Beck. Though awake me still has a few concerns.

I try not to worry, but wind up overthinking absolutely everything to do with our relationship while carrying out my new and enhanced makeup and hair routine. Today's outfit is a pair of black Altuzarra wide-leg pants, a silk shirt, and a pair of Louboutin flats. Diamond stud earrings are accessory enough.

My reflection dazzles back at me from the mirror. And I'm surprised to see it smiling. I guess if this finery is a burden I must endure, then I'll just have to roll with it. I'm stoic like that.

Though there can be too much of a good thing. A white gold and diamond Patek Philippe ladies' watch has appeared in one of the glass cabinets in the walk-in closet. Now that definitely wasn't there yesterday. Mysterious. Google informs me that it's probably worth my firstborn child and possibly the second and half of the third as well. It can stay safely locked away. On the one hand, all of this is pretty and shiny and fun. But I don't want my relationship with money to get warped with all of this excess. I don't want to get too comfortable. It could all go away any minute and then where would I be? Broke and out of work with a Hermès handbag. Life these days is so strange and weird.

While a couple of maids see to the apartment (one thing I do not mind getting used to though I still pick up after myself because hello manners), I head downstairs to see how the staffing situation is today in the bar before making any other plans or settling in with a book. A full complement of waiters are on duty so I'm not needed. However, they aren't happy. This is due to the group of rowdy teenagers seated in the corner ordering alcoholic beverages. And the reason they're being served is Beck's little brother, Henry. The boy's skin is pale and pasty, covered in sweat. This is not good. Other patrons, drinking their morning coffee, are likewise unimpressed with the scene and fair enough.

"Shit," I mutter.

"It's not even ten in the morning. When they refused him service he went behind the bar to get the bottles himself," says the guy beside me. He's a handsome man with a short Afro, wearing a pinstripe suit with a silver tie. Mid-thirties at a guess. He holds out his hand. "Nice to meet you, Miss Lawrence. I'm Aaron Watson, general manager of the Heritage."

"Hi." We shake hands. "Call me Alice."

"All right, then, Alice."

"How should we handle this?" I ask.

His gaze registers surprise, but it's swiftly covered by a

friendly professional demeanor. "As much as I'd like to drag him out of here by the scruff of the neck, I'm supposed to contact Smith to come and deal with any situation. That's how the family likes things done. Unless you have a better idea?"

"Let me tr talking to Henry first."

"They're a long way from sober. Do you think that's wise?"

"I've spent most of my working life dealing with people a long way from sober." I shrug. "But if it all goes to hell, you can tell Beck it was my fault."

Aaron just smiles. There's no way he should have to deal with a mess of the Elliots' creating. But here we are.

Henry and his three buddies are partying hard. One empty bottle and another half full sit on the table. Top shelf single malt, of course. Privileged little shits.

And from the looks of the glasses, Henry's been mixing it with cola. Expensive scotch and soda, that's a hanging offense right there.

"Party's over, Henry," I say with a smile. "Time to go, boys."

Henry, his face red, just laughs. "Hey, it's Beck's latest screw. Sorry. Girlfriend, I mean. How you doing? I'd introduce you, but, honest to God, I can't remember your name. I mean, why bother learning them? None of you last for long."

His friends all chuckle like he's a comedic genius. Drunken assholes are pretty much the same the world over. Age and money mean little once the booze hits your bloodstream.

I pick up the bottle of scotch, passing it to Aaron.

"Give it back," growls Henry, slamming his hand down on the table. "Or I'll have all of your asses fired."

"I don't actually work here, so...not much of a threat."

"I own this fucking place. You and the other basics can leave now."

"Thing is, you don't own me." I smile. The trick with dealing with drunks is confidence. Act like you have total authority and some dark, drunken part of their brain starts to wonder if maybe you do. "You three, Henry's friends, up and out."

His friends shoot him questioning looks. Henry's cheekbones stand out in stark relief. "Gold-digging fucking bitch, you can't tell us what to do! Go find a dick to suck. That's the only thing you're good for."

"Quick question, Henry. Why should I hesitate to call the cops? I mean, I could just call your grandmother, but I'm figuring this would be so much more memorable if you got your sorry asses dragged down to the lockup. And don't think the same doesn't go for all of your little friends."

Now they exchange nervous glances.

"I neither know nor give a flying fuck who any of you are," I say. "Get moving. *Now.*"

There's some muttered swearing and furious looks, but his three buddies eventually get to their feet and stomp out. Part of the problem dealt with, at least. Aaron gives the nod and a couple of security guys follow them. Hopefully they'll get them home safely. I have enough on my plate just dealing with Beck's little brother.

Henry's red eyes are furious.

"Don't make me call her," I say quietly. "I've been on the receiving end of her bullshit. You know you don't want that."

And no matter what a little shit he's being right now, he has to be hurting. What with his father dying and everything. Change is hard. Some of the fight leaches out of him at this, making him more sullen teenager than anything. He gives me a resentful glare. "What are you going to do, then?"

"Where's your mom?"

"Gone."

The hell? "Where?"

He just shrugs.

"Okay. So you and those three drank a bottle and a half

between you?" I ask. "Hope you feel good now because you're going to feel like hell soon enough."

"Like that'll be a change."

Heavy sigh. "C'mon up to the apartment, Henry."

"Will you let me drink up there?" he asks, getting unsteadily to his feet. He's tall like his brothers, but yet to fill out.

"Not a chance. But I will let you lie on the couch, watch TV, drink some water, take some Advil, and sleep it off."

A shadow of fear or doubt crosses his face. "You won't tell Grandma?"

"No."

"Okay," he decides. A hand goes to his stomach. "I don't feel so good."

"I'm not surprised. Let's go."

That's when he throws up on me.

Beck walks in a little after one p.m. with a vase full of red roses and greenery. "Honey, I'm home."

"Shh!"

His brows draw tight as he inspects my lace bra. At least my bottom half is covered in blue jeans. He places the flowers on the kitchen counter. "We talked about you and your lingerie tempting me to sin."

"I'm not here to tempt you. I'm here to stop you from waking your little brother who's passed out in the office. Please keep your voice down."

"Henry?" he asks, with a frown. "What's he doing here? Especially what is he doing here with you only half dressed? That view is only for me."

"He threw up on me a couple of times, necessitating a wash and change, which I was halfway through when you arrived." I gently close the office door on Henry's drunken snoring. What a day. At least I got the worst of the mess off my shoes and the vomit-splattered clothes are soaking in one of the bathroom sinks. Hopefully the stains aren't permanent. "Aaron sent up a rollaway and we put him in here. Hope you weren't planning on working in the office for a while."

"I get the feeling I'm missing the beginning of this story."

"Okay," I say, taking a breath. "So I went downstairs to see if they had enough waiters today and Henry along with some friends of his were having a liquid brunch. I frightened off his friends and got him up here. The end."

"They were drinking here in the hotel?" he says, voice tense.

"None of your people served them. He went behind the bar himself and grabbed some bottles."

He turns away, his expression tight. The man is pissed. Guess it could've been a real public relations disaster for the family if someone had recorded the incident and posted it on social media. The mega-rich have a lot of perks, but anonymity isn't one of them.

"Anyway," I say. "We got it under control."

He is not appeased. "Why didn't you call Smith to deal with this?"

"Who does Smith answer to?" I ask, hands on hips. "Your grandmother, right? The kid just lost his father and now his mom's abandoned him too."

"Giada's gone?"

"Apparently. All of that would be enough to make anyone lose their shit, let alone a sixteen-year-old. So the last thing he needs is Catherine going off at him."

Beck says nothing.

"I get that you want to kick his ass and I agree that he kind of deserves it."

"Kind of?"

"But he reminds me of what you told me about when you

were young and getting left on your own all of the time. That's what he's going through right now."

Slowly, he nods. "Fuck. You're right. I still want to kick his ass, but you made the right choice."

I give him a smile.

"Though I wish you'd called me. I would have been here sooner to help." He slides his arms around my waist, drawing me in for a hug. "Thank you for looking after my little brother."

"You're welcome."

"Next time call me, okay? Let me handle my family's fuckery."

"Okay."

"Sorry he vomited on you."

"Not the first time it's happened." I shrug. "I'll live. Are those flowers for me?"

"They sure are."

"They're beautiful. Thank you."

"I had big plans for us," he says. "Date night plans."

"We can't just up and leave him like everyone else."

"No, we can't." He kisses my forehead, giving me a small smile. "You finish dressing. I'm going to make a couple of calls, find out what happened to his mom, et cetera."

"Okay."

By the time I finish fixing myself up and putting on a clean black T-shirt and Aquatalia knee-high boots (much more spew proof than flats), Beck is sitting on the couch staring off into the distance.

"How'd it go?" I ask, getting comfortable beside him.

"Giada is at a spa in Switzerland."

"So she did just take off and leave her teenage son with the staff?"

"Yep."

Her losing her husband is awful. But to dump her child at a time like this to go get a facial...that I don't understand.

"They clearly can't control him," says Beck, slipping an arm around my shoulders. "He's been off school for the past couple of weeks. Supposed to go back this weekend."

"He attends boarding school?"

"Family tradition." And he doesn't sound particularly enthusiastic about this. "Guess I'll try and talk to him. We used to be close, but he's been pretty much giving me the silent treatment since I got back."

"What if it was a cry for help, his coming here, causing a scene?"

"You're sweet. But stunts like this aren't exactly uncommon when it comes to Henry." He does his usual thing, playing with my hair while he thinks. "One time when he was nine, Dad dumped him at Grandma's while he and Giada went to Monaco. He put dishwashing detergent in the big fountain out front. There were bubbles going halfway down the drive. I've never seen Winston lose his shit like that. It was hilarious. On the other hand, last year at Thanksgiving he drank an eight-thousand-dollar bottle of wine through a straw and reversed a Ferrari into a tree. That was less funny. Little idiot could have been hurt. Or hurt someone."

"Negative attention is still a form of attention," I recite. "I may have done a class on Intro to Psychology."

"Ah."

"We can't just leave him on his own, getting into who knows what trouble."

He sighs. "No, we can't."

"It's only for a few days. He's your brother. It's the right thing to do."

"You're awfully understanding for a girl who got thrown up on multiple times today."

"Don't get me wrong, he behaved like a total ass downstairs.

But I feel sorry for him. Plus, it's not really the first time I've been thrown up on by a drunk. Occupational hazard."

The office door opens and Henry comes slouching out. "Oh. Hey."

"Take a seat." Beck waves at the couch opposite us. "Time for us to have a nice little chat."

"Fuck that. I'm heading back to the mansion." Not home, the mansion. And, boy, is that telling. I get the definite feeling he did not get enough hugs as a child. Which he still legally is. I'm not much of a hugger myself, being average in all things social (same goes for my mom so I guess that's where I inherited it from). But knowing that you're loved and wanted is still crucial. My parents always told my brother and me that we were gifts. Regardless of the various stupid shit we did and whether we were getting along with them at the time. Henry deserves nothing less than the same.

"Sit your ass down," says Beck, voice hardening.

Henry just gives him the stink eye.

"One call to Ethan gets all access to your trust fund cut off. The moment he has evidence that you are not using that money in your own best interests, he is legally bound as a fiduciary to prevent you from accessing it. Your choice."

His little brother glares back at him for a moment before slumping on the couch, doing the same rigid jaw thing Beck does when he's angry. Also, the boy stinks of sweat and vomit. Ew.

"If Grandma heard about you drinking and causing a scene in public with your friends so soon after Dad's funeral, she'd lose her mind. Probably pack you off to one of those hard ass rehab centers in Idaho. A nice high security school for naughty rich troubled kids. Out of sight, out of mind and all that."

"Mom wouldn't let her," snaps Henry.

"You sure about that?"

Henry swallows, avoiding our eyes.

"And we already covered how Ethan would react." Beck sets

his ankle on his knee. "Of course, sooner or later, they're both going to hear about the shit you pulled downstairs. So it's not if, it's when."

"So?"

"I can deal with them for you. Keep them off your back. But, as is the way with everything in this family, it's going to cost."

Henry's gaze narrows. "What do you want?"

"First up, you'll apologize to Alice followed by Aaron and the staff downstairs. Secondly, you'll stay here with us until it's time to—"

"I'm not sleeping on a fucking rollaway in your office."

"Sure you will," says Beck, nice and calm. "It'll be just like glamping and it's only for a few days. Suck it up. Thirdly, when you do go back to school you're going to be a model student. No more day drinking or any other bullshit. Am I understood?"

"You're not giving me much of a choice," he grumps.

"No. I'm not, Henry. Because in all honesty, I'm kind of up-set with you right now." Beck's whole body vibrates with tension. "Let's be honest, our dad was a pretty shitty parent, too busy to be bothered with us most of the time. But he's gone now. Rules have changed. You come into my business, the place where I live and work, and you make this mess?"

Henry's laughter is harsh. "It's always about the business with you assholes."

"If it was all about the business we wouldn't even be talking. Your ass would already be on its way to Idaho or a nice fun mili-tary school, maybe."

Silence.

"But you're my brother and I love you. So here we are. You get one chance with me. Just the one," says Beck. "You're going to follow my three-step plan because you're all out of options. There are no better alternatives for you than this. Do you understand?"

Henry jerks his chin.

"Go shower. You can borrow some of my clothes."

With a heavy sigh, Henry gets to his feet and pauses. "Sorry, Alice. About what I said downstairs and puking on you and all that."

I just nod.

While the teenager slouches off into the bathroom off the main room, Beck turns to me with a quizzical look. "What did he say to you downstairs?"

"The usual drunken nonsense. It's not a big deal."

"Fine. I'll get the details from Aaron, then." There's a knock at the door and Beck rises to go answer. "Or you could just tell me."

"It's over and done with. Let it go."

"Why can't you pander to me like everyone else does?"

My eyes go wide. "Wow. No. I'm afraid you chose the wrong girlfriend for that."

"Not possible. I'll have you know that as of a couple of weeks ago, my taste in women has been impeccable." He opens the door. "Smith, come on in."

The big driver/bodyguard strides in. But really quietly. How does someone so big walk so softly? There must be a trick. "Miss Lawrence."

"Hello," I say.

"Smith works for us now," announces Beck. "Mind taking a seat outside or in the office while I talk to Alice, please?"

The man nods and slips outside, closing the door behind him. He's in one of his usual black suits. No doubt carrying a weapon.

"You stole your grandma's driver?" I ask. "Have you told her yet? What did she say?"

"Nothing. There was just this really long silence." He sits back down on the couch beside me. "I think I'm getting cabbage again for Christmas. Anyway, I was always his favorite. And I doubled his salary. It wasn't a hard sell."

"Good God, you work fast. I wasn't even out of the room for that long."

"You're frowning." He licks his thumb and wipes it between my brows. "There you go, beloved. All better."

I wrinkle my nose. "I'm going to pretend you didn't do that. And I thought I'd made my feelings about bodyguards clear."

Beck winces. "Yeah, but...how do I put this? You're wrong. You see, whatever we decided to do with Henry, we were going to need someone helping us keep a closer eye on him. At least for the next few days until he goes back to school."

"But you're not talking about Smith being here only for a few days, are you?"

"No. And he probably won't be the only security person I bring in." He loosens his tie, pulling it free. "Thing is, if you suddenly became rich, you'd realize quickly that you need to be more security conscious. You'd be a target in ways you never were before. That's basically our reality now. I know you don't like it. But I don't know how else to explain it to you."

I think it over. "You're right; I don't like it. Though I don't want to see you get hurt, or have some nut job try to kidnap you and cut you into little pieces and send you back in gift boxes to me, either."

"That's very kind of you. And it's quite the visual image." He picks up my hand, pressing a kiss to my knuckles. "Now, how do we keep a teenager occupied and out of trouble for the next few days?"

"Good question. I used to go to the mall with my friends or to the library. Neither of those options really strike me as being Henry's thing."

"Probably not."

"By the way," I say. "We need to discuss that watch."

He arches a brow. "What watch? Do you need one?"

"A diamond watch appeared in the closet this morning. It's beautiful, but...excessive. I looked it up. It's a Patek Philippe."

"Rachel must have sent it over." He taps his lip with one finger. "Unless, and hear me out, the closet is in fact a magical portal."

"You think Narnia might be back there?"

"Maybe."

"I have to admit, that hadn't occurred to me."

"If a box of Turkish delight appears, we'll know for sure," he says. "To be honest, it's more likely Rachel and Selah still trying to help you look the part of an Elliot consort."

I laugh. "Consort my ass. You, my friend, are a lot of things. But a king is not one of them."

"Couldn't we pretend?"

"No."

"But you'd look so pretty on your knees."

I give him good side-eye. "You know what you have to do to get that."

"The sex ban will lift in due time," he says, tone solemn. But it doesn't last. "It's your call, dearest. If you like the watch, keep it. Though it might be nice to hang onto it for a while and appease Rachel a little. She seems to like you."

"She doesn't know me. What she likes is you being back."

"That too."

Beck waves his hand and Smith comes back inside. While he appeared to be chilling and taking in the skyline, he apparently also had us in the corner of his eye the whole time. More body-guard magic tricks. Henry comes out of the bathroom on a cloud of steam with a towel wrapped around his waist and dark wet hair dripping in his eyes.

"Your soap and shampoo smells of girly shit," he grouches.

"Good to know." Beck crosses his arms, taking my hand with him. It's not exactly comfortable, but oh well, whatever makes him happy. "Smith is going to take you over to Bertram Street to grab your stuff. Get anything you need for school too, okay?"

Another chin jerk from Henry.

"Get dressed. Closet's through there."

"I'm putting on a suit. A Westmancott, maybe."

"You put on one of my suits, we're going to have problems." Beck looks to heaven. "You really want an ass kicking when you're hungover? 'Cause I'm telling you now, been there, done that, and it does not feel good."

"You got into a fight?" I ask, curious. "When did this happen?"

"There may have been a misunderstanding or two during my younger, wilder years."

Henry claps his hands together. "You mean she hasn't heard about the time you—"

"Rule number four, you will not tell Alice any stories," orders Beck. "I mean it. And anyway, that was a long time ago. I've matured since then."

At this, Smith snorts and Henry's diabolical laughter echoes through the apartment. Thing is, he almost sounds happy. And Beck does one of his sneaky smiles, the kind he tries to hide for one reason or another. But it's there and it's beautiful like everything else about him. If the man was a book, I'd reread him a hundred times or more. Learning every nook and cranny of his mind and emotions until I knew him inside and out. Get to know his history, the things that helped to shape him, like the back of my hand. I don't think I've ever been this curious about anyone before. So wholly taken up with another person. A corner of my mind seems to have been set up just to dwell on this man specifically. It's crazy. This goes so far beyond a crush it's not funny.

When he catches me watching, he gives me a wink. Then his gaze lingers on my face, just staring at me. And the feeling that I'm not alone in all of my wanting means everything.

CHAPTER NINE

T
HE LOUD BANGING ON THE DOOR THE NEXT DAY ALMOST MAKES ME
wish I hadn't sent Smith away. Someone out there is angry.

"Beck," a familiar voice yells. "Dammit, I know you're in
there."

I open the door despite my current aesthetic being messy
bun, no makeup, and sweats. With no plans to go out, today is
all about low key. Fancy can kiss my ass. I'm having a day off. I
already caught up on my long-distance socializing by texting
Natasha and Hanae and calling my mother and brother. I even
listened to my niece gurgle and say something that sounded like
"cat" followed by a screeched meow. Too cute.

As for the jerk on the other side of the door, he can take me
as I am. "Hi, Ethan. He's not actually here."

But the dude has already stormed past me, searching for his
brother. And he's definitely doing the Elliot rigid jaw thing. I wonder if he does the furrowed brow as well. The Elliot genes are
strong. Ethan's coloring is a faded kind of gold. Like someone
who once had a tan, however, it's been a while now since he'd
seen the sun.

Matías enters somewhat more sedately. "Hey, Alice."

"Hi. Is something wrong?"

"Where the fuck is Henry?" Ethan jerks at his usually perfect
tie, pulling it askew. "Is he okay?"

"He's fine. He and Beck went for a drive up to Boulder. They
should be back soon."

"Calm down, Ethan. You're being a dick," says Matías,

making himself comfortable on one of the couches. "Sorry about this, Alice. Emma sent me over to find out what's going on."

"Right."

"You'd think I'd have more self-respect than to let her treat me as her gofer, but here we are." The man just shrugs. He really is handsome. "She's with her mom in New York for some girl time. That's code for shopping. Seeing a show or two. Maybe buying a couple of penthouses or the Yankees, maybe."

"Emma's into baseball?" I ask.

"Not really. She just likes the way their butts look in those tight pants."

"I can respect that."

Meanwhile, Ethan paces. And then he paces and yells, proving men really can multitask. "What the hell happened downstairs, yesterday? Beck leaves me a half-assed message about Henry staying here and that's all I get? And what's this about stealing Grandma's staff? She just about chewed my damn ear off this morning!"

"Considering your father just died of a heart attack," says Matías. "Maybe you should take a couple of deep breaths and calm down."

Ethan ignores him, pulling his cell out of his coat pocket. "Are you going to answer my questions?"

Guess he means me. "No. I think this is family business and should be a conversation between you and Beck. But I'll be happy to ask him to give you a call as soon as he gets back."

The man just stares at me. Part stunned, part pissed.

"If you'd like me to ask, that is," I offer. Because manners. "Henry really is okay. I promise."

"I don't have time for this." And Ethan is heading for the door, opening it, and stalking through it, before slamming it shut. It's quite the dramatic exit.

Matías sighs.

"Feel free to wait if you want." I retake my seat on the couch. My hands are a little shaky for some reason. "They shouldn't be long."

"Thanks. I think I will."

"Can I get you a drink or anything?"

"No. It's fine." His fingers tap out a beat on the arm of the couch. "You'll have to forgive Ethan. He's an Elliot. They're not used to hearing the word no."

"I noticed. He's obviously worried about Henry, though, which is nice."

He just watches me.

"Something on your mind?"

"Though I appreciate your subtle brand of ball busting, you're not still upset about Ethan having you investigated, are you? Or has he been a douche to you in some other way?" he asks. "Apart from yelling in your face just now, of course."

"He's your friend, huh?"

"As much as he allows anyone to be a friend."

"No, I'm not really upset about the report. I understand they need to protect themselves against gold diggers or corporate spies or whatever. Even if it was a gross invasion of my privacy," I say, my voice gaining volume with each word. "And total bullshit in general to attempt to reduce people down to a series of dry facts. Like your credit rating or GPA actually says what kind of person you are. If you're kind or funny or moral or...I don't know."

Matías just waits.

"There actually may be a bit of resentment lingering, now that I think about it."

"It's not easy being the new kid. I was there myself once, you know, and I got the full Elliot treatment too." He gives me a glum smile. "Not the best time to be meeting them, either. Grief is hard. Between you and me, Emma and Rachel are in New York because they need some time away from here. A chance to get their heads around everything and deal with the loss. Jack was Emma's dad, but he and Rachel were also together for a long time. I think it's hitting them both."

"Understandably. So you're suggesting Ethan isn't usually quite this bad?"

He laughs. "Well, he's not usually quite this stressed. Taking over as CEO is big, having however many tens of thousands of people's livelihoods resting on his shoulders, proving himself to the board and shareholders and so on. It's a lot of power, no doubt, but a lot of opportunity to really screw things up as well."

"True." I relax back against the sofa. "If you don't mind me asking, how did you and Emma meet? Were you Denver high society too?"

"No. Not me," he says. "I'm from Florida, originally. Was on a soccer scholarship and blew my knee. Finished my marketing degree and got an intern position. Did some modeling on the side to pay the rent. Emma and I met at a party in Miami and it all kind of went from there. Jack was less than impressed when she bought me home."

"What was he like?"

He frowns, thinking it over. "About what you'd imagine. If you have a cynical, brutal imagination, that is. A workaholic mega-rich asshole with an eye for the ladies who expected his children to do as told and follow in his footsteps. I think he loved them in his own way; he just couldn't tolerate the thought that they might have their own thoughts and ideas about life, you know?"

"Sounds charming."

"Sure. When he wanted something. The man knew how to close a deal. But he could be a mean son of a bitch too. And while he was flexible with moral concepts such as right and wrong, his idea of success and how important it should be in someone's life was set in stone. Didn't leave the people around him with much room to maneuver." His smile is somewhat twisted. "Anyway, I worked for Elliot Corp. for a while. Then I decided I needed to do my own thing. Beck was looking for different ways to invest his trust fund and The Crooked Company was formed."

"I love that name."

"It came about after a particularly long brainstorming session one night involving many beers."

Matías's gaze drops to the gleaming laptop sitting on the coffee table in front of me. It just arrived this morning, and the box and all the other paraphernalia with it are strewn in an untidy heap beside it. "New toy?"

"I made the mistake of asking Beck if I could borrow his laptop for an hour or two one evening." Mrs. Flores's cat knocked mine off a table a few months back and I'd been saving up to get another ever since. "Normally when a guy seems a bit shocked at the prospect of handing over his devices, it's because he's worried about being busted with porn or something, but I think for Beck it was just that he forgets that not everyone owns the latest toys. Anyway, within an hour a delivery guy turns up with this shiny tech. The guy offered to set it up for me, but I figured that if I didn't do it myself, I'd never know how to fix anything when it goes wrong."

Matías nods. "What's your purpose with it? Business or pleasure?"

"The first option."

"Yeah?" He sits up. "What are you working on?"

"My résumé," I answer. "If I'm staying, I'm going to need a job. The trick is making a half a dozen different waitressing jobs sound like it's prepared me for great things. Slinging coffee or beer won't go down well with the fam so it's time to use the degree."

"Mind if I take a look?"

"Sure." I scan my thumbprint and pass the computer. "Any and all constructive feedback gratefully accepted."

He's quiet for several minutes, reading what I've written so far. Which deep down inside I can admit is probably a whole lot of nonsense. But you have to start somewhere. At least if I do get any interviews, I can turn up in a fancy suit and look the part.

"You have a way with words."

I laugh. "Potential employers might not care much about my degree in English Lit. But at least it gifted me the ability to spin beautiful sentences about my lack of useful qualifications."

"Let me show you something." His fingers tap oh so quietly against the keys. He hands the laptop back over to me with a site for a local microbrewery on screen.

"Is this the business you guys were talking about the other day?" I ask. "The beer we sampled?"

"That's right. Tell me what you think."

Taking my time, I scroll through the information. "It looks good, but the content is a little clunky."

"Agreed. Rewrite it for me. Give me something better."

I just look at him.

And the man is serious. Very much so. "The Crooked Company is growing and some of these businesses need a little mentoring. Fact is, I can't keep handling everything on my own and Beck is busy doing his own thing. These are exactly the kinds of jobs I should be handing over to someone else. Someone qualified. So give it a go."

"All right," I say, and get to work rereading the content before beginning. If nothing else, it'll be good practice. Maybe I'll even get a job. Worst case scenario is I'll ask Matías for five bucks for my work and put in a new entry on my résumé as professional internet consultant. Or whatever fancy title I can invent.

An hour or so later, I've got a solid first draft for the content for the microbrewery, and Beck and Henry stroll in all smiles. Thing is, they're not wearing the clothes they left in. Both of them are now in sports type T-shirts, shorts, and weird looking sneakers. Not that any of this actually matters. Because my gaze fixes on Beck, all of the happy hormones are released, and oh boy…the high from simply seeing him again is breathtaking. My whole body wakes up, my defenses crumble, and my plans (if I had any) disappear.

Also, there's a nasty scratch on his cheek.

"Detour to do some climbing, huh?" asks Matías. "Where'd you go?"

"Boulder Canyon." Henry collapses into the chair next to him. "Can I've a beer?"

"No. But I can. Anybody else want anything?" Beck grabs a beer for himself and a bottle of juice for his brother out of the fridge. After passing Henry his drink, he joins me on the couch. "Hello, dearest. How was your day?"

"Did you get hurt because you were hanging off a mountain with little to no safety equipment?" I ask.

He reflects upon the question for a moment. "No, it was more like a really big rock."

"It was lit," says Henry.

"And we were both extremely careful the whole time," adds Beck.

"Glad you enjoyed yourselves." The whole idea still kind of freaks me out, but oh well. "Have you talked to Ethan?"

Beck takes a swig of beer, nodding. "Yeah. Sorry about that. Had him in my ear all the way back home. Eventually managed to talk him around."

"Good."

"How was he when he stopped by earlier?" asks Beck.

"It was fine." I shoot Matías a look in case he's of a mind to contradict me. "He's just worried, you know."

Having already finished the bottle of juice, Henry slams it on the coffee table. "As if he cares. Ethan is a fucking—"

"Dude." Beck scowls. "Language. We talked about this."

Henry gestures toward me with a hand. "C'mon, she used to work in a bar. It's not like she hasn't heard it all before. Right, Alice? You don't care, do you?"

I say nothing. This is between them.

Beck just stares at him, his gaze flat and unhappy.

"You know, you used to be okay." Henry gets to his feet, heading for the office. His temporary bedroom. "But you're turning into an even bigger hard-ass than Dad was."

The door is slammed and Henry is gone. What is it about Elliot males feeling the need to abuse doors today?

Matías raises a brow. "I'm getting the feeling you're no longer one of the cool kids."

"I can live with that," say Beck, voice dour. "He was perfectly happy for a couple of hours. Even talked to me a bit about school and stuff. Now we're back to this."

"Does he like his school?" I ask.

"Seems to. As much as anyone that age does. But mostly he just wants to get back to his friends."

"Having a routine after all of this upset and change won't hurt him either," says Matías. "Anyway, congratulate Alice. She just got hired by The Crooked Company. She is now in charge of assisting with website content and I'm thinking I could train her up to do more. Like take over some of the initial basic research and assessment, maybe even handle some of the interviews."

I cock my head. "Are you offering me a job?"

"Please don't say no." Matías puts his palms together like he's praying. "The thought of having to find someone has been doing my head in. I'll even come up with a cool title for you. It'll be great. Of course, you'll also be monetarily recompensed at a suitable rate for your time and expertise. What do you say, Alice?"

"If you want her going out doing interviews, she'll need a company car," says Beck.

"What? I don't even have a company car!"

"Because Emma bought you a Lamborghini for your birthday last year, you fucking show pony."

"Says the idiot that owns a Bugatti."

"Alice is also going to require in-depth information on health and dental insurance, sick, vacation, and parental leave, and a pension plan, of course." Beck scratches at the stubble on his chin. "I think a yearly bonus and or share in profits would be reasonable."

Matías just gapes. "You're not serious."

"Think it over. Then make her an offer and she'll get back to you."

"For a silent partner, you sure do talk a lot. Some might say too much."

"Just looking out for my girl."

"Which is a clear conflict of interest. You have a duty to your shareholders."

"What shareholders? It's just you and me."

"Exactly. Your loyal business partner needs to be protected from funding the egregious shows of affection that you like to shower upon your better half."

It's like watching a tennis match. My head just keeps moving back and forth between them. Much more of this and I'll hurt my neck. "Are you two finished deciding my future?" I ask.

"For now," says Beck. "Oh, Grandma has also submitted a request. Well, first she tried to brow beat me into handing over Henry. Then she had a go at me about stealing Smith. Apparently, there's an old money tradition that you can't purloin the help. I suggested she embrace the heady reality of twenty-first century capitalism, which went down really well as you can imagine. But then she asked me to ask you for a favor."

"I'm listening."

"Seems she's coming down with a cold. With Giada, Emma, and Rachel away, and Ethan and I busy with the delegation from Amari, she needs someone to represent the Elliot Family Foundation at a charity luncheon tomorrow."

My brows go up. "She wants me to go? Me?"

"It's an emergency. But apparently all you have to do is sit there, eat fancy food, sip fine wine, and make a little light conversation. What do you say?"

"Are you sure your grandma wasn't under the influence?"

Beck thinks it over. "Reasonably so. Yeah. I mean, she wasn't slurring her words or anything."

"Chance to get on Catherine's good side," says Matías.

"But does she have one?" asks Beck. "This is the question."

I just blink. "You're not helping."

"Sorry."

"Okay. All right." All in all, this sounds reasonable and I have no cause to decline. Apart from my innate fear of being judged and/or having to partake in social situations (especially those involving rich people). But I can quash that and get the job done. "I'll do it."

Beck pulls out his cell and shoots off a text. "Great. Letting her assistant know and asking for the details. I'll forward them. Smith can drive you."

"But if I'm going to stay in Denver, I should learn my way around, right? If you wouldn't mind lending me a vehicle that is…"

"I thought we discussed this," he says.

"With both you and me busy, we're going to need Smith to keep an eye on Henry."

"You have a point."

Matías gets to his feet. "I better get going."

"Hey, how'd you go with the soup tureen?" asks Beck.

"I've agreed to surrender the butt-ugly tureen on the basis that she hands over the fertility idol given to us as a wedding present from Lise."

"My mother gave you a fertility idol?" Beck blinks several times. "I mean, of course she did. Please continue."

"Apparently it's meant to manifest abundance or, I presume, a couple of kids. Emma's already filthy rich and isn't sure about children. So she doesn't need it."

"And you do?"

"Eh. Dunno about the kids," says Matías. "But abundance, man!"

"Good luck with that."

"See you at drinks, right?"

Beck pauses. "Right. Yeah."

"Alice, I'll call you."

The door is barely shut before Beck's hands are at my waist, lifting me onto his lap. The man is strong. Hands cup my face and he presses his lips against mine. We kiss like we've been apart for years. Or at least a solid seven or so hours. My tongue in his mouth, mating with his. My fingers in his hair holding on tight. It's all good and right and necessary. And when his hands wander, slipping under the back of my sweatshirt to meet bare skin...a shiver runs through me from top to toe.

We should never not be kissing, never be out of each other's reach. What a waste of time normal life is in comparison to being with him. It's too big to be happiness, yet it's not just lust, but joy too. Bigger and better words are required to describe how he makes me feel.

But not love. Not yet. Just quietly, that word terrifies the crap out of me.

"I'd like to take a moment to thank you on behalf of my libido for wearing baggy unattractive clothing," he murmurs.

"Fuck you," I murmur back. "I'm comfortable."

"Trouble is, it doesn't work. I still want to do you."

"That's sweet."

He pulls me in even closer, wrapping his arms around me

good and tight. "And I'm glad you're comfortable. This is our place and I want you to be comfortable enough to stay with me for a good long time."

I smile.

Henry's temporary bedroom door stays closed. He's probably playing *Halo* or something. When he returned with Smith from the Bertram Street mansion yesterday, the first thing he did was set up a gaming console in the office. And thank God. Beck and I could do with some alone time. Sometimes it feels like I've known him for years. But other times it feels like minutes. Fragile and flimsy and in need of constant attention. Both the relationship and me. Being emotionally vulnerable is such a pain in the ass.

I inspect the scratch on his cheek with a frown. "Did you put antiseptic cream on this?"

"Yes, beloved. Got a first aid kit in the car. Don't worry."

"Don't tell me what to do."

"Obstinate, headstrong girl," he says, pressing a kiss to my chin.

"And what was all of that arguing with Matías about the job?"

"I was just trying to be helpful," he says with the worst attempt at an innocent expression ever. "You interested in the position?"

"I think so. Creating content is fine so long as I can get my hands on the right information. As for the rest, we'll see. And I can handle any negotiations myself, thank you."

"Understood."

I pull back from him, searching his face.

"What?"

"Did you put him up to this? Offering me the job?"

Lines appear on Beck's forehead. "No. Absolutely not. Today is the first I've heard of the idea. I mean, I guess it's convenient because he'd already met you, gets along with you, and knows that you're trustworthy. But believe me when I say that he cares a lot about our little business venture. There's no way he would have let you anywhere near website content unless he honestly thinks you'd be good at it."

"Okay." I relax further against him, my smile coming more easily. "How did things go at the hotel?"

"Good, actually. I think it has real potential. We'll move on to the next stage and take a closer look at the situation, make sure everything's solid. Work out how much it will cost to renovate and so on. But I'm hopeful."

"That's great."

"About the drinks night after next," he says, fingers tracing the ridges of my spine. Higher and higher he goes. It's more than a little thrilling.

"The bra is sensible boring cotton. I wouldn't bother if I was you."

"Ooh, sensible boring cotton. Tell me more. What color is it?"

I laugh. "Black."

"Fuck that's hot."

"Mm-hmm," I say, arms around his neck. "Now tell me about your drinks night, Beck."

"Once a week a group of us get together, have a few, decompress, that sort of thing. If there was anyone you'd like to invite, they'd be very welcome."

"Sounds nice."

"It is."

"You can do stuff with your friends without me, though."

"I know, but I think you'd like it," he says. "It's not like it's a dudes-only night or anything. And I'd like you to get to know my friends."

I nod. "In that case, I'd love to."

His fingers toy with the clasp on my bra. Dangerous territory to be sure. I'm like fifty-one percent sure he won't undo the thing.

But the forty-nine-percent chance of him taking this further has me breathing faster. Someone needs to write a list of exactly what going slow entails. Because there's nothing slow about my pulse rate right now. The anticipation is killing me.

Which of course is when there's a knock on the door. Because the universe hates me.

"Are you expecting anyone?" I ask.

"No. We could ignore it," he says in a low voice. "Keep making out…"

"Your brother's in the next room, remember?" I climb off his lap, heading for the door. And the person waiting is not particularly someone I need to see. At least, not again today. "Ethan."

His gaze is almost apologetic. Almost. Also, he has a bag of takeout food in each hand. "Alice, hi. I picked up some tacos. Okay if I come in?"

"Of course."

"You didn't pick up tacos, your assistant did," says Beck, up and knocking on the office door. "Henry, come and eat."

"Same thing." Ethan sets the bags on the kitchen bench. "Wasn't sure what you liked, so I told her to order a bit of everything."

I start fetching plates and utensils and so on. "It smells amazing."

"I heard what you did down in the bar. The way you looked after Henry," he says, not quite meeting my eyes.

"Yep."

"Thank you."

Beck just watches us with interest.

"You sure you don't mind that I'm here?" asks Ethan.

"No," says Beck, banging on the door some more. "You're welcome anytime, brother."

Henry slouches on out as per his usual. Only when he sees Ethan does he pause and frown. Guess they don't spend much time together. Both of them seem suddenly even more on edge, shoulders stiff and expressions tight. This family is so damn complicated. My heart hurts for them. Mom would make everyone sit down and talk it out. I don't know if that would work here, given how much bad history they have, but eating tacos together seems like a good start.

"Hungry?" I ask.

Henry's gaze shifts to the bags of food and he's in motion again. "Did you get Enrico's?"

"Yeah," says Ethan. "Carne asada still your favorite?"

A reluctant nod from Henry.

Beck just stands back, watching his brothers with wary eyes. When he catches me looking, he winks at me. "Why don't we put a movie on?" he asks. "If you've got time, Ethan?"

"Sure. That'd be good."

"Henry?" asks Beck. "Hang out with us for a while?"

The boy just shrugs, the smell of food luring him ever closer. "What movie?"

"Whatever you want," I answer.

Henry grins.

"You're going to regret that," says Beck.

CHAPTER TEN

"**T**HIS VEHICLE?" I ASK. "ARE YOU SURE?"

"Yes, Miss Lawrence. Mr. Elliot was most specific."

Holy shit. I can't keep the smile off my face. The valet hands me a key fob with a red bow attached. Another gift from Beck. At least, it better be just from Beck. Because if Matías had to chip in for this as a "company car" there's every chance he'd go into conniptions.

It's big, black, and boxy looking. Kind of like a tank crossed with an SUV with a dash of cool thrown in for good measure. I have no doubt it could climb any mountain and contain any shopping trip. The interior is all soft gray leather with plenty of room and all the latest gadgets. Top of the line, obviously. As if Beck would buy anything else.

"Mercedes Benz G-Class," says Aaron, appearing behind me. "It's basically indestructible and has a great safety rating. A good choice."

"I'm not that bad a driver," I joke.

The valet watching us hides a smile. "Good for someone with maybe limited experience in the snow, miss."

"That does make sense. Thank you for bringing it around," I say, handing him a tip. He made a fair enough comment about a Cali girl, assuming I'll still be here come winter. I hope I will be. No one has mentioned what the deal is when you live in the hotel, but I'll just keep tipping hardworking people until I'm told otherwise. Another reason to get a job and have some cash flowing in instead of out.

I wait until Aaron and I are alone before speaking. "Smith is keeping an eye on Henry. I don't think there'll be any problems, but feel free to call me if there is. Beck is in meetings for most of the day so I'm not sure about his availability. But you shouldn't have to deal with their family crap."

"Are you sure?" asks Aaron.

"Absolutely." My cell buzzes inside my black Birkin handbag. I rummage through the makeup, tissues, chocolate bar, book, and other highly necessary items.

"Excuse me," I murmur to Aaron.

He nods. "I'll leave you to it. Have a nice day, Alice."

"You too." The text is from Beck. My stomach does the swooping thing at the mere sight of his name. Even though I only saw him three hours ago. Even though I'll see him again tonight.

Beck: Like it?

Me: It's incredible. Thank you.

Beck: You can pay me back in kisses if you're so inclined.

Me: You're on.

Beck: Paperwork to transfer it into your name is on the passenger seat. Happy third birthday.

Me: ?

Beck: The clothes etc cover your first. The watch can be for your second. So this is for your third.

Me: I would have happily accepted the dick pic for all twenty-two, you know.

Beck: This is why I like you.

Beck: You're going to do great at the luncheon. Try to relax and enjoy yourself.

Me: xx

Beck: Let me know how it goes.

Me: Will do. Good luck with your meetings.

I type the address into the GPS and get moving. Sure enough, the vehicle handles like a dream. A far cry from my old sedan back home. It even has the new-car smell, which kind of gets me high. The ethical implications of accepting all of these gifts is an ongoing concern. But on the other hand, who am I to tell a billionaire how to spend his money? Maybe I am being seduced by the lifestyle. Mostly, however, it's just Beck.

Being uncertain as to what people wear to charity luncheons, I went with a Diane Von Furstenberg wrap dress and the black knee-high boots. Doubt that I'll ever make Instagram Fashionista status, but I feel good. Especially after using eye masks and half a tube of concealer. My shitty night's sleep has two causes: The first being performance anxiety over today. The second being nightmares from Henry's ridiculously gory horror film. "It's by the guy who did *The Lord of the Rings*," he'd said, getting my hopes up but pointedly not mentioning that the name of the film was literally *Bad Taste*. Last time Henry ever gets to pick. Ever.

The event is held at a restaurant in a reclaimed big old brick building. A factory, perhaps. It's all fancy inside with cool modern light fixtures and linen tablecloths. About eighty or so people fill the private room overlooking the river. My presence confuses the maître d' and the woman he discreetly calls over.

"Miss Lawrence is here in place of Mrs. Elliot," he says to the lady. She looks to be in her fifties, stylish with red lipstick and curly gray hair.

"Oh," is all she says.

Awkward. "Perhaps her assistant forgot to inform you," I say. "Catherine asked me to come in her place. Well, she asked her grand-son to ask me. She wasn't feeling well, apparently. Is that a problem?"

The woman just blinks at me.

"Not that she wasn't feeling well, but that she sent me in her place, I mean." Specificity is good, babbling less so. This is not a fortuitous start to my first solo event.

"Of course not," says another woman. She's a decade or so older than me with cool orange glasses. "I'm Yumi Manning, head of partnerships. And this is Debra Stein, philanthropy manager."

"Alice Lawrence."

We all shake hands and the maître d' heads back to the front of the restaurant. Call me paranoid, but I'm getting a bad feeling about this. Grandma Catherine doesn't strike me as the type to hire people who forget to do things. Especially when she went to the effort of requesting my presence here in the first place. What the fuck is going on?

Debra disappears into the crowd the first chance she gets.

A few people stop and stare at me. Perhaps they've seen my picture in the social pages with Beck. Whatever the cause, it makes me even more fidgety and self-conscious.

"Let's get you a drink." Yumi stops a passing waiter.

"That would be great. White wine," I say, because alcohol. "Thank you."

"Hello, Alice." Penny the lawyer who sat next to me at the gala is smiling. Someone is actually happy to see me. Also, she looks awesome in a green pantsuit. "This is a surprise."

"I'll let you two catch up," says Yumi as she too takes the chance to bolt.

I smile, relieved to know someone. "Hi. Catherine sent me."

"Did she now?" asks Penny, tone wary.

"Yes. I didn't know you'd be here."

"I also work with the Elliot Family Foundation."

"Well, it's good to see you again."

Penny licks her lips, looking out over the crowd. "This was one of Jack's causes. Catherine is more inclined toward giving to the polo club and the children's boarding schools and colleges. Their fraternities and sororities and so on."

"Ah."

"Rumors are rife that she's planning on cutting the donation to the libraries by at least half."

"Are the rumors true?" I ask.

"Yes, they are."

Fuck. "That's why she didn't want to come."

"Got it in one. Yumi and Debra were hoping to wine and dine her into a more giving frame of mind," says Penny. "Feeling like the sacrificial lamb yet?"

I down a mouthful of wine before replying. "B-a-a-a."

She laughs.

Oh yeah. This is awesome. I'll just be over here being awkward if anyone wants me.

Lunch is artisanal cheeses followed by red wine wagyu pot roast with sweet potato mash and a fruit tart for dessert. The food is excellent, however, the conversation sucks. Yumi and Debra are seated on either side of me but they spend the bulk of their time talking to the other people at the table. And I get it. With approximately four hundred and twenty-eight dollars in my account, I'm little help to their funding situation. Yet again I am the person no one wants at the party. Woe is me.

I'm ready to say my goodbyes and make a run for it when coffee is served. Then Yumi stands and taps a teaspoon against her wine glass. Silence descends. "As you all know, Jack Elliot passed away recently. His loss has been keenly felt by all in Denver, but especially those of us in the libraries. When our government funding was cut, it was Jack Elliot who first stepped in to help fill the deficit. His support enabled us to keep the lights on and the doors open. Alice Lawrence is here today to say a few words on behalf of the Elliot Family Foundation."

Fuck me.

Polite applause.

Yumi sits back down.

Penny's startled gaze meets mine across the room. Guess

she didn't know about this part either. That makes me feel a little better.

I get to my feet, my hands braced against the table. Something has to keep me upright since my knees have turned to water. Every damn eye in the room is on me. Waiting. Expectant. And this is what Catherine really wanted, I know it down to my bones. Me standing in front of a selection of the city's finest making a fool of myself. Yeah well. Not today, Satan.

"Thank you, Yumi," I say, my smile fixed in place. "It's such a pleasure to be here representing the Elliot Family Foundation. What can I say about Jack Elliot? Good question. Unfortunately, to my great regret, I never actually got to meet him. But I've heard many people talk about Jack and it seems that inevitably they all return to this one defining characteristic...his single-mindedness. The man's drive, focus, and unrivaled dedication to getting the job done. In this way, he is without a doubt an inspiration to many.

"What I'd really like to talk about today, however, is the legacy he leaves behind. Not only through his work, but with his four children who have shown such love and loyalty in supporting each other during this difficult time. I don't doubt that each of them will go on to do great things. And then there's what he achieved through a lifetime spent supporting such causes as the libraries.

"It was the gift of story handed down since the dawn of time that helped us to learn and evolve. It was the invention of the printing press that enabled people from all different walks of life to begin understanding and empathizing with one another. And it's our libraries today and the people who staff them that continue this invaluable work, ensuring everyone has access to the gift of knowledge and the possibility of a brighter future.

"Now, I've taken up enough of your time and your coffee is getting cold, which is unforgivable. So let me finish by saying that the Elliot Family Foundation is honored to support this city's libraries and, in memory of Jack, to continue to meet the donation amount set by him. Thank you."

Yumi shrieks in surprise. Penny's mouth hangs open. Debra drops her cake fork. The applause is thunderous. I've never been so popular in my life and I probably never will be again. To think that all it cost is an unspecified amount of someone else's money and any chance of Catherine ever accepting me. Hard not to smile. That's when the person from the newspaper snaps my picture.

"Let me see if I've got this right," says Beck as he walks in the door, cell attached to his ear. "You sent her to an event with absolutely no information or instructions and she made a speech that she wasn't aware she'd have to make and—rather than rocking the boat in any way—she committed to nothing more than a continuance of business as usual? That sounds to me like an entirely measured position to adopt."

Beck flinches, moving the phone away from his ear. Even I can hear Catherine's reply from over on the couch. The woman is furious.

"You're right, Grandma, that is quite an amount of money. And how wonderful that it's going to continue to be given to the city libraries as Dad would have wanted." He pauses. "Hello? Hello, Grandma? I think she hung up on me."

"Hmm."

He crashes onto the couch beside me, slinging an arm around my neck. "Hello, dearest. I've just been hearing all about your busy day."

"On a scale of one to ten, how much trouble am I in?"

"I don't know. Eleven, maybe?"

I sigh.

"Can't even imagine what you're going to get for Christmas. A lump of coal? Some half-rotted brussels sprouts? That's presuming we're still even invited."

"I'm sorry."

He grins. "No you're not. I saw that picture of you grinning like the Cheshire Cat. Half of the damn city did."

"Oops."

"And, as per our earlier discussion on the phone, nor should you be sorry. She set you up to fail," he says. "But not only does a goodly portion of Denver now love you, but you're making her do the right thing by Dad and those people. You won, hands down."

"You're definitely not angry?" I ask, just checking.

"Nope. I'm proud of you." He smacks a kiss on my cheek, giving me a megawatt smile. "Granny was being mean. She deserved to be taught a lesson."

"I was rather upset with her at the time."

"You're nicer than me. I'd have been fucking furious."

"She'll give them the money?" I ask.

"She has to. You made sure of it."

"Wow. Good."

"I'm just sorry I trusted her and encouraged you to do it," he says.

"You're not some all-knowing omnipotent being."

"A pity, that." His thumb caresses the side of my neck. "But next time I'll do more research."

"Question," I say. "Have you ever thought about doing any philanthropy?"

"Answer. I'm involved in a few things. Why do you ask?"

I reach up, rubbing my fingers over his knuckles, down the length of his fingers. "There was a woman there today trying to get a literacy program funded. Also a guy who's involved in clearing school children's lunch debt."

"You'd like to help them?"

"I just thought I'd mention them to you," I say. "I could be wrong, but your grandmother appears to have a throat hold on the Elliot Family Foundation. A lot of her causes seem to largely benefit the people in her social circle."

"This is true. Not that Dad was any better. He just saw more value in getting the family name on as many public buildings as possible." He looks at me and there's lots going on behind his eyes. Lots and lots. It would be so helpful if I could read his mind. "Let me give this some thought, okay?"

"Sure."

"Penny was impressed with how fast you thought on your feet today," he says. "I'm really glad you're here."

"Me too."

"Don't let my family scare you away."

I shake my head. "Not going to happen."

"Did you like driving the SUV? Because if it's not—"

"I love it. Thank you. It's perfect."

Little lines appear beside his eyes when he smiles and I just get lost staring at him for a moment. At his beautiful mouth and the angle of his jaw. At the colors in his eyes and his dark brows. Then there's the sound of his voice and the scent of his skin and his strong but gentle hands. Everything about him works for me. I am one lucky bitch.

"What are you thinking about?" he asks, his gaze warm.

"Sex."

"Good God, you're romantic."

"You should see the size of the backseat in that vehicle. Just the thought of what we could do back there made me wet."

"I actually bought it because of the safety rating," he says, coming closer. "But I'm glad it has other important features. Now tell me more about the state of your panties."

"Are you sure that isn't against the slow rule?"

"Talk is allowed."

"In that case, I tricked you. I'm not wearing any."

His eyes go large and his hands slip beneath the skirt of my dress. Up the length of my thighs slide his palms until a thumb rubs over the silk of my underwear. "Alice, you lied to me. You are too wearing panties."

"Of course I am. I've been out in public. But wasn't it fun to check?"

His hands stay put as he leans closer, pressing his mouth to mine. I part my lips, giving him entrance, and we're all tongues and teeth and wanting. It's delicious. My hands in his hair and my body aching. While under my skirt, his fingers dig into the flesh of my thighs before roaming higher to trace the edges of my underwear. His thumbs slip beneath the edge of lace and elastic, delivering teasing little touches. He's so close to my mound, but not quite. And the stress of the day doesn't matter. Not when it's me and him getting as close as can be with our clothes on. If my panties weren't wet before, they certainly are now. He does it so easily, turning me on, making me hot for him. My face is flushed and my heart is pounding. He nips my bottom lip before diving straight back in, driving me wild. Beck has kissing down to an art form. The pressure and heat and wetness. It's all just right.

His lips trace over my cheek before his teeth make their presence known once more against my jawline and then my neck. The sweet sting is a thrilling thing, making my skin more sensitive, my mind more shut down to anything that isn't us. We're pressed up against each other, my breasts against his hard chest. All of the air seems to have left the room.

"I think we're getting closer to the time for actual action," he says, voice husky.

"God, I hope so."

"Henry goes back to school tomorrow. We're going to have the place to ourselves. I'm feeling pretty confident about reaching second base."

"I'd hope so considering your hands are up my skirt." I laugh. "But we have drinks with your friends tomorrow night, remember?"

He groans. "Drunken fumbling before bedtime it is."

"I'll look forward to it."

He removes his hands from beneath my dress, slipping an arm around my shoulder and drawing me in against his side. "Did you know Dad married Giada when he was on a three-day bender in Monaco? The old man worked hard, but when he decided to take a break...he went all out. Imagine how fast the lawyers had to work to draw up that prenup."

"But their marriage lasted for well over a decade, right?"

"Yeah, but he cheated on her constantly. They had nothing in common apart from the child they both ignored. Dad thought another divorce would look bad and she liked the lifestyle too much to walk away."

"Not a match made in heaven."

"Nope," he says. "At least he always had a plus-one for parties."

"Handy."

"Right?" He stares out at nothing, lost in thought. "I asked Grandma once how she and Grandpa managed it. What the secret was. Because it seemed so extraordinary to me that a couple could actually manage to just stay together."

"What did she say?"

"She looked down her nose at me and said... he married me for my name, dear. Let's not write fairy tales where there are none."

"But do you think they maybe grew to love each other?"

"Fuck knows."

"And that's what you're scared of...us winding up like that."

He shrugs the shoulder I'm not currently using as a pillow. "Given my family history, I'd be a fool not to, beloved."

"I'm not Selah. You can trust me."

He kisses the top of my head. It's not a confirmation and that kind of breaks my heart. But trust takes time. I'll just have to suck it up.

"Guess we should plan some dates and do this right."

"I love that idea."

Henry comes out of the office, cell in hand. He's wearing his usual ripped jeans and a T-shirt. And those tears were made by a designer, no doubt. "Grandma's lighting up my phone. I didn't even know she could text."

"She can't," says Beck. "She gets her assistant to do it. What does she want?"

"For me to go spend the night at her place and have Winston drive me back to school tomorrow. Since when did Winston drive people around, anyway?"

"Since I stole Smith off of her. Remember how he was trailing you all day?"

Henry smirks. "Right. Bet that chaps Winnie's ass."

"Language."

"What the hell?" Henry's brows go up. "She just sent me the eggplant emoji. Does she mean dick or dinner?"

Beck looks to heaven. "Language, dude."

"Dinner," says Henry. "They're having moussaka."

"That's a relief," I whisper.

"Didn't Greek food used to be your favorite?" asks Beck.

"When I was like twelve." Henry sits on the couch opposite, staring at me and his brother through narrowed eyes. "What did you two do? Grandma's making out like you're a bad influence all of a sudden."

"Alice made her give some money to a charity she wasn't planning on giving it to," answers Beck.

Henry nods all sage-like. "That'd do it."

"If you'd rather go spend the night with her than hang with us, that's fine. I'm sure she'd like to see you."

"Nuh," says Henry. "I mean…unless you two want me gone."

"You're very welcome to stay here." I smile. "I'm cooking pasta carbonara for dinner."

Henry cocks his head. "Do you know how to cook?"

"I'll probably manage not to poison you."

Before Henry can shoot off some smartass reply, Beck is there. "That sounds lovely, dearest. Doesn't it, Henry?"

Henry just shrugs.

"Want me to see if I can get Grandma to calm down and ease up on your cell?" asks Beck.

"Are you kidding me? She hates you right now. Besides, I already texted Ethan. He said to message him if I needed anything, so…" Henry keeps scrolling through his screen. "Otherwise Emma can get it sorted. She called today and we talked for a while."

"That's nice," I say. "Good to see you all getting along."

Henry's brows descend. "Don't make a big deal out of it, Alice."

"Yeah, Alice." Beck massages the back of my neck. He has such strong talented fingers. "I'm still your favorite sibling though, right, Henry?"

"You all pretty much suck equally as far as I can see. Though Alice gets respect for getting one up on Grandma."

"I think there's a life lesson in that," says Beck. "It's possible to piss off your family and still do some good in the world. You could really take a page out of her book."

I shake my head. "Okay. Enough of this. What do you feel like doing tonight?"

"We could watch another movie?" suggests Henry. "There's one I've been meaning to see about a killer clown who lives in—"

"Oh hell no."

The boy laughs his ass off. "You're such a girl, Alice."

I flip him the bird.

"Fine, fine," says Henry. "Why don't we hit a couple of clubs?"

"You're too young to go nightclubbing." Beck shakes his head. "Try again."

"Whatever. We'll play cards. A couple of rounds of poker. How does that sound?"

"Okay," I say.

"Beloved." Beck winces. "I have a bad feeling you're going to regret that."

"Why do you never tell me until after I've agreed?" I ever so slightly yell.

Henry smiles like a devil child.

CHAPTER ELEVEN

"**H**E TOOK ME FOR A HUNDRED DOLLARS."

"Of course he did," says Matías, sipping a single malt. "It's Henry. You're just lucky Beck insisted on a pot limit or things could have got ugly."

"I mean, that's almost a quarter of my bank balance. My rent and utilities are paid up for another couple of weeks. But after that…"

The secret bar is called The Downstairs Bar and is duly located down a flight of steps and behind an unmarked door in the basement of a building a couple of blocks away from the Heritage. We're in the corner of the VIP lounge, behind velvet ropes in a deep and wide black leather horseshoe-shaped booth. Even at nine p.m., the place is filling up fast. It's all very cool and vintage. A lot like the Heritage itself, actually. Only with the latest music playing loud over the sound system and much more mood lighting.

"It's not that I won't miss him, because I will," I specify. "Henry is strangely sweet and endearing and yet a handful."

"Why didn't you warn her?" asks Ethan, who only just arrived. "You never play poker against that kid."

"Henry was having fun and it was his last night before going back to school. I couldn't bring myself to break his black little heart." Beck pushes a margarita into my hand. "Drink this. It'll make you feel better."

"Thank you." I down a mouthful. Ah, tequila.

"I did advise you to throw in some of those hands."

I groan. "But I really thought I had a chance of winning."

"That's what Henry wanted you to think." Matías nods somberly. "He won a ball signed by Pelé off me and he doesn't even like soccer. The kid is pure evil. Can't be trusted."

Beck shrugs. "He's an Elliot. We're trained from infancy to take no prisoners. What can you do?"

"True."

"Don't worry, beloved," says Beck. "I'll have some money put into your account tomorrow. I don't mind that you can't play poker to save yourself and thought you stood a chance of beating my demon brother with a pair of twos."

At this, Matías snorts into his expensive liquor.

"No, I will not accept your money. Though thank you for the thought," I say, with a benevolent smile. "Even though it is partly your fault I lost the money because you should never have let me agree to play cards with him in the first place."

"You're right."

"No, she's not," says Ethan. "That makes absolutely no sense."

Beck shushes him.

"This is just how relationships work." Matías sighs. "You have to be man enough to lie, say you're wrong, and let them kick you in the balls whenever the situation calls for it. Which is anytime there's even the merest hint of a disagreement or they're having a bad day."

"I'd just like to point out that I have yet to assault anyone's nuts," I protest.

Matías holds up a finger. "Being a heterosexual female, the emphasis here needs to be on the word *yet*. You have *yet* to assault anyone's nuts."

"Get your patriarchal nonsense out of my face."

Beck just snorts.

"You're all insane." Ethan gestures to the waiter and orders a bottle of Japanese single malt for the table.

We're getting excellent service and no small amount of

attention from other customers. Lots of admiring glances from women and men alike. Everyone seems to know the Elliots. One woman in particular has now walked her tight ass past the table three times in an attempt to catch Beck's eye. I can tell it's my boyfriend she's after, care of the way she keeps doing this sultry stare in his direction followed by a lick of the lips. Not that he seems to have noticed. If she does it again, I'm going to show how déclassé I can be by putting my foot out to trip her.

Just joking. Mostly.

"Stick to your socialite fuck buddies, Ethan," suggests Matías. "Less demanding."

Ethan scoffs, but says nothing.

"How do you even have my account details?" I ask my boyfriend.

"We know everything about you," says Ethan. "That's the whole point of having you investigated and getting the report."

"Ugh. Don't remind me." I frown, picking up my drink. "Let me know when you have more work creating content, Matías. We'll start casual with an hourly rate and see how things go from there, if that suits you?"

"Sounds good." Matías pulls a gold money clip out of his pocket and hands me a hundred-dollar bill. "I'm assuming this is the hourly rate."

"And I am not going to say no. Pleasure doing business with you." I place the money on the table. At least now I'm partially employed. "It must be my turn to buy a round or is everyone drinking whiskey?"

Ethan and Matías exchange puzzled glances before turning to Beck. Strange.

"That's usually how it works when I go out with friends," I explain. "You guys don't take turns buying rounds?"

Penny slides into the booth beside Ethan and immediately picks up on the peculiar mood because the woman isn't an idiot.

On a quick personal note, I'm delighted to see her because possible friend/female ally in my new life in Denver. Making friends as an adult is hard. But as well as gifting me the opportunity to spend huge amounts of money, the charity speech Catherine forced on me had given me the opportunity to impress Penny. She managed to retain a sense of professional calm amid the rapturous standing ovation that I received. As soon as we were alone in the hallway, however, she started laughing so hard she had to lean on me just to stay upright.

"What's with the weird looks?" she asks, taking off a yellow blazer.

"Good question." I turn to Beck with a questioning look. "My etiquette is apparently off. Why is me offering to buy a round so I'm not constantly mooching off you worthy of such a reaction?"

"Oh," says Penny. "I can answer that. Beck owns the bar."

"You own the bar?" I ask. "Why didn't you tell me?"

Beck takes a deep breath. "Because sometimes, such as just now when I offered to put some cash into your account, it seems like you don't really like the money."

"But this is an achievement of yours and something to be proud of," I explain. "Totally separate to you trying to give me a cash handout."

"Trouble in paradise, already?" asks Ethan. Like an asshole.

Neither of us pay any attention to him.

"The bars each have a manager and then there's a director that oversees things," says Beck, ignoring my praise. "It's not really like I have that much to do with the day-to-day operations."

"But you own a string of bars? That's great."

"Thank you." Beck leans in, kissing me lightly on the lips. "Mm, salty."

Matías shakes his head. "Dude, why are you not just honest with her?"

"What? You think he should give her a full write-up of his investments and net worth?" asks Ethan, his gaze surly.

"Of course not. But she needs to fully understand what she's getting into."

"She's living in a luxury apartment and walking around wearing Prada. What exactly is he hiding from her?"

"It's Dolce & Gabbana, actually," I say of my little black dress. It's stretch satin and gives me great cleavage. You might say I'm dressed for seduction. You wouldn't be wrong. "Not every designer makes things in my size."

Penny pours herself a couple of fingers of the scotch before sitting back and crossing her legs. If anything, she seems amused. "How much did you know when Emma dragged you home for the first time, Matías?"

"About the mindset of people who are born to wealth and inherit even more of it? Not a fucking thing. It was eye-opening, I'll tell you that."

Ethan's jaw does the rigid thing. "Are you saying we don't work?"

"No, I know you're not the types to just sit on your trust fund with your thumbs up your asses. Jack didn't raise you that way. Ambition and competition might as well be the family motto," says Matías. "But you do start out ahead of everyone else and you fail to fully appreciate what you're given. You all take it for granted."

"I'm sorry I'm an entitled asshole," Beck whispers in my ear. "But that dress is shit hot, beloved."

I smile. "I should hope so. It cost you two-and-a-half grand."

"Worth every cent."

"I thought you said this was friends getting together to chat, relax, and have a few drinks."

"Yeah..." Beck rests his head against my shoulder, bringing his glass to his lips. Interesting how his circle of friends are either family or people he works with. Guess finding people with no agenda is tricky. People who won't treat you like an ATM or expect help via some other means. "Did I forget to mention the mostly friendly debate that's often involved?"

"Just a little bit, maybe?" And we both laugh, because for some reason it's funny. Or maybe it's just the alcohol making us loose. God, it feels good to relax.

"Look at these two sitting in the corner laughing at their own jokes," says Ethan.

Beck just shrugs. "We can't help it if we're funny."

"What do you think about the fiscal situation affecting relationships, Penny?" asks Ethan.

The woman narrows her eyes on him, obviously thinking deep thoughts. "Matías has a point. You don't know what it's like not to have money, to be struggling to pay the rent and keep the lights on, because that's not your lived experience. It doesn't necessarily make you bad people, it's just a fact."

Ethan raises his brows. "I can't believe I'm having my humanity debated due to my bank balance."

"Not your humanity, just your level of entitlement," she replies. "Whether your trust funds balance out the pressure of great expectations put on you by your family and the publicity and need for personal security...I don't know."

"I would like to mention, we just broke ground on a new hospital ward because of the money you're shitting on," says Ethan.

"Should I add saint to the start of your name?" asks Penny. The way she takes no shit is a constant inspiration.

There's a smile in Ethan's eyes that is not reflected on his lips. "If you like."

"Everyone's got family drama," I say. "Just because you have money doesn't mean you don't have problems. They're just different from those of others."

Matías raises his glass in a toast. "To these two rich bastards and their beautiful sister who is slowly draining me of my will to live."

"I'm not even going near that," mumbles Beck, drinking just the same.

"You lived without the money for a while." Ethan nods at his brother. "How'd that go? Manage to erase the stain of wealth from your soul?"

"I didn't leave empty-handed. I'm not that brave. No way did I want to go hungry or wind up sleeping on the streets." Beck gives a lopsided smile. "Stayed in some pretty fucking crummy places and worked some shitty jobs. Construction, food service, night-club security, you name it. Even stood on a street corner wearing one of those stupid signs advertising cell phones for sale."

Ethan snorts.

"What did all of this teach you?" asks Penny.

"Well, it confirmed my own privilege," reports Beck. "The freedom was nice and that was a big part of me wanting to leave. Along with proving to myself that I could manage without, at least to a degree. You certainly see a different side of the country away from the five-star hotels and private jets. Meet different kinds of people with different priorities and experiences."

"Hmm," is all Penny has to say.

Matías takes a sip of whiskey. "It widened your world, huh?"

"That it did," says Beck. "Also showed me who I am away from the Elliot name blah blah blah."

"And who are you?" I ask.

He grins. "I'm yours."

I laugh. Public displays of affection still make me uncomfortable sometimes, apparently.

A stunning redheaded woman with pink skin and freckles and Aaron the manager from the Heritage join our table. The woman greets Penny with a kiss on the mouth. Aaron raises a hand in greeting to everyone in general.

"Alice, this is my girlfriend, River," says Penny, moving over to make room her. "Babe, this is Alice."

I smile. "Nice to meet you."

"You too." River smiles back at me.

"What's tonight's topic of conversation?" asks Aaron, pouring himself some whiskey.

"Money," supplies Beck, still resting his head against my shoulder.

River swears quietly. "Who the hell started that?"

"Beck hadn't told Alice about owning this place," says Ethan. "Which lead to Matías here ranting about rich people and their ridiculous lifestyles. Then we just generally started trading insults around the table."

"Of course you did." Aaron shakes his head. "Why can't we talk about noncombative things for a change?"

"Nice weather we're having," quips River.

"Did you hear about how Alice went to war against Catherine the Great yesterday?" asks Matías. "Now that's a story."

Aaron whistles through his teeth. "Lot of money. You'd have to be dead not to have heard about that. The bar staff at the Heritage were particularly proud of you."

I snort/laugh. "Thank you."

Ethan looks at me from beneath his brows.

"You have something to say?" I ask, taking another sip of my drink.

He pauses before shaking his head.

Given the man has not been my biggest supporter, this comes as somewhat of a surprise. "Nothing at all?"

"Not a word."

"Huh," I say. "Interesting."

"That means he agrees with what you did," whispers Beck nice and loud. "But he doesn't want to risk losing his position as favorite grandson by actually saying as much."

Ethan continues to say a whole lot of nothing on the subject, raising his glass of whiskey to his lips. But then he pauses. "Actually, I will say one thing...be careful, Alice. Our grandmother doesn't take losing well."

Beck looks to heaven. "Oh, c'mon. Grandma wasn't actually spat out of the fifth circle of hell."

"Though it wouldn't surprise me," says Matías.

I keep my mouth shut. It seems wisest.

"Well, I think you did the right thing, Alice," says Penny. "I'll say it, just not around Catherine. I like my job."

"Thank you." I smile. "At least it should get me out of having to do any more charity luncheons any time soon."

Penny's gaze skips to Beck before returning to me. What was that? I think it was something, but I've had two margaritas and no dinner. Also, I need to visit the bathroom.

"Excuse me," I say, slipping out of the booth. "Back in a minute."

Penny sets down her glass. "I'll come with you."

As I leave, Aaron asks Beck about the hotel in Boulder. It looks like we're thankfully off the subject of wealth or me for a while.

The bathrooms are painted dark red with old-fashioned fixtures. We both do our business and then meet back at the sinks. Even the hand soap smells good.

"Was there a weird look between you and Beck before at the table?" I ask.

Penny scrunches up her brows. "A weird look? I don't believe so. I especially don't believe so because I'm not only a lesbian, but my girlfriend is also with me."

"I don't mean that kind of look."

She pats her dry hands on one of the neatly folded hand towels. The woman really can pull off a pantsuit like nobody's business. "I did want a word with you, though. Since I haven't seen the contracts come back through, I'm guessing you're still perusing them. While I believe them to be fair and reasonable, generous, even, it's never a bad idea to have your own lawyer look them over. I can't refer you to anyone directly—it would be a conflict of interest—but you might consider asking Matías who he recommends. He's been well-represented throughout the divorce, and might have a few good names."

"Contracts? What contracts?"

She blinks. "Beck hasn't given you the contracts?"

"I guess not."

"Oh, fuck me." The woman stomps back out into the bar. Not stopping until she reaches the table. Here she points a finger at Beck's face with one perfectly manicured nail. "You told me Smith gave her the contracts on the jet. So imagine my surprise when I suggested she source some independent legal advice and she didn't have a fucking clue what I was talking about."

Ethan scowls. "She hasn't signed an NDA?"

Aaron and River get busy either inspecting either the contents of their glasses or the other people in the bar.

Matías just hangs his head.

"Both of you, stay the hell out of it," says Beck, sitting up straight. "It's between me and her. I'll talk to Alice about them when the time is right."

"You don't stick your dick in a woman let alone bring her near the family without an NDA," snarls Ethan. "That's the rule. She should have signed before she stepped foot in Colorado."

"You cannot lie to me about things like this, Beck. I cannot fulfil my professional obligations to protect you if I'm acting on false information." Penny takes a deep breath, visibly trying to calm herself, and slides back into the booth. "Cohabitating even for a short period of time can open you up to possible risks. We talked about this."

"She's not like that. You're both worrying over nothing."

Beck slams his glass down on the table. "Now can you all please get your noses out of my fucking business?"

I don't know what to say. So I stand there like an idiot. They wanted me to sign a nondisclosure agreement? As if I would run off and sell my story to the local newspaper or something. Give me strength.

Beck grimaces, raising his hand to me. "Alice..."

"There you are!" Emma almost knocks me aside in her rush to get at the table. She reaches across, doing her best to smack Matías in the face by the look of things. Only he's on the far side against the wall and she's kind of short. Not that she's giving up. Hell no. The woman basically winds up on her belly with her feet in the air, tipping over the bottles of scotch and several glasses, in her effort to beat the man. Never has haute couture been so badly treated. Ethan jumps to his feet as best he can when scotch pours into his lap and an exodus from the booth begins. But not fast enough.

If people weren't watching when Penny went off at Beck and then he banged his drink down on the table, they definitely are now. What a spectacle. When Emma's hands prove insufficient to the task of killing her estranged husband, Emma proceeds to attack Matías with her purse. And I stand there stunned for a moment because holy shit.

"You moron!" yells Emma.

"What the fuck?" Matías roars in reply. Fair enough, really.

"You got me pregnant!"

Matías scrunches up his face in confusion. "I what?"

Emma bursts into tears. "You got me pregnant!"

Which breaks me out of my trance. There are benefits to being bigger. At least when it comes to hauling around small women. I grab her beneath the arms, dragging her back off the table as gently as possible. Before she breaks some glass and cuts herself or hurts herself in some other way. I can't see her managing to fall off the table. But still...

THE RICH BOY | 189

"Okay, enough," I say. "C'mon, Emma."

Emma raises her purse, about to attack me, before she sees that it's me and not the object of her violent affections. "Alice," she sniffs, leaning into my bosom. Nice to know the little black dress and my awesome cleavage came in handy for something. Tears trail down Emma's pale cheeks. "That asshole has ruined everything."

"He is an utter shithead; I don't blame you for being furious." I put my arms around her and give Matías an apologetic look. Because whatever calms down the crazy pregnant lady who was attempting to beat him to death with designer goods in public.

Right now, the man's eyes are as wide as can be.

"Let's get you out of here," I say, shooting meaningful glances at Beck and Ethan.

Beck at least gets with the program, patting Emma's back. Next he motions to Ethan to take care of Matías. Aaron, Penny, and River do their best to block us from the view of the bar patrons and disperse those who've gathered to watch. Smith and the bar security people are soon here to help. They can also deal with the bastard at the next table who has his cell out and is filming everything. Jerk. Ethan hauls Matías out of the booth. He still seems to be in shock. Not helpful. Spilled scotch has left a wet patch on the front of Ethan's no doubt expensive pants and one of the glasses is rolling around on the floor. What a night.

"Bring the car around," Beck orders Smith.

Best damn idea I've ever heard.

"Say something."

I sit with my legs curled up beneath me on the couch, the contracts in my lap. "I'm thinking."

"Then tell me what you're thinking," says Beck, pacing back and forth.

With the fire on, the room is cozy, the night outside dark and silent. We're on our own since once Emma had calmed down, she decided she'd rather go home. An eerily subdued Matías went with her. At least she's not alone.

"The NDA seems straightforward enough." I take a deep breath, straighten the papers. "Only problem being me not discussing anything to do with you, our relationship, or your family with anyone is somewhat unreasonable. Given how you're supposed to talk about your life with the people close to you and you're a large part of my life right now."

"Right now?" He cocks his head. "Is that a threat?"

Like hell he's making this my fault. "Sit your ass down, Beck."

Frown in place, he sits on the couch opposite. His elbow rests on the arm of the couch, thumb and forefinger toying with his bottom lip. The boy is not happy. Neither am I. This paperwork is a wall between us.

"Time to negotiate," I say. "I'll agree not to discuss your family with anyone."

He nods.

"And to restrict any discussion about the two of us to an agreed upon list of friends and family who will be forewarned not to discuss it with anyone else."

"Forewarned, but not contractually obligated," he says. "What are you going to tell them, exactly?"

"I don't know exactly, but I can do my best to keep things in general terms." My head hurts. At least the buzz from the margaritas has worn off. The whole conversation would probably have been better to have tomorrow. Though I doubt either of us would have gotten any sleep with this hanging over us. "Beck, I don't want this relationship to isolate me. I don't want to agree to anything that runs the risk of me winding up resenting you one day."

An indentation appears between his brows.

"You wanted someone who wasn't after you for your money," I say. "And yet the money is such a big part of everything now."

"What do you want me to do?"

"I don't know."

"Can I have the NDA, please?" He reaches out, rising to his feet. I hand over the papers. Turns out he's off to find a pen. The one he returns with gleams like polished metal in the firelight. Platinum probably. If you're going to sign your name to million-dollar deals, I guess you may as well do it in style. He sits back down, and sets the paperwork on the coffee table. Several lines of text are crossed out with a swift series of authoritative strokes before he writes something at the bottom of the contract. "See if that's agreeable."

"All right."

I reach for the papers, but for a moment he holds on to them, almost glaring at them. Then he takes a deep breath and lets it out slow. "Let me give you some context. About sixteen years back, when he was in college, Ethan started dating this girl. A journalism student. It got serious fast. He was planning on asking her to marry him once they graduated, but it was all fake. Turns out she was writing a book about the family and using him as a means of research. Dad managed to get the book shut down, but that's when the background reports and the NDAs became mandatory for everyone."

I take the papers. "No wonder he's bitter. That's horrible."

Beck sits there, looking for all the world like a lost little boy. Just for a moment. Then his jaw firms, his gaze hardens. "Ethan and Penny are right; I need to protect both my interests and my family here."

"From me."

He says nothing. There is no denial.

And that stings. In fact, this whole fucking conversation is misery. What to do when your boyfriend turns into a complicated and costly legal dispute. Someone needs to write that how-to book. I swallow hard, my throat dry. "While I basically understand where you're coming from, this is a lot to take in."

"What did you think of the cohabitation agreement?"

"It seems pretty straightforward. It's also very generous. A little too generous." I rub at my temples, trying to alleviate the ache starting up inside my brain. "The allowance is a definite no. I'm going to find more work. Sitting at home waiting for you to have time for me in your busy schedule does not appeal."

"It wouldn't be like that."

"There's also the self-respect side of things to be considered."

He presses his lips together for a moment. "All right."

I hand over the second lot of papers and he peruses them, searching for the relevant subsection. This too is crossed out before he signs the contract.

I clear my throat. "As for the dissolution part—"

"That stays. You've upended your life and moved to Denver for me. The settlement should we terminate the relationship is fair and based on how long we're together. I won't negotiate that. You and your future must be protected too." He doesn't meet my eyes. "Have a lawyer look it over. But I'm not open to changing that part of the contract, Alice."

"The amount is exorbitant."

"Some of my exes would disagree," he says, tone cynical. "At any rate, it stays."

"If I sign that, are you going to be able to trust that I'm here for you and not the money?" I ask. "Because if all this does is plant doubts in your head than what is even the point of going any further?"

He just stares at me.

"Well?"

He jerks his chin. "Think of it this way. The more generous

the dissolution settlement, the more financial incentive you have to leave me. If you stay—"

"*When* I stay."

"Then it will be obvious to everyone that you're here for me, for us, and not for the money."

I'm not entirely sure that signing a contract saying I win a jackpot if I walk out really provides evidence of my feelings towards him, but apparently this is the best I'm going to get. "All right. What's next? Monogamy is just obvious. I see that written notice of dissolution of the relationship includes text messaging. That's acceptable, though I'd hope we'd have the maturity to sit down and talk. As for any gifts given during the—"

"They're yours. You keep them. The car, the watch, all of it."

I sigh.

"There's a lot about the money that just complicates the fuck out of my life. But buying you things isn't one of them," he says, face set. "It makes me happy. Okay?"

"Okay. The STD tests and contraception shot makes sense," I say. "I'm fine with doing those as soon as possible."

"I'll have my assistant make the appointment tomorrow. Get it out of the way."

"Okay. I suppose it would be only fair to ask you to have the tests too."

"Of course."

Silence.

"Why didn't Smith give me these on the plane?" I ask.

His eyes are dark in the low lighting. "Because I told him not to. You barely knew what you were walking into as it was. If he'd given you those, you'd have made them turn the jet around and take you straight back to LA."

My heels sit abandoned on the floor. A pair of black leather Jimmy Choo pumps with a pointed toe. So much for my plans of seduction and hopes for drunken fumbling. This night has well and truly gone to shit. "You're probably right. So when were you going to give them to me?"

"I don't know. I didn't want to think about it." He rises, his movements tense, shoulders set. "If you're happy with the documents as they stand, then perhaps we can leave them for your lawyer to look over tomorrow. I've got some work to do. Be in the office if you need me."

Neither of us are romantic or touchy-feely. What not a surprise. This feels more like a legally binding agreement than a relationship right now. I kind of want to scream. Loudly.

Instead, I read the new addition at the bottom of the NDA. The thick blue ink of Beck's writing streaming across hard black print. He accepts my discretion in deciding who and what I talk about to a few to be agreed upon close family and friends. I can live with that. Beck has already added his signature to both documents. After reading over them both twice—a task easier said than done—I add my own signature. Having a lawyer look it over would be the smart thing to do. But in this moment, I'm so fucking done.

After a long shower, I crawl into bed. Still no sign of the moody complicated billionaire. Not that I care (a total lie).

It's when I'm on the verge of sleep, my mind all floaty and finally relaxed (so hours later), that the mattress dips. His chest is against my back, nice and tight. It's comforting.

"You signed the contracts," he whispers in my ear.

"Mm."

"I didn't know if you were going to." He slips an arm beneath my neck, the other going over my middle. If anything, he sounds relieved. I know the feeling.

"Me neither."

He sighs, rubbing his mouth against the side of my neck. Given his stubble, it tickles and scratches in even amounts. Being surrounded by him, by his skin and warmth and scent, makes everything infinitely better.

I put my hand over his, holding on tight. "I'll make you a deal. I'm going to stop being weird about the money and you're going to stop keeping secrets. The ground rules have been set. If something is important then we need to communicate and figure things out together in the future."

"Agreed." There's a smile in his voice. Though it's gone when he says, "What are you going to do about your apartment back in LA?"

"I think it's time to let it go. I'll ask Mom and Dad if they wouldn't mind packing it up for me. It's not like there's that much there."

"Are you sure?"

I nod and the tension of the night dissipates. All of the anger and confusion and everything. And thank God for that.

"Question," I say. "Why did you stop calling me wife after I arrived in Denver?"

"Answer. I don't know exactly." He pauses for a moment. "Guess I got superstitious or something, worried I was jinxing us. I decided I should wait to call you that until you are actually that."

"I think we need to get this dating and living together thing down before we attempt getting married. Though that's a pretty good answer," I mumble, tiredness creeping into my voice.

"It is?" He sounds surprised. "Phew. Glad I got something right tonight. Of course, I was tempted to keep going with it, just to see what shade of purple Grandma would turn."

I just grunt. It's the most I can manage.

"Hey, one last thing before you go to sleep," he says, rubbing his face in my hair and sniffing at me like a pervert. An adorable one, but still. "I L you."

"You L me?"

"It could be *like*. It could be *love*. I honestly can't tell anymore." His teeth bite softly into the tender flesh of my neck. Just enough to get my full and utter attention. As if his selection of a letter hadn't done it already. "There's just this whole mass of feelings inside me about you so I figured I'd put it out there. Full and frank disclosure and all that."

"Beck..."

"'I cannot fix on the hour, or the spot, or the look or the words, which laid the foundation. It is too long ago. I was in the middle before I knew that I had begun.'"

Despite the tight hold he has on me, I wriggle around, turning over to face him. There's going to come a day when I look at him and instead of the rush of giddy hormones I'll see the face of my best friend. Of my longtime beloved. Maybe I wasn't certain we'd get there an hour ago. But I am now. Also, in the meantime, the hormones sure are fun. "Nice use of Austen. I L you too."

CHAPTER TWELVE

"WE'RE STARTING OVER."

Beck leans against the refrigerator, clad in only a pair of loose gray sleep pants. His bare chest is a thing of beauty. He's all hard body and perfect skin apart from a few small white scars. From climbing, probably. Or his childhood hobby of skateboarding. Visually the man is a work of art. Not that I don't respect him for his mind and all. Though there's no hiding suddenly hard nipples beneath my thin T-shirt.

"Why are we starting over?" he asks, shoving a hand through his messy hair. "I didn't think we'd been doing that badly. Is that bacon and eggs you're cooking?"

"Yes. Take a seat." I wave the spatula in the vague direction of the stools on the other side of the kitchen island. "And we're starting over, despite already having been cohabitating, because I'm no longer being weird about the money and you're no longer keeping secrets."

He takes a seat. "Right. Got it. I think."

"Here. Drink some coffee." I hand him the cup I just made for myself before prepping the espresso machine for another. "Your brain will work better."

"Thanks." His gaze stays glued to where his T-shirt, the one I'm currently wearing, brushes against the top of my thighs (thick thighs save lives). It's like his hand is on automatic, lifting the cup of coffee and bringing it to his lips. "I know you're not wearing a bra, beloved, but I'm also pretending you're not wearing any panties."

"Whatever makes you happy."

"I don't know about happy," he mumbles. "But it makes me hard."

Previous to this morning, he's always been up before me. Off to the gym and work to build his empire. Even on the weekends. Guess he's still catching up on the time he was away. But eventually he's going need to slow down some. Still, it's interesting to see him in those first few moments when he's just woken. Beck all rumpled and sleepy with stubble on his cheeks is a delight.

Well worth missing out on the extra sleep. Five stars. Would recommend.

"How is our timeline going on taking it slow with the sexing?" I ask as the espresso machine hisses and spits. The scent of fresh coffee is perfection. "I noticed there was no explicit mention regarding our sex life in the contracts. Of course, the stipulated STD tests are suggestive that some activity will eventually take place. Because when it comes to saying 'let's fuck,' nothing conveys it like sterile needles and blood tests. But even so, there was no mention of when this event shall commence or how often it must be partaken of thereafter."

"Would you have smothered me with a pillow in my sleep if such details had been covered in legalese?"

"Yes."

"There you go," he says, tone placid. "I'm smarter than I look. The timeline is definitely getting shorter."

My shoulders slump in relief. "Thank God."

"Yeah." He shifts on the stool with a wince. "I'm imagining you with your underwear back on. More comfortable for everyone involved, but mostly me."

"I see."

"In my mind, you're now wearing a very sensible red lace thong. Crotchless, of course."

I cock my head. "I'd debate your use of the word sensible, but what's the point? And crotchless? Really?"

He just grins.

"I think you might want to imagine more coverage if you're seeking a flaccid state of mind."

"Are you mocking my staff of love? My pillar of pleasure?"

"I wouldn't dare," I say, trying not to laugh. "Please don't call it either of those things if you wish me to ever take that part of your anatomy seriously."

"Harsh, but fair."

"You seem particularly lusty this morning."

He makes a humming noise. "I had dreams about you. Vivid ones. You may have even been naked."

"Ah."

"So, I was thinking…" His gaze now rests on my ass. It appears my butt has him hypnotized since he doesn't even blink. "I know you said penis in vagina, but how do you feel about tongue in vagina? What if we experimented with some oral first?"

"No."

"It would be for science's sake, of course," he continues as if I hadn't said a word. Typical Beck. "We would have a diagram to mark out your most sensitive spots for future reference. A thorough exploration of clit versus labia. Examine the exact ratio required of licking to sucking."

"Stop talking dirty, Beck. You're not going to change my mind."

"Then there's the whole finger fucking issue," he continues. "That'll need some intense study. Where do you stand on the subject of ass play, just out of curiosity?"

And now I'm waving a spatula around like my mother, which is so wrong given the topic of conversation. "I didn't sign contracts and move states to mess this up with you now."

"But—"

"All or nothing, my friend."

He pouts.

"You wanted me on side with this and now I am. Deal with it."

"Well, what about watching each other masturbate, then?"

"We both go without until the big event," I say. "You felt strongly that this was important. That we build our relationship slowly and thoroughly, getting to know each other and all our little quirks in an effort to limit any chance of problems later. Because we've both been let down before, right? Gotten serious about people who were not who we thought they were and been hurt?"

He's seriously cute when he sulks. "Yes."

"So we're doing it right, the old-fashioned way."

"Dad was born six and a half months after Grandma and Grandpa got married. Pretty sure the old-fashioned way isn't what you think it is."

"Another week or two won't kill us." At least, I hope not. "Just please don't tell me it's going to be more than that or I'll ugly cry."

"I'm not even sure we'll last that long at this rate."

I stop watching him over my shoulder and start frothing the milk. Next comes plating up the bacon and eggs. Toast and butter already sit on the kitchen island. A simple breakfast. Though it smells mouthwateringly good. Can't buy the boy a Rolex, but I can look after him in other ways. Also, he already has like a dozen different designer watches.

"I don't think I've ever had a girlfriend cook me breakfast before," he says.

"Seriously?"

"They either had kitchen staff, we went out, or I declined to stay over."

"Bon appétit." I slide the plate in front of him along with cutlery.

"Thank you, dearest." He picks up his knife and fork, cutting into a strip of bacon. "So, how much don't you care about money, just out of curiosity?"

"Eat your breakfast, Beck."

"This is going to make the family tradition much easier to maintain."

"Oh?"

"Yes indeed," he says, loading up his fork with bacon and egg. "All of us Elliots seek to remain emotionally unavailable while throwing money at the problem."

"Am I a problem?"

"No. You're my Alice."

The easy way he has of saying such devastating things. First last night and now this...he's making a mess of my heart. I don't know what to say. I'm too busy just breathing and not being all overemotional at his casual declaration.

"Do you have meetings today?" I ask, voice quieter than before. Less bold.

"Just one," he says. "At the hotel in Boulder. Was wondering if you'd like to go for a drive into the national park beforehand? Head up to some of the lookouts?"

"I'd love to."

He gives me a lopsided grin before shoveling another forkful of food into his mouth and chewing. Once he swallows, he says, "This is great. Thank you."

"You're welcome."

We have a relaxed start to the day together. It's nice. I've kind of been in a sort of holiday mode since arriving in Denver, but that's over. Time for me to get busy building a future. If I was hesitant in any way about this relationship before, those days are gone. It's an odd feeling, being legally bound to someone. We're documented on paper now, bound by rules and subsections. My signature means I'm serious. Maybe it's how commitment in a relationship is made, with layers of promises, emotions, and responsibility. By making yourself vulnerable. I don't know.

Though a text could end things easily enough. That was in the contract too.

After finishing breakfast and washing off the dishes, he checks his cell. "Nothing from Emma or Matías yet."

"I hope they're okay."

"Yeah." He keeps scrolling through the screen. "Henry is fine and settling in back at school. He says he doesn't have time to text with us basics."

"Fair enough."

"Brian will organize your appointment with the OB/GYN for late this afternoon," he says. "My doctor's appointment will also be done nearby at the same time in the interests of keeping all things equal."

"Is Brian your assistant?"

A nod.

"What if they don't have an appointment available?"

"They will." No trace of doubt in his voice. Then he looks up, meeting my eyes. "You haven't changed your mind, have you, beloved?"

"No."

He just nods, still watching my face. There's a question in his gaze. "Okay. Courier will be by to pick up the contracts in five. Last chance to escape my evil clutches."

"I'll go have a shower and get dressed."

"Remember to bring a coat. It'll get cold up in the mountains."

What I can only describe as a cross between a futuristic rocket ship and a motor vehicle sits waiting at the curb outside the Heritage. It's low and sleek and silver. Waving the valet aside, Beck opens the door for me. The interior is black and equally space age in appearance. I shove my hands into my leather jacket, guarding against the wind. I'm back in my casual outfit of black sweater, blue jeans, and my booties. This weather is perfect, brisk and cool. Given how I hate the sun, I make a shit Cali girl. Though experiencing a full-on winter in Colorado is going to be interesting. Beck wears a sweater (swoon), blue jeans, and boots too. Though his sweater is a forest green that brings out the amber flecks in his eyes. How dreamy.

"This is yours?" I ask, hovering near the door.

"Yep."

"How fast does it go?"

"Very." He smiles. "Want me to show you?"

"Oh, yeah."

He smiles and slaps me on the ass. "Well, let's go."

We slide through the streets, taking corners tight, and weaving in and out of traffic. It's a little weird, sitting so low to the road. I've never been in something like this before and the thrill is undeniable. My cheeks hurt from smiling so hard. Without a doubt, this is as close to a vehicular representation of an orgasm as is possible to achieve. Beck handles the wheel with absolute confidence and precision. And watching him is also a mighty turn-on. I'm all but squirming with excitement.

Once we hit the highway, we speed up, the engine purring as we head away from town and toward the mountains. Tall grass, sunflowers, and clear blue sky.

"Ready?" he asks.

"Do it."

When Beck puts his foot down, we shoot forward, the force pushing me back in my seat. It's like being on a roller coaster only better. My heart pounds and laughter escapes my mouth. He just grins. This is freedom. Moving so fast through the world that no cares or complications could possibly keep up. It's just him and me and the road going on forever.

"Let's not push our luck," he says after a while, slowing the vehicle down. He gives me side-eye and a sly smile. "You know, I think you'd look pretty in a tiara. Might put in a call to Cartier or Sotheby's later and see what they've got."

I scrunch up my nose. "A tiara?"

"Absolutely. I'm thinking diamonds. Lots of them."

The asshat is so testing me. "That sounds great, Beck."

"You on top of me wearing a tiara." He happy sighs. "Just imagine it."

"Mm-hmm."

"Can't help but think that tiaras have been maligned so far as modern jewelry go. I mean, anyone can buy a ring or a neck-lace. How passé. But a tiara, now that's a statement, a reclamation of female power." It's official. He's gone insane. "And they're so practical, right?"

"I have no doubt I'll wear it everywhere."

"You'd be okay with me buying you one?" he asks, tone of voice amused. "Really?"

"Absolutely. Far be it from me to tell you how to spend your money," I say. "So what's your relationship with your mother like?"

Two can play at this game. He's not grinning now. "It's fine. We text."

"Yeah?" And I just wait.

"She's apparently finished steaming her private parts in the tropics and is back in New York getting ready for fashion week and working on her next coffee table book. It's about wellness and all of the possible uses for her line of herbal waters." He pulls over to the side of the road. "Your turn to drive."

"Me?"

"Don't be shy." He opens his door before wandering around the front of the vehicle to open mine. "C'mon, Alice. Cars are meant to be driven. And I know you want to."

"You're right, I do."

"That's my girl."

Sitting behind the steering wheel, my stomach tumbles and turns. But my blood beats hotter and faster too. All of the power at my fingertips. Or toe tips. I carefully pull back out onto the highway, even though the road has been almost deserted. What with this part of the day not being a competition, I don't drive as fast as Beck. But I'm no slouch either, despite sticking to the speed limit. Mostly. It's official, sports cars are damn fun. And while being a passenger in one was great, sitting in the driver's seat is about a billion times better. The sensation of hugging the corner and accelerating once we hit a straight stretch of road. It's over way too soon as we swap back in Estes Park so I can concentrate on the view.

"Being serious this time," he says. "I'm buying a jet."

"The Elliot Corp. ones won't do?"

"A lot of people use those. I think for convenience sake we need our own for work and play."

"Need" is a strong word. But again, it's his call. "Okay," I say.

"You're being so agreeable. It turns me on."

"Everything turns you on today." I smile and turn in my seat to watch him. No doubt the view outside is pretty, but the one inside the car is a singular delight. It feels like one of those special moments. The type you never want to forget.

"What are you doing?" he asks.

"Watching you."

"Hmm." He glances at me, a hint of color staining his cheeks. Oh my God, Beck is blushing. He is the cutest, kindest, and craziest.

My throat goes tight with some emotion I don't want to name. "You must be used to people looking at you."

"Not like you do."

"How do I look at you?"

For a moment, he doesn't answer. "Let's discuss it another time when I'm not meant to be concentrating on driving."

How curious. "Okay."

"You're still staring. Ask me another question. Go on."

I think fast. "How are you dealing with your dad being gone?"

Beck frowns.

"You don't have to answer if you don't want to. How you grieve is your own choice, of course."

"It's fine. I miss him." His fingers tighten around the steering wheel. "Me leaving after that argument...the lack of resolution and everything...I guess it's always going to be a thing. But as I've mentioned before, we never had a great relationship. And odds were, it was never going to improve. He was always so big on trying to control people, yet none of his offspring are what you'd call meek or biddable. It's funny, really."

I keep my mouth shut, letting him speak.

"Then I feel guilty because I'm honestly kind of glad he's not here to give Emma shit about the pregnancy among other things."

"Understandable."

"Is it?" He rolls his shoulders, cracks his neck. "Perhaps I should buy an island. You like the beach."

"Or there are plenty of free ones we could visit."

He gives me a half smile.

"But whatever makes you happy, of course. An island sounds lovely."

"Nice save," he whispers. "Ask another question. Go on, I'm an open book."

"All right. What other businesses do you own?"

"We came into our trust funds at twenty-one," he says. "A bit earlier than some. Dad made a competition out of who could invest it the best. Make the most profit."

"Matías was right. Ambition and competition should be the family motto."

"Just remember to put it in Latin. We get bonus points for being pretentious assholes and all that."

"*Ambitio* and *competere*, then." I shrug. "That's probably wrong. I'm okay on Latin roots, but I never really studied the language or grammar."

"You're okay on Latin roots?"

I narrow my eyes. "Etymologically speaking, yes."

"I love how you have all this random knowledge stored in your head."

"It's not random at all. Just slightly impractical."

The small town and tourist shops disappear behind us as we reach the Rocky Mountain National Park. He lowers the window to pay the ranger the fee. Everything is green and beautiful. Lots of trees and towering mountains. Plenty of tourists and other vehicles on the road as well. Still, out here, the air is crisper and fresher than in the city. The fall colors are spectacular.

"I own a few different properties," he says, his gaze on the twisting road heading up into the mountains. "But I mostly wanted to focus on hospitality and entertainment. I partnered with a production company specializing in documentaries, a recording studio in Denver, and a small record label that have all done well. Then there's the bars and nightclubs, which you know about, eight of them throughout Colorado. Also, I own Downtown Gin. It started out small-batch, but we're looking into expanding."

"You own Downtown Gin?" I ask, surprised.

"I do."

"That's some top shelf goodness, Beck."

"Thank you. I have a small team monitoring things in offices at the Heritage."

"How were you able to walk away for six months?"

"I hire good people," he explains. "And Matías helped. But our investments had to be able to be run as a sideline. Dad expected us all to be full-time at Elliot Corp."

"I'm amazed any of you had time for a life."

"'Sleep is for the weak.' Another one of Dad's quotes."

"Yikes."

"Yeah, well, that kind of workload isn't sustainable. The way he lived his life and his recent death proved as much." His face tenses as his large hands maneuver the steering wheel with precision. "At any rate, Ethan was overall winner on highest profit margin, that's how he got to take over Elliot Corp. He went heavily into building while Emma concentrated on green energy sources. She did damn well too. But I'm happy with what I've achieved."

"You should be."

"Thing with wealth is, you have to be wary of getting carried away with how things look on paper. Most of the money is tied up, some of it long-term, and actual worth is dependent on market value should you sell," he explains. "Actual available cash is less than you'd think."

"But enough to buy a jet, apparently."

"Not that you're judging."

"Never."

High up ahead an eagle rides a thermal, its wings stretched wide. Nature is amazing. Now that we're gradually getting up above the tree line the view seems to go on forever.

"Are you really going to look at tiaras?" I ask, tone dubious.

He laughs, which is not an answer, and pulls into a parking space at a lookout. There's an amazing view behind a low stone wall and toilet facilities. A good thing since the three coffees earlier have caught up with me. More than a few people gather around the car to gawk and admire, which is ironic given the stupendous natural beauty in every direction. Meanwhile, we take selfies of us together with the valley and mountains as a backdrop.

Wind whips my hair about and I cuddle up to Beck. With my arms wrapped around his waist, I can press my ear against his chest and feel him breathe and listen to his heartbeat. Just enjoy the moment. He tucks his hand into the back pocket of my jeans. Hard to say if I've ever been this happy. It's such a gift, getting to have this intimacy with him. I know the sound of his voice and the scent of his skin. How he looks when he's asleep and what he's like when he's excited. He's my fairy-tale prince and I have no idea if I deserve him or not, but I'm keeping him.

Quality of life: Bliss.

Ever so gently, he slips my black sunglasses on top of my head so he can see my eyes. "You have to stop looking at me like that, beloved. It messes with me in all sorts of ways."

"I can't help it."

"Alice." His smile is slow and warm and I feel it deep in my belly. "Ready to go higher?"

"Let's do it."

We have lunch at the hotel he's looking to buy in Boulder. It's an old five-story brick building in need of some love and care. The eighties redecoration with beige carpet and ugly corporate art is something else. Mostly the clientele seems to be budget travelers and sad people attending a conference on insurance broking. I'd be depressed too if I had to sit through that. But the hotel has good bones and an above-average restaurant. Though a hamburger and fries does generally please me.

Up in the national park, we stop at three lookouts until the air gets thin and my head feels weird. The views are spectacular. And the rocks and little growths of fungus and moss up high are fascinating. Penny was right when she said the real beauty was in the mountains. We do a drive-by of The Stanley Hotel where Stephen King got his inspiration for *The Shining*. It's an elegant old sprawling white building with a hedge maze growing out the front. Perfect for an ax murderer to chase his family around. All of the tourists present, however, put us off taking a look inside.

While Beck meets with the owner of the hotel in Boulder, I play with my cell. Which turns out to be a mistake. On Instagram, there's a whole bunch of new followers and I've been tagged in a ton of pictures. Me leaving the library charity luncheon. (Okay, so I'm glad that moment of victory got recorded for posterity.) The group of us outside the not-so-secret bar last night with Emma shielding her face with her hand. Beck and I climbing into his Bugatti this morning outside the Heritage. Every damn time we step foot outside our front door, basically. The level of interest in us is crazy. And the names they call me, the things they say...they bitch about my body, compare me to his exes, label me a gold digger and worse. All of these entitled, opinionated strangers. These haters and trolls. It makes my stomach churn.

I order a vodka, soda, and lime and by the time I've reached the bottom of the glass, I'm in a better frame of mind. Less emotional turmoil, more fuck the lot of them. I delete my Instagram account. As if anyone needs all that negative commentary in their head. Life is complicated enough without this shit.

Next I answer messages from Natasha and Hanae. At least with texting, it's easy enough to keep things succinct and general as per the NDA. And I'm not lying; everything is fine. There's a rambling emotional voice message from the lady I met in the bathroom line at the luncheon the other day thanking me for funding her literacy program. Interesting. Then Brian, executive assistant to Beck Elliot, forwards me an email from the gentleman raising money for school lunches. Said gentleman heartily thanks me for fully meeting their monetary requirements.

Curiouser and curiouser.

I have some questions for my boyfriend, but he's still in his meeting. So instead, I call my mother. All of the family are alive and well. My niece is thriving and now saying "cow" accompanied by a moo. The child is an animal sound making virtuoso.

Our conversation (with my mom not the toddler) is going great up until I ask her about cleaning out my apartment.

"Are you sure that's wise?" she asks. "It's only been a couple of weeks. You don't want to give it a bit longer? We can help you with rent if that's the issue."

"No, Mom. I'm staying in Denver. A commitment has been made."

"Just give it one more week," she bargains. "To be sure."

"I'm not going to change my mind."

"Hmm."

"Also, I signed an NDA last night," I say. "So we have to be careful when we talk."

"What do you mean?" she asks, voice gaining in volume.

"Calm down, it's not a big deal. I signed an NDA to protect Beck and his family's privacy is all."

"What? So you can't talk to me now?"

"I can talk to you. I am talking to you."

"Explain yourself, Alice."

"I just won't always be able to get into specifics about things and you can't discuss Beck or my relationship with him with other people. Please try and understand. It's to protect his privacy."

"What about your privacy?"

"My privacy is fine. I'm not rich and no one cares about me."

Now she starts shouting. "I care about you. Your dad cares about you too!"

"Thank you, Mom," I say. "It's all right, really."

"They can't restrict your communication with your family. You should never have signed it. What on earth were you thinking?"

"Mom." And I can't tell her about how Ethan's ex tried to write a book about the family and sell them out (which would go a long way toward explaining the situation) because that's covered under the NDA too. "It's okay. Please trust me."

"You sound like you've joined a cult."

"It's more like entering rich people land, actually."

"They're taking advantage of your good nature"

"Have you ever actually known me to be good-natured, though?" I ask. "When was the last time you thought to yourself: Gosh, my daughter is good-natured?"

"It's not funny, Alice."

"Sorry."

"Did you get a lawyer to go through it with you, at least?"

Oh, shit. "No. It was...um...well, you see, I felt that I had a thorough grasp of situation and the document. So I—"

"ALICE."

My ear is ringing. Not good.

"I'm coming out there," she says, voice determined.

"Oh God, please don't. Everything's fine."

"No. I'm coming."

"Mom..."

Beck strides toward my table, all smiles. When he sees my face, he stops smiling.

"Perhaps I haven't explained this all very well," I continue, stating the obvious. "I'm fine. I can talk to you. We just need to be careful. Beck is protecting himself and his family in much the same way any of us would. But it's a different kind of world with them being wealthy and all, you see? Some compromises need to be made. And that's all it is, a small little compromise. While I'd love to see you, it's just a bit early for planning an actual visit. How about in a couple of months? Or I could come home for Thanksgiving! That would be nice, right?"

Nothing.

"Mom?"

"I'll text you the details when I have them." And she hangs up.

"Fuck," I mutter.

He takes the seat opposite. "Beloved, what's wrong?"

"My, um, my mom is coming to visit."

His brows rise and his eyes widen. "Your mother?"

"Yes."

"Soon?"

"Yes. At least, I think so."

"Oh." He swallows. "Great."

"That was not convincing."

I've never seen him scared before. Not even during that gory film of Henry's. But the idea of my mom visiting has set off all his alarms. His shoulders are rigid and his face has gone pale. "No, no. It's fine. I can't wait to meet her."

"Okay. If you say so."

He studies me for a moment. "Beloved, you're supposed to comfort me by saying you're sure she'll love me."

"Absolutely. I'm sure she will."

"Has she liked any of your other boyfriends?" he asks.

"No. Not really. Though, I mean, they were all assholes, so…"

"Uh-huh."

"It's just that Mom is no more used to one-percenters than I was. But I'm sure you'll win her over. You're funny and kind and charming."

"Yeah," he says, voice flat. "But I also come with an NDA."

"You come with my heart as well." It's as close as I can get to saying I love him without losing all courage. Bravery is so over-rated. "She'll see that."

He holds out his hand and I take it, holding on tight. "Thank you, dearest. It's just that I'm used to society matrons wanting to get their claws into me for various reasons. Hostile moms out to kick my ass for leading their daughters astray and moving them to Denver are a new experience for me."

"It'll be fine."

He does the furrowed brow thing. Never has a man frightened of my mother been so hot.

"But, Beck, just this once, don't throw money at the problem. With the mood she's in, she's certain to take it the wrong way."

"You think?"

"Yes. Don't buy her anything and I'm sure you'll be fine."

"Okay." He nods, staring off into the middle distance. "It'll be fine."

CHAPTER THIRTEEN

I T'S NOT FINE. AS IS AMPLY DEMONSTRATED AT THREE THE NEXT
morning when Beck wakes me from a deep sleep.

"Psst, Alice." There's a vague scent of whiskey as he nudges
my cheek with his nose. In a move both cruel and unusual, he
switches on the bedside lamp. "Hey, beloved, wake up."

"No-o-o."

"There's something I need to tell you."

"Go away."

"It's important."

I open my eyes, but I am not happy. Not even a little. Though
once I grow accustomed to the lamplight, the view sure is something. His hair is ruffled, his angular jaw lined with stubble. How
do you even get lips so expressive? So flawless? So damn kissable?
Despite the rude awakening, I'm already half on my way toward
smiling. Beguiled by the boy yet again. I'm so easy for him it's a
sin. He's lying beside me on the bed, leaning on one arm, looking down at me. The other arm is slung across my middle, fingers creeping beneath the hem of my sleep shirt to check out my
panty situation. For some reason, he enjoys sliding a fingertip beneath the elastic and running it back and forth. If I said I minded,
I'd be lying.

"Hey," I say, voice slow and heavy with sleep. "How's Matías?"

"Passed out on the couch."

I nod.

Soon as we got back from Boulder and the various doctors'
offices, we found Matías lying in wait. He wanted a drinking buddy

and needed a friend. So Beck took him to The Downstairs Bar. I texted Emma just to check on her. She said she was fine, didn't want to talk, and was hanging with her mom. Therefore I settled in with a new book for the night. Along with an order of dumplings for dinner because dumplings.

"I have something to tell you," he repeats.

I cover my mouth with a hand and yawn. "What?"

"Brace yourself." He pauses. "Are you ready?"

"You're starting to make me nervous."

"Oh no," he says, placing a soft kiss on my forehead. "Don't be nervous, dearest. Everything is fine."

"If you say so."

He smiles. "I panicked and bought a house."

"You...what?"

"Yes. Though it's actually more like a big building. That way your mom can have one floor and we'll have another and no one needs to be in anyone else's face."

Huh.

"What do you think?" he asks.

"A house?"

"Yeah."

"Wow." My mind is a blur. A very sleepy one. And yet... "Why didn't you just book Mom her own room in the hotel but on a different level to us? Wouldn't that achieve the same thing?"

He bites his lip. "Actually, I didn't think of that. Like I said, I'd had a few drinks and I panicked."

"Talk me through this."

"Well, we only just got rid of Henry. Who I love, and who, by the way, will also have his own bedroom and living area when he's back next from school. Great, right?" He gives me a salesman's smile.

"Great." I do not sound convinced. "How big is this place, exactly?"

"It's...actually, why don't we let that be a surprise?"

"Okay." I'm not frowning. I'm just confused. It happens at times like these.

He sighs. "Thing is, when you get right down to it, I just couldn't handle the thought of any more people sharing this place with us. Getting all up in our grill. Preventing us from walking around half naked. Judging our suitability as a possible life partner for their daughter. Things like that."

"I see."

"So I called the real estate agent from the charity dinner thing we went to last week. Asked him what was the biggest property he had available that's still in the heart of the city. Then I checked it out and made the owners an offer. Then I woke Penny up to help rush things." And then he just looks at me.

"You've been busy."

"Yeah." He scratches at the stubble on his cheek. "It'd been on the market for a while so we got it at a pretty good price. It's fully furnished including some artwork and is in a very handy location. The owners had already moved to Hong Kong for business so we can have it right away. Time difference sure came in handy for getting it all sorted."

"Wow."

"You already said that," he adds helpfully. "It's kind of exciting though, right? Our first real place together? A proper home. Much more adult than living in a hotel."

"Mm."

"Anyway, this obviously isn't my shining moment, what with it being brought on by fear of your mother and all. But I think we should just make the best of things."

I have nothing.

The fingers tapping against my ass still and he cocks his head. "Matías thought it was a good idea."

"The soon-to-be divorcé soon-to-be father currently passed out drunk on our sofa thought it was good idea?"

"Yes." He just watches me for a long moment. "Beloved, say something."

"How drunk are you?"

"The buzz wore off hours ago."

"Are you going to regret this decision later when you're fully sober?" I ask.

"No, I don't think so." He flops onto his back, putting his hands behind his head and staring at the ceiling. "Fuck, I'm tired."

I sit up, stretching. "Go to sleep."

"Are you angry at me?"

"No, Beck, I'm not. A little surprised maybe, but not angry." I crawl down the mattress to tug at his boots. First one, then the other, hit the floor with a thump. Matías better not be a light sleeper. I undo his belt buckle, drawing it out carefully before tossing it too aside. "Do you want your pants on or off?"

His eyelids are closed now. "Whatever."

I climb off the mattress, heading into the bathroom. In a good and just world, everyone with a hangover would wake to a glass of water and some Advil waiting on their bedside table. It's only humane. Next, I get back into bed, cuddling up to his side. One of his arms comes around me, hand slipping beneath my T-shirt to rest on my hip. As usual, he slips his fingers under the elastic of my panties. And just leaves them there.

"I'm sorry my mother terrified you into buying property," I say.

He lifts one shoulder in a half shrug. "It's fine. There's a small chance I overreacted. But don't tell anybody else that."

"Your secret's safe with me."

"Turn in here."

"This driveway?" I ask.

He nods and I steer my G-Class into a discreet entry for a big old four-story brown brick building. An art gallery, boutiques, and a coffee shop sit either side. It's only about five blocks away from the Heritage.

Today I dressed for comfort. Plain white leather Gucci sneakers, my secondhand Levi's, and a loose navy jersey pullover I think was bought in hopes of me taking up yoga or some such. Ha-ha. As if I'd bend at the waist for anybody. No makeup. A pair of silver framed aviator Ray-Bans cover half of my face. If anyone was lying in wait outside the Heritage to take pictures then they can kiss my frazzled ass.

"The code is 21145," he says. "It was built in 1934 and has been shops and offices and all sorts of things over the years. The owner of the art gallery next door bought it and started renovating it, turning it into a home about eight years back."

The metal gate rolls up and I head down a steep incline into an underground parking lot half filled with vehicles and a couple of motorcycles. Each and every one of them gleams, polished to perfection. One is the Bugatti from yesterday, but the others are new to me. In the middle are a few empty parking spaces sitting before the silver doors of an elevator. This is where I pull in and turn off the engine.

"Are all of these yours?" I ask.

"Yeah. I had Smith organize to bring them over earlier."

"Where were they before?"

"At the Heritage in a locked parking area."

I nod. "That's a lot of cars."

"I like things that go *vroom*. And you." Once we're out of the G-Class, Beck does a quick inventory. "The Bugatti Chiron you already know. Followed by the Bentley Flying Spur sedan, and the Bentley Bentayga SUV."

"A car for every occasion. You like brands that start with the letter B."

He stuffs his hands in his pants pockets. "Does that make me narcissistic?"

"Not sure. But it does make you a fan of alliteration. I think you have very good taste."

"Thank you," he says. "Dad actually had a huge collection of American Muscle. It drove him crazy that I loved the European car makers. But you see the Maserati GT in the corner? He gave me that for my sixteenth birthday. I'd broken my arm skateboarding in New York a couple of months before. Called him from the hospital to tell him, but he never answered. About a week later he had an assistant call to check on me. Rachel lit into him when she found out. The Maserati was mostly my apology, I think. Or him trying to get his ex-wife off his back. Of course, the Escalade behind it was bought for me by Ethan the day after my birthday so I wouldn't crash my stupid sports car speeding on icy roads and kill myself pretending I was playing a video game. That's an exact quote from him."

"That's sweet."

"It is," Beck agrees with a grin. "He's more bark than bite. Ready to go upstairs?"

"Whenever you are."

Beck points to a door in the back wall. "Gym, sauna, laundry, storage, and the back staircase are through there."

"Right."

And then he presses the elevator call button.

By the time we rose for breakfast some six hours ago, our guest from the sofa had been gone. Beck chugged down the Advil, followed by several cups of coffee, showered and put on a suit, before rushing off to Elliot Corp. for some emergency or other. A meeting with his real estate agent followed. Inspecting our new place had to wait until after lunch. Matías sent a business site over for me to assess so I distracted myself with work. Nice to know his hangover wasn't too bad.

But back to now. Hard to know exactly how I feel about our new home or his reasons for purchasing it in such a rush. Though a tangled ball of emotions has been growing inside of me all day.

When the elevator arrives, we only go up one floor to the ground level. Beside the shiny elevator is a polished wooden staircase winding up and up with a skylight way up high. But otherwise, we've walked into a huge open-plan kitchen, dining, and living room area. Lots of brushed steel with beautiful white stone bench tops in the chef worthy kitchen.

"They're Silestone," says Beck, nodding to the bench tops. "Quartz."

"Huh. Pretty. And your mother would most likely approve."

Something yummy is cooking. A roast, perhaps. The dining table is wood and antique looking, seating ten people. All of the various sofas and chairs look big and comfortable and are done in navy and white. Minimalist modern art hangs on the stark white walls. It's not exactly my style, but it's nice. Beautiful even. Lots of windows and two sets of French doors that let in the light open up onto a back garden terrace type area with outdoor furniture. Hidden away from public view, it's walled in by the neighboring buildings.

"It's like a secret garden," I say, as excited as a child at Christmas.

"Entry and foyer to the side at the front with staff rooms taking up the rest of the front half of this level," he says doing more pointing. "Powder room is over there."

"Staff?"

"Smith and the housekeeper."

"Okay." I have questions. Lots of questions. But I save them for later.

"Let's keep going." His suit-clad ass climbs higher and I follow. He has a nice ass. On the next level he stops, reaching for my hand to draw me alongside him. "Formal dining that seats twenty, second smaller kitchen, bar and wine cellar is at the back. The sitting room that also doubles as gallery space is to the front. Powder room is again straight in front of you."

"Second kitchen?"

"The previous owners liked throwing parties. She often had artists staying with them and her partner was a hedge-fund manager so business soirees and so on."

"Got it."

"Up we go again." And he's off. My calf muscles are going to be bomb by the time we've lived here for a while. On the third floor, he pushes a door open leading into the front half of the building. "Office and library through here with our bedroom et cetera at the back."

"A library? Wow." I say that word a lot these days. I don't see it stopping any time soon. If anything, probably be on the lookout for an increase in usage.

He nods, leading me back into a large bedroom with a sitting area. Antique-looking blue-and-gray patterned rugs cover the hardwood floor.

"They're Persian," says Beck.

"I'm not sure exactly what that means besides them having come from Persia? Wait, isn't it Iran now?"

"It means fancy, old, and expensive."

"Okay." I nod. "All of the furniture and art still here comes with the house?"

"Yeah. I get the feeling that decorating is a passion of the previous owners. She was ready to let this one go and move on to other projects. But as I said, you can change anything you like."

Another orgy-size bed like at the hotel sits covered in white linens dominating the huge room. You could fit my old apartment about six times in this one room. It's crazy. Gray chairs, a three-seater sofa, and an ottoman sit in front of the gray marble fireplace. There's also an antique desk and a discreet bar in the corner. Again, the windows are huge, overlooking the back terrace garden area.

"Bathroom to the left, closets to the right." He leans against the wall, watching me all the while. Like me, he seems to be running on nervous energy.

"Closets as in plural? We have one each?"

He raises his brows. "Beloved. Dearest. Have you seen the amount of shit you own these days? I'm honest to God worried you're going to go in there one day and never be seen again. I'm thinking we need to have a protocol that you tie a rope around your waist and to the door handle so you can find your way out again."

"That wardrobe is not entirely my fault. And it keeps growing, somehow. There was stuff in there this morning I could have sworn wasn't there last night." When the maids came up to pack everything for the rushed move, I did another cull and sent some more things back to Rachel. Like three of the four Chanel handbags that had mysteriously appeared. I probably don't even need the one I kept, but it's so pretty. The orchid diamond necklace in a Cartier box also went back. My soul is stained enough by conspicuous consumption these days. "You need to tell Rachel to stop."

He just grins. His arsenal of smiles is unmatched. "What do you think of the place?"

"What's on the next floor?" I ask, taking a seat in a leather wingback and crossing my legs. Enough stairs for now.

He sits on a long low modern gray lounge opposite. "Three more bedrooms, bathrooms, a media room, and a family room. Then there's the rooftop terrace with a hot tub and plunge pool. That's it."

"No ballroom?"

"Sorry."

"Bummer. Guess we'll just have to do without."

"However will we manage? Henry can have one of the rooms on the top floor. Your mom can stay up there too and have her own space." For a minute, he waits. Before finally saying, "What are you thinking?"

I inhale calm and exhale stress, just like the meditation app says to. "You bought it last night when you were drunk."

"Tipsy."

I frown.

He holds out a hand. "Come here."

The hand guides me onto his lap, where I sit crosswise with my feet dangling just off the floor. It does feel better, getting closer. Rubbing up against the scent and the feel and the everything of him. Beck makes a wonderful security blanket. He wraps his arms around my middle and watches me closely with hazel eyes. "Listen to me. By the time I had papers drawn up and things were being signed this morning I was stone cold sober and only like...half as afraid of your mother as I had been the day before. Three quarters, max. But, beloved, if you don't like the house—"

"I love it."

"Oh, okay. Why are you so stressed, then?"

"This is all happening really fast. Us getting together, me moving out here, you buying this place..." My throat goes tight and my eyes go liquid. Ugh. The last thing I want to do is cry. There's no reason to cry. It's just nerves and other assorted unnecessary emotions. "You know, I've bought things on a whim before. Like a few months back I decided to get a DVD player so I could watch my old movies and some BBC television series I hadn't seen in years. But I forgot to check that it was coded for all regions and then most of my stuff wouldn't play and the place I bought it off refused to let me return it because they're assholes. So it cost me $29.99. Thirty bucks down the drain. I was so angry at myself for wasting that money. Just because I hadn't been careful enough to check. But you...you buy a whole building. A beautiful building, but still. I guess what I'm really worried about is, are you sure about this? Do you really think you could be happy here, Beck?"

He looks at me and then he looks around, taking in the opulent room. "You know, Selah would have hated it. She wanted a big old mansion on Grandma's street. Somewhere she could hob-nob with the rich and judgmental. Sure, this place is shiny and cost a lot. But without the right zip code and neighbors to impress, what's even the point?"

"So we won't invite Selah to move in with us. That's decided," I say. "But what about you?"

"Do you really like it? Really truly?"

"It's like its own little world," I say. "A modern-day castle in the middle of the city."

"Does that make me Prince Charming?"

"Yes. And I am the poor common girl with bitchin' taste in T-shirts who has caught your eye."

"You've caught more than that and you can be the queen of my castle any day." His smile is slow and glorious. And he's so close, it's hard not be a little dazzled. "Alice, you're not freaking out anymore."

"I am not freaking out anymore."

"Good." His gaze is the very definition of serious. "I want this to be our home."

Not sure Beck's ever even had a real home before. Or at least not for a long time. As he said, living in a hotel isn't quite the same. And it's not as if his father (may he rest in peace) or his mother seem to have made much room in their lives for him. Catherine, his grandmother, is somewhat terrifying and ditto with her mausoleum of a mansion.

I smile. "Okay then."

Mrs. Francis is our new housekeeper. She is short, cheerful, and around fifty. Due to the place needing to be kept show worthy at all times for sale, the previous owners had kept her on and recommended we do the same. A cleaning crew also comes through three times a week. Beck can happily continue not picking up after himself. (That is a lie. I will do it because it drives me crazy otherwise.) Mrs. Francis has the staff we borrowed from the Heritage to move our personal belongings under complete control. The woman is an organizing aficionado. She's also sorted new sheets and towels and so on for us and made a pot roast for dinner. There's even a couple of thick pillar candles on the dining table for atmosphere. Once dinner is served, she retreats into the staff quarters in the front half of the ground level, where I presume Smith is also, and Beck and I are alone.

"Grandma has a staff of eighteen including gardeners," comments Beck, apropos of nothing.

"And?"

"It's okay for us to have two, beloved. You'll get used to it eventually."

"I don't want to." I lift my glass of white wine. "May this lifestyle always happily weird me out."

"But is it happily weirding you out?"

I think it over. "Yes, it is. I might still get nervous or anxious sometimes, but that's just me."

"Okay then." He taps his crystal glass gently against mine. "Here's to our first night in our new house."

I take a sip. "Oh, I meant to ask you, why are charities thanking me for funding their programs and inviting me to events?"

"Actually, that reminds me," he says, pushing a lock of hair back from his forehead. "Would you do me a favor?"

"What kind of favor?"

"I was hoping you'd just say yes," he admits with a frown.

"I'm sure you were."

"With the inheritance and everything, I'm in need of someone to head up the philanthropy side of things. Penny's been helping me set up a charity foundation and she suggested that you'd be an excellent choice for director."

"Director?"

"You'd be the public face and have the final word on what happens," he continues, cutting into potato and green beans. "There's money put aside, but someone needs to meet with the charities, decide where and how we can help. What do you think? Probably only take a couple of days a week. You could fit it in around what you're doing for The Crooked Company."

"Shouldn't you hire an expert?"

"I trust your judgment and I'd prefer to keep it in the family, so to speak. People appreciate a personal touch when it comes to these sorts of things," he says. "Besides, you're good with people; they like you. Imagine how much more they're going to like you when you're giving them money."

"But I sucked at that luncheon. Your grandmother still isn't talking to us."

He swallows his food. "Only if by sucked you mean completely rocked it. And Granny will give in and forgive us eventually. I think it quietly pleases her when people don't do what she wants. Gives her something to bitch about at tea parties."

"Doesn't that woman own like half of Elliot Corp.?"

"Not quite that much," he says. "And it doesn't mean she doesn't love a good tea party."

"You want me to do this?"

"Yes. But, of course, it's your call."

I think it over. "That's why Penny gave you a weird look at The Downstairs Bar when I mentioned my dislike of charity luncheons."

He shrugs. It's pure avoidance. What a sneak. "Question is, do you really hate the events, or did that one in particular just freak you out due to Granny's evil machinations?"

"Good question. I'll ponder it." I cut up some meat. "You'd think all of the years in customer service would make me more people friendly as opposed to less."

"Not sure if it really works that way. Plus, people."

"True."

A low resonant tone echoes from the front of the house. Next comes the soft sound of footsteps followed by conversation. One half of the conversation, however, isn't soft or discreet. It's loud and strident.

"Where are you two?" yells a familiar female voice.

"Having a romantic dinner on the first night in our new house," yells Beck. "Fuck off."

Emma marches in with Matías close behind and Mrs. Francis trailing in their wake.

"I tried to explain to her that this might not be the best time," says Matías.

Our housekeeper just stands there looking mildly flustered.

"It's all right, Mrs. Francis." I say to the flustered lady with a smile. "Thank you."

"No matter what this woman says"—Beck points at his sister with a stern face—"never give her a key or the security code, Mrs. Francis. Promise me on your life."

Emma scoffs. "Like I can't strong-arm Smith into giving them to me."

"He's twice your size," mocks Beck.

"Doesn't mean he's not afraid of me."

"Whatever you say, Mr. Elliot." The housekeeper disappears once more. Having staff is odd. I bet she's great at getting rid of door to door salespeople, but feisty Elliots are a different kettle of fish. Whether she'll want to put up with us long-term is the next question.

"This is nice." Emma turns in a circle, inspecting the place. "Never been a big fan of modern art, but the black on white brush style in that piece is interesting. Love the high ceiling. And you can't hear cars or the city sounds at all; the soundproofing is excellent."

"You already own a perfectly fine mansion." Matías protests, slumping into a seat beside me. "Emma, you don't need another property."

"An inner-city apartment, though. Wouldn't that be cool?"

"It's not even a twenty-minute drive from where you already live, Em."

She sighs. "I suppose so."

"She never did like it when other people got new toys," mutters Beck. "Christmas can be all-out war."

Emma also pulls up a seat, inspecting our dinner. "Pot roast?"

"Would you like some?" I ask. Because one of us needs to act vaguely hospitable.

"No." She sighs. "I'm still in the I want to hurl twenty-four/seven stage. It's like being constantly seasick without having the joy of being on a yacht in Ibiza."

Beck points toward the kitchen with a fork. "Dinner's in the fridge if you want any, Matías."

"Already ate. Thanks." Though the man is on his feet heading toward the kitchen and opening cupboards. "I'll have a glass, though."

Emma pouts. "You're just drinking because you know I can't."

"I meant a glass of water," says Matías. "And I'm getting one for you too." Can't tell if he's lying or not.

"I've decided we're having the baby and Matías is going to be a stay-at-home father," announces Emma. "We're going to give both therapy and marriage another go. It's not like we were really into the whole divorce thing anyway. Otherwise we would have actually finalized it at some stage and stopped sleeping together."

"Don't get us wrong, the separation was fun while it lasted." Matías returns to the table with two glasses of ice water. "But we're ready to move on and get back together now."

"Stay-at-home dad, huh?" asks Beck, setting down his cutlery. Matías nods. "Yep."

"Cool."

"We'll have a nanny too, of course," says Emma. "What if Matías goes out or something? I can't be expected to change diapers like an animal."

Beck just blinks.

"Don't get me wrong, I'm more than prepared to love and interact with the baby. I'm not Giada or Dad...or Grandma, for that matter. Did you know she never even fed, burped, or bathed our father? Not once. Like ordering a silver rattle from Tiffany's and dressing the kid in ugly lace frocks to pose for family pictures actually counts as making an effort." Emma folds her arms across her chest. Her boobs do look bigger. Not that I generally notice other women's breasts. But in the low-cut white sheath she's wearing, it's kind of hard not to notice.

"The tit fairy has been," she comments, noticing the direction my gaze has taken.

"Sorry," I say. For the tits or for looking, I don't know.

Matías leers. There's no other word. "They're wonderful."

"Whatever." Emma looks to heaven.

"Back to a topic that's not my sister's breasts," says Beck. "We definitely descended from generations of warm and loving people setting us the ultimate example in quality parenting."

Emma shakes her head. "Thank God for Mom."

"Thank God for Rachel," agrees Beck.

"You'll make a great mother too." Matías sits down and takes Emma's hand.

"I hope so." She frowns. "Oh, by the way, Giada has been spotted in London on the arm of an elderly lord. It's quite the scandal in the British press. The Elliot Corp. PR department are working on damage control, but basically we're all instructed to say no comment."

"Has anyone warned Henry?" asks Beck.

Emma nods. "I called him."

"Okay," says Beck. "Well, he can have one of the bedrooms

upstairs. I don't want him going back to Bertram Street on his own again."

"On that we agree. I'd be happy to have him at my place, but we always end up arguing for some reason."

"I can't imagine why," says Matías.

Emma just flips him the bird.

"Sounds like you'll be busy enough with the baby." I set aside the remains of my dinner. It was yum, but I'm full. "And there's plenty of room for Henry here."

The doorbell rings again and Emma smiles. "That'll probably be Penny and River. They were worried after the drama the other night, so I told them to come on over."

Beck just looks at her.

"What? It's like a housewarming and you didn't even have to organize it. You're welcome." She rises from her chair. "Come on through, guys!"

It's sweet really, how much they obviously missed him while he was away. How much they want to be around him now. For all of the hijinks and shenanigans, some of his family are great.

Along with the two ladies, Ethan walks in carrying a bottle of wine. He looks around, taking in the room. "Not bad. Though there's no real view, to speak of."

"I like it," says Aaron, entering behind them holding a bouquet of flowers. "It's got character."

Emma immediately confiscates the flowers. "They're beautiful."

"They're not for you."

Mrs. Francis gives us a concerned glance before helping Emma out with the vase. I just smile and nod. The poor woman. Guess she's used to actually announcing guests. Perhaps even dealing with people who show some sense of decorum. But she's rolling with it, which is great. Winston the majordomo would be having a meltdown by now. He'd probably attempt to send us all to bed without dinner regardless of age. Soon music is playing and more bottles of wine and sparkling water are being opened and we have a small party underway.

Beck leans closer to whisper in my ear. "Sorry about this, beloved."

"Don't be. This is nice."

It's been a while since I've been comfortable with people in this way. Surrounded by friends. And it feels like that's exactly what they're becoming. Penny and I talk about the foundation Beck has set up while River (who, it turns out, is a pediatrician) answers a barrage of questions for Emma and Matías. Ethan, Aaron, and Beck discuss his plans for the Boulder hotel among over things. It's nice to belong. To be a part of a close group. After the boyfriend from hell experience decimated my self-esteem, I shut myself away. That's the truth. I got hurt so I made my world small and safe. And being lonely was the price I paid. But I don't need to do that anymore and it's such a fucking relief.

Even with Mom coming, and his grandmother hating me, and the various disparities between us—I think everything's going to be okay. I really do.

CHAPTER FOURTEEN

"**M**OM?"

Smith escorts her in midafternoon the next day and I'm sad to say that the vibe is more dismayed than happy reunion. Guess after the phone call it's not a surprise.

I had started the day up in the library (huge, amazing, and full of a variety of books and lots of polished wood) working on a site for Matías. Beck could have the office, I preferred the big mahogany desk, comfy work chair, and general vibe of the library. And having coffee brought to me on a regular basis was beautiful. Housekeepers are the best thing ever, especially when they're combined with your own personal library. Brian, Beck's executive assistant, sent me a steady flow of emails regarding various charities. News of his father's passing and the inheritance that followed had obviously created a lot of interest from various groups hoping for help. So I read through some of those and made notes as well. Just in case.

But then Mrs. Francis asked for my opinion with regards to a few things. Those few things turned out to be dinnerware, silverware, crystal, linen, and a ridiculous amount more. Rachel sent over a sales specialist (not Selah thankfully) along with a bevy of people to carry things back and forth from the vans parked downstairs. A household of this size apparently requires a lot of shit.

And I don't ask for prices and nobody offers the information either. So there.

Beck must not have an opinion regarding any of it or he would have remembered it was happening in the first place. One of these days, when he yet again fails to warn me about something, I'm going to slap the boy right upside his handsome face. Or not so accidentally kick him in his sleep.

I'm helping Mrs. Francis with unpacking all the boxes when my mother arrives. Mom is tall with long gray hair pulled back in a braid. In all honesty, she's sort of a mix of suburban mom and hippie. Worn leather boots, jeans, and a plum-colored twinset. She's staring in either horror or wonder at the vast array of luxury homewares spread across every available surface. Maybe a mix of both.

"Hi," I say, pasting a smile on my face. "You're here. I thought you were going to text me your flight details so I could pick you up?"

Nothing from her.

"Mom?"

Her gaze moves to me. "It was fine, honey. A nice man from that hotel you were staying at drove me over. What is all this? Do you live here now?"

"Yes, we just moved. I'm choosing some things for the house. It came with furniture, but there's still a lot we need apparently." So much stuff. It's overwhelming. And now Mom is here. This day isn't going well.

Smith gives me a nod once it's obvious the woman is who she said she is, most likely isn't a hostile threat (at least physically), and I'm okay with her being here. Then he confers with Mrs. Francis before heading for the stairs with my mother's carry-on suitcase.

"It's great to see you," I say. Still in stunned mode, she doesn't react to me kissing her cheek. "Mom, this is our housekeeper, Mrs. Francis. Mrs. Francis, this is my mother, Heather."

Mrs. Francis smiles in welcome. "Mrs. Lawrence, it's a pleasure to meet you."

"Hello." Mom's voice is faint. Even worse, she looks at me

as if I'm a stranger. Like I've grown a second head or tentacles or something. A bit unfair considering I didn't even dress up today. My hair is in a low-slung ponytail and my makeup is minimal. I'm wearing skinny blue jeans, a flowing white silk blouse with long sleeves by Veronica Beard that makes me feel like I'm a heroine in a book from the fifties (though I've already managed to spill a drop of coffee on the front), and blue point-toe Iriza Half d'Orsay Louboutin flats. With the diamond stud earrings, of course.

All right. So maybe I look a little different. But I'm still light years away from being *Real Housewives* material. I smile. "Beck has gone to Boulder, but he should be back soon."

Meanwhile, two gentlemen carry in what looks to be crystal ice buckets. How beyond extra. The sales specialist, Toya, spreads out a selection of linen napkins. My mother's frown deepens with the arrival of every new luxury. This is so fucking awkward.

"Can I get anyone a drink or something to eat, perhaps?" asks Mrs. Francis. God bless the woman.

"Mom?" I ask.

She shakes her head.

"Why don't we give you and your mother a moment alone to catch up?" Mrs. Francis ushers everyone out of the room apart from my mother and me.

"I haven't joined a cult," I say. "But I have discovered what a salad fork is. Useful information, that."

Mom pulls out a dining chair and flops onto it like a ragdoll.

"How was your flight?"

"What on earth is going on here?" she asks, her brows arched high. "Who are you? What happened to my daughter?"

"Now that's harsh."

"Look at you!"

"I thought I looked nice."

"You don't even look like yourself anymore," says Mom, voice rising in volume.

"You'd be amazed what a keratin treatment can do." I pull out the seat beside her and sit down. "Mom, please, just calm down."

"This place...it's insane. I never..."

"Can't you be happy that I'm happy?" I snap, losing my cool. "Because I am, you know?"

She stops and stares at me. At least there's less horror in her eyes this time, more questioning. The lines of tension bracketing her mouth ease a little.

"I love this house. It's crazy, don't get me wrong. But I love it and this city too."

"Alice." The amount of judgment she manages to pack into one little word is impressive.

"As for the NDA, they just want to make sure no one attacks their family in the press or anything. It's honestly not a big deal." I take a breath. "As happy as I am to see you, I don't need saving."

She sighs.

"I chose these clothes, Mom. Along with the hair and the shoes and all the other stuff," I say. "But most of all, I chose him. And I chose him before I knew he had a black AMEX or had bought me so much as a bunch of flowers."

"Honey..."

"If Beck and I had to live together with no money back in that shitty little shoebox of an apartment in LA then that would be fine with me. It's true we've only known each other a few weeks and this is all moving fast. And it's true that I've been hurt before. But, Mom, that's not what's happening here."

She sighs one more time. "Are you sure?"

"Yes. I really am."

She reaches for my hand.

"I know that you love me and you worry about me," I say. "Thank you for that. But you need to ease up a little."

At this, she sniffles. "You look so grown up."

"I'll still need your help now and then." I smile. "For instance, right now, I'd dearly love for someone to help me choose a gravy ladle and canapé knives."

She gives me a glum smile. The woman is beyond unhappy and not even vaguely convinced. And I was so pleased with my speech too. However, Mom still looks vexed. "But aren't you lonely here without your family and friends? Moving halfway across the country like this with no warning."

Which is when Selah walks in, looking around the room with a faint frown on her face. Like she smells something bad. However, she meets the criteria of being both human and breathing so she'll have to do. I know it's a mistake before the words are even out of my mouth. Talk about making bad choices.

"Actually, Mom," I announce. "You can meet one of my new friends right now."

Selah freezes.

"Selah, what perfect timing. Come and meet my mother."

The petite brunette socialite's face changes from disenchantment to delight so fast it almost gives me whiplash. Fortunate, though, since I had no idea if she'd play along. "Hello."

"You're a friend of Alice's?" asks my mother. And sure, the woman in question is polished perfection, but there's no need for Mom to sound quite so skeptical.

I smile. "She sure is."

"I sure am," echoes Selah. "Alice and I actually have a lot in common."

"So true." Besides our taste in men, that's a complete and utter lie.

"I work for Beck's stepmother. But Beck and I go way back. Don't we, Alice?"

I grit my teeth. This was such an error in judgment. "Indeed you do."

"Rachel actually sent me over to see if you needed any help

making your selections," Selah inspects the table's contents. "Are these the items you've chosen so far? What sweet and simple style you have. I just love it."

"Shucks," I say. "Thanks, Selah."

"And this house!" Her gaze fills with distaste. "So interesting."

"You better be careful there." I fake laugh. "Beck chose this house and he absolutely adores it."

"He has the funniest taste sometimes. You just can't pick it." Her fake laugh is so much better than mine, dammit. "Speaking of Beck, I don't suppose he's around?"

"He's out."

"Hmm. I wonder if he'll put the mansion on Green Way Street up for sale now. It's been sitting empty for so long."

Given I have no idea what she's talking about, it takes me a moment to respond. That she knows things I still don't more than grates. "He hasn't said."

"How many properties does this young man own?" asks Mom, frown back in place. If it ever left.

"A few." I shrug. "Does it matter?"

Mom wrings her hands. "I'd just like to know who it is exactly that my daughter's involved with."

"Might I remind you that your daughter's a grown woman?"

"I don't blame you for being worried, Mrs. Lawrence." Selah smiles politely, doing her utmost to ingratiate herself. Suck-up. "Any mother would be."

"It's just that, relationships are hard enough when the couple have a lot in common and come from a similar background," says Mom.

Selah nods.

Give me strength. "Because enjoying each other's company, physical attraction, a similar sense of humor, and strong desire to be together means nothing of course."

Selah plays with the string of freshwater pearls around her throat. "As for his properties, let's see…there's this place, the Green Way Street mansion next to his grandmother's, apartments in New York, Paris, Oslo, and London, a house in the Hollywood Hills, and my personal favorite…his place in Aspen. We had some wonderful times there. Just really special moments, you know?"

She might as well come right out and say they fucked on a bearskin rug in front of a roaring fireplace. The girl can't do innuendo for shit. Is it wrong to want to turn her to ash and then salt the earth where she stood? Asking for a friend.

Mom's eyes are wide. "He must be very wealthy indeed."

"He's a billionaire." Selah smirks.

"And he's mine," I say, because enough of this shit.

The smirk fades.

"It was kind of you to stop by. But you can let Rachel know that Toya and I are doing just fine here. I don't want to hold you up any longer."

Selah's smile is all sharp teeth. "Of course."

"Could you also please pass on another message for me?" I ask. "If you could tell Rachel that my wardrobe doesn't need any further additions, that would be great."

Her gaze narrows. "I wasn't aware that she'd made any more purchases. But of course I'll pass your message on."

"Thank you."

"Goodbye, Mrs. Lawrence," says Selah. "Alice."

"Selah."

Mom waits for the sound of footsteps to fade before she whispers, "Are you sure she's your friend?"

"Would you believe frenemy?"

She tuts. "Honey."

Insert silent groan here. "Remind me to introduce you to Penny and River and Emma. They're much better. Well, maybe not Emma. Depends what mood she's in."

"These people," says Mom, expression pensive once more, "they're certainly different to what you're used to."

I shrug. "Some of them are good and some of them are bad, but most of them are somewhere in the middle. People are pretty much the same everywhere."

"But all of those houses she was talking about. The lifestyle that must come with that sort of money. The pressures and expectations from his friends and family." This is definitely not the woman who read me fairy tales as a child and encouraged me to wish on stars. This woman is much too sensible and fraught for that.

"It doesn't necessarily change who they are as people."

"It doesn't necessarily not."

"I'm having trouble telling if you think I'm not good enough for him, or he's not good enough for me."

Mom's chin goes up. "The second. Definitely."

"If a gorgeous, kind, hardworking billionaire doesn't measure up to your expectations for me, then heaven help us both!" I can't help but sound cranky, but I take a deep breath and get myself back under control. "Please don't decide you hate my boyfriend before you've even had the chance to meet him. That's not fair, Mom. I need you to promise to keep an open mind."

"Alice..." Her brows lower. "Yes. All right, then."

"Thank you."

A loud yowling announces Beck's arrival a couple of hours later. Dressed down in jeans and a gray Henley, he deposits a thing on the floor. A cat carrier, I guess. A demon cage, perhaps. Whatever is inside is not happy.

"So I found her in an alley behind the hotel," he says by way of greeting. "She'd been abandoned. Can you believe that? People are such assholes."

"Is that a cat or a gremlin?" I ask. "I'm having trouble telling by the noise."

Mom went upstairs to settle in and have a nap while I finished up selecting household items (anything minimal and classic in design could stay and the rest went back). If we lack sufficient champagne flutes, table runners, or diffusers then that's on me.

Beck unlocks the cage door and a scrawny black shorthair struts out missing half of one ear. She gives us both a pissed off glare with her pretty green eyes.

"I took her to the vet and she's a little roughed up, but fine," says Beck. "Got her up to date on all of her shots and everything. The vet said people still think black cats are unlucky and many of them get abused."

"That's awful."

Beck watches with pride. "I named her Princess."

"Of the Underworld?"

"No. Of all things sweetness and light and floofy." He slips an arm around my waist and leans in to give me a kiss hello before stopping cold. "You're not allergic to cats are you, beloved?"

"No."

"Phew."

Princess's tail keeps on flicking.

"Hello, Princess," I say.

The cat hisses at me. Then she makes a run for one of the sofas, diving underneath. Only her twitching tail remains in view, sweeping back and forth. We had a dog when we were growing up, but I've never actually owned a cat before. This should be interesting.

"I think that means she likes you," says Beck.

"Should we try giving her a bowl of cream or milk?"

"I'm sure she'd appreciate either. Mrs. Francis is sorting out her litter and food. How was your day?"

"It was a day."

"Yeah?"

I head into the kitchen, putting out a small bowl and grabbing the cream out of the fridge. Once done, I place my small offering near the chair she's hiding beneath. A cute little black nose sniffs at the air, then a black paw reaches out, dragging the bowl of cream back toward her safe space. Praise be. My humble offering has been accepted.

I wrap my arms around Beck's waist, going in for some necessary cuddling. "I got a start on the latest website and also did a bit of research into some local charities. Then I chose about a billion household items. Thanks for letting me know that was happening."

"Sorry," he mumbles. "Forgot Rachel texted me about that."

"Mom arrived and is currently upstairs having a nap. She's not happy, but hopefully I'll be able to talk her around. And I might have exchanged words with Selah."

"Selah was here?" He frowns.

"Yeah. I think she was hoping to talk to you. Not to be harsh, but she needs to be banned from the house. Wait. Let me rephrase that because I'm done with being nice. Nice is nothing more than a bullshit veneer that hides true meanings. Because every time I think we can get along, she proves me wrong."

He rests his chin on top of my head. "This is your home, dearest, and I want you to be comfortable. I'll let Rachel know that's the rule from now on. She can tell Selah."

"Thank you."

"Of course. You don't mind me bringing home a pet?"

Princess takes the opportunity to dash from underneath one sofa to another. Tail still twitching all the while. Guess she's finished with the cream.

"No, of course not. It's your home too." I smile. "And she's cute in an I'll eat your soul kind of way."

"She is, isn't she? Scratched the absolute shit out of the vet."

"Aw. Our sweet little diabolical fur baby."

He gives me a squeeze. "So the thing is, I had been hoping to take you on a date tonight to the Downtown Grill. Would you prefer I cancel that booking or ask for a larger table? I've given Mrs. Francis has the night off, but we can always order in from somewhere."

"I think ordering in might be safest."

"Done." He pulls his cell out of his back jeans pocket. "What are you in the mood for?"

"Mom likes sushi."

"Sounds good."

"How was your day?"

He grins. "The sale is going ahead; they accepted my offer."

"That's great news. Congratulations!"

He covers my face in kisses, making me laugh. "Thank you."

Mom clears her throat, standing over by the foot of the stairs. Mood officially killed. "You must be Beck," she says.

"Hello, Mrs. Lawrence." He walks toward her, hand outstretched. "How was your flight?"

"Call me Heather." Mom shakes his hand, giving him a still sort of smile. "Fine, thank you."

And then they both just look at me. I have a really bad feeling about this.

"Do you have to travel much for your work, Beck?" asks Mom.

We're drinking beers and making our way through a platter full of sushi at the dining table. Princess is hiding under an ottoman, giving us all the evil eye. Though she did come out to eat some cat treats earlier.

"I'm primarily based in Denver, but travel occasionally," answers Beck. "My mother is in New York and I fly out to visit her every couple of months, usually. I also have family in Denmark I try to visit at least once a year."

"Are your businesses only in Denver?"

"No." He dips a Philly Roll in some soy sauce. "I have interests in other cities as well."

"Such as?"

I shoot Mom a look that she chooses to ignore. What a surprise. Not. This is not table conversation. It's a goddamn inquisition.

"New York, Chicago, Phoenix, and LA," answers Beck.

"Will you expect Alice to travel with you?" Mom picks up another California Roll, placing it on her plate before carefully loading it up with pickled ginger. When Beck offered to open a bottle of wine, she asked for a beer instead. Which is such bullshit. At home she drinks Prosecco. This hyper-paranoid negative version of my mother is doing my head in and then some. She gives me a sad smile. "How are you going to be able to get a job, honey? Or are you planning on being a kept woman?"

"I actually already have a job," I say, voice getting cranky. "Two, in fact. I produce content for business websites, which puts my degree to use, and I'm also the director of philanthropy for Beck's company. It's a new endeavor he's taking on that I'll be heading up. When we travel, I can work on my laptop."

Beck raises a brow. So I hadn't told him about accepting the job. Oops.

"You're giving her a job?" asks mom.

"She earned it," corrects Beck. "Alice represented my family's company at a charity luncheon recently and navigated what could have possibly been a very difficult situation with great skill. She's good with people and they in turn enjoy talking to her. You should be proud of your daughter."

"Of course I am. But is it wise to work together?"

I shrug. "I don't see why not. Beck usually works at his offices at the Heritage or out on site and I'll be working from home. If we travel, I can work from wherever we are on my laptop."

"Surely you want to stand on your own two feet, Alice."

"In this economy?" I raise my brows. "I tried that already, Mom, it involved serving beer to jerks and being hit on."

"But you didn't try very hard. You could have moved back home and taken a serious look at internships—"

"You're right, I could have. I got discouraged and gave up." It's the truth. "That's on me. But now these wonderful opportunities have come my way and I'd be a fool not to take them."

"What if it doesn't work out between you two?"

"Then I return to LA and start over. With a better-looking résumé than when I left." I reach for a Shrimp Tempura Roll with my chopsticks.

Mom makes a noise. "Have a Tuna Roll, honey."

"I prefer these." Instead of just one I take two of the Shrimp Tempura Rolls. I'm mature like that.

Beck stares at his plate, one clenched fist resting on the table. Some bad vibes going on there. I don't think Mom's question about it not working out went down very well with him.

When Mom's frown fails to move me, she moves on to another topic. "Amy found a lot of photographs and nonsense written about you on the internet."

"Tell her to ignore it. I do."

"She's concerned."

"She has a baby and my brother to worry about. I'm sure my sister-in-law will get over it." I take a sip of beer. "How are your classes this year?"

"Oh, fine." Mom waves the question away. "Your typical teenage students. I can't wait to retire and be done with it all."

"I thought you loved teaching."

"I did. I do. I'm just getting old." She gives me a smile. Tired and resigned. But quite possibly the first genuine one since she arrived.

And I'd tell her about Henry. About how much fun it can be having him around. About what a pain in the ass he can be sometimes. Only she'd probably take it the wrong way somehow. See it as yet another reason for me to abandon ship and run home. A soft and fluffy thing winds around my legs. Leaning back in my chair, I watch Princess rub herself up against me. When she spies me watching, she hisses and dashes back to beneath the nearest couch. As you do.

"Did you see that?" I ask Beck.

He blinks. "What?"

"Princess deigned to acknowledge I exist."

"Oh, no. What a beautiful moment and I missed it." He grins. "Next time."

"Next time."

Mom just watches us with a faint frown. "Are you sure the animal is safe?"

"Yes," says Beck, back to his blank expression.

This has to be the most awkward fucking meal ever. Mom was always wary of boys who came sniffing around her daughter. Thinking they could only be after one thing (vaginal access). But by the time the male in question has flown you to Denver, bought a house for you to both live in, introduced you to his family, bought you a wardrobe and a car, and offered you a job...you can probably safely assume that his intentions are earnest. Especially given he has yet to put the moves on said vagina. Not that I'm going to share that particular bit of information with my mother. Our sex life, or lack thereof, can stay our business.

"Why don't we have Christmas here?" I ask, looking around the room. "We could get a big tree, invite everyone over."

"You're not coming home for Christmas?" Mom is aghast. Awesome.

"Would we both be welcome?" I ask.

Her mouth gapes. Answer enough.

"It's our first Christmas together in our new home," I say. "We haven't decided how we want to spend it yet."

Beck bushes his fingers over my hand. "Whatever you want, beloved."

"We could get Princess a special Christmas collar and everything."

"She would love that so much," he lies with great vigor.

"Right?"

Mom looks at us as if we're both crazy. Maybe we are.

"'I must learn to be content with being happier than I deserve,'" I quote. And it's nothing less than the truth.

"Hey, that was my line." Beck rises, kissing me on top of my head. He starts collecting the plates, pausing briefly to look at my mother. His gaze is cool. "You don't trust me. I can understand that. I wouldn't want some rich asshole coming in and sweeping my daughter off her feet either. Moving her to another state. Changing her life in big ways. Maybe you and I will learn to get along or maybe we won't. I hope for Alice's sake that we do. But whatever happens, don't ever again tell her what to eat."

Huh.

Mom stares after him as he takes the plates over to the sink. When she turns to me, the shock in her eyes is clear. Though I don't know why she's so surprised. Guess no one's ever stood up for me before. I've done plenty of it myself. Or did I just learn to ignore such shit? Those times at BBQs when she'd point out what piece of steak had the least amount of fat. Serving me the smallest piece of cake at birthday parties. Things like that. Ugh.

"Why don't I let you two catch up?" Beck heads up the stairs, not looking back.

I just wait, slumped back in my chair, sipping on my beer. How do you respectfully ask your mother to retract the stick from her ass? I knew there'd be resistance to my moving away and everything. This, however, is excessive.

Mom's hands sit in front of her, fingers tightly laced. "I had a friend in college who dated a rich boy. Tori, her name was."

"Wasn't she one of your bridesmaids?"

"That's right." Mom's smile is there and gone. Like lightning. "They were so in love. Just crazy about each other. They went everywhere together. Every party, every football game...you name it. There they were, joined at the hip. He even took her home to meet his family for Thanksgiving and he'd never taken a girl home before. It was fine at first. Everyone was perfectly nice. But then his family decided he was maybe a little too serious about this blue-collar girl. Her father was only a mechanic, you see? Her mother had passed. Tori didn't know anything about fitting in with the country club set. Didn't know the right glass to use. But they were determined to be together. Nothing could stop them.

"So after graduation they got married. She worked as a teacher, supporting them both, while he went to law school. It didn't matter that he'd been cut off by his family and they had to live in some rat-infested attic. They were in love. As long as they had each other everything was fine. For years this went on; Tori worked and he studied. He studied hard, graduated top of his class. His family finally came to their senses and accepted the young couple back into the fold. They bought a big mansion in Bel Air and lived the high life. Parties and galas and business dinners. Holidays in the south of France and skiing in Aspen. She changed to teaching at a private school and drove to work in a brand-new Mercedes and wore Ralph Lauren. It was fine. Until it wasn't.

"All of the little pressures just kept mounting up on her. The pressure to maintain that illusion of perfection. The pressure to always be in the right place saying the right things to the right people. The pressure to fit in and help her husband make partner. And all the while she was surrounded by these rich people living idle lives with poison pouring out of their mouths and not an ounce of kindness in them. I imagine it must have been like living under a microscope, constantly being watched, everyone just waiting for you to mess up so they could talk about it behind her back. No matter how much Tori and her man loved each other, it wasn't enough to combat that kind of constant pressure and stress. The cracks started to show and they divorced in the end.

"You can tell me it's not like that with you and your man. That he and his family and friends are different. That no one expects you to change to fit in. But I watched one of the smartest and strongest women I ever met get chewed up and spat out by just these sort of people. She moved to Scotland and he married a failed actress. The perfect trophy wife. It took Tori years to pull herself back together again." Mom sighs. "I don't want that to happen to you."

"Mom, be reasonable. I'm sorry things didn't work out for your friend, but I can't make choices based on someone else's life. For every possible situation there's going to be a sad story. An example of how it all came crashing down and ended in ruins," I say. "But Beck and I can only be ourselves and do what's right for us. And I need you to respect that."

Nothing from Mom.

"And as for your concerns about us working together...I've been flailing since I graduated, I know that. You and Dad knew that you wanted to go into teaching and that's great. But it's okay if I don't know exactly what I'm going to do for the rest of my life. I just have to make a start somewhere and that's what I'm doing here and Beck is a big part of that. He woke me up. He made me want more for myself."

She reaches across the table and pats my hand. "Okay, honey. My girl...you're just so young."

"You and Dad have been together since like two minutes after birth so..."

"Not quite that long." She gives me a dour smile. "I'm flying home tomorrow; I need to get back to work and your father. In the meantime, I'm going to attempt to be nicer to your Beck."

"I would appreciate that."

"But be careful. Please."

"I will."

"Your father and I are always going to be there for you," she says, looking me dead in the eye. "Do you hear me, Alice?"

My eyes are misting up. Fuck it. "Yes, Mom. Thank you."

CHAPTER FIFTEEN

"T HAT'S A SUCKY STORY." BECK KEEPS DRAWING PATTERNS ON MY back, the other hand tucked beneath his head as he stares at the ceiling. He's particularly handsome when he broods. "No wonder your mom proved so resistant to my charms and devilish good looks."

"To watch a friend go through that kind of thing," I say, mood equally somber. "She made it sound like class warfare. I guess that's how your grandmother feels about me. The commoner sullying her marble hallways. Bringing down the brilliance of her lineage and defiling her legacy and so on."

"I shall be your shield, beloved. Rest assured."

"That's sweet of you, but it's not really how it works. I mean, either I can handle the shit that comes my way or…"

"That sounds dire."

"No," I say. "Just matter-of-fact. I don't think any relationship worth having is always going to be easy. We're two different people with our own thoughts and feelings. The fact that we also come from two very different worlds just adds to the challenge."

"I can see your point. You do know you come first with me, though, right?" he asks, sounding concerned. "You're not doing this on your own."

"I know you've got my back." I smile. "And I've got yours. But this fancy-pants lifestyle of yours has some unique pressures and pitfalls. As Penny once said, there's a lot of competition for my position."

"They can all fuck off," he states matter-of-factly. "I'm not interested in anyone but you."

"Thank you. But you're often busy with work and I need to be able to stand on my own two feet here."

He studies me for a moment. "Alice, am I not home enough? Things have been busy since I got back and I'm hopeful that's going to calm down soon. But in the meantime, are you getting what you need from me attention wise? Because if not, we need to change that."

"I know things are especially busy for you right now. And I'm fine."

"Are you sure?"

"Yes, Beck."

"Okay. Tell me if that changes."

"I will. Oh, by the way," I say, "I hear you have a place in the Hollywood Hills. And London, New York, Oslo…all sorts of interesting places. Including the street your grandmother lives on.

His gaze is quizzical. "Let me guess, Selah?"

"Yes indeedy."

"The Green Way mansion is going on the market." He sighs. "Tomorrow."

"Is it the best time to sell?"

"I don't care. If it's upset a single hair on your pretty head, then I want it gone."

"My pretty little head is tougher than you think. Selling can wait until you're ready. It's just that you talked about how she'd have wanted to live there, but you didn't mention you'd actually bought a place." Let the record show, while I will survive, I am a little disgruntled at him not sharing this tidbit with me. "Guess it surprised me."

"I didn't mean for it to be a secret. Just prefer not to think about it. Like I said, I was serious about her. Right up until I found out she'd been lying about everything. I might not have loved her, but I did trust her." He moves his hand up to my neck, rubbing at the muscles there. Ah. Magic fingers. They go a long way toward forgiveness. "That was enough to make me stop and think about what I was really doing. What kind of life I wanted. What sort of relationship I was signing up for long-term. I don't want to be a carbon copy of my father."

"Mm."

"Are you upset I didn't tell you about the properties?"

"I imagine we would have gotten around to talking about them eventually."

He nods. "Most of them Mom uses more than me. Apart from the New York one—she's got her own place there."

"You didn't want to stay with your mom when you visited?"

"Not since she became a naturalist. Having friends over got too awkward," he says. "Then there was the sunning her perineum on the balcony thing. Plus, some people are really great in small measured doses. Know what I mean?"

"Yes, I do."

Another sigh. "Sorry I lost my cool with your mom."

"That was unfortunate. But she wasn't exactly being friendly." And I don't really want to talk about it. It's been a long day. So instead I listen to his heart beating away strong and steady inside his chest. He's here with me. We're okay. Despite all of the ups and downs and other people's opinions.

"Hey," he says softly. "Give me a kiss."

I climb a little farther up the bed, fitting my mouth to his. The taste of him is my ultimate aphrodisiac. A hint of mint toothpaste and Beck, pure and simple. What started out as closed mouth and easy escalates as swiftly as ever. He rolls me onto my back, opening his mouth and teasingly licking at my lips before diving within. We fit together so perfectly. His warm lips against mine, his tongue playing, cajoling. And the weight of his upper torso, pressing against me all the while. My breasts are crushed between us and they ache. Oh God, how they ache. I wrap one of my legs around his, keeping him in place. A strong hand grips my hip, encouraging me. It's fair to say we have first base down and then some. He kisses me hard and deep, showing me with his tongue what he'd like to do with other parts of his body. What we will eventually do. With my head in a spin, it's hard to remember why we're even waiting. And it gets me so hot, the way he grinds his hardening cock into my lower belly. My sex is definitely wet and wanting. There's so many things I want with him. I want him to touch me and fuck me and call me his. I already get a little of the last, which is nice. But I want it all.

"Fuck," he mutters in a low voice, hiding his face in my neck. "Alice..."

"Yeah?"

"Nothing. I just like saying your name."

"Okay, Beck."

His chest rumbles with soft laughter. "Not much longer now."

"I hope not."

"Hmm."

"Oh, I heard from the doctor's office. My birth control shot is up-to-date and working just fine. No STDs to speak of. A small unfortunate case of the black plague. Highly communicable, apparently, but on the plus side it should limit the amount of awkward dinners we have to suffer through in the future..."

"Good, good." His voice is faintly amused as he rises up to look at me. "Heard from the doctor as well. Both were instructed to send over paperwork so we can both be assured of the all clear. If that's still okay with you, of course, beloved."

"Of course."

"So...we could actually have sex one day."

He makes a happy humming sound inside his chest.

"Question is, are you feeling we've sufficiently bonded? That we've gotten to know each other to your satisfaction during this courting period?" I wriggle around, repositioning myself to rest my chin on his pec. Is it weird that I like sniffing him? Because I do. "You were concerned about these things."

He takes a moment to answer. "We've met some of each other's families and managed to do so without any blood being spilled. We've handled the living together and fitting into each other's lives thing. Though that's kind of more of an ongoing process. But I feel the initial stages have gone well. Have you found you think about it more or less since we decided to wait?"

"Sex? More. Because of course we've been together throughout all of that period meaning you're my specific lust object. At other times, it's more of a general notion to release some tension. Or you take a liking to someone and think why not?"

"Right." His hand slides beneath my sleep shirt to stroke his fingertips over the bumps of my spine. "Any fantasies in particular you want to share, dearest?"

"Well, there's the one of you in a French maid's uniform bending over coquettishly to dust things."

He laughs. "Nice."

"But then there's also the one where you're dressed as a fireman busting down the bedroom door to save me."

"Is the fire in question a metaphorical one happening between your legs?" he asks. "Because I could totally work with that."

I just smile. He makes me smile a lot.

"Gosh, I L you, beloved. Both as a person and as a woman with fabulous tits and a gorgeous ass."

"Why, thank you. I'm quite fond of you too. I think you're hot." I fake giggle. Actually, it's not that fake. Sometimes he does just make me feel sixteen all over again and giddy with hormones. Like I could put a picture of him up on my bedroom wall and stare longingly at it for days.

"I'm very glad you're here." With his other hand, he reaches over and switches out the light. "Sweet dreams of me."

And everything is so perfect and peaceful. I wish things could stay this way forever. Only with added boning, of course.

True to her word, Mom is polite to Beck at breakfast. Perhaps there's hope for future friendly relations after all. Beck almost messes up and offers her the use of the jet when she says her flight's been delayed. But he catches my look at the last moment. Normal people don't lend out their jets. That's a rich people thing. And we're pretending he's normal for her comfort's sake. Just until she accepts that he and I are long-term. Fingers crossed.

I drop her off back at the airport in my G-Class. She tries not to be impressed with the behemoth vehicle, but she is. Her subtle bouncing on the seat and asking about all of the features kind of gives it away. It's nice that she can enjoy some of the perks of my new lifestyle. Maybe it's just the whole house and everything being in her face that was overwhelming. Along with what happened to her friend way back when. Whatever. I obviously come by my worrisome nature naturally.

We part with hugs and she seems okay. At least the cult thing seems to have been put aside. Which is when my cell beeps.

Emma: Why aren't you here yet?

Me: What are you talking about?

Emma: Did I forget to tell you? Ugh. Baby brain. I need you at my place right now.

Me: What's wrong?

Emma: Just come to my place it's URGENT.

Me: Ok. Address?

The address is sent along with a screen shot of a map. Maybe she thinks I can't operate Google Maps. Who knows? And off I go as directed. Her place is past the Cherry Tree Mall in a luxe neighborhood. I'm buzzed through a security gate and drive up to the house. It's old and chateau style like Catherine's house only done in a white stone with a gray slate colored roof. Not as fussy as her grandma's despite the fountain and circular driveway leading to the front door. There's an expanse of green lawn and neatly trimmed trees. And an array of vans and people coming and going carrying bouquets of flowers and white linens and God knows what else.

Selah waits at the front door with a frown on her face. It only grows when she takes in my luxury SUV obviously purchased by my boyfriend. She swallows and pastes on a small polite smile. "Emma's waiting for you inside."

"What's this about?"

"I'll let her explain."

Inside there's a midcentury vibe to the furniture and decorating. It's low-key and cool. A white foyer gives way to a large living room where green velvet sofas and sleek teak coffee tables have been pushed aside to make more room. Arrangements of white and green calla lilies are being positioned everywhere. Champagne coupes are being arranged on a side table. A string quartet is setting up in the corner of the room. It looks like Emma is gearing up for the party of the century.

"Nice place," I say.

"Five bedrooms, eight bathrooms, heated pool, hot tub, cabana, indoor basketball court, gym, wine grotto, cigar lounge, dedicated massage room, and a home theater," rattles off Selah. "She got it at a good price too."

Huh. "Have you ever thought of getting into real estate?"

"My father would have an aneurysm." Selah tucks a strand of dark hair behind her ear. "Working with Rachel is bad enough. It's only barely acceptable because her family is old money and good friends and I refused to back down."

It must suck, having a family that doesn't support you. That tries to keep you contained to a certain role in life. I don't want to feel bad for her, but I do.

"Alice, hello." Rachel kisses me lightly on one cheek. Guess she likes me after all. Or she's doing a very good impression of same.

"Hi," I say. "What's going on?"

Rachel opens her mouth to answer, but is beaten to it by her daughter.

"Matías and I are renewing our vows. It's a surprise, meaning I haven't bothered to tell him yet. I only decided this morning." Emma sweeps into the room on a cloud of elegant shining white fabric. It's sleeveless with a bateau neckline, her hair done up in a simple knot. "I'm not sure about this dress. What do you think?"

Rachel sighs. She looks a little tired. "It's beautiful, sweet-heart. But then they all are. Is it pressing on your stomach?"

"No." Emma pulls a face, wriggling about within the confines of the material. "It's comfortable enough."

"Okay. So what can I do to help?" I ask.

"Oh. You're my bridesmaid."

"I am?"

"Yeah." Emma inspects the room. "I don't actually like any of my original bridesmaids, so you're up this time around."

My brows rise. "I'm honored."

Selah delicately snorts. I don't entirely blame her.

"Of course you are." Emma clicks her fingers. "You, musicians, play something. Let me hear you."

The string quartet rushes into place, conferring quietly before bringing up the agreed upon piece of music on their various tablets. The delicate strains of "Ave Maria" fill the air and Emma groans. "Boring. What else have you got?"

The musicians quickly confer once more.

Next comes "Pachelbel's Canon." I've worked more than one wedding in my time on the hospitality frontlines so my knowledge of this sort of music is quite good. And this is a nice piece. But again, Emma seems unimpressed. "No. Something livelier. A touch of rock, maybe."

The violinist contemplates this with a frown. "How about 'Bitter Sweet Symphony' by The Verve?"

"I like it!" Emma smiles, pleased. "And it's sort of funny, what with this being our second time around and everything. Play it. Hurry."

"I hope they're being paid well," I murmur.

Rachel makes a noise in her throat. "I'll be sure to tip them commensurate to my daughter's rudeness and demands. Now, your dress has arrived. Hair and makeup are upstairs. Selah, will you take her, please? Best behavior, thank you."

Selah's smile is brittle. "Of course."

There's a definite look of warning in Rachel's eye. Taking delight in Selah being treated like an errant child is petty of me, but oh well. Such is life. Guess Beck has been in touch with Rachel about his ex being banned from our house. A good thing. While my boyfriend is excellent at avoiding her, I seem to have to deal with Selah far too often. That needs to end. It still amazes me that Rachel even gave her a second chance given how she lied and manipulated Beck. Rachel's obviously a much nicer person than I'll ever be.

"Lead away," I say.

I've never been a bridesmaid before. And I'm more than a little curious about the dress they chose for me. With all of the people rushing to and fro, it appears this will be one hell of a party. At least things are never dull with the Elliots.

Beck: Heard from Emma. Canceled our restaurant booking again.

Me: I feel like the world doesn't want us to date.

Me: On the plus side, I like you in a tux.

Beck: Describe your underwear to me in great and salacious detail.

Me: Old sports bra with a hole in it under one arm. White granny pants washed about a hundred times so the cotton is really soft with some of the elastic coming undone around the waist.

Beck: Holy shit that's hot.

Me: Smokin', right?

Beck: Absolutely. See you soon.

Me: xx

My duties as bridesmaid include standing still while a seamstress makes a couple of small alterations to my classy cool Christian Siriano Infinite Tuxedo Gown in black (capped sleeves, V-neck, floor-length perfection and I will now be buried in *this* dress thank you). Followed by sitting still while the wonderful Tex yet again does my hair and makeup. Then hanging around for hours waiting for the ceremony to begin. Fortunately for me, I have a new book to read to while away the time.

Even with next to no notice, Emma has managed to fill the house with guests. There's formalwear and bling as far as the eye can see. Clutching a bouquet of white roses, peonies, and small blooming branches, Emma and I walk down the aisle together. It's easier to be brave in the face of all the attention with her striding along, setting the pace. In front of an officiant Matías and Beck stand, waiting for us. We're side by side, despite tradition, which is nice. But as Matías and Emma take their places, it leaves me lined up directly in front of Beck.

And the look on Beck's face is everything. It's love. Nothing more and nothing less.

As for me, emotionally I'm a mess. I know the day and the moment is meant to be all about Emma and Matías, but I can't help this and I wouldn't stop it if I could. Beck's somehow become my whole damn world and the way he's watching me makes me think I just might be his too. My heart hammers, battering against my rib cage. The sensation of falling in love with him is terrifying and wonderful all at once. I don't hear the words that are spoken around me. Don't think to clap and cheer when the happy couple kiss. It had to have been a beautiful ceremony because Emma doesn't do things in half. And despite all of the bickering, she and Matías seem to be deeply in love. They were certainly unable or unwilling to move on from each other.

But again, none of it matters. I stand opposite the man of my dreams and just stare. Guess I believe in the real thing in under a month after all. Because there it is, right in front of me. All that I want and need. When people start moving forward to congratulate the still married couple, Beck comes to me.

"You're doing it again," he whispers in my ear, hand sliding beneath the fall of my hair to cradle the nape of my neck. "You look at me like that, beloved, and I have nothing."

"You've got me."

"No, Alice. You've got me. The good and the bad and everything in between." His lips brush against my earlobe, his breath warm. "Don't let me go, okay?"

"Never."

"I'm going to hold you to that."

Waiters move through the crowd with champagne and sparkling water. Beck grabs us two glasses of the first and the party begins. Music plays and people mingle and it's wonderful. How could it not be with him at my side and my cleavage so perfectly displayed by the notched lapels and V-neck of this dress? Sometimes getting the girls out there and up there makes everything better. Not that I'm at risk of falling out. Rachel's stylists know their job. Still, wrangling the Spanx when I need to go to the toilet is a chore. Along with ignoring the women ahead of me discussing my various flaws when I was standing right there. I'm apparently a vicious bitch out to suck Beck and his family dry. Like

I even have those sort of energy levels. One swore she'd met me and I was nothing more than the low-class, fat-assed bimbo you'd expect. Nothing I haven't heard before. But seriously—what is it about bathroom visits that brings out the worst in people? Why can't we all just pee and live as one?

Though the look on their faces when they saw me was rather comical. Pretty sure I could take them, but like a true lady I refrain from starting a brawl in the bathroom line. Jane Austen would be so proud of me. What do some people find such joy in hating? In the thrill of being cruel?

Actually, I don't want to know.

Tables are set up in a lavish white tent with heaters outside on the patio. A selection of food trucks arrive serving Korean-Mexican fusion, Brazilian street food, specialty grilled cheese sandwiches along with mac and cheese, wood-fired pizza, gelato, and gourmet donuts. This wedding/vow renewal is nothing less than spectacular. There are candles and blooming branches decorating the tables. A bar is set up in the corner with a couple of mixologists hard at work and a DJ is spinning tunes. I've never had pizza with Bollinger before. It's an interesting mix of street and luxury.

With Emma and Matías busy mingling with their guests, we sit with our usual crew of Penny, River, Aaron, and Ethan. Beck goes to line up for our cocktails because he's an exceptional human being and my feet hurt.

I delicately wipe my mouth with a linen napkin, trying not to mess up my lipstick any worse than it already is. "I still can't believe she pulled this together in one day."

"The combined might of Emma's and Rachel's staffs could probably achieve just about anything," says Penny.

"But could they build Rome?" asks Aaron.

Penny laughs. "Nothing would surprise me. Nothing."

River gives me a serene smile. "Alice, don't turn around, but Catherine is sitting at the head table and has you in her sights."

"Fuck's sake," mutters Ethan. He glances over his shoulder and nods at someone before turning back to me with a grim expression. "Might be best to avoid her."

I nod. Nothing I hadn't already planned on doing already.

"Emma publicly coming out on your side and choosing you to be bridesmaid is only going to have pissed her off even more," says Penny.

"She needs to get a hobby." I want the peanut butter and jelly gourmet donut, but my belly is full. This is a problem. Would it be wrong to wrap it up in a linen napkin and take it home?

"Playing the evil dowager queen and interfering in all of our lives is her hobby," says Henry, appearing out of nowhere with a grilled cheese in one hand and a bottle of beer in the other. "Welcome to the family."

I frown. "Thanks, I think."

"That's your last drink, Henry." Ethan tips his chin at the beer. "Understood?"

"Yeah, yeah."

"Grandma probably also thinks this celebration is happening too soon after Dad died," says Ethan with a shrug. "I sympathize a bit there. But life goes on and Emma's always been prone to spontaneity."

"How's school?" I ask Henry.

"It's still there."

"Nice to know you haven't burnt it down yet."

Beck sets a cocktail in front of me. "Your gimlet made with Downtown Gin, dearest. And please don't give my younger brother any ideas."

With a mouth full of food, Henry laughs. Gross. Not something I needed to see.

"Why thank you, kind sir." I smile at Beck, taking a sip of the drink. Yummy.

"And I only had to fight off two mothers and one father

with daughters of marriageable age to return to you hearty and whole."

"Bravely done."

"Speaking of supposed maternal figures, Mom rang yesterday," says Henry, settling into a spare seat. "Wanted to tell me about the old bastard she's doing and how much money he has and the castle she's living in. Fuckin' pathetic."

Beck frowns. "Language. And don't talk about your mother like that."

"It's the truth."

"Let's play nice just the same, okay?"

"People grieve in different ways and not everyone is capable of being alone," says River wisely.

Henry just shakes his head. "So what room can I have at your place?"

"I think there's a cupboard in the basement that's available," answers Beck.

I grin. "I was thinking he could have that space under the stairs."

Henry rolls his eyes. "Ha-ha."

"Any bedroom apart from the master is fine," says Beck.

"Cool." Henry bobs his head. "Did you really bring a feral cat home?"

"Princess isn't feral." With a hand to his chest, Beck actually appears affronted at the thought. "She's just temperamental. You have to understand, she's lived a difficult and tumultuous life. What she needs now is our love, support, and understanding."

"Along with a rabies shot from what I've heard."

"Henry," I say warningly. "Be nice about the floof baby."

Henry snorts.

A throat clears behind me and a familiar voice says, "Ethan, Beck, Henry, your grandmother would like a word with you all."

Winston. Ugh. He's as uptight and unhappy as usual in a somber gray suit.

"I'm currently occupied." Beck meshes his fingers with mine. "But thank Grandma for the invitation."

Ethan sighs. "C'mon, Henry. Let's go and say hello. Leave the beer here."

Henry grumbles, but goes.

"Wonder what that's about," says Aaron, relaxing back in his seat with an Old Fashioned. "Actually, nix that, I don't want to know. Your family drama wears me out. In other news, I talked to that friend who might be a good match for the managerial position in Boulder."

"Excellent." Beck perks up. "Tell her to send her résumé over and I'll give her a call."

"Will do."

Selah is here, but keeping her distance. Hooray for small mercies. However, I can't help noticing the longing looks she's still casting Beck's way. Though I note there's also more than a touch of anger in those glances these days. The girl needs to move on with her life. Whether she's after closure or continuance, I doubt she's going to get either from my boyfriend any time soon.

As for Catherine, it doesn't feel good being at the center of all this drama. The cause of it even. But then it's not as if I started things. If Beck doesn't wish to talk to her, then that's his choice. And I can't really blame him. In days of yore, our elders were revered for their wisdom. Though when the elder in question is a real piece of work, it's hard to summon up the necessary respect. Still, I don't like him being on the outs with her. And for me being at least partly responsible for the situation.

"Are you sure you don't want to go say hello to Catherine?" I ask him quietly.

"Granny owes you an apology before that's going to happen."

As if. "She's already taken hits to her pride and her bank balance. I think that'll do."

He sips his whiskey, watching me over the rim of his glass.

"While I realize an admission of guilt is unlikely, you need to understand that Grandma only really respects strength. If I roll over too soon, she'll see it as a sign that she can keep messing with you. I'm not about to allow that to happen."

"I'm a big girl, Beck. I can stand up for myself. And she is your family. She's also old."

"Old enough to know better." He lifts my hand to his lips, kissing my knuckles. "You're tenderhearted, brave, and ridiculously sexy, beloved. But even family need to respect boundaries. Let's talk about something else."

"Okay." At least I tried. I'm not going to let her ruin our night. And what a night it turns out to be.

CHAPTER SIXTEEN

"**H**OW DRUNK ARE YOU?"

Back at home in our bedroom after midnight, Beck dips me. We're slow dancing to Lana del Rey and there are so few perfect moments in life. But this is one of them. We managed not to make out in the back of the Bentley all the way home. Got to say, having Smith to drive us sure came in handy tonight. No one had to count their drinks or abstain altogether. However, convincing Beck to keep his hands out from under the long skirt of my dress on the drive back was an enjoyable effort. His sly smile and dark gaze affect my head and my hormones both.

"Just buzzed," I say. "How about you?"

"High on life and you."

I smile. "You say the sweetest things."

"And they're all true."

With the Louboutin ankle strap leather high-heel sandals gone due to my sore feet, I need to reach up on tippy toes to kiss him. Not a chore given the reward. His mouth is warm and welcoming. His lips opening over mine and tongue taking possession. And I give, because giving to him is sublime. With my arms wrapped around his neck and him holding me to him I never want it to end. I could happily kiss him forever. It's hot and delicious. My head is giddy and my heart long since lost.

His mouth moves over my jawline, down to my neck, teeth biting just so. And he's hard against the soft of my belly making it all the more exciting. Sometimes romance just does include a hard-on digging into you and this is one of those occasions. The state of my panties is a given. My pussy's wet and wanting, more than ready for this to be done.

And the zip in the side of my dress goes down, the material easing around my breasts and middle, down to near my hips.

"Beck?"

"Do you want to?" he asks in a low voice.

"Yes." The man has no damn idea how much. Or maybe he does. We've both been waiting for just this moment for a while now. I pull back, breathing harder. "Let me just...I need a minute in the bathroom to get out of this."

"Can I help?"

How to explain the strictures of structural underwear and how truly un-erotic it is to this man. If I even attempted it, we could be here all night. I hold up a hand. "Just give me a minute."

"Okay."

In the bathroom mirror, my face is flushed, my lipstick worn away. Hair wild from his hands and nipples standing to attention. Holy shit. We're really doing this. We're actually finally having sex. Thank fuck. Seriously.

Without the seamstress and Selah, it's a bit of a job to wriggle out of the dress. To wrestle with the Spanx. However, Rachel and Emma didn't stint on the nice stuff. My panties are Fleur du Mal black lace with a matching demi-bra. Quick check: My breath seems okay and my pits don't smell. But a spritz of perfume after a long day never hurt anybody who didn't have allergies.

And I'm revealed, all of my lumps and bumps. It's fine. So maybe I pause for a moment, but fuck it.

Beck sits on the end of the bed, jacket and bowtie gone along with his shoes and socks. He looks good disheveled, undoing the cuffs at his wrists. When he sees me his gaze gets stuck, his jaw goes rigid. It's like he's keeping a tight rein on himself. "Beloved."

"Hi."

The cufflinks spill onto the floor as he holds out a hand. "Come here."

No idea what he intends, but I know what I want. I straddle him, breasts brushing against the fabric of his shirt, hands sitting on his shoulders. His grip on my hips is firm, the expression in his eyes full of lust and adoration. It's a good feeling, to be safe and wanted this way. I don't think I've ever had it quite like this before.

He gives to me too. That's what makes this work.

I'm shaking for some reason. I don't know why. My fingers slip over the buttons on his shirt, taking longer to get them undone. Mostly patient, he waits.

"Are you sure about this?" I ask.

"Yes." At long last, I push the shirt off his broad shoulders, revealing the smooth skin beneath. "Are you, Alice?"

I nod.

Unlike me, he doesn't fumble. The clasp on my bra is undone in a moment. The man has skills. "Mouth."

I do as told, kissing him hard, my hands cradling his face. His firm lips move beneath mine, his teeth nipping my bottom lip. Like a tease, the straps of my bra are slowly drawn down my arms. I have to let him go to get fully rid of the thing. Now we're both bare from the waist up and it feels so good. Skin to skin is amazing. He takes my breasts in his hands, fingers kneading my flesh and taking their weight. All the while, his hard cock is right damn there. To ask me to sit still would be impossible. Not when I could be writhing and rubbing myself against him, turning us both on.

My whole body is restless with wanting, primed from needing. And Beck's heart beats so damn hard against the palm of my hand. I'm definitely not alone in this.

"More," he says.

Our kisses get longer and wetter, our mouths battling it out. Only we're both winning. I pull on his hair and he growls. The man actually fucking growls. Hotter than hell. Then he grabs me by the waist and rises, turning and tossing me onto the mattress.

"Up," he orders with a jut of his chin.

I hustle my ass up the mattress until I can rest my head on a pillow. And the show he's putting on meanwhile. I don't even blink. Gaze on me, he undoes the buckle of his belt, the button and zip on his trousers. Down they go, to rest on the floor. Next his thumbs dig into the waistband of his black boxer briefs, tugging them down.

I would pause here to write odes to the magnificence of his dick, but there's no time for that. Or words, apparently. My head is sex scrambled. Pheromones have me undone. Large, yeah, and wow are about the best I've got. Along with gimme, of course.

Like some big animal he climbs on after me. My new expensive lingerie is dragged down my legs and sent sailing to join the other accumulated detritus on the floor. Mrs. Francis would be appalled.

Heated gaze on my face, he grips my calves and spreads my legs wide, making room for himself. Then he's there. He's right fucking there, cock lying against my wet cunt. His hips pin mine against the mattress. But the rest of his body hovers above me as he takes his weight on one elbow.

"You're so fucking wet," he says.

"Yes."

His pelvis shifts back and forth just a little, sliding his length against the lips of my sex. I swear my eyes roll back in my head from the sensation. Not saying I could come from it alone. But it's a hell of a promising start.

"Condom," he says. "Yes or no?"

I frown in confusion. "Condom?"

"It's your choice."

"Ah, well, we're both safe and have done all the tests and everything."

"So that's a definite no?" he asks, clarifying.

"Yes. No." I blink. "Um. What I mean is, that's a no to the condom question. Not that I—"

With nil preamble (apart from everything we've done since we met), he reaches down, grabs his dick, lines it up with my sex, and rams the fucking thing into me. Just shoves it in. No finesse at all. The air is pushed from my lungs, my body suddenly full to bursting. All I can do is grab his shoulders and hang on. And it's so good, having all that heat and hardness inside of me, stretching me just so. To finally be one with him. But still…

"Jesus, Beck."

"I may be a little overexcited." He rests his forehead against mine, face tortured. "Just give me a minute. I swear I know how to do this."

I'd laugh, but there's no air. He's so raw and exposed right now. We both are. I raise my chin, press my lips to his. I also wrap my legs around the man on the off chance he tries to get away. Then I kiss him some more, sweet and soft. "Take all the time you need."

We're both already panting and sweating. He takes the kiss deeper, angling his head, rubbing his tongue against mine. And I like that. While he holds his weight on one arm, the other hand slides down my body, fingers just trailing over my skin. Right up until he grabs my thigh and stirs that big cock inside of me. Holy fucking shit.

He groans. "You feel so damn good."

"So do you."

Then he really starts to move, working himself in and out of me. Pulling that thick length way back until the head of his cock teases the sensitive tissue near my entrance, before gliding back in. He's right, I'm ridiculously wet. And getting wetter all the time. It's the feel of him, the scent of him, and the sound of him whispering dirty things in my ear. Like how he's been needing to fuck me since the first time he saw me. Like how I'm going to be on my back in his bed every day from now on. I heartily approve of both of these things.

With every motion, his chest brushes against my breasts, making my nipples ache. He grinds the base of his cock against my clit and I gasp. No doubt, he knows how to do this. Not that I ever really doubted. He goes harder and faster and everything just gets better. Especially when he reaches down between us, rubbing all around my swollen clit. My fingernails dig into his back. I just need something to hold on to, something to keep me grounded. Because my blood is running hot, everything low in my body tense and tight. I'm right on the edge.

"Fuck. Beck."

"C'mon," he coaxes.

It's like lightning, the sensation he sends crashing through me. Electric and blinding, shocking and real. You could even say it was heaven sent, delivered via Beck. It just feels that good. My mind is blown, my body shaking. He labors on top of me, slamming his cock in once, twice more before coming hard. Then we're two sweaty skins plastered together thanks to body fluids. The weight of him heavy and wanted.

I wrap my arms around him since no other limbs are currently working. Just lie there and wait for my pussy to stop quaking. For some kind of cognizant thought process to kick in. Anytime now. No rush.

Which is when Beck draws his still semi-hard cock out of me and collapses at my side. It's quite dramatic. Nice to know I'm not the only one affected.

"Are you still alive?" I ask.

"No."

"That's sad."

"You killed me."

I roll onto my side and rise up on one elbow. "Oh. Sorry."

His glistening cock lies against his hip. It's quite the impressive appendage. "Stop staring at my dick, you siren. It's needs a minute, then we'll go again."

"Okay."

He winces, lifting one shoulder. "I think you Wolverine'd my back."

"A couple of scratches won't kill you. Stop being such a baby."

"Come here," he says somewhat grumpily. "I want to cuddle."

"All right." I smile, fitting myself against him, laying my head on his chest. His arm comes around me and everything is perfect. It's considered the height of romance and best etiquette to yawn so hard your jaw cracks after great sex. Just ask me. "Sorry. It was a big day."

"Close your eyes, beloved. You'll need your stamina for later."

He's a smart man. So I do what the smart sexy man says. And my sleep is both deep and peaceful.

I wake up aching. Skilled fingers pinching my nipples, teeth embedded in my shoulder. The boy is an animal in bed. He draws an invisible line down my body, from my breasts to my pussy. Teasing and thrilling me along the way. My skin is all goose pimples. The heat of his hard body at my back is such a turn-on. No doubt about it, we should spend as much time skin to skin as possible. It's going to take a while for me to get my fix.

"Beck."

"Hmm?"

"What are you up to?"

He draws my leg back over his, making room for him to slip his cock into me. Sex on your side first thing in the morning is a hell of a hello. He angles his hips, pushing in deeper. Deeper than I thought he could go. His hand is back at my breast, thumb rubbing back and forth over my hard nipple.

"Just making up for lost time," he says, voice rough and low.

"That's what you said at three." I happy sigh as he draws back, before pushing back in again. Adding a little roll of his hips for good luck and good times. "And then again at six."

"It's just after nine now, beloved. Time for your breakfast fuck."

"We should have pancakes." I gasp as he hits a particularly wonderful spot deep inside of me.

"Excellent idea."

Then there's no more talking, because the man is fucking me into oblivion.

I add some more bacon and another pancake to my plate before heading back to the dining table. The same table where Beck is lounging back in his seat watching me with a coffee in hand. A leisurely breakfast after a big night is a beautiful thing.

"What?" I ask with a smile.

"You're walking funny."

"I am not. Shut up," I hiss. "And if I am, whose damn fault might that be?"

"I recommend icing followed by a relaxing tongue massage."

"Keep your body parts to yourself for a while, Beck. I need a break." I wave my fork at him in a vaguely threatening manner. Then I check that Mrs. Francis hasn't wandered back into the room. Because it's all fun and games until the housekeeper hears you talking about sex.

Beck smirks. Bastard.

"And get that look off your face."

"What look?"

"That self-satisfied smirk you're wearing."

Princess dashes out from underneath a couch to hide beneath my chair. I tear her off a small piece of bacon and drop it on the ground. She picks up the food and is gone again.

"That's spoiling her," says Beck, taking a sip of coffee. "You're teaching our firstborn bad habits."

"No, I'm buying her love. It's a different thing entirely."

"Babies, both fur and skin, need these things to be stated in plain language." Beck turns in his chair. "Princess, we love you."

From underneath the couch, the cat hisses.

"Do you think she should have her own Instagram account?" asks Beck.

"No."

"Okay. Want to go back to bed after breakfast?" he asks, all innocent like.

"No. Again." I laugh. "I'm serious. I need a break."

"I meant to nap and watch movies."

"You did not. Besides which, we have a media room we haven't even used yet for that." I load up my fork with the perfect ratio of maple syrup-soaked pancake to bacon. "Keep it in your pants until I say otherwise, thank you."

"It's like you don't care about my large penis at all," he says with a sniff.

"I'm not dignifying that with a response."

"But you don't deny it!"

"The lack of care or the size?"

"Both," he says, faking so much indignation. The clown.

It's hard to keep the smile off my face. "Of course I care and as for the second I can only assume you're fishing for compliments."

His tongue plays behind his cheek. Guess he's having a hard time keeping a straight face too.

"But yes, it's very large," I admit.

He punches the sky in victory. "Thank you, dearest. And just so you know, your cunt is world-class."

"Thanks. Are you really taking the day off?" I put the food in my mouth. Mrs. Francis really knows her way around a griddle and I respect her skills heartily.

"Yes," he says. "We're having a date day."

I finish chewing. So much yum. "What does this date day entail, exactly?"

He sighs and stares out into the garden. Outside is all gray skies and autumn colors. A no doubt cold wind blows the remaining leaves from the bushes and potted topiary trees. "Last night was a big one in all the ways. So I'm thinking we get food delivered, binge a TV show…things like that."

"Sounds good."

Which of course is when his cell goes off. He picks it up with a frown, finger moving across the screen. "Shit," he mumbles.

"What?"

"I'm needed in at Elliot Corp." He frowns. "Emma's on her emergency second honeymoon in Paris and Grandma's laid up with a headache. Ethan needs me to go in and sit in on a meeting. Be the second signatory on a contract. It shouldn't take long. I'm sorry, beloved."

"It's fine," I say. Something that turns out to be the biggest lie of all.

CHAPTER SEVENTEEN

"**M**RS. ELLIOT."

Catherine looks around the library with a we-are-not-amused type of expression. Lips a fine line and gaze cranky. The Queen of England couldn't beat her for attitude. She's in a white Chanel suit with low matching pumps. You couldn't ask for better armor to intimidate your opponent. Especially since I'm in jeans, white T-shirt bodysuit, and the blue Louboutin flats. None of them are up to defending me against Beck's grandmother when she's in a mood and wearing haute couture and a frown.

I give Mrs. Francis a nod and she backs out of the room, closing the door behind her. But not before I spy Winston waiting outside. Neither of us is smiling. Catherine sure has a way of setting a room at unease.

Since Beck had to work I figured I might as well also. The latest website from Matías is finished and I've identified a local newspaper doing solid journalism and a food bank who could both use donations from the foundation. It feels good, spreading the money around. God knows my boyfriend doesn't need it all.

"Beck isn't here right now," I say, standing at the desk.

"I know."

I just wait. Whatever her game is, I'm not playing.

With all due elegance, she perches on the chaise longue. Unlike the office at her place, there's no real throne-like chair here for her to rule from. Sucks to be her. "An interesting choice of home."

"We like it."

"All of the noise and filth of the city right outside your doors. I daresay you do."

Ouch. I retake my seat because keeping the desk between us seems wise. The woman might be elderly, but she's also nasty. She looks down her nose at me and I just want her the hell gone. "What can I do for you, Mrs. Elliot?"

"You and my grandson looked very cozy last night."

Again I say nothing.

Her jaw shifts. In anger or frustration perhaps, I don't know. "Alice, you've had your fun. It's time for you to go. I had hoped Rachel would see to getting rid of you, by money or might, but that wasn't the case. She's always had a weak spot for Beck. I should have known better than to entrust the task to her."

I take a sip of water for my dry throat. Conflict always sets me on edge. "Did you really expect Rachel and me to arm wrestle it out or something?"

"I expected her to see to the family interests in this delicate time so soon after my son's death." Her nose goes higher in the air. Much more and she'll give herself a nosebleed. "Not support Beck in his endeavors to make you palatable. As if a makeover and some decent clothes could fix the problem. Let alone his having Matías offer you a job."

"Beck didn't ask Matías to—"

"Of course he did," she says, voice cold as ice. "He couldn't have you serving beers to drunkards in some dive. A waitress... how ridiculous. I'm surprised there aren't peanut shells on the floor in here to make you feel more at home."

I frown and keep my mouth shut.

"Did you truly think you'd been given the job on your own merit? How laughable. You with neither experience nor a clue. Of course, Matías has always been hostile and treacherous when it came to the family. The perfect example of why not to marry outside one's class." She smiles and it's a cunning, malicious thing. "Beck forgot that people talk. They listen and look for an ear to whisper in."

"You spoke to Selah at the party," I say, and it all makes sense. How many conversations have Emma and Rachel had in front of the woman, not suspecting what she might do with the information? Broken hearts and dreams can turn to rage and cruelty so easily. To think I'd almost felt sorry for the bitch.

Catherine continues on, "It's amusing when you think about it. He detested Selah for wanting his wealth and power. Yet he used the same damn lures to draw you in, to attach you as securely as he could to him and this place. A job to keep you busy and make you feel important. A charity foundation to ingratiate you into his social circle. All of the clothes and jewelry and the car to make you hunger for more and more."

"That's not true. The clothes were from Rachel. And the jewelry. They were her doing."

"Where do you think the money came from? The authority to buy it all? From me? From Ethan?" She scoffs. "Don't be a child."

I can only stare.

"Not that I imagine it took much to reel you in. He had you hooked the moment you set foot onto the private jet."

It doesn't make sense. Except it does. Beck's been lying about so much. So many big and little things both.

"And Beck never had any interest in establishing a charity foundation until you came along. I love my grandson, but he's always been a soft touch." She pauses for effect. "Writing checks for anyone who puts their hand out. No, it was all to prop you up. I'd imagine he told you otherwise when it came to that too."

She's right. Not that I'm about to admit it.

"So here's what we're going to do," she announces, hands clasped together over the top of her walking stick. "You're going to take what you've been given and go back to California where you belong. The contract you signed will ensure you're well recompensed for your trouble. You will not contact my grandson ever again."

Beneath the desk, my hands are shaking. "And if I don't?"

"Why would you want to stay? He's lied to you and controlled you from the first moment you met. He won't change, because it's in his blood. It's all he knows."

I glare at her and repeat myself through gritted teeth. "And if I don't?"

"You seem to care for him, despite knowing the truth. Hardly a surprise. That's the point of control, after all. That's why he does it. Why we all do." She smiles grimly. "So let's test that affection, shall we?"

"What are you going to do, Catherine?"

"First, I'll ensure he's voted off the board of Elliot Corp. I love my grandson, but I won't tolerate disloyalty or any further poor choices from him at this time." Her rheumy gaze narrows. "Secondly, his new enterprise, this chain of boutique hotels he's so keen on establishing. I'll ensure he's outbid every time."

I snort. She has a fucked-up way of looking at the world. Of loving people.

"Thirdly, he'll no longer be welcome in Denver society if you're by his side. Do not underestimate my influence here."

"You don't know him at all," I whisper.

"What? What did you say?"

"I said, you don't know your grandson at all." I sit back in the seat, forcing myself to relax. "He walked away from the company, the money, the power, all of it...and that scares the shit out of you, doesn't it?"

"Watch your language," she hisses.

"Why is it people like you always call for civility and niceness while behaving like absolute assholes? It's phenomenal." I shake my head. "Get out, Catherine. Go back to your castle and count your money. No wonder the only people who stand at your side have to be paid to be there."

Slowly, she rises to her feet. "He will tire of your vulgarity and scheming. Mark my words."

"Scheming? Me?" I laugh. "Wow."

"You are nothing but a leech to be broken beneath my foot."

I look to heaven, but there's no help forthcoming. Not much of a surprise. "'Are the shades of Pemberley to be thus polluted?' Blah, blah, blah."

She screws up her wrinkled face. "What?"

"Let me summarize." I get to my feet and march to the door, throwing it open. "Get the fuck out!"

"Beloved, why are you sitting in the dark?"

A fitting metaphor for my state of being. I'm in the chair at the desk where I've been for hours. It's not night yet. Not quite. Through the tall windows, the last of the gray evening light filters through, casting the room in long shadows. A half empty bottle of Downtown Gin and a fine collection of empty little tonic bottles surround me. Just like the ones you get in hotels. Classy.

"Mrs. Francis said Grandma came calling. Are you okay?" Beck switches on a lamp, illuminating the library. He kneels next to my chair, so handsome in his black suit. It hurts to look. The cut of his cheekbones and the love in his eyes. How badly I want to touch him, to just be with him. But here we are, all fucked up.

"You've been lying," I say, voice dead of emotion. My eyes hurt from crying and my throat feels scraped raw. "Haven't you?"

His dark brows lower.

"It wasn't Rachel's idea to take me shopping and shine me up. It was yours."

"Alice…"

"And it wasn't Matías's idea to give me a job either," I say.

"You asked him to find me something. But I bet that's not all. What else have you been lying about, Beck?"

His jawline goes rigid. But he doesn't deny it.

"The watch and the diamonds and all of those things that just appeared in my wardrobe that you swore you had no idea about. No wonder Rachel looked confused when I asked her to stop. I'm so stupid."

"You're not." He wraps a hand around the armrest of the chair I'm sitting in. His knuckles stark white from the fervor of his grip. "Alice, listen to me, okay? Just listen. I wanted you to be happy here. That's all."

"That's all," I agree. "But what else have you been lying about to achieve that aim, hmm?"

He pauses, turning his face away. Every line of him is tense and stressed. "It wasn't because I was ashamed of you or didn't think you were enough."

Does it make it a lie if he won't meet my eyes? Or is that my old insecurities creeping in? Hard to tell. I can't imagine there have been many moments like this in his life. When he's clearly in the wrong and being called on it. When lawyers couldn't be called in or money won't make it go away. I'm not sure his parents ever cared enough to censure him and no one else probably had the guts. He's on his knees, but his broad shoulders shift agitatedly beneath his suit jacket. As if he'd like to rip it apart at the seams Hulk style and just start roaring.

"Look at me and tell the truth," I say, my smile false. "You wanted to hook me on the luxury lifestyle too. Throw me some diamonds to keep me pacified like your daddy used to do."

He stares at me from beneath his brows. So locked down. I can't read him at all. His gaze is like a shut door. "That's not true. I wasn't trying to buy you."

"Bullshit," I say. "Of course you were; it's what you know. All of your good intentions, your search to find someone apart from this. Then you couldn't help but drag me in too. And I fell for it. How long do you think it would have taken before you resented me the same as you do Selah?"

"I wouldn't—"

"You would have. I've been sitting here for hours trying to figure out why you felt the need to lie, but it's just what you know, isn't it? It's what you've seen and been taught. You spent six months wandering the wild lands away from all of this splendor and learned absolutely nothing." And I sound bitter. So damn bitter. "Now tell me. What else did you lie about?"

His nostrils flare like some pissed off bull. Confession clearly isn't his thing. "It wasn't Penny's idea to make you head of the foundation, it was mine," he admits. "I thought you'd be more open to it if you thought it came from someone else."

I nod, breathing hard.

"The watch and those things like you said."

"Yes," I say.

"I didn't find Princess on the street, I got her from a shelter."

"Why the hell would you even lie about that?" I scrunch up my nose. "Seriously, it's insane. What's wrong with you? Are you a compulsive liar or something? Can you not help yourself?"

"I just wanted you to stay," he shouts, the words taut like they're being ripped out of him. "I thought the more reasons I gave you, then the greater likelihood that would happen."

"The jewelry wasn't working as well as you'd hoped so you thought you'd try a pet. Holy hell." I sag back in the chair. "Beck…"

"They were just little things."

"Were they, though? Were they really?"

He looks so lost, like a little boy. I kind of feel bad for him. For both of us.

"I don't think so. Because to me they were everything. They were what we were trying to build a relationship on."

My laughter is devoid of humor. "God, you're such a hypocrite. You wanted to be so careful, take your time and build our foundations strong, and you were lying all along?"

"I just wanted to give you reasons to stay."

"You were my reason. Just you. Don't you get that?" I ask. "God, I am so fucking angry at you right now I can't even think straight."

His grabs my arm, his grip bruisingly tight. "Alice, please."

"You're hurting me. Let go."

Without a word, he does as asked. We both stare at the lingering red marks left by his fingers. He swears quietly. "I'm sorry. I didn't mean to...I'm sorry."

"You should know, your grandma threatened to have you thrown off the board at Elliot Corp. if I stayed," I report. "She also said she'd ensure you were outbid on any further hotels you tried to purchase and would be *gasp horror* unwelcome in Denver society. Just so you know..."

A deep line sits between his brows. Like for a moment, he's not even sure if he believes she could spew such poison.

"Do you want me to leave?"

"Of course I don't want you to leave." His fingers curl into fists. "It's bullshit. She doesn't have the bids or the necessary level of support to oust me. As for the rest, I'll deal with it. You don't need to worry about any of that."

"Okay. I'm tired...I just...I want to sleep," I say, wavering as I get to my feet. He reaches out to steady me, but I hold my palm up in a stop signal. The alcohol didn't help in the least. I'm not numb. My heart is a raw open wound. Messy as fuck. "The bitch of it is, I thought you got me, I thought we understood each other. I felt safe here and now that's all shot to shit."

He rises, moving in slow motion like he's hurt. "Tell me what to say. How do I fix this?"

"I honestly don't know."

"What are you doing?"

It's around eight the next morning when Beck looks up at me. "Alice. Hey."

"You slept on the floor?" I ask, standing in the doorway to one of the fourth-floor guest bedrooms. Still wearing yesterday's clothes. They're crumpled, since I slept in them.

The fourth level is set out much like the ones below. An open area in the middle with a sitting room and powder room. Bedrooms and bathrooms to the back of the building, and media and games rooms at the front. But Beck isn't even lying on the nearby couch. Nope. He's sprawled out on the floor with his suit jacket balled up and put to use as a cushion beneath his head. Princess naps on a nearby antique side table.

After our talk, I'd needed some space. Guess he either didn't get the message or figured a few yards would do.

Still nothing from him.

"Beck, you slept on the floor outside my door?"

"Yeah."

"Why?"

He winces, sitting up. "Several reasons."

"Such as?"

"Well, firstly, if you'd needed something during the night then I could have gotten it for you." He climbs to his feet, shoving a hand through his messy hair.

"I didn't even know you were here." I frown. My system is running on insufficient coffee and Advil for this level of crazy.

"But you would have found out if you'd opened the door. Like you just did. And also if you'd wanted to tell me off some more I'd have been right here within easy hearing."

I shake my head, stepping around him to head for the stairs. "I can't deal with this right now."

"Is there anything I can do?"

"No."

"I, ah, was pretty surprised when you weren't in our bed last night." He follows close behind, down the steps and into our room. "You didn't have to go upstairs. I would have given you your space if you'd said that's what you wanted."

A grunt from me. Hangovers make me surly. Same goes for being betrayed.

"If you'd just said—"

I make an about turn outside my closet. "I want space."

"Oh. Okay."

Inside, I grab some clean jeans, a long-sleeve tee, and boring cotton underwear. Today the glamor care factor is so low it wouldn't even register. Today I officially do not give a fuck. And all the while, Beck stands out in the bedroom and watches. How this is giving me space, I don't know. But I don't have the energy to argue.

"Alice, I'm sorry," he says, his expression blank. "I promise I'll never lie to you about anything ever again."

I sigh.

"I called Emma, got the name of her favorite therapist." He swallows. "Later I'll get an appointment."

"That's a good idea."

I make for the bathroom on the other side of the room. Of course he follows. But I'm excellent at ignoring people when I choose to do so. Just watch me go. I dump my clothes on the bench and grab a pack of Advil out of the cupboard before downing the recommended dose. Next I brush my teeth, because gross. Gin, mornings, and heartbreak do not make for good breath.

He leans a shoulder against the door jamb, watching me all the while. I don't have the heart to shut the door in his face. Maybe I should, but I can't. In the mirror, his forehead is furrowed. "Are you planning on leaving me…just out of curiosity?"

"I'm still here."

He nods, thinking it over. "It occurred to me that perhaps I hadn't groveled sufficiently given the situation and everything. I haven't particularly had occasion to grovel before. If a girl was pissed at me over something then I tended to just ignore it or move on. But I have reason to believe that should I apply myself to groveling I would be quite excellent at it. If you'd give me a chance?"

I finish rinsing and spitting.

He clears his throat and says, "'You are too generous to trifle with me.'"

"Do *not* quote Austen at me!"

"Sorry."

I get busy stripping out of my clothes. Almost strangling myself with my tee due to anger management issues. "I want honesty and apologies. Nothing else."

"Yes, Alice. I'm sorry. I never meant to hurt you."

Hot water is the best fix for my current situation. Hot water and lots of it. I step into the shower and get busy, using my favorite facewash and a soap that smells of rosehips, washing and conditioning my hair. The end result is that I'm still angry, but I smell much better. Towel wrapped around me, I stand back in front of the mirror and drag a brush through my nest of hair.

"Please, stop. You're tearing it out," says Beck, taking over the job. Being tired and cranky, I let him. He's much gentler with my locks, carefully working out the knots with a look of concentration on his face. "Just between you and me, I was kind of terrified you'd leave and I'd never see you again. That's why I was camped outside your door. I figured at the very least, you'd trip over me in the dark and I'd slow you down. Imagine my surprise when you didn't even attempt to make a run for it."

"I don't forgive you yet. But like I said, I'm still here."

Gaze on his task, he nods. The man works diligently until the brush pulls easily through my long hair. If he decides being a billionaire isn't working out, he might just have a future as a lady's maid. We don't talk for a while. It's enough to be near each other. And despite all of the shit he's put me through, I still want to be near him. Love sucks. He hands me back the brush with a small sad smile. "There you go."

"Thank you," I mutter.

"Can I say just one more thing?"

"What?" I ask. Without a word, he gets on his knees before me. I back my towel clad ass up against the bathroom bench, but there's nowhere really for me to go. "What are you doing?"

"You didn't totally nix the idea of groveling so I thought I would try some. Very sincere and apologetic groveling at your feet."

"Beck…"

Then the idiot grabs the sides of my knees, leaning his forehead against the slight round of my belly. He's basically talking straight at my barely covered crotch. "Alice, I'm so fucking sorry I lied. You were right, I was following my father's handbook. Doing things the Elliot way without even giving it a second thought despite all of my bullshit about wanting to be different."

I don't know what to say.

"I acted like a dickhead and you deserve better."

"Yes, you did. And I do."

"Let me make it up to you." He presses his face into one of my thighs, his hands sliding up the back of my legs. His warm breath brushes against my sex. "Please, Alice."

"You knew your grandmother was out to get me and you left a wide-open fucking hole in our defenses with your bullshit and lies."

"Yes."

"You're meant to be my person. The one who's always on my side. And yet you were working against me this whole damn time."

"I'm sorry."

"God, would you stop this and get up?" I groan. The tickle of his breath against my crotch is confusing me. Turning me on when I'm trying to shut him down. Of course, the problem is that after waiting for weeks we'd only just started sex and now we've crashed headfirst into this wall. My body cannot have what it wants. Not right now. "I feel like shit and I need coffee. Once I'm thinking straight, then I'll decide how we're going to handle this and what it will take for you to fix it."

"I can smell your sweet cunt." He takes a deep breath. "Let me start making it up to you now."

I press my thighs together.

"I can make you feel better." He looks up at me, gaze so hot and full of promise. Just the sight of him on his knees before me makes me wetter. This is so confusing. My anger is righteous and all consuming. On the other hand, I'd kind of like to ride his face. Dammit. This cannot be happening. Being attracted and wanting him right now when we're in crisis and need to be dealing with serious shit is ridiculous. What a weak-willed woman I am when it comes to him. Though the weeks of deprivation, minus one night, don't help. His hands grip my ass cheeks, massaging the flesh. While his nose nudges my mound. "Let me do this much at least. Let me make you feel better."

"I am *furious* at you."

"Understood. I deserve it." He nods his head eagerly. "But let me lick you. Then later, once you've come, you can kick me to the floor. Hell, I'm already halfway there. It'll hardly take any effort on your part at all."

"Shut up."

His hands pry my legs open just a little. Just enough for him to tease around my clit with the tip of his tongue. Tingles shoot through me at the sensation. I'm not going to win this battle. I am going down. Or rather, he is on me.

The stubble on his cheeks grazes my inner thighs and

everything low in my belly tightens. My stance widens further, giving him better access. I grab hold of the bench behind me. He guides one of my legs up onto a nearby antique wooden chair. Because rich people have fancy chairs in their bathrooms for some damn reason. And he doesn't hesitate, shoving his face into my pussy. Like the first time we had sex, his hunger apparently outweighs any desire for finesse or skill. He just wants what he wants and what he wants is me. Fingers spread open my sex and Beck eats me like a man starving.

"Fuck," I gasp.

His tongue lashes me from my back entrance to my clit. Over and over he does it as if he can't get enough of the taste of me. The muscles in my thighs quiver and pleasure shoots through me. Any alcohol in my blood is probably long gone. But this high is even better. Hot and heavenly. His lips suck at my labia, lavishing attention on every single inch of my cunt. No part of my sex is neglected.

"I am s-so mad at you."

With one hand he tears the towel from my body, exposing my hard nipples to the cool air. Then he makes a humming noise and jams his tongue into my opening. In and out, mimicking the fucking he'd no doubt like to be doing. Given my shaky hungover condition, it's a wonder I don't take longer. Make him work harder. But the pressure inside of me mounts and mounts. It's like sunlight and rainbows and the sweetest of daydreams. Only it's coming at me like a cannon ball. Sensation tearing through me, racing down my spine. My mouth opens on a moan and every part of me tenses. I draw tighter and tighter, each molecule in me singing. Until the wave of bliss rushes through me. And still he doesn't stop, but he does ease back a little, giving my sex gentle licks and soft kisses. Every so slowly my brain comes back to Earth. My panting echoes in the quiet room and a fine film of sweat covers my skin.

Beck just looks up at me, the lower half of his face damp and glistening. I have magic come in this lighting, apparently. Nice to know. The way he looks at me is reverent. Hopeful, even. But when he speaks, his voice is subdued, "I know...you're still pissed at me."

"Not even great head can fix everything."

"Great?" He raises his brows. "Well, thank you."

The need to touch him is second nature. I can't help myself. I reach down, running a fingertip across his wet mouth, down to his damp chin.

"Pussy juice," he says, licking his lips. "Best facial moisturizer in the world."

I just shake my head. I honestly don't know whether to smile or cry or what. Coming hasn't helped anything. There's still this ominous storm inside me. A break in my beating heart.

Slowly, he rises to his feet, grabbing me another towel. He wraps it around me, tucking it in at the front, as if I were a child in need of care. Then he hands me my pile of clothes. "Why don't you go get dressed, grab some breakfast," he says. "I'll be down soon."

And I want to say something, but I don't know what.

Holy hell, this sucks. We're both hurting so badly. But if I forgive him too soon, too easily, will it happen again? Am I setting us up for failure? We're talking a lifetime's worth of bad habits and a crappy family culture he needs to take a long hard look at here. And yet we're both so damn miserable. Not to forget, it hasn't even been twenty-four hours. No wonder some people run away when things go wrong. This is hard.

"We need to talk," I say.

"Okay. Go get some coffee. I won't be long."

Guess this time, he needs some space. A chance to deal with what's straining the front of his suit pants, perhaps. Under normal conditions, I'd offer to return the favor and make him come. However, these aren't normal conditions. What is the sexual etiquette when your relationship is the thing that has been fucked?

I nod. "See you downstairs."

CHAPTER EIGHTEEN

"WE'RE STARTING OVER," I SAY, CUP OF COFFEE NESTLED BETWEEN my hands. "Again. And we need to get it right this time."

Beck sits opposite me. His hair is still wet from his shower and he's dressed in jeans and a tee like when we first met. "I'm listening."

"I'm moving into the bedroom on the fourth floor for a while and I'd prefer it if you didn't sleep outside the door again."

A barely perceptible flinch from him. I'm hurting him and that sucks to unreached depths, but this is where his lies have brought us. However, he doesn't try to talk me down or anything and I'm so damn grateful for that. There's hope for us yet. There has to be.

"I think we should go back to the start and try dating again." I take a sip of coffee. My hand is shaking, dammit. Now is not the time for weakness. "Things were so rushed between us. We haven't even known each other a full month."

A nod.

"That's it. That's all I've come up with so far."

Mrs. Francis made a pot of coffee and set out a plate of pastries before disappearing. I can't even stomach the idea of food. The sun shines in dully through the floor-to-ceiling windows. Today the whole world seems cold and gray. His cell sits on the table buzzing, but he ignores the thing.

"Okay," he says, the words coming slowly. "I'll stay off the fourth floor, but I'd like to have breakfast and dinner with you each day. Let's consider them dates."

"That's a lot of dates."

He shrugs. "How else are we going to get past this if we don't spend time together?"

"All right. Agreed."

"Thank you."

"And you're going to regularly start seeing a therapist?"

Another nod. "I'd like us to do couples therapy eventually."

"That sounds like a good idea." I keep my body contained to my side of the table. Because as comforting as it would be to hold his hand, we need to establish some boundaries. Especially after the accidental oral. "I also think any use of the word 'love' should be delayed for now. I'm confused enough."

"You want total honesty from me?" he asks, gaze set on my face.

"Yes, but..."

"But what?"

I swallow. "It's just a lot right now."

"It is, however, the truth," he says. "And that's what's important, right? I love you. That's a fact. I don't think maybe I'm in love with you or there's a chance of strong emotions in me regarding you at some future date. I love you and that isn't going anywhere."

"Beck, we—"

"I belong to you whether you want me or not." His shoulders are set, his gaze sure. There's no hedging or doubt in his voice. "That's the truth, Alice."

I shake my head; it's too much too soon. Or maybe I'm just scared. A bit of both, perhaps. "I need to feel like I can trust you with me again. And right now, I'm sorry, but I don't. Let's just...let's talk about it later. What are you going to do about Catherine?"

"I'll deal with her. You don't need to worry about that."

"Since she dragged me into this, I'd like to know."

He takes a deep breath. "Full transparency."

"Yes."

"Okay," he says, gaze narrowing on me. "I made some calls last night. The first one was to my grandmother to strongly suggest she stay the fuck out of my life. She was surprised, to say the least. Guess she'd thought she'd run you off and I'd never hear about her threats and other assorted bullshit."

"Huh."

"Makes me wonder what else she's gotten up to in the past that never made it back to me." His fingers drum against the table. "Then I called Ethan to let him know Grandma might be attempting a hostile takeover."

"She'd try to take over the company?"

"As I might have mentioned before, Catherine isn't used to not getting her way. Her reaction to me calling her out was…intense. So there's no telling exactly how far she might try and take this," he says. "Some people will never be okay with hearing no."

I raised my brows and downed some more coffee. This mess just kept getting bigger and bigger. On the table, his cell buzzed. "Beck, should you check that?"

"This is more important."

"You should be in at Elliot Corp. sorting this out right now, shouldn't you?"

"No, Alice. Talking to you, working us out, is more important."

"But she could kick you off the board."

He shrugs. "She can certainly try."

I slump back in my seat and just take a minute. No matter how much I'd like life to slow down, it's not going to happen anytime soon. This is the reality of our situation. Me bitching about it or dreaming it was otherwise won't help a thing. Mom always said you had to recognize the things you could and couldn't change. What lies within your purview? Beck is a busy rich man dealing with big important things. Not that my life, wants, and needs don't matter. But you support your partner. My own parents showed me this time and again. How you present a united front to the world and have each other's backs. No way will I accept less in my life. "I'm here. I'm not going anywhere. I'm giving us a chance to sort this out."

And on his face there's the hint of a flinch again.

It hurts my bruised heart to see it. "Hey, I'm serious. I've been fighting people for the right to be here with you since I landed in Denver. I'm not giving up now, no matter how mad I am at you. Now check your phone."

With a sigh, he picks up his cell. "Ethan's called four times."

"Go take care of business. I'll see you for dinner tonight."

"Are you sure?"

My smile is small, but it's there. "Yes."

"Ask me why I'm not in Paris."

"Emma?" I sit at the small antique desk in my new bedroom on the fourth floor. Mrs. Francis and Smith helped me move some clothes and other assorted necessary items. We found the chair and desk on the second floor. After yesterday's drama, I'm not ready to face the beautiful library again just yet. Using the desk and chair is much more adult than working sprawled across the bed (despite being super comfortable). Especially since it seems to agitate Mrs. Francis if she can't make the bed up with half a dozen decorative cushions and keep the room in some semblance of order for me. "What are you doing here?"

The petite blonde stands there in a red sweater dress and black knee-high boots. Hair and makeup immaculate. Behind her lurks Matías, leaning against the doorjamb like he's posing for the cover of GQ.

"Good God, Alice, you look terrible. Grandma called me. Then Beck called me. Then I called Ethan followed by Mom. Lots of opinions, emotions, and hot takes, let me tell you. Phew. Now

296 | KYLIE SCOTT

it's time for you and I to talk." She points an accusing finger at her dapper husband. "You wait out there. You withheld information. That was a poor choice on your part, Matías."

He sighs. "So you said the entire flight back from Europe."

"Apologize to her."

He turns his handsome visage my way. "Sorry I lied about the job, Alice. But you were really good at it and I'm hoping that you'll agree to continue with the work."

"I don't know," I say, despite the fact it's what I'm currently working on. All of the males in this family get away with shit far too easily, in all honesty.

"She'll consider your offer. But you'll need to at least double her rate of pay. Now stand out there and think about what you've done," instructs Emma before shutting the door in his face. "Idiot males."

She frowns at my new room. It's neither as big nor as grand as the master bedroom, but I didn't think it was that bad. Perhaps it's just that I'm using a different room. Makes sense.

"When was the last time you ate?" She opens the door once more. "Matías, Alice needs some lunch. And some sort of green smoothie to help her complexion and energy levels. She looks like hell. Go. Fetch. Hurry."

There's grumbling, but he goes.

I just watch. "I appreciate the concern, but the fact is we barely know each other. Why are you really here, Emma?"

"Because my idiot little brother messed things up with you and someone needs to fix the situation and that someone is apparently me." She turns in a slow circle, taking in the room with her brows drawn. "He's at my therapist's office then he's heading back into Elliot Corp., by the way. I find it can be useful to keep track of them. Have you thought of putting an app on his phone?"

"Beck's with your therapist already?"

She nods, still looking around, her expression vaguely un-impressed. God knows what she'd have thought of my old apartment back in California. Horror, most likely. "You're really moving out, but staying in the same house? How does that even work?"

"It's between Beck and me."

She continues on, ignoring my comment completely as only an Elliot can do. "Why don't I make some calls and we'll have a spa day. Girl talk, massages, the whole shebang. We'll get this shit sorted out and get things back to normal in no time."

"Emma, I appreciate the thought, but please stop."

Her shoulders sink. "He really screwed things up with you, didn't he?"

"Yeah, he did."

She takes a deep breath. "So how big an apology present are we talking? Ten million? Twenty?"

I channel some calm. "Emma, I know you mean well, but we're going to have to sort this out on our own."

Her bottom lip trembles. "But if I can't fix things then I'm going to feel very out of control and unhappy. Do you really want that on your conscience?"

Fuck me.

"I'm pregnant. My mood swings are very violent and I'm meant to stay calm," she says, voice rising in pitch at an astounding rate. "Beck and you fighting is not making me calm, Alice."

"Okay, okay. He can buy things to help make it better. Just not for me."

"Not for you? Okay, I can work with that. Let me think." She pulls her cell out of her handbag, shooting off a text. "This is all such a mess. Beck called yesterday wanting the number for a therapist. Then Grandma called wanting to know if she could rely on me if a certain family matter she refused to name came before the board. I told her there was no way I could make a decision without more information. Next Ethan rang to warn me Grandma was being cagey and not to commit to anything. I mean, no shit."

"Right."

"And Grandma called Mom and went off about your foul language and general unsuitability. Told her all about the conversation you two had because Grandma has never understood when she's gone too far. Mom told her off for interfering. Gave her quite the serving apparently. Mom also finally kicked Selah to the curb for repeating conversations and other information she'd overheard in the workplace. A total privacy violation. The stupidity of the girl is awe-inspiring. By that time I figured we just needed to get on a plane so I could come sort this all out. Are you going to give me your version of events or what?" Emma takes a seat on the edge of the bed. "Talk to me, Alice."

"Basically, he lied and some of the things he lied about wouldn't have even mattered to me, but he still felt the need to lie."

She shakes her head. "What you need to understand is that males are just naturally less intelligent. Especially when it comes to emotions and relationships and...everything really. The list is endless."

"I'm not sure that's backed by any actual science."

"No. But it makes sense, doesn't it? Do you know why I kicked Matías out over a year ago?" she asks, head cocked. "Because his assistant was in love with him and he refused to see it. She'd text him about work at all hours. Make overly familiar little comments. Even cooked for him. Casseroles, cookies, you name it. I can't cook for shit, but like we didn't already have a chef on staff. And Matias refused to see it, flat out would not set boundaries with the woman. Even when she turned up for the second time all dressed up with surprise urgent documents for him to sign when she knew that I'd be out. Such bullshit!"

"Huh."

"He suggested we go to therapy to deal with my jealousy issues. When all along, he just needed to tell this woman it was never going to happen."

"I had no idea," I say.

"Nice guys are the worst. So clueless. It wasn't even like I was insisting he fire her or something. He just needed to wise up and set some limits."

"That's very reasonable of you, really." I'm not saying I'm surprised, but I am. "Not sure I'd be that nice in your shoes."

"Don't get me wrong—I wanted to kick the girl's ass. But she's not the one who made me promises. He was. And the thing is, despite all of this, he's still the one. I knew it all along. There he is in my head, up on a little pedestal flashing me his smile." She groans. "I can't help it. I love him. A thing Mom once told me that seems pertinent is this: even heroes fuck up sometimes. At the end of the day, they too are only human."

I snort. "She has a point."

"So, tell me everything that went down between you and my little brother. Don't leave out a single detail."

"Oh, I'm not sure—"

"Alice, I like you. I don't like many people," she states. "I especially don't like many of the people who've tried to date my brothers. Even the rare ones who did happen to make them happy upon occasion. Maybe you and Beck will get back together, maybe you won't. But sometimes you just need to lay everything on a friend. I'm sitting right here. Let me be that for you."

And regurgitating the whole thing is going to hurt. That's a given. But then, keeping quiet and isolating myself has done me absolutely no good in the past. The exact opposite, in fact. It's a bad habit I need to break. Because I haven't even tried reaching out to my own family or friends yet. Meanwhile, Emma just waits, her gaze patient and understanding, even. She's been here too. That was the point of her sharing the story with me. Heartbreak sucks and keeping it to yourself doesn't make it any better.

"Okay," I say, the stupid tears coming all over again. "All right, I'll talk."

In the afternoon, Mrs. Francis delivers an item of mail. Only my first name is scrawled on the front. Inside the envelope there's a copy of the contract I signed. Someone has helpfully highlighted the section on what my payout would be should the relationship with Beck be terminated. There's also a smaller envelope full of ashes, weirdly enough. NDA is written on the front. Guess I'm no longer bound by that. There are also copies of emails detailing donations to the various charities and businesses I'd been recently researching. Which is great for them. It's a start.

Living in this bubble of depression sucks. I want to shake it off, but it keeps right on weighing me down. If the harm done by the idiot in my last year of college stung, then Beck's betrayal is about a million times worse. Every part of me feels hurt and I hate being this fragile. That's he's in pain too just makes it a million times worse. I also hate not having an answer for how to instantly fix things between us. Maybe I should go back to college and do some more psychology. Learn about relationships, maybe.

Someone, however, who isn't in school where he belongs is Henry. "Fam," he yells, banging on the bedroom door. "Open up."

I do as asked. The expression he gives my messy bun, jeans, and tee is not so polite. First Emma and now him. No shit I don't look my best. I'm going through some things right now. Sheesh. Also, Ethan is waiting silently nearby. I also spy a black tail swishing agitatedly beneath a nearby sofa. Poor Princess. It can't be easy being a floof baby when your newly adopted parents are going through some stuff. She has to be picking up on the weird vibes. Or having a weird dream while she naps. Or has gas. One or the other.

"What the hell are you doing up here?" asks Henry.

Such a judgmental family. I frown. "Why aren't you in school?"

"Why are you and Beck fighting?"

"It's complicated."

"Bullshit."

"Language," I say, warningly. Then I reach out to touch his hand. He allows this contact for like two seconds before giving me a you're being weird look. Teenagers. What can you do? "It's good to see you, Henry. Are you okay?"

"What do you think?" he asks, tone somewhat aggressive.

Ethan raises a hand. "Hi, Alice. He called and said he needed to talk to you so I figured I may as well just bring him."

"Hi, Ethan."

Henry slides past me and slumps onto the bed. His dark hair is slicked back, his usual smirk replaced by a somber expression. "Grandma wants me to support her in taking control of my shares from Ethan."

"What?"

"Even if she did, she still wouldn't have the votes necessary to kick Beck off the board," says Ethan. "Don't worry."

Thank goodness for that.

"It's all such bullshit," says Henry.

"Language."

He rolls his eyes. "Whatever. You need to fix things, Alice. Beck is miserable. Grandma is harassing me. Everything's wrong."

"I'm sorry."

"Then talk to Beck and sort things out."

I shake my head "Henry…we're working on it, okay? It's just going to take some time."

"Fucking adults." He looks to heaven. "You're always messing up everything and making it ten times more difficult than it needs to be. He's sorry, okay? He's an idiot; of course he screwed up. Look at our family history—we're bound to be terrible at this sort of thing. But it's nothing you two can't fix."

I turn away for a moment. "How is school going? Is everything all right? It's really is good to see you."

He curls his upper lip, body tense. "You're being fucking selfish, you know that?"

"Henry," snaps Ethan. "That's not okay. Apologize."

But instead, he kicks back hard against the base of the bed before throwing himself out the door and pushing past Ethan. Hoodie pulled up, he heads for the stairs.

Ethan sighs. "It's a tough situation for him. There hasn't been a lot of stability in his world lately."

I just nod. My throat is tight and sore. Again.

"I get this is none of my business, what's going on between you and Beck," he says, not looking at me. "But don't underestimate how important you are to him."

"Thank you."

"Henry had a point about us not learning anything good from some of the authority figures in our lives. It's not an excuse, but... just keep it in mind."

"Yeah."

He lifts a hand goodbye. "If you need anything, call me. I mean that."

"Thank you." And I'm crying once more. God, this sucks. It completely fucking sucks.

There's a knock on the door around seven and Beck stands there with a tray. No idea why the sight of him still sets me metaphorically on my ass. Angry or not, I turn into this gasping swooning creature around him. A woman who needs to ease up on the emotions. Because it can't be healthy, going from heaven to hell and back again several times in the course of one day. However, something in me eases at the sight of him. Some anxiety that's been churning inside of me all day. He's still in the jeans and tee, only with an added cool black leather jacket. And seeing him reminds me of what Emma said. About how even heroes fuck up sometimes. Because Beck is definitely my hero, set up on a pedestal inside my head. It's a fact and it probably doesn't make life or being in a relationship with me any easier for him. Maybe we both need to bring our expectations down to a more reasonable, livable level. Neither of us is godlike or infallible.

"I come bearing food and this disgusting-looking drink for some reason," he says.

"Apparently my complexion is shit."

"Ah." He braves a smile, but it doesn't quite stick. "Well, I brought my dinner up as well since we said we'd eat together. Would you like it in the room or…"

"Why don't we sit out here on the couches?"

He sets the tray down on the modern-looking glass and metal coffee table, taking the seat across from me. Princess lurks beneath, watching us with those pretty green eyes. Dinner is salmon with béarnaise sauce and steamed vegetables. Two slices of pecan pie with whipped cream sit on the side. My stomach grumbles at the scent of food. So I've been surviving on drama and caffeine. As you do.

"Heard you had some visitors today," he says.

"It was a day, all right. Almost your whole family dropped by. It's nice that they care. Though I'm a little worried about Henry."

"Try not to be. Ethan promised to take him snowboarding on the next school break. I might go along with them."

"That's a good idea. I think he'd like that." I spear some potato with my fork. "How did it go talking to the therapist?"

"It was enlightening." He frowns. "I'm still figuring things through, thinking over what he said. We'll meet again tomorrow." I guess my face registers surprise, because Beck nods. "Told you I was serious about fixing things."

"I know...I just...I don't know." Then I make the huge mistake of picking up the khaki-colored drink and taking a sip. "Oh good God, that's revolting."

One side of his mouth edges upward into a smile. "Looks it."

"It's even worse than the one she made me drink at lunch. Tell me, am I beaming yet? Is my skin translucent and radiant?" I joke.

"Absolutely."

"Beck..." My timid smile fades as soon as it appears. "You're not meant to tell lies."

He pauses. "If you're imagining you ever look anything other than beautiful to me, you're wrong."

I finish chewing my potato, taking my time. Too many feelings, dammit. "You're beautiful to me too."

"Thank you." Which is when my cell starts going off in my back jeans pocket. Like seriously. My whole butt cheek is vibrating.

Beck raises a brow. "Sounds like you should get that."

"Yeah."

Mom: You okay?
Me: Yes.
Me: Mostly.
Me: Beck and I are just going through some stuff.
Mom: Sorry to hear that. But it is interesting. Your brother's mortgage got paid off today and $500k was put in the college fund for your niece.
Me: Huh.
Mom: I also just heard from your old neighbor re your plant

she's looking after. Mrs. Flores won a luxury apartment near the beach in Santa Monica and will be moving. Said she won a sweepstakes.

Me: Wow.

Mom: There's more. An anonymous donor also funded a new library for my school.

Me: Okay.

Mom: Sounds like someone's trying to buy his way back into your good graces.

Me: Guess so.

Mom: What do you want to do? Should they accept it?

Me: He can definitely afford it and is doing it willingly, so yes.

Mom: Do you want me to call? Do you want to talk about this?

Me: No. Let me think it over for a while. Thanks.

Mom: xx

It's a lot to take in. Mrs. Flores will be happy. No more shitty view of the building next door, the stink of the bins, and the city fog. The security it will give my brother and his family is not to be underestimated. Then there's just the joy that is a new library coming into the world.

"You've been busy," I say, setting aside my phone.

He just keeps on eating.

"College funds and libraries and apartments and all sorts of things."

He looks up at me from beneath dark brows, but still says nothing.

"Thank you."

He uses the side of his fork to break apart the fish. "Can I make just one highly apt literary quote without pissing you off?"

"Sure. Why not."

"'I hoped to obtain your forgiveness, to lessen your ill opinion, by letting you see that your reproofs had been attended to,'" he says, voice subdued. "'I can only hope that your good opinion, once lost, is not lost forever.'"

"That's two literary quotes. Don't push it."

"They're sincerely meant." His smile is fleeting. "Your friends Natasha and Hanae have also had some unexpected windfalls. They both won hundred-thousand-dollar payouts today."

"That'll make a big difference in their lives. By the way, I also did some more research into local and national charities today. I have plans to give away some more of your money."

"Good. Do it. Hoarding money has yet to actually make anyone in my family happy." He thinks for a moment. "You wanted to know about the therapist. We talked about my family and you and life in general for a few hours. The general message seemed to be that I can't blame lack of affection and attention from my parents for screwing up everything for the rest of my life. My bad choices caused this situation."

"I see."

"So I need to accept and let go of the fact that Mom spent most of my childhood being too busy to deal with me and Dad wasn't any better. Did I ever tell you about the time he forgot I was visiting and went on holiday without me?" he asks. "Guess you could say I haven't had many positive adult or relationship examples in my life. Not that it's an excuse. I shouldn't have lied to you."

"No, you shouldn't have," I say.

"Shitty parents messing up your life only works so long, then you've got to sort your own self out. I think that's what's called being an adult."

"True."

"You were right when you said we would have been fine if I'd just let us be," he admits.

My throat is dry all of a sudden. Stupid emotions. "I was

never there for the diamond watches or luxury vehicles, Beck. I was there for you."

"I know that now."

"Not that they weren't fun, but they were never necessary. Being with you, having your attention, working through what was between us and building something for the future, that's what matters to me."

"I hear you." He nods. "I've never been in love before. I've never loved someone like I love you. Again, not an excuse. But I'm hoping when you've had a chance to think it over, you will see it as a reason to maybe give us another chance."

My frown feels mighty indeed and my head is abuzz. So many feelings and thoughts spinning around and around. "You know, I've never been good at saying the right thing or doing the right thing or managing to exist correctly, apparently. Except with you."

His gaze is so sad. "I'm sorry, beloved. I'm so fucking sorry."

All I can do is stare. A chunk of his hair has flopped over his forehead and his gaze is all tense. The need to throw myself at him is immense. To just be done with all of this division.

"How do I trust you?" I ask.

"I don't know." He blinks. "I can keep on apologizing and promise that I'll never lie to you about anything ever again, but...I don't know exactly how we get past this and I fucking hate that because it's all on me."

My throat is all tight, my eyes itchy. Emotional upheaval is an unrelenting bitch.

"Though, just briefly going back to the sex thing. I've been giving it some thought and I think I was wrong to make us wait. I underrated the importance of physical intimacy."

"Oh?"

"You quit your job, moved states, and started a whole new life for me. And in return, I did not have your back in the way I should have," he says. "There was always family and business shit distracting me. I failed to support and fuck you like a good boyfriend would have in the same situation."

I think it over. "Okay."

"That's all you've got to say?"

"What do you want me to say?"

"That you love me too and we can get back together now would be nice."

"And then there's the whole trust issue still, Beck."

"If you think I'm ever going to lie or mislead you again, you're wrong," he says, tone emphatic. "I just spent the worst twenty-four or so hours of my life trying to figure out how I could have been stupid enough to mess things up in the first place."

I sigh. "I'm not going anywhere."

"Keep me telling me that. I need it." His jaw does the rigid thing and for a moment he turns away. When he looks back at me, there's a fire, a passion in his eyes that burns right through me. I am ash. And he is still everything. "You have no idea how fucking grateful I am for it, for you still being here even after I hurt you and messed things up. Because maybe, just maybe, it means you're as crazy about me as I am about you. And if that's the case, then we're definitely going to get through this."

I hang my head. Now my damn throat is tight and sore.

"Beloved?"

"Don't call me that."

"Wife?" he asks softly.

"Don't call me that either." My nose is not running. There's just something awkward going on in there. I rub it with the back of my hand like a four-year-old because I'm stylish like that.

"But I want to call you that. I've wanted to call you that since I met you," he says, reaching into the coat pocket of his leather jacket. "Don't freak out, but I panicked and did something."

Oh, no. "What?"

A black Harry Winston ring box is placed on the couch

between us. He draws back the two halves of the top of the little box, exposing a large square solitaire diamond ring set in a platinum band. It sparkles and shines and generally blows my mind.

"Holy shit," I mutter.

"I know I can't throw money at this problem and fix it." He picks up my hand, sliding the ring on the relevant finger. "This isn't me buying you. It's me giving you me."

"Oh my God."

"Would you do me the honor of allowing me to be your husband?" he asks.

I shake my head. "You can't...we shouldn't...Beck."

"You don't need to answer right now."

"If we have any chance at all then we need to rebuild the foundations of our relationship properly this time. Fix the trust issues between us and have total honesty. You can't just jump ahead like this."

He just stares at me, his gaze sober.

"Did you even listen to me when I said we needed to take it slow like a hundred times?"

"Yes," he says. "But I didn't agree."

"Plainly!"

"You can trust me, Alice. I swear it."

I sniffle. "And this ring is ridiculous."

"It wasn't the biggest one they had. It was just the best quality diamond. Because that's what you are, a diamond." His grip firms on my hand, not letting go. "Though it is bigger than anything Grandma has because I felt that was important for various reasons."

"I only just moved into the other bedroom."

"Don't worry about that. Besides, sleeping without you made me fucking miserable. I'm not even sure I could have stopped myself from trying to be near you again. I'd probably sleep halfway up the damn stairs so I wasn't breaking your terms," he confesses.

"Question: Were you planning on breaking up with me any time soon?"

I frown. "No. You know that."

"Okay. Another question: Do you love me?"

"Beck." My spine curves as if I'm caving in on myself. "I don't know."

"I think you do. I think you're just worried that if you say it you're going to get hurt again. But I'm promising you, that is never going to happen." He waits and watches, still and patient. Like this conversation, me hesitating, could go on forever and he'd never move an inch. Not until he gets his answer. The stubborn, beautiful, heartbreaking boy who I am absolutely crazy about. "Do you love me, Alice?"

"Fine," I growl. "Yes."

"Good. That's good." And he's holding back a smile. I can see it.

For fuck's sake, I'm crying again. I'm so sick of crying. But at least they're not sad tears. They're more along the lines of what the hell just happened tears. When it comes to him, I never stood a chance. This is a fact.

"It's okay. Come here," says Beck, basically grabbing me and dragging me onto his lap. Things are knocked over on the table. Most noticeably the green drink of death. But none of it matters. Big hands cup my face, thumbs wiping away the tears. "Emma said you're an ugly crier, but I think you're lovely. She's just jealous. You know how she gets."

"Your family…"

"Our family." He stops. "Oh, that reminds me, I've got some major sucking up to do to your mother. Probably your dad too, yeah?"

"I haven't told them what happened. But it wouldn't hurt."

He nods. "I'm up to the task. You love me. I can do anything."

I just smile. "What about your grandmother?"

"She can either get with the program or get lost. I am not messing around." He tucks a strand of hair tenderly behind my ear with a satisfied smile. "How do you feel about getting married tonight?"

"No. Absolutely not. I haven't even said yes to that yet."

He scowls, the indent appearing between his brows. "But it was implied, right? And what if you change your mind?"

"I'm not going to change my mind. I love you."

"And we'll get married eventually," he demands, gaze narrowed. "Promise me."

"Yes, okay, I promise. If you keep seeing the therapist and we keep working on things and everything goes all right."

"Agreed. Though that's a lot of conditions."

"Deal with it."

And his mouth is on mine, kissing me stupid. Taking my tears and my fears and everything in between. It's so good, getting my hands on him, reveling the taste and the feel of him. His breath and mine are the same and for some reason it feels like it's been forever and a day since we were like this. Our tongues duel and my fingers in his hair. His are meanwhile slipping beneath my tee, pressing into my back, urging me closer. The sensible thing is to straddle him. To get us lined up in all the ways that matter. Physically at least. I'm done with doubt and despair. We're going to work this out one way or another. Right now we just need to be together. He strokes my back, my shoulders, my neck. It seems like his hands are everywhere, settling me alight. Meanwhile, the growing hardness in his pants is fast turning into nirvana against my sadly clad crotch.

Who even invented clothing? What a loser.

"What do you want?" he says, voice harsh and urgent.

"You."

The smile he gives me. It just might be my new favorite. So hot and hungry. "Get undressed, beloved."

Best damn idea ever. And I nod because I'm not an idiot when it matters. However, I do need him to steady my hips as I attempt to stand and tear off my top and bra at the same time. Multitasking in this sort of situation is a trial. Especially once hormones and urgency come out to play. Everything needs to be faster, quicker, now. Not to say making love slow and gentle isn't nice and sweet. We should definitely do it later. Though fucking definitely has a time and a place. Like here and now.

Our fumbling urgent hands are all over each other. With Beck, being the perfect gentleman, ripping open the button on my jeans and so on. Both jeans and underwear are soon being dragged down my legs. In a feat of great dexterity, I step out of them without falling on my ass. Yes. Naked. Only there's a problem.

"You're fully clothed," I push his jacket off his shoulders.

"Right."

He stands up, his jacket thrown in one direction, his tee going another. Then there's that grin again. It's a delightful mix of lecherous and love. Makes my tummy turn over and my knees go weak. I can't not cover his face in kisses when he looks at me like that. Impossible. So we're making out and trying to get him undressed at the same time, which is a little haphazard. And all the while my heart is pounding inside my chest so hard I could swear it echoes throughout the house.

Our fingers clash at the buckle of his belt, but I take over. Since he's so set on soul kissing me, I attempt to deal with his pants situation. Just as well given he's also busy playing with my breasts. He's pinching and kneading them in the best way possible, making me a wet squirming mess. I grab hold of his cock, pumping him with a twist, rubbing the pad of my thumb over and around the head of his shaft. It's perfect, how his skin feels like velvet. How hot and alive he is in my hand. His dick swelling and hardening further. The need in him only excites me more.

The knot in my pelvis drawing tighter and tighter. I'm wet and swollen between my legs, more than ready and we've barely begun.

This must be love...being so desperate for each other you could die, needing the physical and emotional connection more than you need your next breath. But also being willing to work at it and not give up. Being in love, loving someone, would have to be the most dizzying, terrifying, and thrilling thing to ever happen to me.

I think love is big and complicated and all encompassing.

I also think I need to ride him like a pony.

With his jeans shoved far enough down, I helpfully push him back onto the couch and climb onto his lap. Life is full of potentially embarrassing moments. That my inner thighs are already wet with my juices. That bits of me wobble. That someone could come up the stairs. But fuck that shit. Life is first and foremost to be lived.

"You need anything?" he asks, gaze dark and thrilling.

I just shake my heads. Words are beyond me.

Then he grabs my hips, guiding me. Though it's not exactly necessary. His dick is large, upright, and demanding attention. It's not like I can miss it. I leave one hand on his shoulder for balance, using the other to guide him into me. And oh hell, the first feverish brush of him against me. The sensation of him pressing into me, stretching me, filling me just right. It's exquisite. My eyes roll back in my head and my mind goes to a galaxy far away.

"Christ, you're beautiful." He mumbles against my neck, breath hot on my skin. "Love you so fucking much."

I rise up a little, testing the feel of him inside of me. Squeeze him with my inner muscles and bite my lip on the way back down. Yes, yes, yes. This is exactly what we need. Just me and him together.

He groans. "Alice."

It's as natural as breathing, working myself on him. Taking his cock in deep before raising my body back up again. At first we kiss, mouths pressed tight together. My arms wrapped around his neck, his fingers digging into the flesh of my sides. I was wrong about fast and furious. Slow is amazing. Just savoring the rigid length of him buried deep inside of me. Over and over I rise, gradually gaining in speed. Hair disheveled and eyes dilated, he's so carnal. The way he's collapsed back against the couch, watching me fucking him. Like I'm his own private porn queen and fairy-tale princess all wrapped up in one.

It's a powerful and potent thing, being with him. His thigh muscles tense beneath me. The buckle on his belt jangling every time I bounce. Being on top is awesome. And all the while, what we're building between us gets higher and greater. My toes curl and my back arches, thrusting out my breasts. Beck growls and grabs me tight. The raw animal expression on his face is a thrilling thing. But I can't keep my eyelids open when it hits. It's too much. The heat and power of it burns through me from top to toe. My orgasm is a sparkly shining thing of wonder blasting away all of the crap of the last day with ease. Only this warm, glowing, shimmering sensation remains. Ever so slowly it fades from my body. First leaving my fingers and toes, receding until only the great ball of emotion inside my chest remains. It's not uncomfortable. Nope. It's right and good.

Damp face on his shoulder, I lie plastered against him, learning how to breathe again. His arms wrap around me, holding me tight. "We should never leave the house."

"Hmm."

"Seriously, though. You ready to put the ring on your finger now?"

"Eventually."

"Eventually," he mutters. "You're going to make me work for it, aren't you?"

"Yep."

His chest shifts beneath me as he laughs. "Fine. Whatever. Do your worst. I love you. I can take it."

"I love you too."

But the drama train isn't done with us yet.

CHAPTER NINETEEN

"THIS IS A BAD IDEA."

"It's a great idea," says Beck, passing me a gin and tonic. "It was your idea, beloved."

"Don't remind me."

"It's already done so you might as well relax." Ethan pulls on the cuff of his shirt. "She should be here any minute."

Henry looks up from his cell with a smirk. "Entertainment with a capital E."

Matías gives me a wink. None of it soothes my nerves.

"Hand me that bread roll." Emma points to the one sitting on my side plate. I do as told. You don't mess with a hungry pregnant woman. Not if you want to live. "Thanks, Alice."

"Do you want another juice or something, honey?" asks Rachel. The woman is going to make a great grandmother. You can tell.

"Iced water please, Mom."

The Elliot Corp. Christmas party is every bit as swanky as you'd imagine. A ballroom at one of the grandest hotels in Denver and hundreds of people present. Tuxedos and formalwear and crystal chandeliers. In years past, the family would sit at different tables, mixed in with board members and so on. But this year we're all together at the one big round table. Beck and I, Emma and Matías, Ethan, Henry, and Rachel. Everyone is present.

Penny and River surreptitiously watch from a nearby table. They got married at Thanksgiving. I'd never been to a surprise Thanksgiving wedding before, but it was fantastic. Though Beck knew about it because he lent them his place in Aspen for the event. He didn't tell me, though. Apparently Matías and Emma's last-minute vow renewal inspired them to do it all on the sly. Giving people no warning does seem to cut down on a large percentage of the crazy. But I'm thinking eloping to an island could be the way to go. I could rock a wedding bikini. Beck has yet to agree to the idea, however. I suspect my mother threatened him with regards to any sneakiness regarding our wedding. She wants a small ceremony in California with family and friends and then whatever else we want to do in Denver.

Keeping everyone happy is never easy.

"You look beautiful." Beck picks up my free hand, lacing his fingers with mine. He's in a tuxedo so of course I want to bang the boy. Though my need to sex him has been a constant since I met him. Some things never change.

"Thank you. So do you." For this most portentous event I chose a calf-length black stretch sequin fitted tee dress and Louboutin platform stilettos. Makes me feel like a futuristic disco queen with ass kicking capabilities. My only jewelry is the diamond stud earrings and the bling on my wedding finger my fiancé is currently kissing. I laugh. "I thought people only did that to the pope."

He grins. It's the cunning one I've learned to be wary of because Beck. "Beloved, you well know I relish the nectar of your body and live only to worship daily at the temple of your sweet wet—"

"Not. In. Public."

Henry frowns. "Huh?"

"Nothing. Go back to staring at your phone."

Ethan just blinks at us before turning away. His blank face is full in force. It's an Elliot thing along with the rigid chin. Guess it's that kind of night. But he's here with us and that's all that matters.

"What are you two on about?" asks Emma, slathering my/ her bread roll with butter. Yum.

Matías straightens himself. "She's here."

I haven't seen Catherine since the day of the event. When she visited our home to lay down the law according to her and diminish me with insults to the best of her abilities. Once Henry, Ethan, and Emma made it clear that they wouldn't support any attempt by her to kick Beck off the board for insubordination, she backed away from the idea fast. Things between her and Beck have been mostly cordial from what I'm told. Guess at heart she doesn't want to lose her grandson even if she doesn't approve of his life choices. Which is the way it should be.

She wears a green silk suit the color of money and is dripping diamonds. Every inch the dowager queen of Elliot Corp. And sure enough, people bow and stoop, hoping for the blessing of a moment of her precious time. So maybe I'm still a bit bitter about the whole thing and her in general. Who could blame me?

When she reaches our table with Winston accompanying her, clearing the way, she stops cold at the sight. All of us, gathered together, facing her as a united front. Like a family, if you will. Her eyes dart about, taking in every face. Oh, the expression of outrage when her gaze settles on me.

Beck stands and pulls out a chair for her at the table. "Grandmother."

"I explicitly asked to be seated elsewhere."

Emma cocks her head. "We explicitly overrode you."

"We even all arrived early to ensure there'd be no shenanigans," says Beck.

"This ends now." Ethan gets to his feet. "Alice and Beck are announcing their engagement later. She is and will be a part of our family and you will accept it."

Catherine's nostrils flare in outrage, but she says nothing.

"Mrs. Elliot, would you like me to—"

"Fuck off, Winnie," drawls Beck. "You're not a part of this."

Whoa. The majordomo's face blanches in outrage.

I take a sip of my drink. "Sit down, Catherine. We're putting all of this unpleasantness behind us."

Her eyes widen at my impertinence or whatever.

"Sit, Grandma," says Emma in a softer voice. "This is your family, whether you like it or not. I'm about to add a third generation to it and I won't tolerate this infighting and other assorted assholish behavior."

Rachel sighs. "Language, honey."

But it's Henry who has the last word. "You're either with us or against us, Grandma. Which'll it be?"

This is it, the moment of truth. Once again, her gaze skitters around the group, searching for some sign of support. But no go. She is, without a doubt, the one on the outside looking in right now. I almost feel sorry for her. Despite all of the bullshit, she must love her grandchildren. Her way of expressing that love is the thing that sucks.

Will she take the olive branch or not?

People at neighboring tables are watching with interest. There's going to be some gossip going around tonight for sure. But then, there always is. A rich dynasty like the Elliots are always a topic of interest. Such is life.

Catherine's chin goes up, her gaze icy cool as she moves toward the chair. "Of course I'm delighted to sit with my family."

There's almost an audible sigh of relief. An unwinding or easing of tension from everyone at the table. The vibe is definitely one of oh thank fuck. In-house fighting doesn't help anyone.

Winston pours Catherine a glass of champagne. "Engaged."

It's not a question so much as a statement. Beck retakes his chair, holding my hand once more. And the look he gives me, the love in his eyes...he still makes me giddy. I think he always will. "That's right. Alice finally accepted yesterday. We couldn't be happier."

Catherine just sniffs.

"It's a beautiful ring," says Rachel.

I smile. "Yes, it is."

"Makes me second most eligible bachelor in Denver." Henry's tongue plays behind his cheek. No one's heard from Giada lately. Lord knows what she's up to. But Henry knows he's loved and wanted by all of us. That's what matters. The boys only got back from their snowboarding trip a few days ago and a great time was apparently had by all.

"Don't let it go to your head." Ethan sips a whiskey. "I'm still number one."

A grunt from Henry. "Looks like the love bug is going around Ethan. Be careful it doesn't bite you on the ass."

Catherine scowls. "Language, Henry."

"Not going to happen," says Ethan, voice deep and sure. "Emma's supplying an heir and Beck and Alice will keep society busy with wedding plans. I'm off the hook for now."

"We'll see." Beck gives his brother his most irritating grin before kissing my hand again. "All good, beloved?"

"I'm just fine, thank you."

Catherine turns away with a sour expression. So she's still neither looking at me nor talking to me. But never mind. So long as she plays nice. I didn't imagine she'd welcome me with arms open after everything. However, Beck and I are happy and the family is no longer an active war zone.

"Actually, I'm better than fine," I correct, leaning in closer to my fiancé. "I'm so happy."

"'We are all fools in love.'" Then he gives me the smile that is ever only for me. My favorite smile of them all.

"I'm not a fool. In fact, I think I'm quite smart to have caught you."

He raises a brow. "And here I always thought I caught you."

"We caught each other." I grin, leaning in for a kiss. And he gives it to me, regardless of where we are or who is watching. Nothing matters beyond the press of his lips against mine. How neither of us closes our eyes until the last moment. The way his hand strays to the back of my neck. As public displays of affection go, it's a good one. Sometimes love can suck. We both know this. Life together won't be without its bumps. We're going to be attending couples therapy and working on things for a long time to come. Building up that trust and maintaining it. Working on our communication skills and spending quality time together. But tonight, our love is perfection.

"Whatever you say, almost-wife."

PURCHASE KYLIE SCOTT'S OTHER BOOKS

FIND KYLIE AT:

www.kyliescott.com

Facebook: www.facebook.com/kyliescottwriter

Twitter: twitter.com/KylieScottbooks

Instagram: www.instagram.com/authorkyliescott

Pinterest: www.pinterest.com/kyliescottbooks

BookBub: www.bookbub.com/authors/kylie-scott

To learn about exclusive content, my upcoming releases and giveaways, join my newsletter:

kyliescott.com/subscribe

Keep reading for a free sample of

LIES

ONE

"YOU'RE GOING TO BREAK HIS HEART."

"No, I'm not," I say. "That's sort of the whole point. If I really thought leaving him would break his heart, then I probably wouldn't be leaving him in the first place."

My best friend, Jen, does not look convinced.

Boxes fill a good half of the room. What a mess. Who knew you could accumulate so much junk in only twelve months? At least we weren't together so long that I can't remember who owns what. One year is about the sweet spot for this issue in relationships, apparently.

"The fact of the matter is, we're not in love. We have no business being engaged, let alone getting married." I sigh. "Have you seen the packing tape?"

"No. He's just such a nice guy."

"I'm not debating that." I climb to my feet, then head up the stairs to the second bedroom. Thom's unofficial workout room/home office. Not a room I normally go into. But it only takes a bit of rummaging to find what I'm looking for. Whatever else might be said about them, insurance assessors are organized. The bottom drawer of Thom's desk has a neat stash of stationery. I grab a couple rolls of thick tape.

"And leaving him this way..." Jen continues as I head back down.

"How many times have I told him we need to talk? He's always putting it off, saying it's not a good time. And now he's away again. I've been messaging him for the last week and he barely replies."

"You know he has to drop everything once a job comes up. I realize he's not the most exciting guy, Betty, but—"

"I know." I smack down a line of tape with extra zest, sealing the lid of the last box. In this Operation Abandon Ship Posthaste, I know I'm definitely slightly the bad guy. But not totally. Say sixty/forty. Or maybe seventy/thirty. It's hard to tell to what degree. "I do know all of that. But he's always busy with work or away on some business trip. What am I supposed to do?"

A sigh from Jen.

"When you realize you've made such a monumental mistake, it's hard to sit and wait to fix things. Nor is it fair on either of us to keep up the pretense."

"Guess so."

"And the fact that he's yet again made no effort to prioritize our relationship and make a little time for me in his busy schedule is just further proof that I've made the right choice in ending this now before it gets any more complicated. End of rant."

Nothing from her.

"Anyway, you're supposed to be on my side. Stop questioning me."

"You wanted to get married and have children so badly."

"Yeah." I sit back on my heels. "I blame it all on playing with Ken and Barbie's dreamhouse when I was little. But it turns out that being in a relationship with the wrong person can be even lonelier than being alone."

Jen and I have been friends since sharing a room in college. We've witnessed the bulk of each other's dating ups and downs. For some reason, I'm the type of girl who guys will go out with, but don't tend to stick with. Apparently, I'm fuckable—just not girlfriend material. Maybe it's my smart mouth. Maybe it's the whole not fitting current societal expectations of beauty i.e. I'm fat. Maybe I was born under an unlucky star. I don't know; it's their loss. Like anyone, I have my faults, but all in all, I'm awesome. And I have a lot to give. Too often in the past few months, I've had to keep reminding myself of this fact.

"There are just so many jerks out there," Jen says. "I was happy that you'd found a good one."

"I think I'd prefer a jerk who was genuinely into me than a nice guy phoning it in. Honestly, I'd rather go adopt a dozen cats and settle into old age and isolation than be with someone who treats me as if I'm an afterthought."

She looks at me for a long moment, then nods slowly. "I'm sorry it didn't work out."

"Me too."

"Time to start filling up the cars. Boy, do you owe me."

I smile. "That I do."

Jen stands and stretches before picking up one of the boxes labeled *kitchen*. "I just didn't want you to do something you'd regret, you know?"

"I know. Thank you."

Alone in the two-bedroom condo, everything is silent. My parting letter sits waiting on the coffee table with his name written on the front. A slight bulge in the envelope betrays the shape of my engagement ring. It's a sweet, simple ring. One small diamond perched on a band of yellow gold. My hand feels wrong without it. Naked. They say there are different love languages and you have to take the time to learn your partner's needs. It's like he and I never quite got there. Or maybe I'm just crappy at relationships.

The bridal magazines I'd collected are in the trash. Perhaps I should have taken them into the florist shop where I work so someone could get some use out of them. But this feels more symbolic, more definite. My family are a couple of states away, and I have only a few of what I'd classify as good friends. Being an introvert makes it hard to meet people. A boyfriend, a husband, would mean I'm no longer alone. Someone cares about me and puts me first. At least part of the time. Only Thom doesn't any of the time, so here we are.

I tighten my ponytail of long dark hair. Then, in a rare display of dexterity that my yoga instructor would be proud of, I stack three boxes in my arms and head outside into the hot afternoon sun. Jen's Honda Civic is parked at the curb, the trunk standing open as she moves things about inside. My old Subaru sits in the driveway waiting to be filled. Birds are singing and insects chirping. It's your typical mild autumn day in California.

That's when the condo blows up behind me.

I come to on the front lawn, sprawled across crushed boxes. Guess they cushioned my fall. A ringing fills my ears, smoke billows up into the sky. The condo is on fire. What's left of it, at least. This cannot be happening.

"Betty!"

I try to turn in the direction of Jen's voice, but one of my eyes won't open. When I touch the area, my fingers come away bright with blood. Also, my brain hurts. It feels as if someone picked me up and shook me around hard.

"Oh my God, Betty," she says, falling to her knees beside me. She's fuzzy for some reason, her familiar features indistinct. "Are you all right?"

"Sure," I say as blackness closes in.

The next time I wake, I'm lying down in a moving vehicle. An ambulance, by the looks of it. Only things don't seem quite right. A woman shines a small light in my eyes before tossing it over her shoulder. And instead of a uniform, she's wearing tight black pants and a tank top.

"Lucky girl. Just a mild concussion and a small cut on her forehead," the woman says with an English accent. Next she rips an antiseptic wipe out of its packet and starts cleaning up the blood on my face none too gently. "She's certainly not his usual type."

"What were you expecting?" asks the driver.

"I don't know. Something a little less plump and homely, perhaps."

A grunt.

"And she's awake," the woman says.

"That's inconvenient."

"I'm on it." She drops the wipe and reaches for a syringe.

"W-wait," I say, my mouth dry and muscles hurting. "What's going on?"

Without any preamble, the needle is plunged into my arm, the stopper depressed. It all happens so quickly. I try to move, to push her away, but I'm no match for her strength. Not in my current condition. As darkness closes in once more, I see a discarded paramedic uniform sitting off to the side.

"Who are you?" I mumble, my lips, face, and everything else going numb.

"Friends," she says. "Well, sort of."

The driver just laughs.

Consciousness comes slowly. It's like I'm underwater in an ocean of night. This time, however, I'm upright, seated on a chair in a large and dimly lit room. My feet rest on the cold bare floor since someone's stolen my shoes. Everything's woozy and horrible. My hands are tied behind my back, the restraints painfully tight. The shadows disappear as a blinding light is shone in my face. It's dazzling and awful, shooting pain through my already pounding head. Next comes a bucket of ice-cold water thrown in my face.

"Wakey wakey," yells the shadow of a man. "Time for us to talk, Miss Elizabeth Dawsey."

I cringe and shiver. "Wh-where am I?"

"I ask the questions and you give me answers. That's how this works."

"Is all this really necessary?" the woman with the British accent asks. Her voice comes from farther back in the room. "He's not going to be happy."

"Keep your mouth shut," growls the man.

With the light blinding my eyes, there's little I can see. My bare feet rest on concrete and the air is dusty and still. I could be anywhere. "I don't understand. Who are you people?"

Heavy footsteps come toward me; then *smack*! His hand connects with my cheek. Fothermucker. I've never been hit before. It's a hell of a shock. My face throbs and there's the taste of blood on my tongue. I must have bitten it. But then everything pretty much hurts to one degree or another.

"I wouldn't have done that if I were you," says the woman.

But the man just ignores her, stepping back beyond the light. "What does the word 'wolf' mean to you?"

"Wolf?" I ask.

"Answer the question."

"I don't...what do you mean?" I shake from more than fear, ice-cold water sliding down my skin beneath the drenched clothing. "As in the animal?"

"What else?"

"Fur? Teeth? House Stark? I don't know."

Laughter from the woman.

"Tell me about your fiancé," he demands. "Everything you know about the man."

This makes no sense to my already-addled brain. "But why? Thom hasn't done anything. He's an insurance assessor, for Christ's sake. Whenever there's a fire or a flood or something, he goes and helps people with their claims. That's where he is right now, assessing damage from that hurricane in Florida. It was on the news and everything."

"Are you sure about that?"

"What are you saying?" A sudden surge of fear grips me. "Thom's okay, isn't he? I mean, he couldn't have been in the explosion. He's on the other side of the country."

"He wasn't in the explosion, no. Tell me more about him."

"Ah, we met in a bar downtown, been together for just over a year. He's a hard worker. He likes watching football and going for morning runs. His favorite food is lasagna and he drinks Bud Light even though it's trash."

"MORE."

"I don't know what you want," I cry. Never in my life have I been so scared.

"Describe him to me."

"He's just an average guy. Average height. Fit, but not bulky. He has brown eyes and hair. Thirty-one years old."

"Tick-tock, tick-tock," says the woman. "You're running out of time."

"Whose fucking fault is that?" hisses the man.

"Guess I gave her more sleep juice than I meant to. Oops."

A grunt. "Keep talking, bitch."

My head pounds. "I, um...he sleeps on the right-hand side of the bed."

"What weapons does he keep in the house?"

"Like guns? None. I hate the things. We both do."

Again, the woman laughs. "Not the brightest, is she?"

"Keep talking," repeats the man.

"Thom's a decent person. He's nice...polite. Doesn't do social media. Has no close family." Nothing I'm telling them is damning or even particularly interesting. Still, I feel guilty for answering at all. But what the hell else am I supposed to do? "Is this what you want to know? I don't understand; what's he done? What's he involved in?"

"Who says he's involved in anything?"

"The fact that I'm here and you're questioning me says something's going on."

"Watch it. I don't think you appreciate how nice I'm being," says the creep. "Things could get much worse for you very quickly. You have no idea exactly how bad things could get."

"I don't know what you want. Are you the ones who blew up the condo?" My heart is pounding and I can't seem to get enough air. "Are you going to kill me?"

"Asking me questions again. Tsk tsk. You just never learn. Perhaps you'd like to try some waterboarding, hmm? Does that sound like fun?"

I choke on a sob.

"Got to say, it really messes you up. Feels just like you're drowning. You start suffocating and water gets in your lungs, which fucking stings, let me tell you. And your sinuses feel like they're going to explode. Eventually, Betty, you'll lose consciousness. Then I'll wake you back up not so gently and we'll start all over again." The sadistic prick laughs. "I hate to do it. But I just don't think you're being entirely truthful with me, you see? It's sad, really. All of this football-and-lasagna bullshit, it's just surface information. You must know more about the man you live with, the man you're going to marry. You'd have to know all his secrets by now, wouldn't you?"

I shake my head. "Thom doesn't have any secrets."

"Everyone has secrets."

"No, not Thom. I mean, he hates his boss and he takes his coffee black." I'm babbling now, the words tripping over themselves in their haste to get out. "He's a bit of a loner. Only has a couple of friends f-from college, work…I don't…oh, God."

"Do you talk to your friends about Thom?"

"Well, I talk to my friend Jen. Wait, where is Jen? Have you taken her too?"

"The friend checks out," says the woman. "She's clean."

"Is Jen okay?" I repeat. "Did you hurt her?"

"Your nosy little friend is fine. Took a lot of talking to keep her out of the ambulance," says the man. "Maybe we should have brought her along. I think you just need a bit more encouragement to help your memory."

"Are you sure about this?" asks the woman.

"Use your head," he snaps. "If they've found the condo, then they know about this one. If they know about her, they'll have tried to compromise her. Get her on the floor."

"Oh, no. I'm observing only," says the woman. "You're on your own with this."

The light clicks off and white spots dance before my eyes. I blink and blink, but it's a while before I can see anything. In the meantime, there are noises. Water running from a tap. More heavy footsteps. The near-silent hiss of the frigid air-conditioning turning on.

Slowly, gradually, things swim into focus. We're in an empty basement by the look of it. Small barred windows set high. Bare brick walls and a concrete floor. Over by a laundry tub, the man stands with his back to me. He's tall with a shaved head, dressed in all black. Meanwhile, the woman leans against a wall inspecting her nails. She's petite with short dark hair and golden-brown skin.

This isn't real. It can't be real. Everything hurts. And it's about to hurt a lot more.

Someone jogs down the stairs, coming into view a bit at a time. First are the black boots. Next is blue jeans. Then a gray T-shirt hanging loose. Finally, I see his face...

And it's Thom.

Relief rushes through me. He's here. He's okay. Oh, thank God. Though, now that I really pay attention, he seems different than normal. My addled brain can't figure it out exactly. As if it's Thom's doppelgänger. Because it looks like him, but the expression on his face...

Oh, shit. What if they're going to hurt him too?

"Thom," I gasp. "No."

He spares me only the briefest of glances. "What's going on?"

The creep turns, mouth set in a distinctly pissy line. Water keeps pouring out of the faucet into a bucket, presumably, and he's holding a piece of ripped towel. "Wolf."

"Spider," says Thom.

"Since we had to pick her up, they wanted a threat assessment." The woman continues to lean casually against the wall.

"It's sanctioned," snarls the man. Spider.

"And you decided that meant tying her up and torturing her?" asks Thom. "I don't think so."

The woman sighs. "For the record, I told him it wasn't a good idea."

"You were right."

"Hey, now." The man lifts his hands in a pacifying way. "I wasn't actually going to do it. I was just messing with her head. You know how it works, you've got to—"

It all happens so quickly. The work of a moment, no more. Thom's hand lunges for Spider's throat, crushing his windpipe. The man doubles over, choking.

Unhurried, Thom draws a gun from his belt. One smooth, graceful arc, and the gun's butt strikes the side of the man's head. He drops to the floor.

"I've been wanting to do that for years," the woman says. "He always liked hurting women a little too much for my tastes. Such a rubbish human."

It's the last straw for me. I'm not used to all the threats and fear and violence. In movies maybe, but not actual real-world stuff. Acid climbs my throat and I lean to the side to throw up. Vomit splashes the side of my leg. I'm too freaked out to feel the usual disgust. Instead, I feel frail and hollow. Like I might cave in on myself at any moment.

"Fox, get him out of here," orders Thom in a calm voice.

"Fuck's sake. I hate carrying dead weight." The woman, Fox, pulls out a cell, thumbs moving across the screen, sending someone a message instead of following orders. Perhaps she's checking her social media first. I don't know. Nothing about this makes sense.

Thom strides toward me, his face hard, eyes cold. I've never been afraid of him, but I am now. He produces a knife out of nowhere and squats down to cut the ties on my wrists. Then he grabs my chin, inspecting me.

I push him away, wipe my mouth clean with the back of a hand. My world has suddenly turned upside down. Thom the kickass fighter and me almost blown-up and waterboarded. What the hell?

"Thom…" I breathe.

His dark hair is this cool artful mess instead of following its usual dull, neat lines. And there's a focus to him, a determination. No, a confidence. That's the difference between this man and my former fiancé. He stands tall and strong. Ready to conquer nations, to take on anything and win.

Holy shit. Who is this guy?

Because this isn't my Thom. It can't be.

"Your eyes are blue," I say.

"I wear contacts around you."

"No. You're his evil twin or something." This makes total sense. Sort of. "That's it."

"Don't be silly," he replies shortly. "It's me, Betty. Your fiancé."

"I know Thom. He's nothing like you. He would never…"

He pauses, then sighs. "You've seen my scars. You know them."

"I know Thom's scars, but…"

Without a word, he pulls his T-shirt up and over his head. Thom's always been fit, but in the shadowy light, with the gun tucked into the waistband of his jeans now exposed, the rippled body before me looks hard and dangerous. However, the scars are indeed there. Every one of them. One on the shoulder. A slash on his upper right arm. Four across his stomach, like a little constellation.

I shake my head. "Thom would never take his shirt off in public. He's too self-conscious. We didn't even have sex with the light on."

"Self-conscious about the damage from the car accident, right?"

"Yeah, and the scars from playing sports and a surgery when he was younger."

"I don't care about them." He sighs. "It was just too much of a risk that someone might recognize gunshot, knife, and shrapnel wounds if they saw them."

Huh. "Thom?"

"Hi, babe." He gives me a sad, sort of contrite smile. For the first time, he looks exactly like my Thom.

"What the hell is going on?"

He says nothing. But his gaze moves over me, taking in my battered face, my bruised body. It stops, however, at my hands. "Betty, where's your ring?"

"I—I took it off. I was leaving you."

For the first time, this scary alternate version of Thom seems almost surprised. A little shocked even. "You left me? Why would you…" Then he looks over his shoulder at Fox, who is carrying Spider away, holding him over one shoulder, fireman style. She's obviously stronger than she looks. Thom leans in close, his voice harsh and low. "Tell no one. Do you understand?"

"What? But why?"

"No one. Your life depends on it."

Returning without Spider, Fox wanders over. "All organized."

"Good," answers Thom.

"Of course, this is all your own bloody fault," says Fox. "You're the one who wanted a white picket fence and suburban family for a cover. Yawn."

Thom draws me to my feet and I sway like I'm caught in a storm. He slides a strong arm around my waist, drawing me against his body. I don't want to touch him, this stranger who uses violence so easily. But my options for staying upright and getting out of here are limited.

"The internal leak is being investigated," says Fox. "We should have something for you soon."

Thom just nods.

"What do I say to Spider when he regains consciousness?" asks Fox.

"Tell him if he ever touches my fiancée again, I won't be so diplomatic next time."

Fox snorts. "Whatever. Cheerio, Betty. No hard feelings, yeah?"

Thom hustles me out of there as fast as he can.

"I know you've got questions."

What an understatement. We're upstairs in one of the many bedrooms inside the sprawling old ranch house. It's somewhere in the wilds of one of the canyons, at a guess. No neighbors are in sight. Apart from Fox, the unconscious Spider, and a man working at a serious array of computers in the great room, the place seems empty. There's basic furniture only. No pictures or keepsakes. Nothing to indicate it's a home.

And it's all so surreal. I want to keep pinching myself, but I hurt enough already. Which reminds me: "Was anyone else harmed in the explosion?"

"No."

"It was meant to kill?"

"As best we can figure, the bomb malfunctioned. Went off early."

"Someone actually tried to blow us up. I wonder…I went into your office looking for tape. I don't usually go in there."

His nostrils flare. "That could have been it."

"So there's a leak in your organization and someone wants to kill you," I say, voice shaking. "Or you and me both?"

"You were paying attention back there."

"I'm not as stupid as you think I am." I almost laugh. Or cry. One or the other. "At least, I hope I'm not."

"Babe—"

"Do not babe me."

He takes a deep breath, pushing a hand through his hair. The past few months, he's been so busy it's longer than normal. Way overdue for a cut. "I never thought you were stupid, Betty."

"No. Just desperate."

He says nothing. Confirmation enough. Not that I needed it.

"Well?" I ask.

"Until we can identify who's passing off information, we won't know if the target is just me. It would, however, make the most sense."

"Unless they wanted to kill me to hurt you. Though it wouldn't hurt you, would it?"

His lips thin ever so slightly. "Given I cold-cocked the last person who harmed you, I think we can assume I care at least a little."

"A little. That's big of you." I sit on the side of the king-size bed, trying to ease the nerves, tiredness, and pain. What I wouldn't give for Tylenol or something stronger. A bottle of medicinal vodka, maybe. "What happens now?"

"Now we wait to see what the searches Badger's doing on the computers dig up. We're safe here for the moment."

"Badger." I snort. "Is there an Otter?"

"Not that I'm aware of."

"You and your friends are a regular fucking zoo."

The following silence is thick and heavy. Not comfortable at all. And to think I'd planned to spend my life with this man. This stranger.

"She referred to me and our life together as your cover. Does that make you a spy or a government agent or what?"

"Something like that."

"Oh my God, are you a traitor?"

"No, Betty. The ones I work for...they're an international group dedicated to keeping things as unfucked as possible. That's really all I can say."

"And these people, you kill for them?"

There's the slightest of pauses before he answers. "When it's necessary. There are some dangerous people out there. But other times I just gather information. Each job is different."

"They usually involve you pretending to be someone you're not, though, right? Lying to people?"

"Yes."

"Hmm. You're very good at it." I watch him carefully. "So are you doing this for the good of humankind or for the money?"

"Can't it be both?" he asks all smooth-like. New Thom is slippery.

"What did you mean, my life depended on not saying anything about leaving you?"

"You know too much now. The only thing keeping you alive is that they, the people in charge, think you're loyal to me and that I'm committed to you. If those beliefs change, then they will review their risk-reward calculation about keeping you alive."

"All I know is that you name yourselves after animals and answer to some mysterious organization referred to as 'they.'"

"That's enough."

"It's ridiculous they'd want me dead just for knowing that." I want to beat him with my fists. Scream and howl in rage. Maybe later when I've got the energy. "Is Thom Lange even your real name?"

"Thom is my name."

"But Lange's not your surname."

"No." He pauses. "Why did you want to leave?"

"Does it matter why I attempted to dump you, since we're apparently now stuck with each other?"

"I thought you were happy." The weird thing is, he sounds almost hurt. Which is crazy. "I know I've been busy lately, but—"

"You do remember this is a fake relationship you're talking about," I say between clenched teeth. "A lie that you manipulated and tricked me into believing."

For a moment, we just stare at each other. Neither of us is happy.

"Given how badly I held up under pressure, I can almost forgive you for not telling me the whole truth. But I really don't think I can ever forgive you for starting this relationship in the first place."

"Everyone breaks under torture; it's just a matter of when." He doesn't address the second issue. Doesn't even go near it.

"Great."

"You're exhausted; you should sleep." He nods to a door on the other side of the large bedroom. "Bathroom is through there if you want to clean up. I'll check on you later."

"Okay."

"I'll be right outside. You're safe, Betty."

I don't know what to say. This new Thom doesn't feel safe at all.

And then he's gone.

I have no idea where we are or how far from civilization we might be. And I have neither money nor shoes. My chances of making a successful getaway are slim to none. For now, there's no other real option but to stay put and figure out this situation. My supposed fiancé seems to want to keep me alive and in one piece. It's something, I guess.

The woman in the bathroom mirror is pale and pasty, battered and bruised. I turn on the shower, testing the temperature with a hand. Red marks line my wrists, further reminder of the crazy and violent day. My clothes stink of smoke and vomit, but there's soap and shampoo, towels and a fluffy white robe. It'll have to do. I need to put myself back together and deal.

Only the first tear leaves a trail in the soot and general mess of my face. A second tear follows fast. Soon my vision wavers and I step into the shower, hiding the sound of my crying with the running water. It'd be great to be able to handle this, to stay strong. But first I apparently need a minute to let it all out. All of the anger, stress, and horror of the past few hours. All of my fear.

Because I'm trapped. That's what it comes down to in the end.

LIES

is available now!